Praise for Kathryn Rose

Camelot Burning

"[*Camelot Burning*] offers up magic, alchemy, and an epic struggle along with vivid writing and a brave, intelligent lead character."

—*Booklist*

"The perfect blend of romance and action."

—*School Library Journal*

First Edition
First Printing, 2015

Book design by Bob Gaul
Cover design by Kevin R. Brown
Cover illustration by John Blumen
Interior map illustration by Chris Down

Flux, an imprint of Llewellyn Worldwide Ltd.

This is a work of fiction. Names, characters, places, and incidents are either the product of the author's imagination or are used fictitiously, and any resemblance to actual persons living or dead, business establishments, events, or locales is entirely coincidental.

Library of Congress Cataloging-in-Publication Data
Rose, Kathryn.
 Avalon rising/Kathryn Rose.—First Edition.
  pages cm.—(A Metal and Lace novel; #2)
 Summary: In the aftermath of Morgan le Fay's war on Camelot, Vivienne, Merlin's former apprentice, secretly builds an aeroship which the Lady of the Lake believes will ensure success in the quest for Avalon and the Holy Grail, but when things go wrong, Vivienne comandeers the aeroship for a rescue mission.
 ISBN 978-0-7387-4489-6
 [1. Courts and courtiers—Fiction. 2. Automata—Fiction. 3. Airships—Fiction. 4. Knights and knighthood—Fiction. 5. Lady of the Lake (Legendary character)—Fiction. 6. Magic—Fiction. 7. Camelot (Legendary place)—Fiction. 8. Kings, queens, rulers, etc.—Fiction.] I. Title.
 PZ7.R71715Av2015
 [Fic]—dc23
                                             2014040974

Flux
Llewellyn Worldwide Ltd.
2143 Wooddale Drive
Woodbury, MN 55125-2989
www.fluxnow.com

Printed in the United States of America

———■ *a* METAL & LACE NOVEL ■———

AVALON RISING

KATHRYN ROSE

Woodbury, Minnesota

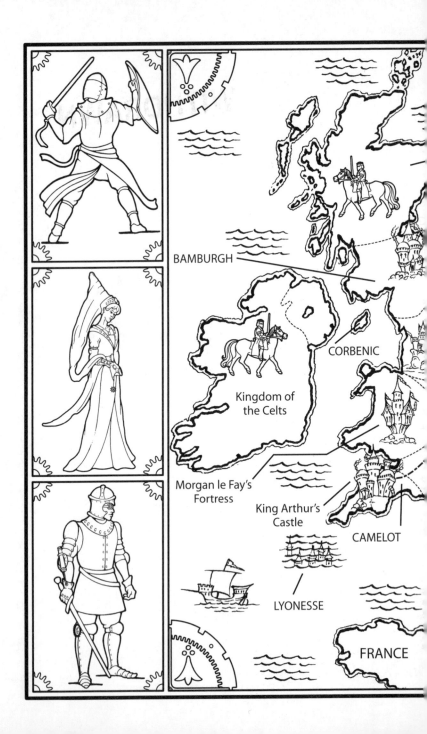

BAMBURGH

CORBENIC

Kingdom of
the Celts

Morgan le Fay's
Fortress

King Arthur's
Castle

CAMELOT

LYONESSE

FRANCE

CALEDONIA

Castle Blanc

Fisher King's Castle

Perilous
Lands

Grail Quest
Road

Refugee
Villages

ASTOLAT

SARPENIC

GLASTONBURY

BRITANNIA

N

W E

S

For Papa Devlin

ONE

Frost has the good sense not to test my patience by settling on my tools.

Nevertheless, a half-dozen gas lanterns line Merlin's desk as precaution. They illuminate iron beams, steel gears, and my own chapped hands when ensuring no snow touches my bounty of metal. Cold air has been my companion for several months, but it doesn't bother me; it's the same air Marcus is breathing on the quest for the Holy Grail. And he has less of a chance for any warmth while I at least have Guinevere's forgotten wardrobe. Amongst it, a selection of strange black-and-white furs I can drape over my shoulders.

Today is a windless morning in the tower Merlin decapitated when he became the spirit of Victor, the ghost in the mechanical dragon, and this lets me keep close watch on that jagged bit of land concealing my newly built aeroship from curious eyes. On clear days with a pale sun high in the sky, I can lift my viewer north to see if anyone will return, half a year after aeroships evacuated Camelot's subjects to safety. If the Lady of the Lake will stroll in with her warped cane in hand to tell me it's time to leave for Avalon now that my aeroship is finished. Which it is—almost.

But she hasn't passed through Camelot in weeks.

My viewer is heavy and unused in my dress's pocket, but my work lies before me, a small flame hovering above to illuminate the words. I release the long, cylindrical quicklight with its small lever from my gloved grip—it rolls a few times and settles atop the table, the words *To Marcus* facing up, engraved in my own penmanship. My hands, freezing despite the tough leather of Merlin's falconry gloves, reach across for scraps of parchment to brainstorm the enigma that has plagued me for days—*how on earth does one create* jaseemat?

I rest my chin on my folded arms and glance at Merlin's safe, inside of which the last of Azur's own blend sits. I ponder the alchemic properties the sorcerer taught me—*what is the precise make-up of charcoal? At what temperature does newly forged gold best keep shape?*—and flip through the hastily scrawled notes. But what I seek is nowhere to be found. The sorcerer made sure of that.

"Merlin," I mutter to myself, "this would be a much faster endeavor if you hadn't been plagued with paranoia."

Perhaps the sorcerer intended to start me on a wild goose chase when he hid those instructions, though to think in such a way might bring about an irreconcilable madness. Outside this insanity, the new-falling snow is as gentle as always for Decembers in Camelot, and that quiet is unnerving.

December. Three months longer than the knights claimed they'd need to beat the Spanish rogues, and not a word from them since autumn.

It's left Lancelot more than worried, but I'm sure plans simply didn't go as expected. Secondary and tertiary tactics became necessary, and although my heart seems to swell with unease every time I think of how long it's been since I last saw Marcus, he and the rest of Galahad's infantry are knights. They can certainly find their way home.

That isn't the only reason for Lancelot's worry, though. Every month, it seems, I watch from Merlin's tower as more knights leave for neighboring kingdoms, carrying messages to aeroship ports on the coast of Britannia. These knights are not going after the Grail; they're tracking down the ships from the kingdoms of España that took Camelot's subjects to safety before Morgan's war. It has slowed the rebuilding of our castle, not having them back yet. And now, with few left in the kingdom, and not a whisper about where the rest might be...

I squeeze my eyes shut. I have to believe my mother is on her way back. "Focus, Vivienne."

Volumes of correspondence between Merlin and Azur lie amongst the cogs and wheels at my fingertips. Caldor I resurrected after Morgan's war, and it tiptoes to my side, every creak and whistle of copper talons amplified through the tower's silence. Its plated feathers are innocently tucked against its belly, but I keep a close eye on my pet nevertheless, in case it were to suddenly broaden its wingspan, knocking the tools and shimmering steel clear off the table and into the clouds drifting beside us. There are still some loose ends to tie up in its machinery or it'll forever be an awkward plaything.

Steam whistles, and the dying sound of Caldor's *jaseemat* stutters empty. I cast some of Merlin's blend into the falcon's copper heart. Then I lean close. This is the best part.

"Yaty ala alhyah." Come to life.

Caldor's feathers shine reddish-gold, and the copper

plates bounce with the chilly morning air. Its neck stretches, twisting until beady black eyes can blink themselves awake with an extra surge of life, even though they're the only parts still reminiscent of a machine. Less clacking are its wings now; when alive through alchemy, they're as fluid as a real bird's. I smile, and my gaze pulls back to my scribbling in front of me.

A knock on the door's frame surprises Caldor enough that the newly alive falcon spins on its talons to face the intruder. I glance over my shoulder at the tall, black-haired knight Gawain standing where there was once a red door. His jaw is square, his eyes are deep and black, suspicious in this space he hasn't grown to know. And his new arm, welded together by the blacksmith, is due for a fix-up.

"I don't disturb, Lady Vivienne?" His middle-aged voice is rough and low, matching perfectly his ruddy face and traveled eyes.

I straighten in my less-than-ladylike leather bodice atop one of Guinevere's cherry gowns, jagged furs about my shoulder and neck, and hair piled up in my trusty steel netting. But Gawain ignores how I look. Those who stayed in Camelot, working to remake it what it once was, have grown accustomed to my dress.

"Of course not." I must force a gentle smile. I wish my thoughts hadn't been interrupted.

He glances around at the remains of the tower. "When will they rebuild it?"

Perhaps when knights and subjects walk the cobblestone streets of Camelot again. "I don't think it's a high priority."

He frowns. "Terrible weather up here, especially if a strong wind were to hit. Why not work in the main castle?"

I hesitate in the ruins that have evolved into a strange sort of sanctuary. Because this is where I feel at home. This is my refuge from the kingdom and reminds me of a time when Camelot might have been a prison, but at least sported life and happiness at every turn.

Gawain notices my discomfort. "Apologies. I don't mean to pry."

I gesture to the chair across from mine and gather a leather-bound set of tools from a table nearby. "Please." I switch out Merlin's falconry gloves for my own fingerless set made of wool and leather and studded with pearls to work on the intricacies of Gawain's arm.

He obeys. "It's incredible what you've done to this old thing," he says, unslinging the immobile arm. "Next time you wish to try your luck at sword play, I don't think I'll need to rely on my left."

I smile. It's nice to hear appreciation for the less than conventional route I've taken. "I'm glad it suits you."

I roll up his sleeve and regard Gawain's arm. Black iron to the shoulder, welded to the bone in the same manner Morgan would have done to construct her dying son, Mordred. I don't know how the man-machine bore it when his mother brought out the soldering torch and pressed the red-hot tip to his flesh. Nor do I know if Mordred had been human enough to scream as Gawain did, despite the tough leather Lancelot gave him to bite down on.

But such gruesome memories have been erased from Gawain's face, a little more each day. He watches plainly as I adjust the elbow: the joints twist in my hands, and black oil softens the creaks until they go silent. There's a mechanism at the base of his wrist that attaches fine wires to the intricate iron fingers and thumb the blacksmith constructed, based on my design.

Gawain shivers. "Ten minutes in this tower is as frigid as an entire day in the north. Did I ever tell you about that journey? We searched Viking-dense airs for the Grail, and that took an entire fortnight. Had it been a day longer, one less arm would have been the least of my bloody problems."

Gawain is the first knight I've met who will talk freely about any and all aspects of the quest without any thought to censor himself in front of a lady.

"How far did you get?" I ask as I lay out the appropriate tools.

Gawain looks over my shoulder at the mountains. "This time around I didn't get farther south than the French territory." His eyes are cold, but also alive, exhilarated. "But last time, it was as far as you could go before you'd reach the end of the world. A land where the sun clung high in the sky for days on end."

I light a small burner Merlin would use to melt metal; the fire dances like a child at a feast. A strange device composed of copper wires I rescued from my unsalvageable mechanical falcon Terra heats up and glows red, but it does not warp. The wires are reinforced with plated steel. I pour in a slow stream of water, and the instrument catches a lightning bolt, as though from Zeus himself, and cages the bolt. From the mechanism, I pull a steel wand connected to a fine wire and set it to Gawain's palm. The elements create a charge that singes all five fingers of Gawain's hand to his flesh. Instantly, the appendages drum against the table, his iron hand now in possession of the lightning's power. I wish my mother were here so I could show Merlin's former apprentice what her daughter is capable of building now.

"We stood out horribly, though. Our markings as Arthur's knights made us easy targets, and the thick furs to hide our inked necks suffocated us." Gawain blinks at the memory. "'Course, there were some with gentle hearts; those who didn't want to see Morgan claim the Grail offered hospitality, but for the hundreds that loved us, there were those who hated us more fervently."

Now it's time to ask the question that's lingered on my mind for weeks. I clear my throat, hoping my fear won't betray me. "The knights. Where would they be now, if they haven't sent word to Lancelot?"

He scratches his thick mop of stringy black hair. "Don't know. If they've been gone this long, perhaps they're being tested. The nearer you get to Avalon, the more you feel its siren's call. Maybe that's where they are. Or maybe they've never been further away."

A response that returns me to the limbo I found myself in not minutes ago. I shake off the disappointment and dip into a forgotten opium box of Merlin's. Inside lies a reserve of Azur's *jaseemat*, more than enough for Gawain to use his iron arm for months. Just a little less than what I've kept in Merlin's safe for my aeroship.

I think of it then, hidden in the woods from Camelot and pillagers alike. Furnace and copper veins inspired by Merlin's catacombs and the mechanical dragon we set against Morgan's drones in June. White sails made of the lightest silk I could find, although their skeletal extensions and retractions are not yet as smooth as I'd hoped. The body of the ship is wood, to counter the heavy iron necessary to reinforce the vessel. Dry kindle and gas lantern oil ready for the voyage. My voyage.

When Gawain sees the small box, he leans forward and pulls open his tunic, right at the heart, presenting a small iron door that's been surgically set into his torso. One of the door's chambers is locked with a pocket attached to his ribs that lets the *jaseemat* pass through his body, like real blood. It ignites his mechanical arm, but not permanently.

The instructions to bring the dust to life are soft whispers I emit without thinking. I pour in the *jaseemat*. The arm flexes, and Gawain nods in approval as he rolls the sleeve back down, breathing fully as he feels the contortion of the elements elevate his blood. People have gotten used to his iron arm, but when the aeroships return with Camelot's citizens, there'll be a new batch of strange looks.

I close the box, and his words hit me again. "The knights are being tested?"

Gawain ties up his tunic and tightens the black furs around his shoulders as a chill overcomes the *jaseemat*'s warmth. "The Grail is protected. It won't be found easily. In order to claim it, the knights will have to go through tests the likes of which you could never imagine. Even with what you know about Merlin and all."

The Lady of the Lake never mentioned this. "What kind of tests?" My wobbly voice might have alerted someone who knows me better—like Merlin or Marcus, or even my brother Owen—to a secret I've kept since Galahad's infantry left six months past. But Gawain might assume my nervousness is for the idea of Avalon, and not the coordinates to it etched onto my mind, but locked from me. I firm my lips in frustration at that.

My own mind kept from me, part of it held hostage, until I don't know when.

Gawain looks me right in the eye. "All men have vices, things of sin they cannot live without. The Grail's holiness purifies anything that comes near it. All desires will be made stronger so those seeking it might overcome them. A swordsman will slit his friend's throat. A drunk will search for a pint. An adulterer will seek a bed ... " His mouth promptly closes. "Begging your pardon."

I'm in a kingdom of men six months without any other women. I've heard worse. "Go on."

"It makes the Grail impossible to seek. Only someone pure of heart will find her. Someone with no tainted soul."

Like a legend or a fairy tale Owen might have told me as a girl. I want to laugh at the audacity of such a person existing. But after what I've seen and done, I know better.

"This ... " Gawain says, gauging the iron fingers on his arm. They stretch and bend at his will. "This is the closest I ever got to it. This right here."

I don't ask his vice. It's well known that knights have always sought the pleasures of food and drink, women and opium. And the swollen cheeks of a forgotten drunk in front of me could never lie. "How did it happen?" I ask. This is the first time I've found the courage to ask.

He's not bothered by my question. "You ever hear of the Spanish rogues?"

"Of course." Every child in Camelot grows up hearing the stories of air pirates from all corners of the world who took over a kingdom of España while the rest of the country fought to take it back. For years, Arthur sent knights to help.

"What about the captain of the rogue aeroship *MUERTE*?" Gawain adds.

I shake my head. This I do not know.

Gawain shifts to the side of his chair, glancing out at the snowy land as he speaks. "We call him the Black Knight because of his suits of iron and dark silks. Who knows what his real name actually is? Something damning, I'm sure. Some say he was once a demigod, soulless and without the ability to feel, who now walks the earth as a man seeking the Grail for his own purposes. They claim he wants to sell it to the highest bidder." Another twist of his mechanical arm. "All he needs is to find it, and he'll do whatever it takes to have it in his possession. Even if it means tempting a man with but a pint to learn Avalon's coordinates."

Coordinates. Coordinates the world believes were hidden inside Camelot by a demigoddess who wanted Arthur to find it. Like the song children sang in the village, when children were plentiful in Camelot. Coordinates the Lady of the Lake told me lie within a realm of my mind I cannot yet explore. But there's no way the Spanish rogues could ever know that.

They might be close to finding out somehow. But besides that, I cannot lead the knights to Avalon until I receive word that the Spanish rogues have been defeated. Nor can I go until I've replicated Azur's *jaseemat* so my aeroship can fly all the way to the Great Sea of the Mediterranean in Greece, but the endeavor is impossible. When Azur heard of my task to build an aeroship powerful enough to soar above the skies, he was quick to tell me stories about inventors in Jerusalem— accomplished and trained, and certainly never handmaids— whose attempts at such a feat by utilizing the mechanical arts and the ingenuity of advanced aeroships were massive failures. They fell from the sky and into horrifying legend. Modern aeroships can only fly as high as the boldest falcon.

The whole thing is impossible, and so I rebuilt Caldor, the detailed carving taking up an entire evening. A means to distract myself when the task of finishing such an aeroship becomes too overwhelming to bear.

Gawain's face goes somber. "It was just one pint. We were so close to Avalon, and the Black Knight had a different sort of chalice in his grip. One just for me. And it drew me in."

I lean closer. "You knew how to find the Grail?" I whisper. Cannot be.

He opens his eyes to mine. "No," he says. "That's why they took my arm."

TWO

Winter mornings are best for sword fighting.

Most knights agree, Gawain tells me. *Habit.* On the quest, his infantry would be up an hour before dawn, the best time to get used to a new day before risking hot summer weather that would render a knight lethargic by noon. And so began the practice of riding at night and sleeping come sunrise. Conveniently enough, this is also the only time my father is guaranteed still to be asleep. Dawn was hours ago, but the courtyard might as well be a graveyard, host to the phantoms of Camelot, and never the few left here.

I don't complain about the cold. It was difficult enough to convince Gawain to teach me my way around a sword. He'd suggested archery, but I refused. I couldn't bring myself to rebuild my miniature crossbow. It reminds me too much of Morgan's war and the lives I stole. Of the witch herself seizing it from my grasp and sending in into a nearby tree. The exact moment I thought I was going to die.

"Check for frost," Gawain says, rolling his shoulders and pacing the courtyard. His own blade is easy in his grasp. It was the first thing that struck me once he agreed to teach me: he's just as good with a weapon in his left hand as his right.

I run the blade across my skirt, smoothing Merlin's prized

sword until it's shining and dry. A silent weapon, the sole reason we decided on swords rather than firelances or fusionahs whose blasts would echo for weeks in the ruins that is Camelot. Anyway, Merlin's pistolník went missing when he became the ghost for the mechanical dragon Victor.

Gawain gestures to my stance. "Hold your blade high. Like I showed you. Both hands on the hilt."

My knuckles go white with my grip. Gawain walks casually toward me and lifts his own blade over his head, letting it slam down on mine. I jump and swing Merlin's sword against Gawain's. He frees our blades and steps back.

"Good. But don't flinch. Your footing makes you awkward; you look as though this is the third or fourth time you've ever held a blade."

I glare at him. "It is."

He cocks a lighthearted smile and sends his weapon through the air, the point straight at me. Instinctively, I lift my sword vertical, and our weapons clash. We both hold. If I hadn't moved, I would have lost an ear. My mouth goes agape.

"Faster next time." His eyes gleam.

I find my breath again. The clock tower chimes eight o'clock and surprises me, and I glance over at the still-missing numbers near its top.

"Don't turn away from your enemy," Gawain warns.

I look back, but he's already advancing and swinging his sword. A rush of irritation turns my blood hot from my error in gauging his speed. His blade strikes mine, and his heavy step moves me backward, giving him the advantage. The steel spins around my wrist and nearly peels my grip free.

Hold on—he's done this before. I know his next move.

I grip the hilt tighter and force his sword away. Our jaws firm, our blades dance, and the steel sings. There's a split second where I can grab control and push him back. His eyes widen in surprise, and I slam my blade against his, once, twice, again, again. Finally, his sword falls, and I grin.

His arms lift in surrender, the mechanical one slower than his left. "Well done," he says with a proud smile.

Progress. I gaze past my blade's disguise to see it for what it really is: a tool, fundamentally speaking. Something I can study, learn, understand. And then, perhaps, one day, master. "Your words made me angry."

"Then you'll be better once you learn to fight with a clear head."

The snow flutters around me. I pull Guinevere's white furs tight against my shoulders. My ears are frozen. My fingertips, likewise. But my smile at Gawain's words, confident.

"Lower the drawbridge!" someone calls.

Gawain and I glance at the northern gates as guards peel them back. Someone is riding for Camelot, and my first thought is a mixture of hope and preemptive disappointment. With every reason: the rider is too tall to be Marcus, even if the newest Knight of the Round Table is already rather tall. Nor is it Owen, as this stranger's shoulders are much broader than my brother's. The rider's hair is long and dark, and his beard suggests he's been away from any kingdom for months. He gallops in on a near-flying stallion, and I make out the tail end of a dragon tattoo on his neck when he turns his head.

From the main castle, Lancelot steps out, visibly fatigued, with gray weaving through his hair from running a kingdom on the brink of collapse. He's lost weight and sleep since Arthur's death and Guinevere's departure. Anxious wrinkles line his face like a map.

My father, Lord William, steps out beside him, and the two men converse with somber looks about them.

At the gates, guards call, "Sir Kay!"

"I'll be damned," Gawain mutters. "The last time I saw Kay, I was about to lose an arm, and he an eye. Seems my luck was worse that day than his." He glances sideways at me and inclines his head: "Lady Vivienne." And then he leaves for the main castle. But I don't hesitate in following.

One recent night at dinner, Lancelot spoke about Arthur's step-brother, Kay, who was born to coal miners in a village beyond Camelot's borders while Merlin kept harm and the wrath of Glastonbury far from Uther Pendragon's first and only son. Kay was raised with Arthur in the English country-side before Merlin arrived on Arthur's fifteenth birthday to tell him of his true purpose: grasp the gauntlet wielding the blade Excalibur and run a kingdom destined to find the Holy Grail.

Lancelot told the story through pints of ale and miniature goblets of absinthe, through tears of regret for a betrayed friendship and a torn marriage. It was a story I'd never heard before. Sir Kay, a character in Arthur's journal of life I'd never read.

And now he's here.

My breath is a fog as I reach the steps of the main castle. I keep far from the guards and the commotion; as the only lady in Camelot, I haven't decided if they'll let my place be amongst them, as Gawain does, despite my role in Morgan's war last June.

But then my father catches my eye and beckons me to his side. He has finally given in to fashionable gentlemen's jackets, or it could very well be that his practical cloaks were destroyed during Morgan's wrath. I catch up with him and Lancelot as they march toward the opening gates.

"You spend too much time in that tower, Vivienne," my father says as he clears his throat with the proper aura of a king's advisor.

Lancelot's eyes meet mine only briefly. "Conduct your work in the main castle, my lady. It'd ease all our minds."

I shake my head, foregoing the expected curtsy. "The main castle doesn't have what I need, Sir Lancelot. I'll stay in the tower." Neither Lancelot nor my father knows it's for the aeroship I'm building.

I don't miss the knight's jaw clenching at my disobedient words, but he doesn't dispute me. He saw what world lies beneath Camelot's surface when he assisted in cleaning up Merlin's catacombs. And with few knights left to send to Galahad's infantry or search for the subjects gone too long, the problem I am to him is a low priority.

Sir Kay approaches with deep-set eyes of brutal charcoal, nearly ten years on Lancelot, and a strong face in need of a good cleaning.

"Lancelot." Kay dismounts and hands off his horse to a waiting guard.

Lancelot's eyes crinkle with happiness long forgotten at

the sight of the dead king's brother. "Kay," he says with a brotherly embrace. The name coming off his tongue might as well be Arthur's. "You've had a long journey."

Kay's eyes fall to the snow-covered ground as more falls from the sky through a quiet wind.

"A journey months too long, if I'm not mistaken," Lancelot adds.

"No," Kay says. "Years. Pour me a drink, Lancelot. I have much to tell you."

THREE

Sir Kay's booming laughter gets in the way of his reminiscent storytelling that evening.

"We'd just arrived in Corbenic when Lancelot decided the ale from the night prior deserved to make a reappearance!" Kay shouts as his cheeks redden from drink. An array of dried meats and whatever bread we've managed to scrounge up from the banquet halls lies in front of our company, composed of Kay, Lancelot, Gawain, my father, and me. But only Kay eats.

"A brew of ox piss always does," Lancelot mutters, wiping away bittersweet tears at the memory.

"You should have seen the look on Arthur's face—utter horror! He couldn't believe his finest ale was coming back up with the braised pork!" A loud laugh shakes the table and Kay's stomach until he must clench it.

Lancelot hides his smile by drinking from his pint. "Piss, Kay. It was piss."

Story after story about Arthur, carefully collected and lying in front of us in such detail that one might think the king was alive. Lancelot was the one to confirm Arthur's death upon Kay's arrival, and at the news, the older knight's eyes grew heavy, and his lips quivered. But then he smiled at the wealth of tales that would ensure Arthur of Camelot would live on.

Finally, Kay lifts his pint. "To Arthur."

"To Arthur," the lot of us reply.

"To Arthur." Lancelot drinks quickly and regards the main hall of Camelot, losing himself in its decrepit architecture. Suits of armor stand guard in a castle whose twisted copper candelabras have darkened, and where the silence of cold smokestacks is too loud. The mechanical arts and their influence over the way we lived were destroyed in Morgan's war, leaving us in an archaic world.

Kay eyes Lancelot carefully, the aura of mourning now passed. "I stopped at Corbenic several nights ago. I remembered Pelles as a man of life and joy, but when we met again this time, he was a ghost of himself."

Lancelot traces the rings in the wooden table. My father clears his throat. "Le Fay's attack on Camelot left our kingdoms' alliance fractured. Pelles mourns his fallen men with the rest of Corbenic."

I stare at my own untouched pint and clench my skirt in my fists until I'm certain my nails will weave the threads into my skin. The scrimmage Morgan stirred up between our kingdoms was the setting of my first kill; the war that followed and the scores who died showed me how crucial it was for Camelot to find the Grail, that which Merlin said could end death and balance the scales between magic and the mechanical arts. An alchemist's dream.

Kay leans back in his chair, clutching his heavy leather belt across his stomach and glancing at the desolate rafters.

"Shame. It was always a fine kingdom to visit. Its festivals were wonderfully entertaining, how they would twist the mechanical arts into vivid illusions. Your squire Marcus enjoyed it there."

At those words I straighten, and Lancelot glances wearily at me.

"You know Sir Marcus?" I ask.

Kay searches the table for the one who spoke and regards me as though I'd been invisible this entire time. "*Sir* Marcus?" He chuckles once and turns to Lancelot. "Don't tell me that whirlwind of a boy has proven his worth already! With all the attention the girls of Corbenic gave him, I half-expected him to follow in your swaggering footsteps, Lancelot." A sly smile skirts to the side of Kay's face as though yet another memory has come to mind. "Wasn't too long ago that I bet three bags of gold you'd be the first to relinquish knighthood for warm, feminine arms, after all. Even if it'd mean banishment from this godforsaken iron-and-stone prison."

I feel my eyebrows shoot up. Marcus? A favorite to the girls of Corbenic? "Surely, you're thinking of someone else," I hear myself whisper, but I've been forgotten now. I consider the barn, Marcus's arms holding me against the wall, my fingers woven in his rain-soaked hair, our swollen lips. *"I've never done that before,"* he'd said. Was it true?

Lancelot's face darkens. "That's enough, Kay."

But Kay is much too interested in Lancelot's philandering past now. "Especially that one maiden who was particularly fond of you. What was her name? That girl at court who disappeared after Pelles's festival earlier this year? I never knew what happened to the likes of her. Didn't Pelles say she eloped—"

"Enough," Lancelot repeats.

I turn to the knight who apparently was a heartbreaking scoundrel even before Guinevere. He'll certainly clarify what Kay meant about Marcus. My father clears his throat and sets a scrutinizing eye upon a muddled spot on the side of his goblet.

Kay will not let up. "Mara? No, that's not it. Blast it all, I can't remember! She was madly in love with you, swore to make you her champion if only you'd love her back." Kay turns to dramatics to imitate the poor girl's memory, his ruddy fingers soft and delicate in midair as he punctuates the words.

Lancelot finally gives in. "Elaine. She didn't understand the knights' vow."

"Elaine! That's it! Long black hair, curves only a real man would—"

"Sir Kay!" my father erupts, hands clapping over my ears, but I pull free. "Talk like that! It's undignified!"

Kay blows air through his lips, letting the ruffle declare his indifference, but resettles in his chair. "Very well. To matters of the Grail, then. You said, Lancelot, you've sent word to Arthur's allies concerning Camelot's missing subjects, but communication with Jerusalem has suddenly stalled, and no one seems to know why. Might I inquire about the wizard? I'd heard that once again the bastard lost his mind to magic—"

"That's not what happened," I say sharply. How dare Sir

Kay speak against Merlin after all the sorcerer sacrificed for Camelot?

Kay regards me with curiosity, and I realize I'm still wearing a uniform that outsiders would see as inappropriate. "We have yet to become formally acquainted, my lady."

Lancelot clears his throat. "Lady Vivienne was the queen's lady-in-waiting before her majesty took to the north."

Kay casts a suspicious glance at Lancelot. "Yes, so I heard. Guinevere's left Camelot, hasn't she? She is well-missed?"

Lancelot nods, losing himself in the light of the lone gas lantern sitting in front of him. "Very much so."

Now they won't bother correcting themselves concerning Merlin's reputation, and so I must do it myself. "Merlin sacrificed himself so Camelot could defeat Morgan le Fay."

"Vivienne—" my father mutters.

I couldn't care less now. My status in Camelot might have already been decided tonight, but I won't let Kay think me a simple-minded handmaid.

"Without him, le Fay would have claimed the kingdom and gone after Sir Gawain's infantry, bringing with her mechanical monsters you could never imagine. Her thievery of magic knew no bounds." And perhaps it's the cold or the waiting on end with no word, but my nerves are shot, and I don't want to be thought of as invisible anymore. "I don't know where Merlin is now, Sir Kay, if he's alive or doomed, but you owe him a hefty debt. We all do. I only hope I do him justice by continuing with his work."

Out of the corner of my eye, I see how my father cringes ever so slightly. He allows this only because he fears Merlin's magic more than his own tarnished reputation, but just barely.

I glance at Gawain, and he nods, an ally in my corner. Kay sees the silent interaction, and when Gawain lifts his pint to drink, the four of us stare at the iron arm holding it to his lips.

Kay faces me again. His smile is one of condescension. "You have a strong will, Lady Vivienne, if you've taken up the mechanical arts. Was it your own lady who convinced you to study them? Or the sorcerer's rhetoric? Perhaps you can fix the hilt on my sword, polish it—"

"We have a blacksmith in the village, Sir Kay, if it requires iron or fire," I say shortly. "I work in the clock tower."

"I see," Kay continues in a louder voice. "I was hoping to turn to these sorts of matters when *my lady* had retired for the evening, but it seems you're going nowhere. I bring up the question of Merlin because he was Arthur's most trusted advisor and was to help us find the Grail while serving as a liaison to the Kingdom of Jerusalem. Now, these tasks go unfulfilled, as though Merlin's protégé is unaware of her newfound responsibilities."

My face should feel warm, and I should be a mess of insecurity, but I'm not the same girl I was in the spring. "His protégé knows that," I say, "and she's worked under the guidance of both Merlin and his mentor from Jerusalem—"

"The alchemist? Azur?" Kay interrupts. He leans forward. "Lately?"

I hesitate. It's certainly been some time since I last communicated with Azur. "Well, no, but—"

"Then forgive my boldness, Lady Vivienne," Kay says, his eyes turning to fire, "but I have one more question. What could alchemy possibly do for the knights when some of Galahad's infantry had already gone missing by the time I finally found him and Percy?"

FOUR

Missing.

The word is an executioner's drum thundering in my mind.

"What do you mean?" My voice wavers. It was only months ago that I last felt Marcus's hand in mine, and suddenly the idea of never holding it again...

My father eases closer, as though preparing his daughter for bad news before worst. "We don't know for certain they're missing," he whispers, sneaking a sharp eye toward Kay while Lancelot drinks his ale faster now.

Kay leans back in his chair. "Then where are they, Lord William? Did they vanish into thin air? Did they seek Camelot's subjects and become lost in the same void? Did they find the Grail?" He scoffs, shaking his head before taking a large gulp of ale. "They've missed their checkpoints. That's what you get when you send a company of fools with Galahad. He's too inexperienced, Lancelot, and not nearly aggressive enough. I've told you this before."

My father leans over the table. "Do not insult Sir Galahad's infantry, Sir Kay. My boy is out there."

"Yes, so I heard. Master Owen, Galahad's squire." He swallows a mouthful of ale and sets his goblet on the table. "I must admit, you couldn't ask for a better mentor than *Galahad the Pure*. But where is Master Owen now?"

My breath bursts from my lungs as though someone punched me. "Owen?" To hear this spoken of my brother is much worse than what my mind could conjure up on its own.

Lancelot glances at me. "The group split up. There was a conflict. Not relating to the Spanish rogues, but from within." His eyes look disturbed. Galahad is a brother to him.

All eyes watch me. I glance at Gawain, who with one look tells me he, too, has known of this for perhaps days. He mentioned tests. How a man of the sword might slice the throat of his companion. What sort of sinister dangers might have fallen upon Galahad's infantry?

I force myself to breathe, and it feels like I'm drowning. "You all knew." I'm too angry to form words. "When were you going to tell me?" But instead of facing my father, I face the one who would understand more than the rest.

Gawain holds my gaze for a long moment before speaking. "If we heard from Sir Marcus."

I should say something, but no words come. My lips form the letters, but no breath races to help. I need to be strong like the men sitting around me, but I've never felt more like a child.

Finally, I find my voice. "Marcus is missing, too?"

"Yes," Lancelot says. "Word arrived two nights past of an argument between him and Owen that started it all. Your boy is headstrong, William."

My father sits back in his seat. This was not news to him, but he doesn't like hearing it again.

Lancelot's attention returns to me. "Owen has a thirst for power. Who knows what was said amongst them?"

I watch the scene in my mind's eye: my brother unleashing rage upon Marcus after Owen found error in something as simple as a mistake in direction. The crossbow on Owen's back suddenly aimed at Marcus's throat. I think of Marcus forced to unsheathe his sword, crafted by the blacksmith when he was knighted, unexpectedly vicious and strong when he needs to be. Perhaps something worse happened— like their brawl over Owen betraying Lancelot and Guinevere resurfaced. A spiteful remark about loyalty from Marcus. A quick jump to violence from Owen. Merlin did say there were sleeping demons in my brother.

It's easy to imagine Owen reacting violently, but not Marcus. "What sort of conflict would they fight over?"

Lancelot reaches into the pocket of his gentleman's jacket and tosses a thin strip of black lace on the table. Each of us looks at the small trinket, but I'm the only one to recognize it. Without even a touch, I remember its delicate feel as I tied it around Marcus's wrist before he headed into Morgan's war. Owen told me to be careful when it came to my heart and how Marcus made it flutter, but when my brother told me what deal Marcus had made with Lancelot about finding the Grail, and how it would let him relinquish his knighthood, I'd thought all was forgiven.

But the truth very well may be that the knights disbanded over something as simple as Marcus and me.

Now, Lancelot doesn't hold back. "All the messenger knew was that Marcus was the first to go missing, one month past. No one's heard from him since."

Guinevere's furs fall from my shoulders to the snowy ground, but the chill doesn't affect my sprint back to the clock tower. My father bellows at me to return—he's much closer than I thought. Suddenly, his hand grabs my arm, and I spin to look at him.

"Let me go," I say with not an ounce of emotion stitched into the words. "Let me go. Now. Please."

"Stop this!" he growls in a low voice striving for patience. His worn blue eyes are heavy with worry and fatigue. "Enough, Vivienne. You're wasting your time up in that clock tower."

He won't let go of my arm, but I haven't given up. "I can save them. I can find them. Will you *please* let me go?" My voice jumps three octaves into the quiet Camelot night.

But my father's grip stills me into place, and I hold my breath, waiting for retribution, for discipline, for the order to become a lady whom a lord of Camelot might desire for a wife.

"No. That was the last of it, daughter," he says in a low voice he uses when there's sadness attached. I've mentioned my place in Camelot too many times, and it's caught up to me. My father glances about, as though expecting perhaps a nosy stable boy eavesdropping. But we're alone. "I cannot bear to worry about your safety here. A fortnight past, I sent for an aeroship. It'll arrive in the morning. You'll go to the north to be with Guinevere until the others return."

The others. My father's name for those who left the kingdom for safer grounds and who haven't returned. To go to the same northern nunnery Guinevere fled to after Morgan's war would save my reputation once Camelot is a united kingdom again. Certainly a more ideal option than to be found as the only lady in these ruins for six months. Quite possibly I could be married off by the time Camelot is rebuilt.

To speak higher than a whisper might mean a scream of protest. "You would have me leave my home all because Sir Kay didn't like how a handmaid argued with him?"

My father's gaze is not one of anger at my words, but one of pity. Of perhaps wishing I could have instead been born a boy to follow in his political footsteps. "You would have done well as an advisor."

I scoff, wishing away the lump of sadness in my throat.

My father could rebuke me for that, but he finds patience somehow. "The world we live in is unkind, even here, in a place that should have been paradise." He sets his hands on my shoulders so that I look at him. "It won't be this way forever. Our allies in España, Caledonia, and the Druid lands are helping us search for . . . for them. It won't be much longer now."

I feel my eyes well, but not because of what being sent away would mean for Marcus and me. But because there is no argument I could give my father that would change his mind, regardless of whether it could save his only son. The morning is only hours away. I could be on the northern shores by the next nightfall.

"Please don't ask me to do this," I whisper.

My father touches my cheek in a tender way. "It's for the best. You don't belong up there." His eyes shoot up at the clock tower, but he'll never say the words himself. "Let Lancelot deal with Owen and the…" He trails off, and I wonder if he and Lancelot have spoken much about Marcus's affection for me. "He's a knight now, and he was only a serf. Please, Vivienne. You'll thank me one day."

I want to speak up, to defy him, to tell him I won't live a life decided for me, but the words are lost on my lips, and all I can manage is a bitter response. "No. I'll never forgive you."

My father straightens, guarding himself from my words, though certain I won't leave the castle. And so there's no reason to keep tight to my arm: no one in this wretched place would accompany me should I try to escape anyway. I run through the snow to Merlin's tower before my father can see me cry and know that perhaps he was right in believing this skeleton of a kingdom is no place for a girl.

———

Night is descending, and Camelot will grow colder. Irrelevant—I must leave tonight, before the aeroship my father sent for arrives. For that, I'll need *jaseemat*. And a hell of a lot of it.

According to my specifications, only *jaseemat* as sophisticated as Azur's can power my own aeroship to fly high enough to kiss the heavens, fast enough to chase Apollo across dawn's sky. To reach Avalon. When Merlin and I used the alchemic powder as blood in the copper veins of Victor, it rendered much power. To hell with waiting for a signal from the Lady of the Lake. I need to find Marcus and Owen or I'll be sent away at the first sight of dawn. A month missing without returning to Camelot? Marcus wouldn't do that. He'd find a way to send word.

In the clock tower, the wind blasts a tornado around me, its voice taunting me that it might already be too late. I ignore it for the scattered journals and leaves of parchment on Merlin's desk, scanning the alchemic incantations I've come to memorize. But I've already gone through these volumes. There's nothing here about turning charcoal into gold, let alone *jaseemat*.

Azur. I need Azur, though it's been weeks since I could last reach him. But he might have heard something. And he needs to teach me more about alchemy.

I pick up Merlin's looking glass. A small one the sorcerer cherished for as long as I'd been his apprentice: rounded, metal back with hammered texture and handle inspired by ancient Druid art. I know how to use alchemic properties for communication; to stay in touch with Azur, it became necessary to learn how. As my soul is unblemished of magic, it works perfectly.

The looking glass reflects the haggard look in my eyes, the dark circles beneath, the gaunt cheeks—I haven't been eating enough. The wind forces me to draw a blanket nearer to my face, tucking against my skin the wild blonde strands that have loosened themselves from my steel netting. I look away from my reflection.

I'll have to sacrifice some of Azur's *jaseemat* for this, as Merlin's is not nearly strong enough, even though to fail at reaching Azur again would be the risk of spending it. I open Merlin's padlocked safe and seize the mortar and pestle, tossing a pinch of *jaseemat* atop the looking glass. *"Yaty ala alhyah."*

The dust shimmers in cool clumps. It strikes the looking glass and vanishes into its surface.

"*Ahlohnfu* Azur Barad," I whisper, emitting the conjuring instruction in Azur's native tongue. The alchemy's alto voice whispers the name back. The surface shimmers like water, and the ripples reveal Azur's eyes, as though from the bottom of a pond as he stands at the surface. I can't help but smile through my worry at seeing him, at *finally* seeing him.

"Vivienne," he says in a voice unnaturally concerned, vowels jagged from his accent and warped through the watery reflection. "This is a surprise."

The looking glass is now a window to Jerusalem, Azur's world. And in that world, explosions abound as the alchemist takes cover in a fast crouch. Aeroships move against the skies like hawks: unsuspecting, fast, deadly. I've found Azur in the midst of chaos, and suddenly I know why no one in Camelot has heard from the Holy Land.

"Quick, child! I have but minutes."

"Oh God, Azur. What's happening? Why haven't you sent for help? No one here has heard from Jerusalem in weeks!"

His eyes are heavier now, full of things he's seen since Morgan's war, perhaps more horrid than the torture the witch inflicted upon Camelot. With a gaze saddened and tired, he breathes for a long, long second, enough time for that gaze to turn vengeful. "Where Camelot was the birthplace of magic, Jerusalem is the inception of mechanical progress, but with that comes vulnerability. We have sent word with a knight from Camelot who was stationed in Jerusalem. He was supposed to have arrived by now. Tell Lancelot to send his knights. I beg of you, Vivienne. The Druids will send warriors to help with this siege—"

"Is it rogues, Azur?" I run Azur's instructions through my mind over and over, grasping at every image it shows me of cannons and clashing swords. The images I conjure up are stronger than the alchemist's words, but I must remember them. "Why would they do this? They seek the Grail, like the rest of the world!" And Avalon is certainly not in the Holy Land. That has been long established.

Azur's face falls with confusion, like perhaps one of the most tragic aspects of this attack is how he doesn't understand it. "Send help. Please."

My hands are shaking, and the cold is no longer the culprit. Another strike of lightning to Jerusalem's ground, and I realize too late it's an array of bearings falling like rain. I can help, though it might delay any aid I could be to Marcus and Owen; nevertheless, I raise my voice to match the echoes of cannons. "My aeroship, Azur. I can fly to Jerusalem and get you out of the city! Tell me how to create *jaseemat*—"

But then the blood-curdling scream of a monster trumps the atmosphere, forcing Azur's eyes shut and me to cover my cold ears with colder hands. Beads of sweat line the parts of Azur's face I can see. "By Allah's grace we will be saved."

This is no longer the spoils of war I'm hearing. This is something worse.

Merlin's spirit is caged in an iron vault in Jerusalem, anchored to the ground by Azur's alchemy and the part of the sorcerer still yearning to be a man. A necessary confinement Merlin would agree to, surely, lest his uncontrollable, dragonesque soul were to attack his old friend or others. I don't know how Azur will return Merlin to his physical body, and I'm not sure I want to.

Azur turns quickly as though to prevent an ambush. "Merlin is drunk with magic and refusing to cooperate." His eyes turn fierce. "It is nearly impossible. By interfering, I might be damning him to a limbo not of this world, and he was already at risk for a month, when the demon inside him managed to find freedom. Now, with these attacks, I am not as strong a man as I once was. But leave this to Lancelot and the Druids warriors. You, with the coordinates to Avalon, cannot leave Camelot."

"Riders!" comes from the gates. I pull back to look upon the citadel, where a messenger bearing the rust-and-ivory colored garments of Sarpenic arrives, calling to the few guards left. One guard runs for the main castle. *"Rogues have overtaken Jerusalem!"*

And so now Lancelot will know, even though word from the Holy Land never made it here. Though knights from Camelot are lost or missing or seeking our subjects with the kingdoms of España and Caledonia, the Druid warriors are allied with Jerusalem and will surely help. Perhaps Azur is right, though, and the coordinates in my mind would render me a more interesting capture than Jerusalem itself.

But then I can search for Marcus and Owen. If the rogues are attacking Jerusalem, there might not be many on the Grail quest. The news about this attack will serve as a way out of this decrepit castle unseen, but if I am sent away first, I can do nothing.

My hands tremble as the bravery I need comes over me. "Azur. I won't sit here, useless—"

"Vivienne, I cannot teach you how to create *jaseemat*. The line between alchemy and magic might not be as distinct as I originally thought. It could very well be a border drawn in the sands, now gone up in a windstorm."

My thoughts race back to how many times I've touched *jaseemat*, so close to how my gloved hand feels when pressed against the Norwegian steel, singing into my skin a song so alluring.

Azur continues. "Now that I have had the chance to study the fall of Lyonesse, I have learned alchemy might be the darkest path to magic!"

I grip the edges of the looking glass. "No. Alchemy is instruction to the elements, not something that would tarnish souls—"

"According to alchemy! Believe the liar, Vivienne, and I will show you the fool!"

There's another cry behind him, and it could very well be that Merlin's only gotten worse, a shimmer of his form thrashing against the iron vault, begging for opium and magic. His mind might no longer be in limbo, but completely gone, dead. Morgan might have stolen his very being.

"I must go now," Azur says. "Or he might free himself—"

"Wait!"

But Azur disappears, and I drop Merlin's looking glass. It shatters into an ocean of jagged edges.

FIVE

I stare blankly at the broken glass. My breath is stuttered, and when I take a deep breath, it releases as a sob. My fingers fly to cover my mouth. Warm tears slice my cheeks into freezing glaciers in this wintry haven at the very thought of never speaking with Azur again. Not only that; I'm chained to this spot with no way of finding instructions to create *jaseemat* in Merlin's writings. Blast.

Blast, blast, *blast!*

I breathe in an ugly way, inhaling the cold air and slamming the heel of my boot into the shattered looking glass, over and over until my reflection is nothing more than uneven lines and edges. I'm as useless to the knights as ever, sitting amongst the high winds in a rickety tower, while angry shouts from the main castle tell me the Spanish rogues have seized Jerusalem. Why did I think for a moment that I could be of any help to Camelot?

I shut my eyes, and right away I see Marcus, even though he's so far away. But to dive into my own memory brings us closer.

═══════

"Tell me a story," I said, shuffling on my side to relieve the discomfort of hay digging into my skin. I leaned on my palm, and my other hand snapped dried bits in half while we waited out the storm in his family's barn.

When the fire was strong enough to burn without Marcus tending to it, he moved next to me, close enough that I could smell the sweet rain on his skin, but far enough away that I wouldn't see it dry. The flickering light shone in his eyes, speckling the violet with natural bits of gray and gold. A smirk appeared. "I'm not a very good storyteller."

"Anything." I didn't tell him I needed something to distract me from the contours of his cheekbones and the way his mouth parted every time he looked at me.

But he must have caught on because his eyes were too long absorbed in mine, and suddenly his temperament changed to a lighter one. "All right. There was once an old serf. He enjoyed roasted duck. His wife preferred pork. But he didn't give a—"

I pushed him away before he could finish, feigning horror. "The language on your mind!"

His lip cocked up in a mischievous grin. "You don't know the half of it." When his body swayed back, he was closer.

I could feel the heat from his skin, and my voice shuddered into a whisper. "Then tell me about your home. It's only fair. You watched me work in the clock tower for years."

He was bold in how he reached across to set a lock of damp hair behind my ear. His eyes drifted on every detail of my face, and I should have felt vulnerable, but it wasn't with judgment that he looked at me.

"Only fair?" he challenged me, his voice striving to tease, but too quiet to fool me. "I told you my life from the tops of parapets, nearly falling to my death. All to make sure you wouldn't leave to carry out some tedious errand."

"And nearly fell twice!"

He shrugged. "All right. I could tell you about my father. He didn't always live in Camelot. His life was a secret one my mother and I know little about. I grew up hearing few stories about his life." His eyes were shining at the nostalgia surrounding us, but as it dawned on him what tales those would be, he grew more serious.

"Stories about his time in Lyonesse."

———

My eyes open, staring at nothing. "Stop this."

The black lace is still in my hand, and I wrap it twice around my wrist, securing a ruthless knot. I lean on the desk, and my arm brushes against the skeletal form of Caldor. I glance at its petal-like copper feathers, at how meticulously I engraved the veins of each. But all I see are flaws in such an ugly machine. The hinges on the wings are too creaky. The wingspan doesn't extend as fluidly as it did before. And when Caldor looks at me with those dark beady eyes full of *jaseemat* life, I see the face of a creature who might wish its true creator had fixed it, not a handmaid.

A rush of fury comes over me. "I should never have wasted time on you, stupid falcon!"

I shove Caldor away, but its feet are much closer to the

table's edge than I thought, and it trips, catching the wind with its wings, but too late. Caldor spirals as it strives to reach flight, but crashes straight into the wall, falling to a nearby windowsill. Its pitiful black eyes stare emptily across the way, and its wing falls broken, reflecting the village below.

I sigh in annoyance at myself. That'll be a few hours' worth of repairs.

A dark shadow passes in my periphery. I glance back at Caldor's cocked wing in time to see the shadow's reflection in the copper. That of a man, but warped in the rounded wing of the falcon, upside-down and smudged.

I step toward the window for a better look. The mirror's glass crunches under my boots, but all I care about is the village below. When I reach the window, I pull Caldor aside and peek down for myself.

The blacksmith is still at work, despite the chaos. I frown at the late hour, the furnace still hot. In the same spot where Azur's aerohawk landed six months past, he lifts his mask from his face, but the gas lanterns in the street are too dim to make out any features. He doesn't seem bothered by the cold in only a white tunic and brown trousers, typical serf wear.

I look closer. He goes behind the workstation and pulls up the door to the cellar, stepping down.

And then a realization hits me, and I curse my lack of foresight these past few months and my habit of leaving the swinging stone door *open*.

The catacombs. Oh, how Merlin would scold if he knew. It never occurred to me that the blacksmith would come across the stone door on its axis to the world beneath Camelot.

I don't know which is worse—someone prodding at my alchemic work or someone in a realm with magic still lingering there.

I don't give it a second thought and run down the stairs for the cellar. My feet land squarely in front of the stone wall leading to the catacombs. It's wide open, chilling my blood and cautioning me about the possibility of forthcoming danger. As I peer down, I watch the fiery dance of a lantern move about with each step the blacksmith takes. I clench my fists to gather courage and set my hand to the steps' wall to follow him.

My footsteps are soundless because of the inferno dancing on the pyre. But then I must pause as the blacksmith's words silence the flames in exactly the same accent Merlin would employ. "*Ahzikabah.*"

I gasp. The blacksmith knows how to ask of the demigods safe passage into the catacombs. Impossible … unless he's followed me before.

He presses onward, and so do I. The doors open, revealing the pitch-blackness of the fireless room. When he walks inside, the flames from his lantern jump for the wall, illuminating the entire space until they reach the heavy, iron furnace across from the door.

The blacksmith reaches the center of the catacombs and turns, his silhouette distinguished against the rubble of broken cobblestone and gemstones torn free by Victor's iron claws. I pause at the door, hidden by darkness. The blacksmith is perhaps twice my age, tall and burly. His hair is pitch black, and he runs his fingers through the back in a manner I find remarkably familiar. He studies the room and continues on to the other side.

He stops past the furnace, pressing his palm against the wall, and glances up, muttering. The wall shudders and unhinges from the labyrinth of pipes and metalwork. Through a long, humming creak, they move backward into an empty space.

I thought I knew these catacombs well, but there's so much more that Merlin never told me—unless he didn't know about this passageway himself.

My eyes follow the moving wall to the ceiling, where once there was the gemstone mosaic of a dragon that is now no longer whole, but an assembling of sparkling amethysts that survived Victor's blow. There's a sharp break where the ceiling ends and where a long roller chain with rotating sprockets reveals itself. I glance at the blacksmith in time to see him disappear through the break in the wall, the white of his shirt the only indication he'd escaped.

Then the walls churn to close the gap.

I certainly won't be left behind. I close my dress into my fists to lift the hem and run. The stone pulls forward and the sprockets rotate faster. The break is pitch black, but the orange glow of the blacksmith's lantern lets me see a path. The wall's reassembling speeds up. My feet move faster.

Goodness, what am I doing? I might be crushed to death!

I twist to the side in time to pass through, fingers nearly caught in the stone wall as it slams back into place. Merlin did say there were traps about for curious fingers.

There's a familiar crack, one that sounds when you

switch on a common gas lantern to catch flame. One by one, lanterns line the corridor. At the end, the light is bright.

There's nowhere to go but forward. But when I reach the end of the path, the burly shadow of the blacksmith steps in front of me, his lantern lifted high, revealing his unmasked face. His face fills with surprise. But he can't be as surprised as I am.

Because the blacksmith has Marcus's violet eyes.

SIX

Those violet eyes turn to fire. The blacksmith steps toward me, just as shocked as I am.

"What are you doing here? Why did you follow me?" His voice is heavy and raw from so many years working with fire and soot in his trade, but also mixed with the French-sounding pronunciation Guinevere had.

His surprise sets me back several steps. I reach for the surface of the walls for balance.

"You're—" I cannot say the words for fear I might be wrong.

The blacksmith turns away. Marcus told me all he could find in the farmlands was his mother's apron. There was never any mention of his father's body in the fields that Morgan's drones burned. I wonder if I didn't just see in the blacksmith what I wanted to see, rather than the possibility that Morgan le Fay actually failed in killing both of Marcus's parents.

But then the blacksmith glances back at me, and there's no denying it.

"It's been you all this time. Does he know you're alive?" I step inside the dimly lit room, where the walls are covered with iron workings, trinkets that would catch the wind and turn it into song, twisted black poles morphed into cold, decorative animals. Clocks with cuckoo birds whose delicate iron sculptures surpass Caldor in realism. Wrought-work stools with cold, black blossoms for feet. And a scene of miniature people in a festive, wintery village. All of it, the same decor I saw only once in a barn that no longer stands.

The blacksmith's face falls, as though he's given up on his secret. "No, Marcus doesn't know I'm alive." His eyes grow heavy, and he looks away. His face is larger than Marcus's. Wider. But his walk and height are identical. "By the time I'd returned from the infirmary, he was to be knighted. How could I show myself and encourage him to refuse such an honor, when it was to be but a few months before all was said and done? We were serfs. He had the chance to be something better."

I'm more furious at my own inability to see the truth when it was standing right in front of me than the blacksmith's deception, and yet. "All this time, you never told me. *He* never told me. You watched me sneak in and out of Merlin's clock tower for five years, and you said nothing. Did Marcus at least know you worked here?"

I follow him further inside the workshop. In the dead center, he stops in front of an ironwork cross. One made with meticulous detail. With love. In the middle, the name *Elly* formed in long, thick, iron strips and sharpened to angled points. The blacksmith kneels. He glances at me with tears wet on his face. "Give a mourning husband a minute of peace."

A wave of shame washes over me as he goes quiet.

There are a few moments of whispered prayers. Then he

clears his throat and stands, shoulders curving into a hunch as he regards the cross's craftsmanship. "Of course Marcus knew of my trade."

I remember the horse-drawn cart departing from Camelot with Marcus's mother in it. I remember her bright blue eyes as she glanced at me, a stranger, a noblewoman, and how she looked elsewhere when she didn't recognize me. Naturally, Marcus's eyes would come from his father, who'd congenially slapped his boy on the shoulder before returning to his work. "Why are you still here? Why did you work in the castle as a faceless man, but keep your name under the guise of a farmer?"

"I needed to be close to the wizard," he says. "You weren't his only apprentice, my lady, and that is something Marcus does not know. Merlin chooses those who would be of unique and practical use to him." His eyes dive into an old memory he never entertains when he could choose happier ones instead. "I promised the old fool we'd both see the Grail in Camelot. If I'd found the coordinates to Avalon, I might have been able to bring my family inside the castle. To be a blacksmith wasn't enough on its own. Bribery, threats. I tried everything." He leans on the table, and his arms carry a leftover summer tan that would brand him as an outsider. But an iron-masked blacksmith would fade into Camelot's background when brightly dressed nobility and dandies strolled the village streets.

I step forward. "But Marcus was a squire—"

"Yes, and so Marcus had to become a knight. For his mother's sake." His face goes dark with thoughts of the past, and his eyes flicker again to the wrought-iron cross. "Damn the Grail, and damn the idiots who seek it. I'd give anything to see my boy safe now. Six months gone—they were supposed to be back after three!"

I see Marcus whenever I think of the dangers unconquered on the quest, and it is nearly too much to bear. The blacksmith's fingers weave through his hair, messing it up. For a moment, he looks like his son, and I can no longer watch. I wonder if he knows Marcus is missing. "My lord—"

"You can call me Rufus, my lady."

I nod, knowing if I were to extend the same offer he'd likely refuse, as Marcus once did. "Sir Kay brought news of Galahad's infantry."

"I heard. And now it seems Jerusalem has fallen to pirates of the skies. Word spreads quickly when there are few lips to pass it on." He rolls up the sleeves to his tunic as though he's about to get to work. It reveals tattoos across his forearms in an old style. A choppy alphabet scrawled in thick black ink. Fragments of symbols I can't decipher, symbols I recognize from the linings of Guinevere's vestments. Alphabets that were etched into the back of the sorcerer's skull.

Rufus sees me studying them. "Lyonesse … it was a place of magic. To appear as one of them was the safest way to live."

I look up, unable to stop my eyes from asking the most obvious question. He reads me easily.

"No, I didn't dabble. I got the markings to protect myself in hopes I'd be left alone."

He gestures to the pathway. Together, we make our way to the streets in the village. I glance in the distance at the gas lanterns' glow spilling through the windows in the main hall. My father is there with Lancelot and the others, the only ones left. And the messenger from Sarpenic, surely, to discuss what must now be done about the attack on Jerusalem. The snow continues to fall, but the breeze has subsided, letting flakes drift wherever they will without the force of wind to guide them.

"Forgive me for taking all this time to finally speak with you. I'm sure you understand, though." He squeezes the bridge of his nose with his thumb and forefinger. "These damned eyes of ours... I couldn't risk having Marcus discovered as the son of a man who'd lived in Lyonesse, who had the inked skin of someone who lived there. It would have been next to impossible for him to become a knight if word got of who I was."

I sift through my recollection of Marcus staring at me in the grand hall during the royal wedding and the way his eyes were so strange. So captivating. So unusual. How I came to be entranced by them.

"Word has it that..." Rufus stops there, unsure of how to arrange his words, his foot tapping restlessly on the ground. "Marcus won't be a knight forever, then."

I find it hard to hold the blacksmith's gaze. Even harder to recall the memory of Owen telling me so himself. "No," I say. "That was Marcus's condition of knighthood—it'd be temporary. Only until the Grail was found. And only if it was by him."

And then, what? We haven't spoken of what would become of the two of us, if he'd join me in escaping to some wonderful place once the Grail is safe in Camelot. Although, that was before rogues attacked Jerusalem.

Rufus squints as he regards the midnight blue of the sky. In the light flickering from the gas lanterns on these streets, snow whispers to the ground. The blacksmith kneels in a crouch by his shop as he might have in the middle of a blustery day with nobility passing through, calling to one another with insincere waves and smiles all the more so. Phantoms of serfs might have tipped their ruddy hats toward one another, atop of which goggles would have held together with whatever they could find.

A sadness falls over Rufus's eyes. "What I wouldn't give for him to know I'm alive."

Neither of us is foolish enough to believe that just because word hasn't gotten to us means Marcus is safe. They'd surely notify Camelot if a knight was killed, no matter what Marcus believed. *"No one will remember me if I don't return."* But the simple inconvenience of not having the same communicative alchemic abilities as Merlin and Azur is dreadfully frightening. If Marcus is dying right now, we wouldn't hear of it until at least a month has passed. A month of his body freezing in the wilderness. I need to find Marcus fast. Before any of this could happen.

"There is a way," I hear myself tell Rufus.

SEVEN

The blacksmith tilts his head in my direction, waiting for my explanation. I step closer, eyes glancing about with care in case my father were to spot me and promptly take me back to the main castle to await the forthcoming aeroship.

"Before Marcus left…" I don't know where to begin, or even if Rufus should know what task the Lady of the Lake set upon me. I don't know if I can trust him—he went years without revealing his identity. But he's Marcus's father, and we both want the same thing, and by God, if I can do nothing for Azur in Jerusalem or my missing mother, I can do this. "I was to build an aeroship."

"For the knights, I imagine." The blacksmith faces me. "You accomplished this feat, my lady?"

I hesitate. "Not exactly. Mostly. There are still some missing elements." Like the *jaseemat* I'll need.

"In Lyonesse, when an inventor responded with such uncertainty, by nightfall the next day, he was already a slave to magic." Rufus loses himself in the idea for only a second before returning to the present. "One could use this ship to find the knights?"

"Better," I say, my usual defiance vanished for zeal, even though my aeroship certainly merits no form of boasting just yet. "One could use it to find Avalon." To sell my creation to Rufus might make all the difference.

A rare smile shapes his solemn face into a younger one, showing me a stark resemblance to Marcus. "Once you rebuilt Merlin's copper bird, I knew you'd soon be up to something else. I understand what it's like to lose yourself to the mechanical arts."

And he must understand that I need help. "To complete my aeroship will take knowledge and experience I do not have. Help me turn it into something the likes of which would even impress Azur."

The blacksmith stiffens when I mention Merlin's mentor. "Don't compare yourself to men who might be too wise for their own good, my lady."

I ignore the comment. "The vessel is nearly complete, resurrected out of the Norwegian steel Merlin and I stole for the mechanical dragon." Picking apart Victor like a hungry vulture was a bleak affair, but reforming its brass and copper into a ship to glide across the sky was exhilarating. Seeing it from the height of Merlin's clock tower is enough to yearn to escape on it forever. "It needs alchemy to work, and I need Azur's help, but he's in Jerusalem, and he's trying to save Merlin, and I need—" I stop there, lost in worry over the sheer possibility of Azur fending off rogues as I speak.

But then, "*Jaseemat*," Rufus says with a knowing nod.

"Yes," I breathe.

He firms his lips into a line and looks up at the gas lanterns decorating the cobblestone streets. The lights flicker against his violet pupils, highlighting the gray, and my breath catches. I've never missed Marcus as much as I do right now.

"For years, I warned the sorcerer against alchemy. He was convinced it was a way to use nature to its fullest potential. But in Lyonesse..." He pulls his sleeves over his wrists. The inked images disappear like one could ignore the choice between right and wrong. "What else do you need?"

"What?"

"You said you built an aeroship. Where is it? The catacombs are empty, and it's certainly not in the clock tower. And when the old fool built the aerohawk, it was an enormous inconvenience behind my shop. Yet I stand here unbothered. Where is it? And what else do you need?"

I run my own scrawled blueprints through my mind. The sails are finely made, a delicate arrangement of drapes that once shielded Merlin's bed, with the addition of fine dresses Guinevere will never again wear. The farmlands offered plenty of space, and everything I constructed remains outside of Camelot, hidden by autumn trees. The aeroship's cabin is stark and bare, but it has my touch and the attention to detail that Merlin would never consider, like the navigational piece on the helm. The engine is a remarkable reworking of Victor's leather-encapsulated iron lungs, expanded to work with a charcoal furnace to propel the ship faster. The clockwork heart's veins spread throughout the ship, up to the sails. But no, it's not ready. The wings are too weak, and the vessel might be too heavy to take flight.

"I need to reinforce parts of the ship to prepare for high winds, and, yes, *jaseemat*," I confess. "God help me, I need *jaseemat* in order to get the ship high enough to..." To reach Avalon, the castle in the clouds, truth be told. But no, Rufus can't know that just yet. And although Azur needs help, I can be of no use in a war where the knowledge in my mind is a clear prize.

And so, "Help me find instructions on how to make *jaseemat*, and I will find your son," I hear myself say. A solemn promise. A promise Marcus would hate hearing me make.

Rufus's expression changes. He doesn't regard me as though I were a lady of Camelot; now, he sees me as an artisan like himself. "Show me."

———

I lead Rufus through the break in the citadel wall Marcus showed me in the spring, the blacksmith with a heavy satchel of tools strapped to his back and the same copper-tipped hook he used in Morgan's war tight against his hip. *"There are no knights to protect us now, my lady,"* he tells me. And with the new threat of rogues foregoing their own Grail quest to attack cities and kingdoms, I can offer no argument. With thick black furs long enough to be feathers around his shoulders, Rufus stalks after me like a raven hungry to find an unlucky mouse. I pull my cloak closer to my face and breathe into my gloved hands to keep warm.

I come out on the other side of the dry, bristly bushes, my boots crunching the snow with each step. I lift my hood over my hair and steal a glance at the wall—no guards are keeping watch. I can escape into the woods without fear I'll be spotted. I run, pushing aside the paralyzing fear that comes about as I let my mind drift to the idea of Marcus missing, of Azur being cornered by danger, of an aeroship on its way for me. Rufus is not far behind.

We reach the woods that surround the lake. As we approach the snow-covered cellar where I hid my aeroship in pieces—the dug-out ground a forgotten casualty of Morgan's war—I lower my hood, glancing about for the demigoddess who once told me she made her home in this very spot. But she's nowhere to be seen, a ghost these six months past. Above, the stars are breaking through the clouds, and I remember how so long ago, Marcus and I stood under this same sky with starfish as constellations.

"Where is it?" Rufus demands.

I pull from fantasy and return to the logical mindset I embraced as I built the vessel. "This way." I march along the side of the lake—the ice strong enough to carry my weight—and disappear into a lining of dead trees. Rufus follows me into a sparse patch of muddy snow and sleeping foliage. To him, there is nothing to be seen.

But before he can impatiently demand again, I kneel and brush away some branches. Under my feet, I reveal a door built into the ground, one locked with a device of my own craft, similar to Arthur's *l'enigma insolubile*, a most precise and fussy locking device that once guarded Excalibur. But this one has a contracting feature that would allow for the entire door to swing deeply into the ground as soon as the correct sequence is engaged. As I tug on the iron rod and arrange the gauges with no need for a key—damn all keys forever—the door pulls free.

Rufus's eyebrows lift. "I'm impressed."

I shoot a grateful smile one could only offer another inventor. I steady my palms on my knees and lift. The door reveals a trench I can easily step into, a practical use for a part of broken, cratered land that was never refilled when Victor sprung from the catacombs. I crank a spring-loaded copper lever to raise the platform where I built the lighter parts of my aeroship. The floor rises. Once it parallels itself with the land, I step onto the deck and release the wings that will wave high and mightily across the sky. They crack out, slow and wobbly, and certainly a problem once strong winds would hit them. I climb up the ship's bow to check on the status of the wood—dry, thankfully. As is the bucket of charcoal for the furnace.

Rufus circles my aeroship—a small English ship styled for the oceans but made for the skies—his eyes darting from one detail to the next. From the rounded wooden beams that come to a point at the ship's bow, to the arched walls that extend toward the main sail. No words come from him; he moves his lips like he's trying to find speech, but it's nearly impossible. While not as beautifully crafted as Caldor, whose feathers were tediously sculpted out of softened copper, it's a good ship capable of rising above its aesthetic appearance.

"You built this?" Rufus finally manages.

I nod. I think of the days after Galahad's infantry left Camelot. Of the incredible loneliness that came about when my father disappeared into the main castle to plan what would happen next to this forgotten world. How they'd searched for Camelot's subjects for weeks on end, and how every day it grew more natural not to hear a single voice in the village.

Building my aeroship kept me occupied. It kept me close

to the Grail quest. I could not yet leave Camelot for the life in Jerusalem I'd dreamt of, but it was something.

I point up. "Its wings must be strengthened, but to do that would require reinforcement I worry might be too heavy."

"Yes, but if you were to use a lighter metal—perhaps more of the king's steel, if you can spare some—it would work." Rufus is a blur of mumbled notes to himself as he tests the vessel's strength. Then he glances at me, and even in the dim moonlight, I see him light up with an idea. "Let me fly it."

I frown. "You?"

He jumps on the deck and seizes my shoulders. "Yes. I can find Marcus with a vessel such as this, and you would never have to venture into dangerous territory."

Certainly he can't be so naïve to think I'd simply let someone else fly my own aeroship?

Like he can see my refusal for himself, he speaks again. "*Jaseemat*. I know how to make it." A grimace falls upon his face, like a tittering scale in his mind has shown him the less painful of two choices.

And it seems unlikely. His words, deceptive. I narrow my eyes at such a statement that shouts of its falsity.

But, "I swear it. Merlin entrusted Azur's instructions to me once the old fool had the steps memorized for himself." To prove it, Rufus searches his satchel and withdraws a scrap piece of yellowing parchment decorated with unfamiliar script. An emblem I recognize has been stamped onto the back: a phoenix in green ink with a twisting Celtic design around it. The Druids created this stamp for Merlin's correspondence with them.

I'm instantly struck with envy at the idea that my mentor would give something so precious to someone else. "Why would Merlin do that?"

"I don't know," Rufus says. "Honest, I don't. But you must be nearly out of the *jaseemat* you got from the alchemist in Jerusalem if you've been maintaining Gawain's iron arm these past six months. I'm sure you have a reserve for the aeroship—"

"Of course, but not enough."

"All right. If you give your aeroship to me, I can find Marcus and bring him back. It'd take but a few days at most, I wager. I'll bring him back, my lady, and then you could have the instructions to create *jaseemat* for yourself and whatever inventions you'll create in Merlin's tower, but don't you see, you could also—" And here, he pulls away. He turns, running his hands over his neck. A long sigh follows. "I cannot lose him, too, Lady Vivienne. All I want is for Marcus to live a long, happy life." He glances at me. "And he wants that, too. Especially if he can have it with you."

My heart skips a beat. I knew this. Marcus never said it out loud, but I already knew. He wanted us to escape together, to live a life that would let me be happy the same way I was in Merlin's clock tower. A life of exploring the mechanical arts in a way I could never live proudly in Camelot's village streets or main castle. I want that. I want to see Jerusalem defeat the Spanish rogues, and I want to work with Azur. I want to touch Marcus's raspy cheek, fall asleep in his arms.

"Stop," I say, but it's to myself. *Stop it, Vivienne, with these torturous thoughts.* I feel guilty enough that the coordinates locked in my mind are preventing me from getting Azur out of Jerusalem. "Why would you offer me *jaseemat* when you fear it?"

Rufus's face darkens with the ghosts he might have left behind in Lyonesse. "A father would offer the world to the devil himself if it meant his son returned safely."

I think about his offer. "You cannot take my aeroship, but you may accompany me." I wait. I wait for the wrath of the Lady of the Lake to come upon me for declaring this when her very clear instructions indicated the exact opposite. "If you refuse, I will not show you how it flies, and so it would be meaningless to try to steal it." I want to fall to my knees in happiness for setting another *l'enigma insolubile*-like puzzle into the lock that releases the lever, setting the aeroship in motion. "A faster option would be to build your own."

Rufus looks at the aeroship and sets a large hand to its surface, feeling the smoothed-out wood, but steering clear of the Norwegian steel that still has a bit of hum to it. After a second of utter frustration, he turns back to me. "Please. I offer this so that you and my boy will be alive."

He cannot know there's an aeroship on its way for me. "You don't know me, Rufus. You don't know what I'm capable of."

He shuts his eyes. "No. It's not that. It's that you don't know what sort of a world lies outside Camelot. Not because of your own ignorance, but because of your own experience. You don't know, and Marcus, neither did he. Not really. Not when Lancelot led him through parts of the countryside that craved the knights' attention instead of resenting it. You are capable of surviving such a world, Lady Vivienne, but that world will not look kindly upon you. Not the protégé of Merlin. Nor a noblewoman of Camelot."

I feel a hard swallow in my throat. *Nor someone who might know the coordinates to Avalon, I suppose.*

Regardless. "That is my offer."

Rufus takes a breath and then a step forward, hands on his hips as he studies my aeroship. "You overestimated how ready this vessel is. Forget the sad state of the wings, the bow needs metal stronger than dragon's scales, and the ship'll need a steering mechanism much more sophisticated than the one you've built. Yes, there's much work to be done, Lady Vivienne. But I'll need steel as light as a feather. I trust a lady of your stature could handle a task like that on your own."

Without waiting for a response, he drops to the ground and shrugs off his heavy satchel, pulling out a set of black-smith's goggles, an iron mask, a soldering iron.

I smile. *Of course I can.*

EIGHT

The safe shuts. The echoes are riddled with the usual clinks and whistles of *l'enigma insolubile* retracting itself to keep out unwanted visitors. With one last tug of my stolen horse's saddle, I know Merlin's wagon is secure. Already, the air is sharply scented with early morning, only two hours later, and Rufus and I must be on our way.

"Certainly, you can move faster than the wind," I whisper close to my horse's ear, kicking the soles of my boots into its side. We ride off. The frigid air is ruthless in such stark wilderness, and I hold my hood tightly over my head to ward off the prickly chill. It bites at my eyes, forcing them shut, but my horse knows the way back to the castle, and we'll find relief traveling through the nearby woods. Morgan's curse has fallen now, so I can come and go as I please. Though I cannot deny how it still frightens me to see the same twisted trees and arm-like branches that were once alive with magic.

Finally, we reach the refuge of rough-barked maples standing like soldiers as I duck under their branches. Months ago, these parts were lush with emerald green, but no more. The horse slows as the wagon shifts past the trees, and we continue on in a slower trot. It's impossible to stay focused when in mere hours I might be away from Camelot, possibly for good. I've committed to this idea without thinking it through. That's not like me.

My knuckles tighten in Merlin's falconry gloves. At dawn, I'll be in the skies with Rufus, en route to finding Marcus and Owen while the rogues' attack on Jerusalem provides a diversion from the Grail and the girl who carries the coordinates to it. Assuming Marcus and Owen are already heading home, it might take but a few hours—God willing, my aeroship will prove to be alarmingly fast if the tests I obsessed over in the downfall of autumn leaves is any indicator.

Or it might take days, weeks. Weeks away from home.

How could I return to Camelot? Certainly, my father would keep an aeroship waiting so he could carry out his intention of sending me to the same nunnery Guinevere went to. But then what?

"I need the Grail, too," I hear myself whisper. And it's the truth. Because otherwise, there'd be no way I could return home, after wars are fought and wars are won, with a knight who before that was a serf. If Camelot were to be victorious, I don't know what Marcus would do—he might want to stay in the kingdom with his father. Or he might be as enthralled as I am at the idea of exploring the Holy Land once it's saved and learning from Azur the ways of the mechanical arts.

A strong jolt throws me forward in my saddle, and I snap free from my thoughts. My horse neighs in annoyance, and I search the grounds, but these parts are dimly lit. A wave of worry flutters through my stomach at the thought that perhaps the ghost of Morgan still wanders the woods and has found an opportune time to reveal herself to snatch vengeance upon the girl who took her life. Not just any girl: *an apprentice, a handmaid.*

I reach into my pocket for the quicklight I made and snap it against the saddle. The tiny light flickers dimly, only able to illuminate a few feet in front of my eyes, but I've set a gauge to its side that heightens the flame. It rises tall from my hand, and suddenly, I see the reason for my horse's dismay.

The frozen ground beneath my horse's hooves melts under each step. *Melts*, turns the snow into ugly, brown mud under which is a sandy consistency unlike any land I've ever seen.

"What in God's name…"

My horse's hooves dig into the earth, and the animal tugs at its reins violently, trying to free itself. Its wild head sways, and its bray calls loudly into the early morning sky.

I search the woods. If I can find a source, I can find a solution. But there's nothing to be seen.

"Steady, steady," I tell the horse and swing my legs over the saddle, ready to jump. But the land all around turns into the same sticky mud my horse is drowning in, and I realize if I were to leap from this height, I'd be lost in it, too.

I resettle myself and tug on the reins. It's a foolish thing to do, but I don't care. I don't know what else—"Move, you stupid beast!" I shout. *"Move!"*

"It'll only be faster that way," a sharp voice calls, splitting the ice-cold air in half. Familiar, honey-coated, with a distinct accent. "It's been many months, daughter of Carolyn."

I feel caught, guilty. There's a rustle of jewelry. A heavy step. I sit straighter in my saddle, seeking the demigoddess in these foggy woods, but her voice is omnipresent, and she is nowhere to be found.

"I didn't expect to find you here," the voice continues. "Not when I specifically ordered otherwise."

The Lady of the Lake ordered otherwise because to have the one entrusted with the coordinates to Avalon outside of her protection might cost Camelot the Grail.

But I find taunts enormously irritating. "Show yourself, old woman. Show yourself, and remove my horse from this trap. Do it, and then tell me what it is you expect me to wait for."

My body flies forward. I'm thrown into a large, dead tree; I hit the trunk and fall, my palms holding me up. My hair drapes around my face, and my hood is lost around my neck. I look at my fingers, clawing into the ground. Frozen again, and my nails white, covered in snow. My horse finds its balance and scuffs its hooves into the land, scampering in place through its shock. The ground it stands on is solid.

More rustling of silver. I breathe my gasp and turn my eyes toward the sound. Through a light fog comes the wooden cane, the long, ornamental clothes, the starfish earrings lying against her shoulder. Her blue eyes pierce through the air, intrusive and enticing, like with one glance she could control me as easily as Morgan le Fay sought to.

"Daughter of Carolyn," the Lady of the Lake says with a slight curtsy, inauthentic in its sentiment. "You find yourself far from home."

I try to stand, but she's trapped me to the ground with icy fog locking me to it. I take a breath and search for my last ounce of patience. "Release me."

"Why did you leave the safety of Camelot?"

I might not be able to trust her with the truth. "The knights—"

"I know they're missing." She darts her bright ocean-hued eyes at me, holding the wrath of a thousand hurricanes. "I know the Spanish rogues have laid siege upon Jerusalem; I know the Black Knight has resorted to everything in his power to beat Camelot to Avalon. I've known since the beginning of time and the rule of the demigods. And so what?"

I feel my blood grow hot against the ice in my hands. "I cannot fight the Spanish rogues, nor can I save Azur's city, but I have the means to find Marcus and my brother. You're the one who commissioned me to build a vessel. My aeroship is more than capable—"

Instantly she's in my face. I gasp in surprise; I don't know how she could move so quickly, like her magic might give her the flight of a demonic hummingbird. Her finely arched brows draw together through her fury.

"Don't let pride claim you, girl. You don't know what sort of world exists beyond the shores of Britannia. I told you that your place in this plan was to bring the knights to Avalon after the war against the Spanish rogues was won. And yet the Black Knight still walks the earth. He'll find the coordinates unless you stay in Camelot."

She doesn't say it's to protect me, and perhaps the demigods don't care about such things. Not when something as important as the Holy Grail is at stake. Are we pawns to them?

She peels back and resets herself in a strong, confident

stance. "Perhaps you were the wrong choice for this. Perhaps I made a mistake."

I feel like my heart might explode with anger. "Let me do this."

"You do this, and you change the future in a way I cannot know!" Her voice is loud enough to shatter dead branches back to life, and I'm terrified of what wrath she could unleash upon me. For a long moment, she stills, eyes white and motionless. "In fact, you already have. Stubborn girl! By seeking Arthur's Norwegian steel today, you've completely changed the fate of the world!"

"How? How have I done that? I've been to the safe in the mountains many times since the summer. I've built my aeroship outside the walls to avoid my father. How is this any different?"

"You did what was needed to complete the task I gave you. But now your actions dictate another plan. It's no longer to build your aeroship; it's to disobey the order I gave. Now, it's uncertain whether Camelot can claim the Grail, and, oh!" Her eyes widen, and a flash of dread passes through them.

My fingers clutch the icy ground at seeing an entity of power and might harboring such terror. *For what?*

She blinks away whatever vision came over her and shoots a look of pure anger at me. "Sir Marcus." The way she speaks his name is akin to a blackness settling over a world already full of desolation. "His fate has changed, too. A great loss is looming. One of betrayal or death—I can't see which."

My blood is chilled, but not by the wind or the snow under my knees and palms. "I don't understand."

Her eyes are two pools of lake water staring into mine. "If only you'd listened, girl, his fate would be that much surer. And now ... " She looks elsewhere, and I catch a hint of worry I've never seen her employ. "Death or betrayal. I'm not sure which. One path is certain."

My lip quivers. Death is nothing new to me. Not since Morgan's war, where I killed not one man, but several— fathers, sons, brothers, perhaps some who were but boys in their iron armor, chained by Morgan's magic.

If that isn't enough, the memory of Morgan's dying eyes still haunts me as I sleep.

But *betrayal*. The meaning is vague, and I have to know more. "What sort of betrayal?"

She glances over her shoulder at me. "Unknown. But each of these paths is equally possible."

Marcus would never betray Camelot. He didn't want to be a knight, but he knows the Grail cannot fall into the wrong hands. If for no other reason than to avenge his mother's death, he wouldn't.

"Yes, I chose the wrong person." The Lady of the Lake stares at me as one would study blueprints: objectively, curiously. "I should confine you to where you are. Keep you locked until your destiny can be fulfilled while I fix all this." Inch by inch, she moves closer, and I feel myself grow smaller and smaller. I struggle to free myself, but it's useless—

A slam against the earth forces a scream out of me, and I curl over the ground as much as I can. A slow thump and then another passes me by, and I lift my head to look. A wistful spirit drifts across the snowy land, a fog dropped from the sky. But this spirit is in the shape of a man, and it takes solid form before blitzing back, like a bolt of lightning that hasn't decided if it yearns to be sunlight. Long, pressed trousers resting atop scuffed black boots step toward the Lady of the Lake. I catch the surprise in her face and the long cloak of an otherworldly being with a hood atop its head.

"Impossible. The alchemist locked you in a vault in Jerusalem," the Lady of the Lake declares, a tremor in her voice.

A pair of old hands rises to the spirit's transparent hood, and the ghost becomes flesh. I blink at the knuckles displaying their familiar ink, and when his fingers draw back his hood, his shorn head reveals the same tattoos as when he was a man.

Merlin faces me, the phoenix feather in his goatee as bright as the sun, even as it flicks in and out of existence. His blue eyes are two golden-mooned prisms shadowed by arched eyebrows, all too aware.

"Get up, girl. The floor of an icy forest is no place for an apprentice of mine."

With one flick of his finger, the Lady of the Lake's trap releases, and I'm able to stand.

"Merlin." I step closer as I watch him fade in and out of the ghost his thievery has paid for. "How can this be?" I consider the use of stolen magic that released me and how the alluring voice of it marks my skin with warmth and happiness. When it disappears, I find myself almost missing it.

Merlin smiles, and it's a strange one: a smile of deceit, accented with an untrustworthy friendliness he'd offered few in Arthur's court. "Azur's iron vault has only alchemy to guard me. The magic I stole is much stronger than that."

I should be terrified to speak to a thief of magic, but it's Merlin. It's my mentor. "The Spanish rogues have attacked Jerusalem. Azur told me you were missing for a month. That you won't return to your physical form. Why won't you cooperate?"

With that, the Merlin I once knew fades into something terrible. His eyes are full of magic that swirls the same white and gold I saw in both Lancelot and Guinevere before their affair. Merlin's arched brows furrow with his cunning smile of opportunity. "There is so much power in this world, Vivienne." And nothing more. He shoots a look at the Lady of the Lake. "She's on the right path. How dare you threaten her when this is the right future for all of us?"

I frown. "What?" Can he see the future where the Lady of the Lake cannot?

The Lady of the Lake snarls as they both ignore my question, and I'm not sure which of them is speaking the truth now. "This isn't the way it's meant to be played out, wizard. You know this; you knew it when you were a man, weaning yourself off magic."

"Vivienne was never meant to dwell in Camelot. Her fate must take her north, where the Fisher King waits to be cured. She must be tested."

I breathe in the thought. *The Fisher King?* "Whom do you mean, Merlin?"

Merlin angles his jaw at me. "A thief like myself. Find him in the Perilous Lands so you and your lover can find Avalon. These demigods"—he juts a thumb over his shoulder at the Lady of the Lake—"captured him and set a curse upon his land." With that, he twirls back around to face her. "You play unfairly, demigoddess. When one of us finds a means to use magic, you make a prime example of him. He had to watch everything around him die: queen, children, subjects, land. Doomed to become dust while alive as it happened." The anger in Merlin's loud voice cannot hide the sadness it strives to conceal.

The Lady of the Lake watches the spirit of Merlin circle her, and she sneers. "He was a knowing thief who took what didn't belong to him. Ask any demigod you might meet. Men have no concept of the power they're trying to wield. It's not meant for them!"

I shake my head to collect these staccato thoughts. "What has the Fisher King to do with Avalon?"

"Nothing," replies the Lady of the Lake.

"Everything," replies Merlin at the same time.

I don't know whom to trust. Both the Lady of the Lake and Merlin stare at one another with such authority in their stances, with power in their voices, but Merlin is a thief of magic once again, and perhaps by default, he's a liar as well. But to me? When I was a child, it was Merlin, and Merlin alone, who found amusement in the aeroship I forged from pieces of his hookah. It was Merlin who saw in me the potential to be a student of his, and then an apprentice. Even when he stole magic to conceal Marcus and me from Morgan, even when he stole more to get us out of the woods all together, he wouldn't lie. Not my teacher, no matter how much of a scoundrel he is, no matter what Azur said about alchemy being the darkest path to magic. He wouldn't lie. Not to me.

But now he growls at the Lady of the Lake like she's no better a foe than Morgan was. "We both know it has to be Vivienne. Don't deny it; don't you dare deny it again after what happened last time." His transparent fingers tighten around her wrist, holding her still as he flickers between spirit and corporal form.

Last time? I don't understand why a demigoddess and a sorcerer would ever fight about me.

She narrows her eyes on his ghostly features. "That is not for certain, *thief*." Her lip curls on the insult. "The most direct route is the safest for the bearer of Avalon's coordinates; to gallop to each corner of the known world might mean those coordinates are lost to another. We *know* this. No matter how long it takes for the rogues to be defeated, no matter what might happen in the meantime, Vivienne cannot leave Camelot, and I stretched fate enough by allowing her to be the one to construct the aeroship. She must wait until the rogues have been put into their place, the Black Knight, slain. The Fisher King is not a necessary cog in this plan."

I won't let them talk about me like I'm not standing right there. "But people I love are missing, and I have the means to find them. You must understand how important it is that I go! I cannot risk wasting time going after a thief of magic who—"

"You want to find your beloved and your brother," Merlin interrupts, "and after that, you want to help Jerusalem defeat the Spanish rogues. To do so, you'll need the Grail. If you need the Grail, you'll first need the Fisher King."

I feel my resolve falter as his words fly at me. "That'll take time, and the longer I'm outside of Camelot—"

"Yes, it will take time, and it'll be quite dangerous." Merlin rolls his head on his neck. His eyes flash gold and white and then return to the blue ones I knew. The fiery anger he bore abandons him for curiosity. "The Lady of the Lake knows what sort of evils lie outside of this castle, Vivienne. As do I. Are you ready to see the harshness of the world, a girl such as yourself?" If he weren't an emotionless thief of magic, I'd have wondered if he was actually a bit worried.

But I've had people worrying about me long enough. "I'm not a child."

With a toss of the Lady of the Lake's wrist, he storms toward me, and when he's no more than a foot away, the coolness of his spirit surrounds me in a way that's awesome and frightening. "But you *are* a child. You're a girl who found my work interesting, curious, and now you seek something greater. I told you what the Grail's powers contained. Tell the truth, girl. Are you ready to see what sort of magic you'll be up against?"

My eyes well at his harsh tone, but I lift my chin high. I know this is a test. Gawain said those on the Grail quest would be tested. Why should I be any different? "Yes."

Merlin cocks an eyebrow, and a smile skirts to the side of his face. "So be it."

The Lady of the Lake's face darkens with fury. "She cannot leave, wizard, or all will be for naught! If you send her away, you'll have my wrath to face! I will find her!"

Merlin seizes my cloak and pulls me close so he can

whisper in my ear. "Get to the north, to the Fisher King. Save him—it must be *you*. He can unlock the coordinates from your mind and give you something I've hidden with him. You'll need it to find the Grail, and you must guard it with your life." Then his temperament changes with the taunting lift of one eyebrow. "There'll be no hope for Azur or Jerusalem or anyone else if you don't heed my commands. But if all this proves to be too much, and you can no longer bear such magic in a ruthless world, turn back. Won't you?"

His eyebrow lifts higher. This is a challenge. He wants to see what I can do.

I narrow my eyes. "Do not patronize me," I whisper back.

The Lady of the Lake lifts her cane high. Her eyes turn white, and her hair follows suit: from root to tip, it paints itself with the hues of snow and starlight, and her tea-colored skin sparkles with a sort of magic I never saw in Morgan. Magic that could never be reined by a human.

"Hancashi feramitanouski mittererasha intsoh gehenna-mach!" she shouts in a voice that sends a force of power against the trees and flattens them. "Get to hell, thief!"

Merlin spins in place and points his emerald-stone cane at the Lady of the Lake. The light bounces off his hand and rushes back at her. She recoils, stepping away from the power. I look out from under the hem of my cloak just as Merlin's eyes turn completely red with dark magic.

"Hell is no place for me, demigoddess," he growls. "I have work to do." He finds me again, and we struggle to stare at each other with the red magic around him. "Go now, Vivienne! Do not leave without my journals—you'll need them."

I've searched those journals a million times for the instructions to make *jaseemat*, but they've come up empty—what could I need them for? "Why? Merlin! I don't—"

"Fly north!" he says, and I do not miss the touch of shame that draws his eyebrows together, showing me the bit of humanity still left in him. But then he faces the Lady of the Lake again, a vision of great whiteness that nearly blinds me with power and deafens me with her angry cries. Even when Morgan le Fay unleashed drones and drones and fire onto Camelot, I've never seen such power and might before.

I know there's no time, and if I don't leave now, the Lady of the Lake might hold me here forever. With a final look at my mentor, I jump onto my waiting horse's back. It whinnies with surprise and soars across the ground, hooves clamping on snow and rock and ice. We ride through the woods. Only once do I risk a look over my shoulder at the magical battle. I'm shaking like mad, as though the cold has seeped through my skin and into my bones to forever haunt me with its cruelty. I feel my heart fall into a fit of devastation at the thought that Merlin might forever be a ghost seeking magic to sustain him. I don't know how he escaped Azur's vault, if Azur will seek a way to bring him back. If Azur is even alive. I don't know if my mentor is forever gone, and I don't know if I'll now be seen as a thief of magic myself, having followed the orders of Merlin.

My horse breaks through the woods, and we ride on through the countryside with Arthur's Norwegian steel trailing behind. At the cusp of the forest before the lake, I spy Rufus waiting. He's set an iron exoskeleton about my aeroship with the thinnest rods he could forge, and he's strengthened the main sail. There's already a fire burning inside the aeroship's furnace, ready to come to life.

To see my aeroship in all its grandeur is nearly enough to make me forget the very real and very awful possibility that I might never see Merlin again. But if this was to be the last time, I can never forget what he did. For it is only through his defiance of the Lady of the Lake that I'm able to leave Camelot.

Perhaps Merlin's soul was the price for me to know what world I'll soon face.

NINE

Rufus calls my horse to a halt. There's no sign of Merlin or the Lady of the Lake, though in the woods behind me, there are occasional thunderous slams to the earth, like lightning bolts striking the ground. Strange lights appear, too bright, and for a moment, I watch. "Oh, Merlin."

The blacksmith takes the reins from my hands. "We have to hurry." His eyes are all-knowing, like perhaps he anticipated our shared mentor would return to ensure our escape. And, at that, I have to be resilient against the path my father designed for me, or the Lady of the Lake. Because if it is true that Merlin is my only ally other than Rufus, then by God, I'll hold on to what I can.

My aeroship's wings have been strengthened and tightened, and they wave about in the skies, ready to combat the wind. Almost ready: Rufus will have to reinforce the vessel with Arthur's Norwegian steel. And I should help.

But my eyes catch sight of the clock tower, and a tug at my heart won't let me leave this soon. Besides: *his journals.*

Merlin told me to bring them, though I'm not sure why. Beyond the obvious fact that the instructions to make Azur's *jaseemat* have evaded me, I found in his journals no maps or blueprints.

Rufus glances back at the castle. The guards patrolling the walls are plentiful now that they've heard of the Spanish rogues' attack on Jerusalem, and from this distance I can see my father's window in our quarters and the illuminated gas lanterns. It's only a matter of time before he'll notice I've left. He might send guards after me to ensure I find myself on the aeroship he sent for.

It can't matter, I decide. "I'll return as fast as I can," I promise Rufus. I have to get Merlin's journals, even if it might bring me face to face with my father one last time.

"Wait, my lady—"

But I've already seized my horse's reins and ridden off.

―――――――

Mornings in Camelot have been silent as of late; the gardens and courtyard are akin to graveyards. I reach the wall and tie my horse to the brambles hiding the break. My hood atop my hair, I rush for the village by way of the gardens, running past each snowy tree along the path I know all too well. I keep to the outskirts of the village, avoiding the few serfs who stayed after Morgan's war to assist in the infirmary. The fully healed squire Stephen helps two priests ease a hurt knight to his feet, slowly back to walking. Finally, I reach Rufus's shop and climb the steps to Merlin's clock tower.

At the top, the heavy winds have fallen asleep, letting me sift through stilled papers and journals and scrolls and tools on the sorcerer's desk. Merlin's leather holster I blasphemously buckle around my waist, and his long, antiqued blade goes inside with a spare firelance secured at my hip. The goggles embroidered by my mother I hang around my neck. I'll need them as I steer my aeroship through the clouds. My stomach flits with excitement at the thought—the wind, the skies, the world outside Camelot.

A slow, sputtering puncturing of air splits the blue and gray of the sky, growing louder and louder. I duck toward the window just as a large body of polished wood with bird-like sails soars by. It sends a gust of frozen wind into my hair, freeing it from its steel netting. The aeroship ordered by my father to take me north.

"No," I think I whisper, but do not hear. "No!"

I have to move faster. There was never any time to come back. *Damn you, Merlin!*

On his work desk is his leather satchel. I pour inside all the tools and journals and scrolls—familiar or not—I can find. Scrolls which, God willing, might contain maps to the land of the Fisher King. Steel wire, a knife, Azur's reserve of *jaseemat*. If only I had Merlin's pistolník...

My viewer is on the table where I built my long-lost mechanical falcon, Terra. I seize it. Caldor, with its broken wing because of my stupid wrath—I cannot leave it behind. Besides, if Rufus and I are to be flying over the seas, we'll need something to navigate us in case the device in the helm should fail.

I fit my fingers around Caldor's dislodged wing and twist it once so it fits inside the falcon's shoulder. It won't be permanent, but it'll hold for now. I pour some of Merlin's *jaseemat* inside. I store a small velvet purse with more *jaseemat* inside the falcon's belly and shut the metal gate.

"*Yaty ala alhyah.*"

An awareness comes over Caldor's beady eyes, and it cocks its head, feathers ruffling against its copper body.

"To the aeroship," I say, and Caldor takes flight from the window, spiraling through clouds heavy with the weight of a million snowflakes.

I sling the satchel over my shoulder and flee the tower. As I climb the cellar steps outside Rufus's workshop, the iron door's clatter is dreadfully loud, but the aeroship's propellers are even more thunderous. I gauge my surroundings. The vessel that'll try to take me north is heading eastward, toward the docks.

I glance up at Caldor flying over the trees; it'll reach Rufus at the lake before I will. Its caw pierces the might of the air, and with it, I hear male voices shouting orders to one another. As I race for the gardens, I realize one of the voices is my father's.

"Where is she? With all of the Holy Land under attack, who knows if Camelot won't be next? She needs to head north. Vivienne!"

I'm running as fast as I can, and when I reach the threshold of the gardens, I see out of the corner of my eye the slick gentleman's jacket of Lord William as he strolls through the courtyard, Lancelot not too far behind. I duck under a tree. My eyes dart to the wall where a pair of patrolling guards makes their way closer to the break that was my only plan of escape. *Blast.*

"Vivienne!" my father calls again, louder now.

I peer around the tree at my pacing father.

His old eyes search about in worry, in fatigue. "Ready to leave in a half hour's time. She can't be too far." He marches in the direction of our family's quarters. As I turn to the walls of the city, there are now six guards patrolling and searching, but they've paused at Lord William's instructions, and have likewise turned their backs to me.

I run for the break in the wall where squires would buy their *shisha* from passing gypsies. I run from Camelot and from my father, whom I realize I won't have the chance to say goodbye to, despite the chains he'd give me if he could. I reach the lake. I've made it. I've made it, and God willing I have all I'll need to find Marcus and Owen and the Holy Grail.

Nevertheless, I can't help but wonder if I've left my entire life behind.

━━━━━━

By the time I reach Rufus, he's tightening the main sail to stand strong against the growing wind and shoots me a look of urgency as my horse stops. "Start the aeroship! Where's the *jaseemat?*"

I hold up the satchel as I leap from the horse and send it running back to Camelot. "We don't have much time left!"

Rufus glances twice at the castle behind me. "Less."

I whip around. The drawbridge is lowering. I spot my father atop the citadel wall as he looks out at the horses riding toward us. To the east, I see the floating aeroship waiting to fly north.

It can't be like this. I turn back to Rufus, but I don't know what to say. He might try to make me stay.

But he doesn't. He hesitates, and then, "Get aboard."

Caldor lands on my shoulder with the blacksmith's words. I climb the steps to my aeroship and head straight to the helm. On the far side is the hot-burning furnace, and I throw back the grate. I add more charcoal to the iron lungs and light it with the quicklight I'll give to Marcus as a birthday present if I find him—*when*. I open Azur's reserve of *jaseemat*, and the old alchemist's whispered words bring the golden dust to life. It floats around the fire and spiders throughout the aeroship's body. At the helm, I ignite the engine. It sputters once and finds its rhythm, ebbing and flowing like a wave with the alchemy's song.

And still, there are calls, shouts, warnings, my father's pleas booming through the air. He's never used such an angry voice when it concerned me; all of these growls had been saved and carefully reserved for his annoyance with Arthur's council. Ahead, in the woods, the flickering flashes and eerie songs of a magical battle play on between Merlin and the demigoddess, and this distracts me from the knot in my throat, courtesy of a father who might be too angry and too worried ever to soften his tone.

Beside me, Rufus gives me a solemn nod. "She's ready."

I look up at the grandeur of the aeroship that only existed in my mind before this as a tiny hookah-pieced model when I was only twelve, in the blueprints I'd agonized over for weeks before gathering the courage to construct. The sails are secure, taut, incredible—taller than Camelot's gates. The *jaseemat* brings a strange bit of fortitude and luminescence to the copper helm and the ship's iron linings, and I must remember what Merlin told me: it cannot bring to life that which never had the potential for life to begin with. Arthur's Norwegian steel is abundant with song and glory, covering most of the wood and hammered into the crevices to keep it strong.

I know I couldn't have done this without Rufus. "Let's go, then," I say.

I have my foot on a pedal that churns *jaseemat* further into the furnace, and I face the lock on the lever that will bring the ship to life. There's a small assembly of eight gears attached to a face I'll turn clockwise, and then counterclockwise, and then back again. Three clicks, and the contraption unlocks.

With a sharp tug of the lever, I start the stout wheels under the vessel until they move. Faster, and then faster still. The wings on either side of me jet outward from the body, and I gauge the bare land in front of us—we'll have to take flight soon, much too soon, lest we would find ourselves in the thick of the woods. Oars lie on the inner side extended with beams of iron, letting me adjust the angles from the helm. Sixty degrees should do it.

"Ready!" I call to Rufus, manning the sail.

Behind us, Lancelot, the faster rider in Camelot, is gaining speed. "Lady Vivienne, stop!"

I face Rufus. His nod is encouragement enough. My boot slams on the pedal of wood and steel, and suddenly, the aeroship's bumpy ride becomes smooth. We lift off into the air, higher and higher and higher, and then the home I once knew changes. Now, it is only a speck of gray in the distance.

I tear around and seize my viewer from my pocket.

Extend it so that the citadel walls are in view. Lord William watches my aeroship's ascent, though I'm certain he does not see me from so far away. But then the angry brows drawn together soften with defeat or surrender, and he retreats slowly to the castle until only his gentleman's jacket is visible, and the arms that would embrace me when I was a girl.

I free my gaze from Camelot, blinking away the tears that have sought to ambush me, and I think of how once, my father never gave up searching until he found me hiding in an elm tree.

———

I stand for a long time at the ship's bow, studying the borders of the world that separate castle from farmland, wheat from cattle-grounds. There are trees and mountains to distract me from the melancholy lurking in my heart, and mostly everything is covered in snow, but there are also great lakes that haven't frozen over yet. The ocean far off appears as though we'd peeked around a corner, and its waves are dances of wind and water that disappear into the blue horizon of this new day. I've never seen anything like it before.

I don't miss the detail of the gears and pulleys surrounding the copper-plated helm or Rufus's new tug connected to the main sail that'll adjust our direction with the wings more smoothly, not to mention the reservoir that'll send an extra burst of *jaseemat* into the furnace whenever I might desire a sharp increase of speed. Of course, this means I'll need to know how to make *jaseemat* at these heights. And soon. Otherwise, to exhaust that option, we'd run out in minutes.

But to worry about such things at a time when I'm feeling the winds of the entire world is not what I plan to do. I breathe, letting my sorrow rise from my heart until it's expelled, sent into the air, the currents gliding over me like I've never felt before. We're soaring, and I reach out to grab the wisps of white and gray clouds. The tendrils drift over my fingers, leaving them cold and wet. A flock of northern birds is late to head south, and I'm nearly tempted to add a bit more of Azur's alchemic powder to my mechanical falcon to send it into the skies. How on earth could I ever feel so conflicted when the world lies static beneath me?

"Lady Vivienne?" Rufus calls from the helm, bursting my bubble of awe. "We'll head due south until we reach España."

I turn, recalling Merlin's instruction to head north. "No, we must..." I pause, my gaze latched onto Rufus's. What I say might let him connect me to the Lady of the Lake. What can I tell the blacksmith, and what might be too much? I have to lie. "In Merlin's clock tower, I used a spare looking glass to get in touch with Azur."

Rufus shifts nervously. "He would have been furious to know you left Camelot."

"On the contrary," I say quickly, "Azur said we should make for the north to the Perilous Lands, the land of the Fisher King. Marcus likely went there, as Galahad's infantry was already on their way."

Rufus's eyebrows rise. "The Fisher King?"

"You know of him?"

Rufus shakes his head in a way that tells me he might not want to think about it. Though he steers us onward, he's a million miles away, perhaps at the bottom of the sea in the midst of these clouds, revisiting ghosts of Lyonesse who want to ensure the time he spent there will never be forgotten. "Damn it all!" he shouts.

I frown at the angry response. "What do you know of him?"

But Rufus shuts his eyes and does not answer for a long time. Then he sets the helm against a lever that keeps the aero-ship northbound and comes to my side at the bow's railing.

"He was a king who stole magic to make his castle fruitful. Had a remarkably strong queen and two warrior sons who married princesses and gave him a wealth of grandchildren. Loved and respected by his people, his land in the north was amongst the most prosperous in all of Britannia. But the crime of magic caught up with him, and he was found out by the demigods, who punished him by destroying all he knew and loved before turning him into a living statue." He leans on the railing as the clouds spill around us into a beautiful, calming blue. "Sometimes death is the merciful option, Lady Vivienne."

I take a breath. What Rufus said brings the boy-machine Mordred to mind. "Azur said by curing the Fisher King, Avalon could be within reach."

Rufus clenches his fists. He rolls up his sleeves, and I watch the dancing of mystical, tattooed symbols as he clenches again in worry. "Why should I trust the alchemist anyway?"

I cannot tell Rufus all of this is so I can go after the Grail myself once we find Marcus. A quest that might mean a way to save Jerusalem, and perhaps even grant me my freedom in the eyes of my father. "What if the fastest way to Avalon was for Marcus to backtrack first? We both know he would do whatever it took to return to Camelot."

Rufus thinks about my reasons and grunts once, and with that, I know my logic has aligned with his. The aeroship reaches a higher altitude, and the quiet of the air so close to the heavens is finally enough to let me feel a bit of hope.

We're on our way.

TEN

As the aeroship flies high over the clouds, I poke and prod at the embers in the furnace. The mechanism Rufus built to expel more *jaseemat* into the ship helps us climb the harsher winds as we fly north. Once we find our momentum, I set up a workspace at the ship's bow so I can properly fix Caldor. The mechanical falcon has fallen still, out of *jaseemat*. Its cold, beady eyes stare at the sky as I oil the hinges connecting the wing to its body.

Rufus stands at the helm, silent and brooding as I search the leather satchel for Merlin's journals and scrolls. I run my fingers over the thick leather binding and the pressed words nearly worn out through so many years of use. The letters are not ones I can read properly—it might be written in Azur's own alphabet. But inside are Merlin's scratches and jottings; I've read this volume at least eight times since June, but only now do I feel like I'm intruding. I remember the sadness on the sorcerer's face before I ran from the woods—I don't know where that sentiment would have come from.

I open the journal and search carefully for any writings on the Fisher King. I smooth each page, and when my palms touch the rough, thick parchment, a sensation of wonderment and awe comes over me. I yank my hand free.

The blacksmith is watching me—I can feel it. I glance sideways over my shoulder. I'm right. "You could have left me behind, and you didn't."

Rufus straightens, his hands tight on the helm. "We had an agreement. Plus, you would have been chained to a parlor with a gold ring around your finger courtesy of a complete stranger. I don't think I could have faced Marcus knowing I let that happen."

After all this time, he still has hope his son is alive. "Marcus spoke highly of you," I say.

The blacksmith chuckles in a low tone, a sound of pride mingling with grief. "He's a good boy. I'm tempted to breach etiquette and say you're lucky."

The silence between us is long after that, filled with unspoken—yet identical—worries.

I pass the time soldering Caldor's copper feathers to hold his wing in place. A bit of Merlin's own *jaseemat* brings the falcon to life before I return the small box to the compartment inside its belly, and I speak of the Perilous Lands to my little friend to help navigate us. I make sure the blacksmith sees Caldor flit to the aeroship's bow, where it perches. Once we run out of *jaseemat*, navigation will prove to be more difficult if the cloudy skies don't let up.

I don't want to think about that, but once I push that worry to a far corner in my mind, I'm reminded of an even bigger concern: the danger Azur and the people of Jerusalem have found. I turn in my seat, noticing the blacksmith's shifting feet, his hesitant breathing at seeing the falcon.

To distract both of us, I ask, "Did others in Lyonesse

know about the Perilous Lands?" I'm envious of all the stories Rufus might have.

His gaze rests on the horizon. "Legends like that can't help but be passed down. My grandfather was just a boy when it was already ancient. And the tale only grew by the time I was a young man in Lyonesse." He loses himself in a forlorn memory. "Some said the kingdom was destined to find the Grail, despite what efforts Merlin put forth for Camelot. Many said there was an undeniable connection, but it'd only come about once the kingdom sank."

It must be because of the wind that I feel my skin prickle. I turn back to my work, my fingers shakier now than before. Briefly, I wonder why something so removed from my own life in Camelot would affect me so. "The queen never spoke so freely of Lyonesse. She was more protective of her home."

"She would have been. She had status."

I don't turn, but my eyes flick upward until they're locked on the wooden grains of my table. "What do you mean?"

"Only that a princess of Lyonesse, set to marry Arthur of Camelot, would never dwell upon the horrors in her home."

I force a smile. "You make it sound as though she was as guilty as Merlin when it came to stealing magic." And of course Guinevere never did.

"Well," Rufus says, "I suppose it'd be inaccurate to say I was the only innocent one in Lyonesse."

The implication that Guinevere might have stolen magic doesn't sit well, but I don't speak up on her behalf. For some reason, even to think of doing so feels like I'd be lying.

Thicker clouds touch my skin with their cool, wet breath, reminding me that I'm soaring like Caldor as gears and cogs pedal us through. Just like Victor, this creation needs a name, and since she flies as high as the heavens, the stars, the celestial sky, I silently christen my aeroship *CELESTE*.

"It flies well, Lady Vivienne. I commend you," Rufus says, as though he's just as captivated as I am by this glorious vessel.

I offer a meek smile and turn back to my work.

"Could have used some of my own touches, though."

He speaks in a strange way now, in a low voice I cannot place, and instantly I turn back, almost defensive. "I beg your pardon?"

Rufus blinks. "I said the aeroship flies well. I commend you."

"No, after that."

Rufus inclines his head in question. "I didn't say anything else."

"'Course he didn't," the voice speaks again, and I'm not sure how I could have mistaken it for Rufus. I whip around, expecting to see Merlin, but he's not there.

"My lady?" Rufus asks.

My heart pounds wildly against my ribs, or it's stopped entirely, and the realization of whose voice it was comes over me slowly, like how night tends not to show its face until it's already conquered the sun. I must be going mad, but I offer Rufus that same, weak smile again. "Must have been the wind."

We return to our tasks. I fumble with Caldor's copper wing. In a silence that only permits that wind's eternal cry, I think about why I'd hear Merlin's voice. If it really was

Merlin. I think about the woods—did he defeat the Lady of the Lake? What became of them? And why would a duel between a thief of magic and a demigoddess come to pass for the sake of a girl, even if she does know where Avalon lies?

I don't realize until too late how sharp the feathers of Caldor's wings are, and one pricks my finger, letting a few drops of blood stain my skin. "Blast."

I find my focus again and glance at the scrolls. There's nothing in them about the Fisher King. But then a whisper of wind teases Merlin's leather-bound journal, and I seize it just as several pages to fly open. My hand flattens the pages in place, and I realize I'm looking at one I missed: a sheet folded in half toward the journal's spine.

I unfold it. An entry detailing a conversation with Azur, and the hastiness of Merlin's scrawled words in this particular passage draws me toward it. I settle in my spot and draw my furs around my shoulders, hiding the parchment from Rufus.

"Azur—could alchemy stop death if we fail in finding the Grail?"

My eyes go wide. Merlin's penmanship is shaken, yet practiced, as though he couldn't have been bothered with the prospect of taking the time to write legibly.

"I wonder if you aren't letting the thought tinker away in your mind. We've already changed charcoal into gold. The next task is to utilize that gold in new ways. You claim to have found mystical properties in it, in the form of a powder that could bring temporary life to inanimate things. When I receive this element, I will test it on the falcon I'll finish constructing before Arthur's bride arrives in the coming week. I know we tread a

fine line here, but you assure me there's nothing to worry about. Despite the incantations we'd recite to activate its life, it's simply an instruction to the elements to work in a new way. There is no magic here. I should be safe."

The scribbles end on the first page, continuing on to the second.

"Azur, you have been silent. I wonder if bringing life to inanimate objects would be any different from bringing life to what once lived. One could argue it was also inanimate. But would it be the same life, or a new one? This endeavor reminds me of the pagan magic I escaped; in particular, one spell that could bring life back to those who'd died no more than an hour prior, with no countereffects. Only to the enchanter after a month's time. A difficult feat, and the most intrusive thievery of magic I've ever witnessed—"

There are no words after that. I leaf through the pages to see if it continues anywhere else, but the rest are blueprints of Caldor, of quicklights, of simple gas lanterns.

The most intrusive thievery of magic ...

The sputtering furnace pulls me out of this world of astonishment. We're running low on charcoal. Merlin's falconry gloves keeping my hands warm, I pull open the grate and use an iron fire poker to turn the whitened bits to dust.

I must think of something other than Merlin's past thieveries of magic. "When will you give me the instructions?" I ask Rufus, the aura of alchemic mystery clinging to my thoughts. "I might as well use this time to create more."

Rufus doesn't waver. "I promised you'd have it once we found Marcus." But he cannot look me in the eye as he speaks the words, and suddenly, I'm not sure he's being truthful. But then I remember the parchment in his pocket with the sorcerer's seal.

I'm careful not to get any hot bits of charcoal from the open furnace onto my skin or furs. Inside is the connection to the clockwork heart I used in Victor, but that alone won't be enough forever. "With the Perilous Lands so far away, we might not find Marcus unless I make *jaseemat* first."

Rufus still won't budge, but now, he looks at me with an aura of suspicion that is, at least, honest. "I would give anything to spare you the danger of making it, my lady. You must understand."

I turn back to the furnace to reattach the grate, feeling the insult dig into my bones as though perhaps Rufus thinks of me as nothing but a child. A brief moment of wonderment strikes my mind, that of Rufus possibly knowing about these notes of Merlin's. If the blacksmith might have had a change of heart by remembering these words laced with danger.

The action of reattaching the grate is nearly automatic, but I'm irritated by Rufus's refusal. "Don't insult me, blacksmith. You don't know—"

"I do! I was Merlin's apprentice, too," he says, and with the frightened force of his voice, he's lost control of the helm. The aeroship twists before stabilizing itself, and I grip the grate to keep balance.

I stare at Rufus. So much of Marcus springs free in the passion behind his words, but in a way that's terrified instead of enthusiastic. When he sees my reaction to his outburst, he lowers his chin until he's staring at the helm, now back in his grasp.

"I saw for myself what sort of danger there was in alchemy," he says. "How it led to magic. Did Merlin tell you nothing?"

No. But Azur did.

I don't say it aloud. We cannot afford safety solely in the mechanical arts, not when the Grail still has yet to be found. Alchemy must be employed.

"Merlin told me it was an instruction to the elements," I say. When I blink, I see a flash of the sorcerer's face after he'd stolen magic. How he'd hammered a mask to his jaw to conceal his fading features. What sort of torment took hold of his soul? "I've seen magic, blacksmith. Not as much as you, I realize, but I can certainly tell the difference."

My voice must carry notes of challenge or rebuttal, because Rufus's shoulders fall. "I don't mean to insult. I fear this task for you; I wish there could have been something else that would lead us both to Marcus. Do not ask me this now. We can certainly reach the Perilous Lands with the amount you've provided."

I don't want to wait. I can feel the knowledge only feet away, calling to me, tempting me with the revelation the stamped parchment boasts. This is torture.

"I promise," Rufus says, "I'll give you the instructions. Besides, you'll need a stable surface to create *jaseemat* before I leave to find Marcus if he isn't in the Perilous Lands yet."

I turn my head quickly, in time for Rufus to realize the gaffe in his statement. "*We.* Not *you*, blacksmith," I assert. As was the agreement.

He has goggles around his neck and sets them over his eyes. "Aye, my lady. That's what I meant."

But I don't believe him.

It didn't take long for Marcus and myself to forget we were meant to be hiding from Morgan in that barn.

"He never spoke much, even when I was a child," Marcus said of his father. His stories were few and vague, but compelling and mysterious all the same. "My mother was born and raised in the farmlands of Camelot, but when my father arrived as a man, alone and with no name for himself, she was caught up in the mystery, I suppose."

My eyes were heavy with fatigue as Marcus spoke, but I wanted to hear more. I rested my cheek on my arm, facing him as he mirrored my position. His fingers plucked at the bits of hay between us, and his eyes went back and forth between the dancing fire and me.

"He said there were people who knew about the Grail's powers and could attest to how incredible they were. They wanted it for their own reasons. I'm sure to continue stealing magic was one of them." He shrugged lazily. "Lyonesse knew of alchemy, but I don't think those living there saw much difference between it and magic, to be honest."

"Why did he leave?" I asked in a whisper. "And what made him decide upon Camelot?"

Over the course of Marcus's storytelling, he'd certainly become exhausted by my many questions, but Guinevere had never told me what sort of life she'd had in Lyonesse. Only brief words in passing about her former handmaids, the luxurious animal skins and linens they'd use for ornate clothing, foods so different from our Jerusalem-styled feasts.

She'd never said anything close to the likes of what Marcus just admitted.

He hesitated and raised a corner of his lips in an awkward smile. "Aren't you glad he did? Otherwise I might not have been here to save you from this storm."

I pushed him away playfully, my fingers lingering at the ties of his tunic, passing them between my fingers like weaving a loom. "Watch your pride, squire. You saved me from nothing."

He shrugged again, his smile broader now. After a long breath, we both remembered my question. "It was dangerous to be there. Full of sorceresses turning men into wraiths a knight would have to slay with mechanical weapons. He didn't want to turn into the likes of…" He might have almost said Merlin's name, but his voice was a lullaby I could fall asleep to, and I'd already felt my eyelids growing heavy. "You might stop me if I'm that dull of a storyteller."

My eyes fluttered open again in time to see him shuffling closer. We had to be careful. But outside, there was still a thunderous storm and an angry witch eager to find us. We weren't about to leave for a while.

He smiled again and rested against the hay bushel, his arm opened to me. "It's all right. I'll wake you when the rain stops."

I knew it might be the only time I could feel his body near mine. I knew this sanctuary from the rain was all we could claim for ourselves. For now, possibly forever. I shuffled closer and set my cheek against his beating heart. His arm pulled me in; he took a long, deep breath like he was memorizing this moment, as I was.

I was desperate not to fall asleep.

─────────

The low and winded voice of Merlin returns with the force of crashing waves. *"Not only did you nearly ruin your reputation that night, you let down your guard and risked our plans of construction."*

My eyes snap open. The sky is dark from night; I missed any sunset to the west, but the clouds wouldn't have let me see it anyway. We've been flying for nearly an entire day. The chill is terrible, and I draw my cloak closer, wrapping Guinevere's black-and-white-striped furs around my shoulders. Caldor lies fixed in front of me, but as dead as the winter land. My breath is a fog, and Rufus manning the helm shivers violently. I glance at the furnace, still relatively warm, but the charcoal pieces are fading fast. We need an active fire.

"Here." I stand to hand him my falconry gloves. He holds up a palm to refuse at first, but reconsiders and nods in thanks as he puts them on. As they were once Merlin's, they fit him well. I kneel in front of the furnace and set my goggles atop my eyes so I can open the gate and toss in a few more lumps of wood and charcoal.

"We'll arrive shortly," Rufus tells me. "I'm steering her toward the sea to keep us from the blizzard heading south."

I look out at the wrath of galloping, thunderous clouds of gray and white and sculpted out of rock by whatever god might have forged them. Snow comes quickly, and soon, we're covered in it—sails, railings, Norwegian steel reinforcements. Everything.

We hit a current, and the aeroship wobbles. I glance at the ship's frame, in case I might have forgotten to tighten any bolts. The creaks of wear and tear are alarming, but everything holds. A particularly violent current strikes, and I reach for the railing. My hand falls upon the Norwegian steel that sings its magical song into my skin. It's an opera of celestial music, and I want to feel it forever. But I must focus.

"Rufus! The wings!" I shout into the song of the gale as the silk sheets rustle. I used the strongest silk I could find in Guinevere's and Merlin's towers and sewed expertly enough that my mother would have been proud. But it might not be enough.

The ship dips suddenly, and with its strength, I'm thrown across the floor as the winds turn violent. I slam into the side. Knock the back of my head. Cringe and inhale sharply.

"Damn it!" Rufus curses, holding tightly to the helm. "You all right?"

I nod and climb to my feet, clutching the steel railings for support. The only emotion I see on Rufus's face is through the gritted teeth he bares like a lion: he's determined, but perhaps uncertain we'll make it.

The port wing flails wildly, its strength fading. If we lose one wing, it'll send us spiraling toward the ground. There's not a moment to lose. There are lines secured over each side of the aeroship for this very purpose. But I should have tightened them long before we left.

"Keep to starboard!" I call, setting my goggles back over my eyes and making for the wing.

"What are you doing?" Rufus calls.

"I need to fix it!"

"No! You'll fall!"

But I've already opened a window right above the wings. I squeeze through, and instantly the wind nearly knocks me onto my back. There's the fraying end of a thick, white line, and I could tie it to the wing's base, and perhaps that'll hold us until we land. I stretch my arm toward it, feeling the icy death grip of winter's ire, and immediately I regret giving my gloves to the blacksmith. But it cannot matter now. The silk whips like mad, but my fingers touch it, nearly catching it. I can do this.

"Just a little more," I whisper.

"If the worst should happen—"

"Never mind that!" I shout back. I need to focus. "A little more," I whisper. My hand stretches further, and my fingers are turning blue, and I might lose my arm, but I'm nearly there and suddenly, I feel the silk.

"Yes!"

I tie it to the base, and the wing stretches and catches the wind. I jerk back inside and set my back flush against the wood. Rufus looks at me in amazement, but he wasn't there when I activated Victor. He doesn't know what more I've been able to fix myself.

"We're nearly there," Rufus tells me through his awe.

I nod. "Land her."

ELEVEN

The storm won't ease up as we descend from the clouds—on the contrary, the winds quicken, like my aeroship is nothing more than a wayward butterfly. I lower my goggles back over my eyes, but only seconds later, they fog up. As the storm spins us into a vortex, Rufus and I grab the helm to hold the ship steady. He's wearing my gloves, and my hands are blue with frost, and I'm cursing the copper—not wooden—spokes, which hold the cold dreadfully. My face is frozen, but I cannot tell if it's from the ice storm pattering around us or from the great speed at which we're falling to the earth.

"We must find the current!" I shout, as Rufus and I coax *CELESTE* to stay upturned.

"No use! Take cover!" he growls loudly enough that even the winds subside to his tone. "We're going to crash."

I'm nearly blinded in this gray and white lightning-rich storm, but I shake my head. "We're not." My fingers grip the helm tighter, and then I spot the edge of the storm: a border of flashing lightning and a curve of clouds. "Fly south!" The rounded glass navigator bolted to the helm confirms our direction; the arrow rattles wildly against the glass.

CELESTE's wooden beams shudder, and the furnace's piping loosens from the ship's skeleton. Out of the corner of my goggled eyes, I spot the wings holding tightly against their beams; they're buoyant and the sails are strong enough, and yes, we're going to make it.

A gust sets us on the edge, and Rufus and I put all our weight onto the helm to keep it steady. We break free of the winds, and now the winter sky is peaceful. I whip around to the storm's darkness behind us as we fly onward. My shoulders settle in relief, and I feel a smile grace my face as I look at Rufus.

He throws a fatherly arm around my shoulder and kisses the top of my head. "Well done. Well done."

We glide over smoother currents, and I watch the eastern sky as the sun peeks over the horizon. The air is blistery and cold, and every breath is an inhale of icicles and an exhale of fog. But the view—the view is exhilarating. There are pinks and oranges and roses, and light fluffy blankets of clouds expanding toward the moon and stars about to go to sleep. It's remarkable.

"There!" Rufus calls, pointing north. I follow his gaze.

"Oh," I whisper when I spot what we seek. The Perilous Lands.

Endless infertile land. Not even desert, but muck and dirt and dead trees with no hope of ever a spring. There's a lone castle in the distance, tall and black with too many pointed towers and not enough breaths of color. *CELESTE* drifts lower, and the closer we come to the realm of the Fisher King, the fewer the skeletons of trees and foliage, as though God himself might have seized everything lush and alive and cast it aside, leaving only a spectacle of silent, iron grandeur.

"Does no one come here?" I face the blacksmith, his expression of mourning and worry as heavy as his iron mask.

"Would you?"

I turn back to the view. "Let's be quick about this." Already, there's a sensation of magic—the same eeriness I felt when Merlin and I strode through the woods for Arthur's Norwegian steel. But this is different. The aura of death is powerful, but sentient, as though ghosts might still dwell. The aeroship's tattered wings flap against the breeze as we hover over the ground. I help Rufus steer until we find a good spot to land, outside the castle walls, directly in front of the moat. Inside, there's a labyrinth of pathways and streets. I don't know how we'll find our way through to come upon the Fisher King.

Like Rufus might be thinking the same thing, he speaks: "Maybe you should take another quick peek at the sorcerer's scrolls and writings in case Merlin had a map."

I nod without turning. I cannot pry my eyes away from such desolation. "Yes. There must be something."

Surely there must. Because the only other way to survive such a place as this would be to steal magic, for goodness sake.

And certainly Merlin wouldn't put us in that sort of position.

═══════

The aeroship lands in front of the southern entrance with little trouble, and once we've sputtered still, I extend the steps and find my footing on the ground, a little wobbly at first. I tighten my cloak and furs as I survey the damage my aeroship suffered in the ice storm.

A sharpness hits my stomach when I see how much worse off we are than I'd anticipated. The sails are tearing badly, and I'm left wondering how we ever managed to land. The wings are no better. The ship's bow received the brunt of the damage, but Arthur's Norwegian steel was resilient enough even to combat the most gruesome winter winds. The ship's entire body will need to be reinforced. The steel kept it strong, but just barely.

"It'll be too heavy to fly if we add more," I whisper to myself, thinking of how Rufus had to be very careful about the amount of reinforcement he added.

Rufus steps down from the aeroship, wrapping the ropes around his palm and elbow into a tidy bunch. "We'll worry about it later," he says with gravity in his voice.

I scan Merlin's scrolls and journals, not seeing any maps. A sense of worry about Rufus taking my aeroship once he's realized we're here for the Fisher King, and not for Marcus, settles on my shoulders.

"Lady Vivienne," Rufus says as he turns, making his way to the castle. "Let's not waste time."

I roll up Merlin's scrolls, nod, and grab my satchel. Caldor is inside, inanimate, but fixed. "I haven't forgotten you, old friend," I whisper. I sneak some of Merlin's *jaseemat* into Caldor's steam valve, and the mechanical falcon returns to life.

If Rufus objects, I'll simply argue that we need a guide.

———

We walk in silence toward the drawbridge, my right hand never leaving Merlin's sword at my waist. The Fisher King's castle is much grander than Camelot, but in a hellish way. It looks like it was built out of iron that's fought the elements for eons. Now, we stand in front of these walls so tall that even the much-taller towers behind them are no longer visible. Caldor soars above to the highest point. The traitor.

Inside, it's a mad inventor's paradise. I look up, up, up at the sky concealed by countless statues hanging over windowsills, nightmarish monsters with ugly faces, something I would expect to see in the catacombs. I feel eyes upon me; I feel the aura of festivals that once were, of knowing there's a man in this kingdom who's slowly turning to stone or dust. I feel the bone-chilling sensation of shadows wanting to spring to life. I feel eyes staring and perhaps monsters waiting for the right moment to attack.

For a moment, I wonder if we haven't stepped into the dismal, forgotten lair of Morgan le Fay in Glastonbury, but the dried-up river dissecting the castle is a clear indicator that this land was once alive with plants and animals. This is where the Fisher King lived. This is where the fertility of his lands and the prosperity of his wealth were celebrated amongst nobility and serf, royal and servant.

"Remarkable," I say.

Rufus scowls inwardly at the signs of magic scattered about: pagan symbols like Merlin's tattoos scratched into wooden doors we pass, crystal balls, and hanging burlap dolls with eyes X-ed out with pins poking through their hands and necks. Trinkets and apothecaries lined up in the village. And a strange element of the mechanical arts that doesn't feel natural like it does in Camelot, but forced upon the people who once lived here. I see no shops where merchants might have sold spectacles or firelances. Instead, wires cross overhead, connecting the windows like fishing line. Puppets have been enhanced with brightly colored paint and bolts in their arms and legs, wind-up levers on their backs so they could move about independently of their puppeteers. I should be able to hear the sound of children laughing, of gossipy subjects, of merchants playing with fiery tricks in the streets, of the same festivities I knew in Camelot and saw last at the wedding of Arthur and Guinevere.

An eternity ago.

Something draws my focus, and I dart my eyes to the left. Just in time to see a dark shadow disappear into an alleyway. "Rufus," I breathe.

He follows my line of vision as I will the shadow to show itself again. It won't.

"What was it?" the blacksmith asks.

But I've already got the firelance from my waist tight in my hand, and my feet are tiptoeing after the figure. I force myself to be weightless, a silent ghost as I follow. Rufus's quiet steps barely stir up an echo behind me. We reach the slate-gray corner of a decrepit tower, and there, I pause. I set my cheek to the brick and listen. My eyes shut, and around me, a gentle wind rises from the ground, lifting dead leaves into my hair and snapping them across my face. But then, there it is: a breath. A simple breath. But not an exhale. A whisper. One word, and in a language I do not know.

It could be rogues. But better to find them now than the other way around.

I glance at Rufus, and he nods, holding tightly to his iron hook with copper plating on the point.

Taking a breath I pray will give me courage, I step into the alleyway and lift my firelance.

Staring back at me are six men standing around the wreckage of what must have been an exquisite aeroship. They all have sun-kissed skin like Azur, all in the same dress as the traveling alchemist from Jerusalem. Contrasting white and black tunics with silver-plated shoulder bands. Curved swords gleaming against the ugly white sky. Their eyes are on me, and I'm about to speak, but then a particularly tall middle-aged man with a silk turban the color of blood and the beginnings of an ash-blond beard steps in my direction.

And lifts a silver firelance back at me.

I breathe my surprised gasp, and Rufus steps in front of me quickly, his iron hook held high. "Lower your weapon, pilgrim."

The man's eyes won't drop from mine. Though his firelance remains lifted, his gaze is peaceful, curious. "You find yourselves a long way from home, friends." His voice commands obedience, and he speaks English like anyone in Camelot might. When I glance again, I realize his eyes are too light to be native of Jerusalem.

My firelance is steady; my gaze is focused. "Though perhaps not as much as you."

A smile cocks to the side of his face as he studies me. "I've only ever had women in Jerusalem speak to me with such authority, and yet you come from the south of Britannia, am I right?"

He still won't lower his firelance, and neither will I, but there's nostalgia lingering on his voice, and I wonder if I could end this stalemate. "My name is Vivienne. I come from Camelot."

"My lady," Rufus scolds. I don't care.

The man's eyes flicker with curiosity. "A noblewoman from Camelot outside of the kingdom? Unlikely." He regards me with Azur's familiar propriety.

I lower my firelance to indicate that what I speak is the truth. "And yet when she's the daughter of Arthur's advisor and served as apprentice to Merlin, it's very possible."

At that, he sheathes his weapon in a thick leather holster. One quick glance at Rufus tells me he believes the blacksmith to be my guard. Then he studies me, eyebrows raised, but only out of polite curiosity. Jerusalem is no stranger to female inventors and alchemists. "Sir Tristan."

Tristan. My father spoke highly of him when feasts were plentiful and absinthe was cold. Sir Tristan's story as a Knight of the Round Table was cut short once his heart fell to Isolde, a married noblewoman in a Druid kingdom, and from then on he devoted his life to searching Jerusalem and its neighboring countries for the Holy Grail. A creature of loneliness.

Now he stands before me with few clues that would tell me of his Britannia heritage. His restlessness has vanished for poise; his eyes are focused instead of spontaneous. "Why would an accomplished lady such as yourself ever come to this place?" His voice trembles upon the verge of discipline, like he might set me atop my own aeroship faster than steam bursts from the valves on Caldor's belly.

Rufus speaks. "We're searching for my boy. Sir Marcus of Camelot."

A blankness falls upon Tristan's face. His eyes turn elsewhere as he searches his memory for such a name. "I don't know him. Why would he be here?"

It's my turn to speak before Rufus might realize my white lie. "Sir Galahad's infantry was to come to the Perilous Lands. To free the Fisher King."

Sir Tristan's expression is one of amused pity. "That legend is an old one, my lady, and I'd wager it remains only that. No one else has been here in the time since we arrived in this desolate place. Why would Galahad bother?"

I take a breath and answer him with confidence. "It would mean finding Avalon."

Tristan breathes a low laugh. "This castle is empty. Abandoned. It's only served as refuge from these damned winds, particularly irritating when you've had to land unexpectedly while an alchemist waits in Jerusalem—"

"Azur," I say. "Azur Barad." So Tristan was the one to bring news of Jerusalem's attack to Camelot, then. This is why he never made it.

Tristan looks at me in surprise. "Yes."

I recall the last time Azur and I spoke, and I do not trust my voice to hide my worry. "I know him, my lord. All too well. Camelot has only just found out that Jerusalem is under siege. But there's no one in the kingdom to send to help." To speak this bad news puts my heart into a vice.

Tristan shuts his eyes tightly, as though to think of what might occur in the Holy Land is devastating. He turns to five other men standing at the Arabic-styled aeroship decorated with ornate gold and fine wings, the same style Azur sought to improve upon the rough and practical aerohawk Merlin and I built for him. The aeroship has a deep break in the starboard rails, and its wings are halfway to being reinforced.

"If that's the case, we'll return to Jerusalem. Six extra warriors might not make a difference, but perhaps they could." He faces his warriors. "We'll leave at dawn."

Rufus steps closer to me. "My lady, we must—"

I lift a hand to silence Rufus. "Has no one in Jerusalem evacuated?" Though I know Azur would stay, if for no other reason than to ensure Merlin is brought back to his natural form, there are thousands who would have to seek refuge elsewhere.

Tristan shakes his head. "All ports have been claimed by the Black Knight's rogues." Then his eyes focus on mine. "Leave here, my lady. You and your manservant. This is a place of death, not exploration, and the Black Knight's whereabouts are unknown—"

A wail blasts our ears. I drop my firelance, and it clatters to the cobblestone. Tristan searches the skies. I look at Rufus, whose gaze rests on the windows of the high towers in this kingdom. He won't blink—he won't let down his guard. His copper-plated hook lifts higher as Tristan shouts orders in Arabic to his men, who lift their firelances and crossbows and curved swords to the skies in response. Then Sir Tristan turns back to me. "Get out of this place."

I shake my head stubbornly. Though I can feel the blood rushing from my cheeks, and though my hands shake uncontrollably, I cannot give up. Especially when to return to Camelot would mean my father sending me away. "No."

"Clearly your Sir Marcus is not here! Keep to the outer citadel and we can escort you and your manservant back—"

"No," I say again, and seize my firelance from the ground to aim at him.

The reaction is stalled, but immediate once I click back the weapon's hammer: Tristan lifts his hands, his weapon dropping so he can kick it a few feet ahead. Unarmed. "Lower your weapons," he tells his men behind him.

Rufus's eyes rest on the knight as he leans in close. "My lady, Marcus is—"

"We're not going to find your son here, blacksmith," I declare. The truth must be known, and the agony inside at withholding something so important from Marcus's father slays my heart into a million brittle shards of glass. "But if we find the Fisher King first, the path to Avalon would be revealed." Somehow, what Merlin has ordered me to do will lead me to Marcus, and then to Azur.

Rufus draws away from me, a shadow falling over his eyes. "You knew he was never here, didn't you?"

I stare for too long at the blacksmith, and the truth of my lie is too painful to admit. I lower my firelance, tuck it into the holster at my side, and storm toward the main castle with two sets of footsteps on my heels.

"Stop!" Rufus growls in a voice too father-like to adhere to etiquette when addressing a noblewoman, but I don't blame him for his anger. Nor would I expect anyone in his situation be any less volatile. "We're leaving this kingdom and returning to Camelot at once!"

I reach a set of iron-lined wooden doors at the top of five stone stairs. They're noble and grand, but when I reach the rings and pull, they're locked. "Blast."

Sir Tristan's gloved hand presses against the doors, as though it isn't the lock keeping me out of the castle, but him. "My lady, get back to your ship." His voice is disciplinary with a quiver desperate to remain polite. "This is no place to explore."

"I'm not *exploring*, Sir Tristan," I reply, my words abrupt and terse. "I was sent here. This is the only way we can hope to find the Grail."

Light flashes in the sky, followed by a burst of thunder, like God himself might be just as furious at my sins.

Tristan jumps ever so slightly, and his eyes fall shut in relief. "Just thunder." But no rain to accompany it in a land so dead.

Something catches my eye on the wall behind him. I blink, glancing at Rufus at the base of the steps as he holds tightly to his iron hook. Then I circle Tristan to get a closer look at the wall.

"My lady—" Tristan begins.

There's a smudged window there. I grip the sleeve of my cloak to wipe it clean. "Rufus!" I call. Behind the glass is a scroll entitled, *DO NOT VENTURE INSIDE THIS KING-DOM DAMNED.*

Rufus hesitates, but only for a moment. It might be curiosity that comes over him, or his acceptance that to free the Fisher King would mean saving his son. "Guard your eyes." I lower my goggles, and Rufus throws his elbow into the glass; it breaks easily, letting him grab the scroll. He hands it to me.

My fingers unroll the parchment. I read out loud.

"Our king has been cursed to die slowly, in a way no man would wish for. We'll be emptied of generations before he takes another true breath. To save him has proven impossible. They've guarded our sire with three tests—VALOR, INGENUITY, and RIGHT JUDGMENT—that a soul of true bravery must pass in order to free him from these earthly chains. Many have come and tried; none will succeed. To endure this hellish existence is the destiny of the Fisher King."

I lower the scroll. Rufus is watching me, and the regret in his eyes is palpable. "A kingdom turned into a trap. We never should have come here."

"Didn't you know this in Lyonesse?" I ask.

Rufus shakes his head. "But I should have expected it."

Tristan steps backward, glancing up at the height of the tower. How strange to regard something so immense, so grand, so cold and inanimate, but come to realize that inside is danger alive and just waiting to be found. "This cannot be," he whispers.

Despite the sharp cold, I lower my hood, my eyes returned to the door. "Open it." Merlin's sword was once at my waist, but now it's in my hand. The old fool said I'd be tested, and certainly, these tests are his. Let it begin.

Rufus works quickly at the lock as a selection of tools rests at his feet. The gadgets are small and intricate, and I can't help but envy how quickly they snap the hinge and unlock the door. He throws his heel into the wood. The door bursts open and slams against the wall inside the stale entrance.

"Wait," Sir Tristan says. He turns to his crashed aeroship and the men slowly making their way toward us. "We'll search this place, not you." He whistles loudly and beckons over the rest before facing me. "I cannot let a noblewoman fight in my place."

Without waiting for my response, which was most assuredly to be one of insult, Tristan takes the five steps needed to speak to his men. The music of their conversation is trumped by the occasional outburst, like they might refuse to embark on this side quest.

As they quarrel, Rufus and I step inside. What were once lush red carpets are covered in sawdust and tattered scrap metal. The remnants of suits of armor lie about as though something had seized hold of the knight who owned it and torn him limb from limb. I inhale sharply at the splintered bones in a glove.

"Hold on," I say. "If they were able to get inside but no further, that means—" I turn on my heel.

Too late, though. The door slams shut, as though alive itself, and mends the hinge the blacksmith destroyed, securing it tighter.

I run to the door, my palms against the rough surface as I listen to Tristan pull at the iron rings. Pound his fists. Call, *"My lady! Damn it all!"*

Rufus likewise yanks on the rings, but it's no use. "It won't budge." He swings his gaze over to meet mine. "My tools—"

His lock-picking tools are on the other side.

We could try slamming the welding iron from my own satchel into the hinges, but it would never be strong enough.

"Forget it," I say in a voice unsure of itself. The sense of protection Tristan's presence gave me vanishes into the dank air. We're alone in this. "There must be another way out then."

I hold Marcus's quicklight high, leading the way with the point of my sword piercing the space in front of me.

Then there's a gentle tinkering sound, like how the wind rustled my aeroship on its currents. Like how a castle will settle when all is silent. Like how a man in a suit of armor will walk when his squire hasn't properly oiled the hinges.

"What is that?" I whisper. I'm tempted to fall back, to let Rufus be the one to face this test, but Merlin told me to find the Fisher King.

It must be you.

And if Merlin believed I could past these tests, then it is quite possible I might come out of this alive.

In the distance is a set of descending stairs beautifully lined in red carpet that hasn't yet lost its shade, with sculpted gold railings leading to the main tower.

"This way," I say.

But then the squeaking becomes louder, and now it's more rhythmic. Like footsteps, slow and heavy. They march one after the other until finally, one foot of black iron steps from the staircase in perfect view of where Rufus and I stand. I lose my breath.

"My lady," Rufus says in horror.

The armor's other foot takes the next step, and when my quicklight's glow is bright enough to illuminate against it, I see the intruder—a walking, moving suit of armor with a long sword withdrawn and held high in a gloved hand. But the most frightening part is how its helmet looks, particularly its visor.

Because that visor is lifted high, and there appears to be nothing inside.

TWELVE

"That's impossible," Rufus says. "Wraiths fell when magic did." My eyes widen as I face him. I wonder if these are the same creatures Marcus spoke of when he told me stories in the barn of his father in Lyonesse. And then Rufus's gaze settles on something behind me. "Vivienne, get out of the way!"

I turn back as the wraith lifts its sword and leaps from the staircase into my path. Rufus steps in front of me, wielding the same heavy iron hook that served him in Morgan's war. The wraith slams its blade against Rufus's weapon. Throws him off. The iron hook slides down the hall, clattering against stone.

Shadows surround me, vanishing as soon as I turn to them. They're in the corners of my eyes, cold fingers falling upon my shoulders and neck. They whisper, *It will die, it will die,* slow in speech, but quick to avoid me.

The shadows leave, and I hold my blade high, just as Gawain taught me. But the wraith is merciless and stalks for me once it's sent Rufus into the wall, a stunning clanging of metal against metal ringing through my bones. I hold tightly to the sword and keep the point between us. The wraith moves as quick as lightning, striking its weapon faster than I can follow, refusing my attack.

"Rufus!" I shout.

He finds his footing and scrambles to a skeletal body, rotted away long ago and dressed with brass chest plates and a shield. Grabs the sword still shining at the waist. There's a sharp whistle when he's able to free it from the sheath, and the wraith jerks at the sound. Rufus readies to charge. "There's a way to beat it—"

But before he can say how, the wraith casts its arm toward the blacksmith, and suddenly, a bolt of translucent white light charges the air and sends Rufus onto his back. His head smashes against the stone floor, and he falls still.

Then the wraith turns to me. It inclines its head, and in the visor I see the faint wisp of black smoke in the shape of a wicked face staring. Rufus isn't moving, and I'm not sure if he's alive or dead, and I can't think about that anymore.

I align one boot in front of the other and grip my sword tightly. Perhaps this is the test of valor; if so, there must be a way to pass it. There has to be a solution. I think back to what I had to learn quickly about war and its many faces. The wraith wears a suit of armor. That's all. Twisted metal easily flawed. I know from Gawain that there are weak links under the arms and in the neck. But before I can consider a plan of attack, more shadows appear and vanish, like black lightning. The whole kingdom falls silent—now there's no sound of Sir Tristan and his men desperately trying to get through to us—and each flash of blackness draws closer as the seconds pass. The wraith seems not to notice. The shadows are for me alone.

"It will die, it will die."

I swallow my fear and clutch the sword tighter. A burst of smoke-like light breathes me in, and my head goes light and warm, and it says those words again in its whispered voice, but this time, different.

"Estakah mortuusashay estach, estakah mortuusashay estach."

Oh God, it's magic. But I'm completely intact, and the words haven't slain me.

And then I realize what the shadows mean for me to do—I must steal magic to win. *It will die.* That spell will kill the wraith.

And then it approaches again, a blade ready to strike. When it does, I lose my balance, the toe of my boot catching on the carpet. I fall to the stone floor with a burst of air forcing itself from my lungs. The wraith straightens in its suit of armor, its head turning slowly but with tenacity nonetheless. I panic. Yank the satchel's straps from my back and the cloak restricting my breath. Another step closer, and this time, the blade's shine is blinding against my dropped quicklight. I shuffle backward on my palms and heels. My teeth grit and grind, but then the quicklight illuminates a gleam of silver I'd forgotten about. The firelance at my waist.

I regard this hallway and the many suits of armor torn apart. None of them had embraced the mechanical arts. And how much would the demigods despise that mind-boggling world their own creations would be powerless against?

Maybe this is how I win. By refusing their temptation of magic in favor of something I know much better.

The wraith is coming closer, but the frost has stuck

my firelance to its holster. I only have time to reach for my dropped sword. As my blade clashes with the wraith's, I remember all Gawain taught me. The wraith spins the blade against mine until my wrist bends painfully.

My grip loosens, and my sword goes scattering across the stone floor, thumping against Rufus's stilled body. "Damn!" I cry.

The armored suit steps closer.

I must be quick.

My hand returns to the holster at my waist. Yanks at the firelance again. The wraith's footsteps are thrusts of thunder echoing against these cold walls. Its armored glove grabs my throat and lifts me off my feet. Finally, the firelance loosens, but dangles from my hand. The grip on my neck hurts, and it's cutting off my breath, and I can see the hints of dancing shadows in place of what should be a face, but there's no face, and my boots are kicking in fierce protest, but this might indeed be how I share the same fate as the others. How could I think I'd ever pass a test the likes of which *knights* failed?

An uncontrollable surge of anger comes over me at this pathetic doom. "No! I will not die because of an empty suit of armor!" I sputter.

I drop my hands from the wraith's grip, risking the seconds without air to further yank back its steel mask. I set the firelance's barrel inside. I pull the trigger.

The blast echoes, slicing through the back of the helmet, drawing the wraith's suit back from the recoil.

The wraith drops me, and I scramble to my feet again. I watch as the armor falls and comes apart at the seams.

Melts like water, vanishing into the carpet with only its helmet atop of what appears to be a long harpoon, shining like a crescent moon that drank the stars.

The only sound I can hear is my own breathing, rapid and shaken. No wind passes through the windows, but nonetheless a bitter cold refuses to let up. My hands tremble, and my teeth chatter. I'm certain all of this is a nightmare and not the real world I thought I knew. But that certainty falters as the shadows vanish, leaving behind the stark, white light of overcast skies pouring through the frames. Dead and still as always in the Perilous Lands, though without the hauntings that wished for me to become a thief of magic.

Rufus groans from the corner. I run for him. "Rufus!"

He sets a tender hand to his head where a deep gash parts his skin. Furrowing his brow, he looks around. "I've had worse. Where is it?"

"Gone," I breathe. "It needed to be slain by a firelance—something tied to the mechanical arts. We passed the first test."

His eyes dart around in disbelief, at the steel helmet and the harpoon atop that appeared out of nowhere. A smile crosses Rufus's face, and then he is the image of Marcus my heart cannot forget.

"You passed it, Lady Vivienne. Not I."

<hr>

The cold is persistent in this kingdom, and so for now, I give up on warmth. Furs tight around my body and Merlin's sword re-holstered at my side, I lead Rufus up the stairs. My right hand carries my firelance, and my left holds the harpoon at the blacksmith's insisting. It's heavy and awkward, but it would do great damage alongside Rufus's reclaimed iron hook that's once again strapped to his back.

I haven't told him about the spell the shadows whispered to me. I don't know how he would react to that, and besides, we still have yet to discuss my horrid lie. But now is not the time.

"The scroll implied the second test would be one of ingenuity," Rufus says in a low voice, hardened with a scoff. "When was the last time philosophers and thinkers lifted a weapon to solve a puzzle?"

"Perhaps it won't require one, then," I answer.

We reach the next floor. My boots clack on the stone, polished to shine like a sun that would never find its way through such narrow windows. Ahead are two wide and heavy doors, made of wood darker than any I've seen. Carved into them are visions of land and rivers and fishermen. I imagine what sort of life these people had in a kingdom plentiful of happiness and prosperity. And how the Fisher King himself might consider this scene just as torturous as his plight.

"Lady Vivienne?" Rufus says, arriving at my side.

I take a breath, hoping it might inflate me with the courage I desperately need. "Let's get on with it, then." I grab the iron rings of each door and push them open. A gust of icy wind nearly throws me off-balance, and I stumble. My foot feels for the floor, and suddenly I realize it's crumbling beneath my weight. "Oh!" I cry.

"Hold!" Rufus says, grabbing my arm.

Once the gust passes, we look down at a dark abyss below my boots. Above us is a wonderment of windows and arches bordering delicate oil paintings upon the ceiling, fading from sunlight and time.

"There's no way to pass," I breathe. I search for a way to cross to the door on the far side of the room, perhaps a catwalk or a set of stairs on either side of the walls, but there's nothing. "We must be in the wrong place," I add as an echo follows my voice.

Rufus points. "I don't think so, my lady."

The doors across the blackness slowly open, revealing a third set of brightly lit stairs. There's no one standing on the other side, but it's enough to convince me we must continue onward.

I nod. "Then we'll have to use what's been given us." But how? The second test is *ingenuity*, and frankly, the cleverest thing to do at this point would be to turn around, head straight back to the aeroship, and leave this desolate place. I could return to Camelot and live a life of safety in a northern nunnery.

But I saw my father walk away when I made the choice to leave. That life is gone now.

I take a breath and gauge my options. Like the armored wraith, this is a test, and I've beaten the first one. Let the second do its worst. I grab hold to the door's frame and lean over the threshold, listening to the echo of nothingness below. The stench of mold and the stickiness of humidity are potent, clinging to my skin and suffocating my breathing. But they're also clues.

"Water," I say, tilting my head as the whisper of waves rises to my ears.

Water far below, like in a canyon or a grotto lost and forgotten for eras. Glancing up, I spot a rowboat hanging alongside the wall, as though to taunt the Fisher King after his curse came upon him. Then there's a sound, like an exhale—a gasp, something breaching the surface for air. I'm quick to straighten. The gasp rises twice more. It could be one creature, or it could be three.

"The demigods ensured we wouldn't be able to use that," Rufus says, his eye on the rowboat.

I ignore Rufus's assertion and look to the ceiling, lifting my quicklight high enough to illuminate the entire canopying stone. Shadows form when they cross the sculpted wooden beams, adding dimensions to the painted scenes. I realize each panel is a story, one chapter at a time, and when fire is added to the equation, there's another tale to discover: one that was initially hidden.

"Rufus," I breathe. "Look."

The first panel by itself is a vision of a banquet, nobility and princes dancing with longhaired girls whose flowing dresses and lacy bodices could only belong to princesses. There is a purple-robed king sitting on a wrought-iron throne, laughing and lifting a goblet quickly enough that red wine spills over the sides. His queen dances with their children, and minstrels play around them. When I lift the quicklight higher, a shadow appears as the beam separating each panel corrupts the image. Now the king's face is distorted, melting, and the queen and their children have spears and harpoons piercing their hearts. Their faces of laughter, once jovial and celebratory, are now twisted with tears and blackened mouths. A vision of death.

I cover my mouth and drop the quicklight. It clacks against the smooth stone floor and rattles before falling still, the flame vanished. I don't speak, and neither does Rufus. But I feel him watching me and lift my chin. "Is this what happened?"

"Try the next panel, my lady."

We look to the right, at the next panel without shadows. A scene of fertile landscapes: the countryside with farmers and mechanical harvesters and wheat and hay and livestock being led down dirt paths by happy serfs. The sky is powder blue, and the grass is fresh and alive. A river dissects the fields, and in it are fish and children playing in its turquoise waters.

"Now the quicklight, my lady. Nothing to be frightened about; it's just a painting."

I know this, but the sense of horror is prominent in this place, and it's gotten a ahold of me. Nonetheless, "Right," I say, snapping the quicklight against my boot and lifting it high.

The beams cross the image, and the shadows show a dried lake, a dead lake. One of the children has morphed into a monster. A monster with a long neck and a rabid tail, with sharp teeth and fiery eyes, with scaly fins and razor-sharp gills. Livestock is black with disease, and serfs are made skeletal by the shadows, as though starving. The sky is overpowered with rainclouds, and the grass is painted with blood.

"What kind of beast is that?" Rufus asks in amazement.

We might realize at the same time that the splashing beneath us has grown quiet.

"Is this what happened? Is this the curse of the Fisher King?" I ask. The first panel shows what was; the second shows the demigods' wrath. What will the third reveal? "Rufus, you must know more. What did they say in Lyonesse?"

His face is white. "I didn't think it was as bad as this."

"What is the third panel?" I demand, because I can't bear to see it for myself. This curse could have fallen upon Merlin. Merlin might have been mere days from the same sort of fate as the Fisher King the moment the sorcerer decided to give up his thievery of magic. This could have been Camelot. This could have been my home.

"Let's see for ourselves," Rufus says. "As the first two have shown us what the curse entailed, perhaps the third will show us how to lift it."

I push aside the sudden rush of fear and glance up. The third panel is of a girl, possibly no older than I am. She's got white-blonde hair and her dress is asymmetrical, bright crimson. The features are pasty and unclear, and she's holding something in her hand, something that resembles a half-moon perhaps. Or a smile.

I shake my head, confused. "Is she a demigoddess? One of the Fisher King's daughters?"

Gently, Rufus takes my quicklight and lifts it high, and the beams of wood send shadows soaring across the details. And then the girl changes. Her features become more refined. Her eyes catch rays of bright blue that resemble those of the advisor to a dead king. Her hair darkens until it's honey-blonde. Her dress isn't red at all: the shadows have painted it blue to render the garment purple, and it dips low to her chest. Something of a Lyonesse style, but one I find remarkably familiar.

And in her hand is no moon at all: the shadows have darkened the canvas, and what originally appeared to be a crescent is actually a cup. Not just any cup.

It's the Holy Grail.

"Oh my God," I whisper.

I take the quicklight and lift it higher.

"It's me."

THIRTEEN

Rufus gives me time to internalize this strangeness. The silence is eerie and unsettling, and I nearly wish the creature swimming in the waters below would breach the surface again if for no other reason than to interrupt my shock.

I realize the blacksmith might have figured out what I've kept from him. And I'm right.

"It's you, isn't it? You have the coordinates to Avalon." He rubs his tired eyes with callused hands. "All this time I carried guilt about keeping my own identity a secret, and you've been keeping not one but two lies from me. Was it the wizard who told you?"

"No," I whisper. "The Lady of the Lake, before Marcus left with Galahad's infantry."

Rufus scoffs, and it turns into an ironic laugh. "That was six months ago. Six months since my boy trotted out into the wild unknown, looking for that damned cup."

"I didn't know what I could trust you with."

"But you knew not a day ago I'd been searching for those coordinates for years! Coordinates which might have saved Elly's life!" His anger bounces off the stone walls and comes back at me.

I should feel ashamed, but instead, the entire truth

springs out of me. "I told you I didn't know until Marcus was about to leave. How might it have saved your wife's life? Don't you think I would have told you had I known who you were, had I known it could save the life of the boy I—"

I stop there. I haven't addressed these feelings for Marcus yet, or how deeply they run through me, but now is certainly not the time. "You weren't there when Marcus saw your home burn. You didn't see his devastation; instead, you hid from him and let him believe you were gone. I would have done anything to have delivered him from such anguish!"

Rufus slams his fist into the wall with a loud cry of anger and loss, and bits of rock and stone chip free, flitting onto his sleeve. His breathing is unstable and wobbles with the weight of grief.

"I apologize," he says in a low voice. "Truly. I don't know what sort of role you have in these games of demigods and idiots, how they'll make you into pawns if they must, but if I could spare you from such a life, know that I would."

He speaks with such conviction, with such clarity in the words he chooses, that I know it's the truth.

When I don't answer, he casts his violet eyes at me. "A father should never have to bury his son. I'm selfish enough to live my life in a way that ensures that never happens. Know that."

There's a longing for me to understand such a love in Rufus's eyes, but I cannot respond. I'm still wondering if this might be a game to demigods, as he said. Enough to tempt those who would defy them to steal their magic. Maybe the Black Knight is just as influential as the Lady of the Lake. Maybe this is why there's a painting of me on the ceiling above. Maybe this is why Marcus is lost, searching for the Grail, or perhaps not.

Perhaps the blacksmith would feel differently about me if he knew I wanted to leave for Jerusalem instead of staying in Britannia.

With a heavy sigh, Rufus regards the bewitched room. "You said this was a test of ingenuity." He faces me with a cocked smile so much like Marcus's. "This'll be your area of expertise then, surely."

I respond with a smile that's much more somber, that also wants to see his son outlive the man in front of me. Certainly, if we can find the damned king himself, he might explain how to find Marcus or why I'd be of any importance in this world. The only way Rufus and I could ever hope for answers now is by confronting these horrors head-on.

I ignore the taunting panels and their threats. Instead, I consider the barriers and beams. "Your satchel."

Rufus shrugs it from his shoulder, tucked under the iron of his hook.

I think about the tools a blacksmith would carry, excluding the lock picks left outside the main castle; I think how I could use them. "Do you know how to build a pulley system?"

"Of course."

I let a smile of that desired and elusive *ingenuity* flit across my face. "Then we have work to do."

My plan is not complicated, but guarantees much danger if something should go wrong.

A rowboat hangs on the wall. I remove my furs and cloak, exposing my bare arms to air as cold as Merlin's insults and as dry as Azur's desert. My breath is a fog in front of my face, and my heart pounds. Rufus and I empty Merlin's leather satchel, and I affix it to the door's frame so I can lean against its weight into the room without any fear of tumbling into the abyss. I suspend myself above the slick and watchful water and reach out to see how the boat is attached to the wall.

"Be careful, my lady," Rufus says quietly, as though a word out of him might send me into the water below. But it must be me to do this, as I'm much smaller, and the leather is not terribly strong.

I stretch my arm to see if I can reach the wood, at least *touch* it, just once—

A hand. A wet, gray hand with nails long and pointed and black as coal seizes my wrist. A pair of waterlogged eyes on a girl's dead face look out from the edge of the rowboat. I scream, and my balance wobbles, threatening me with a watery grave.

Lips do not rise from behind the mildew-coated wood of the boat, but still a voice speaks. *"It will disappear, it will disappear."*

My eyes widen, and it's like I'm drowning, Rufus's voice calling my name from so far away.

The girl suddenly turns to water and spills over the rowboat's side. Her hand is the last to melt, and when it does, I draw away.

"Vivienne!" Rufus shouts, pulling me back. I clutch the edge of the door, grounded on the landing and shaking from the cold on my hand. Glancing at my wrist, I see no water, no marks from the tightness of the girl's grip. *But she was there!*

Rufus likewise peers at my wrist. "What the hell was that?"

But I already know. "They want me to steal magic." And this time, I know exactly what the forthcoming spell will do: the water, and the monster in it, will disappear. All I'll need is to utter the spell soon to come.

Rufus is silent, and for this to be his response is unnerving. He moves to the edge, looking at the rowboat hanging there. It wobbles on two long iron nails, hammered into the wood. A strange way to decorate a ballroom in a castle with such fine paintings on its ceiling, unless you might need a way out of it.

Rufus glances sideways at me. "We will not take their magic." He spits the words and stretches his iron hook toward the nail. With a long reach and a strained voice, his hook detaches the boat and catches its side.

Instantly, I grab his other arm, knowing the sudden influx of weight will fling him into the water. "Hang on!"

There's sweat beading across his forehead, and he grits his teeth, anchoring himself with a long grunt. I consider the chances he'll be lost to the water, food for whatever creature from hell swims beneath us. But the blacksmith is stronger than I give him credit for, and he manages to grab the boat's edge with his free hand to pull it high. With a long, heavy cry, he heaves, and it slams against the stone.

The boat is one a fisherman would use on the Lord's Day. It should fit both of us easily, with added room for the leather-rimmed wheel Rufus constructed using the spokes in the staircase and a loosened doorknob. We took the leather from Merlin's falconry gloves, as they're good and tight—the old sorcerer will have to forgive us. Simple steel wires from my satchel will weave through the slot at the end of the harpoon, and I'll send it flying through the countless beams, straight at the wall. But that begs the question of how to spring the harpoon into motion.

"I have an idea," Rufus says, dropping to a knee to search his satchel. When he finds a certain tool in his possession, he pauses, like he might be tempting a squirrel with a trick acorn. He withdraws a miniature crossbow from his belongings.

My miniature crossbow. I draw in a quick breath.

He shrugs. "Perhaps it's time to become reacquainted."

I search his eyes. "How?"

"After Morgan's war, I returned to the farmlands while the rest of you buried the king. To see Elly." His words tighten before he's able to push his heartbreak aside. "On the way back I saw your broken bow at the base of a tree, and I remembered how brave you were. How you went up against the witch herself, even though you could have been killed. She broke this; slammed it straight into the tree. After I'd seen you work so hard on it."

He holds it in front of me, and it's exactly as I remembered. The same wood, only reinforced with veins of iron, highlighted ends with copper. Even the latch is pulled back to a proper place, rendering the string taut. Through my melancholic amazement, I smile. It's what Marcus told me needed to be fixed.

"Thank you," I say with every ounce of sincerity I can manage.

Rufus inclines his head.

My crossbow can certainly launch a harpoon. And after defeating the wraith, I won't spend any more time thinking about the lives I stole—had to steal, was made to steal—all because of a witch.

Rufus unravels the ring of steel line. He counts under his breath enough for the volley there and back, and adds about fifteen extra yards for the weight, the security, and the margin for error.

"Ready." He loops one end through the harpoon and uses a clamp to melt it back onto itself. He ties it thrice and tests it with a heavy pull.

I affix my crossbow to my arm and peer through its sight. It's a clear path of triangular wooden beams. Not an easy shot, but at least a straight one. The harpoon lies against the string.

"Steady," I tell myself.

A sudden burst from below loosens my footing. The monster breaches the surface, and I have to regain composure or fall. Then, a splash of water—but, no, it's not water. It passes over me and returns to the depths just as quickly.

"It will disappear, it will disappear."

I'm afraid, but I will not let this overcome rational thought. Some of the paint from the ceiling falls onto my hair, just like the old incantations in Merlin's catacombs when

Victor came to life. I narrow my eyes on the sight again and reset the harpoon's trajectory. It'll slam into the wall, but there's a small, off-balanced mechanism I've applied to the base that'll act as a boomerang through pure force of momentum, unclipping itself from the arrow and slamming back.

"Steady," I say in a barely-there whisper. When all triangular beams have disappeared into one, I release the harpoon.

It flies straight and it flies true over each of the beams and slams into the frame above the door on the other side. Instantly, the mechanism disconnects and loops the steel back around and catapults the line back toward us.

"Move!" I cry. And once again, the monster below us slams against the water, and the harpoon's point wavers in midair. I dive to the floor, covering my head in case the worst were to happen; Rufus does the same. There's a loud *thwack*, and I jump. Silence falls.

I look beside me. The harpoon is clear through the wall no more than several finger-widths away. I give it a pull to check its strength and hitch the boat to the steel. My crossbow twists against the length of my arm and tucks under my cloak.

In my hands is another contraption: a crank. A simple gadget able to clamp over the dual strings and rotate them through two separate sprockets. With a little more wire, we tie our boat to it, and soon, we're on our way across the hall's watery graveyard.

When we've reached the halfway point, I take in more of the beautiful yet horrible panels that have included me in their story. I think of how Marcus might have been astounded by the third one, and how he might have made a light comment to break the tension—anything to make me smile.

But then, there's another shudder of land and castle, and I look over the side. I blink. Then once more.

Because the shuddering doesn't stop. And it feels as though the wire might be stretching, or the space around us might be collapsing, or our boat is sinking further. My eyes snap up to our pulley system. Perhaps the steel line was too long; perhaps the wooden beams were too weak to hold our weight, even with the added anchoring of stone walls and iron. But that's not it.

"The water is rising!" I shout. The crashing water is deafening, and the voice calling for me to steal magic so omnipresent and bittersweet lulls me. *It will disappear, it will disappear.*

It slices through my mind like whatever evil in this place has thrown the edge of an axe into my skull. I wince from the pain, the intensity of the voice, the semblance of magic behind all of it, calling me to indulge in what it could save me from.

"Rufus!" I call, pressing my hands to my face as though it could alleviate the pain. When I pull my fingers away, a streak of blood accompanies my hand. More pours from my nose, and a weightlessness comes over me, making me dizzy. Oh God.

Rufus's eyes go wide, and he turns the crank faster and faster so we can get to the other side. But suddenly the scaled gray skin of something belonging to hell rises and falls beneath the murky surface. I inhale sharply, suppressing a scream that wants to unleash itself.

The watery eyes with their dead gray pupils flash in front

of me. A pair of ice-cold hands clutch my neck. *"Estakah evanesqui estach, estakah evanesqui estach."*

Magic. Certainly magic. And with a sharper edge than Morgan le Fay's spells or even those of Merlin. The voice is old. The words are ancient and heavy.

I cry out as the shadows fall over me, but Rufus's ever-searching eyes tell me he sees nothing.

"Don't!" Rufus says. He wastes no more strength, but I know what he means: *Don't steal magic.*

I throw the hands off. The siren screeches and falls into the waters. I glance at the door. We're nearly there, but we're dreadfully slow, and I must do something to help.

The crossbow. Inside the compartment is a spare bolt from Morgan's war. Right away, I reinforce it with an additional line that might let us abandon this boat. I run the line through my palms, and the steel is sharp and fast and slices at my skin. When I've reached the end, the room is still rising. I aim through the doorway at the stone wall on the other side. With any luck, the bolt will break through and hold us steady.

I twist my crossbow, aim, fire. The bolt flies. Finds its target. And holds.

"Go!" I cry.

We're close enough that the blacksmith can jump and climb to the other side. He does so and reaches for the boat's edging to bring me to safety. Another shuddering of this hellish castle, and I'm gathering my weapons and tools, and there's water spraying in my face and slippery gray skin brushing up against my leg, coming around either side of the boat. My lip quivers; my teeth chatter. The blacksmith reaches for my hand, and I move to grasp it, but suddenly, the bolt in the wall comes loose, and the boat falls.

I might scream with my drop, but I don't hear a sound; instead, I feel wind rushing around me and the sturdy grip of Rufus's hand around my wrist. He yanks me to the other side just as the body of a monster leaps into the air with as many teeth as I could ever count, just missing my feet.

I scramble backward. The monster falls. All is silent.

"We made it," the blacksmith says, crouched beside me. "I didn't know if we would."

We crossed water by commandeering a boat across a ceiling and were nearly destroyed by whatever hell-beast dwells in the castle of the Fisher King. We refused a siren and a wraith the chance to steal the magic they guard. On another day, I'll panic more about what fates I barely missed.

"We haven't made it yet," I whisper. "We still have one more test."

FOURTEEN

Stairs wind up around an empty space. They climb to the top, opening to the wintery sky. No ceiling. Just like the room with the Round Table back in Camelot, which Marcus showed me, and which brought me the same sense of heart-pounding thrill. I'm not sure what third test Rufus and I will face, but this is only path for us now.

"Right judgment, then," I say, gripping my sword tightly as the harpoon leans against my shoulder, propped in my other hand. "I don't know what that might mean."

I don't expect Rufus to answer, and he doesn't; his silence is enigmatic and vast with possibility as I take the stairs with him following. The gold railing is sublime, carved into mermaids and swordfish, crustaceans and seaweed. The bottom of the ocean brought to the surface. But while some spots are covered in wet, sticky moss, others are dry with chipped gold plating, rotting wood underneath. At each landing, there's a window looking over the Perilous Lands, endless, with no sense or feel of ocean or sea. I keep my eyes skyward and remember that each step brings me closer to finding the pathway to the Grail. And Marcus. And it will also lead me to understand why I'm here, why I'd ever be painted on the ceiling of a castle as old as this one.

Why on earth would Merlin have ever sent me here?

It feels like eons have passed by the time we reach a landing leading nowhere. I glance up, seeing how far we are from the top. As the walls lift into the sky, I see more floors, more railings, more rooms I could explore. How curious. I reset my eyes on the doors, lined in thin iron and decorated with cogs warped and stretched like they might have found themselves fighting a wrathful sea.

This is it, I think. The third test.

Right judgment might not include monsters or death, but it might be something all together more terrifying. And I'm not sure what sort of demon or magic will be there to ensure the last test is where I fail.

Inside is a dusty room that resembles the main castle in Camelot where Arthur would meet with his advisors. There, it was decorated with red and gold tapestries boasting the Pendragon emblem, tables of wrought-iron candles and wine and dishes, the king and queen's own magnificent thrones trumping any gossip or talks of war from nobility and knights who'd enter.

But this room is bare, empty. Nothing other than cobwebs and a set of arched cathedral windows on one side with columns on the other. My eyes adjust to the strange sunlight spilling in; I watch as heavy dust from years of settlement dances in the beams. There's a lone flag, the color of dull ocean water that might have been bright and bold once. I lift the silk, and a silver trident stares back at me. The symbol of the Fisher King.

I don't understand why the pathway would bring us

here, and I'm about to speak, but first, three long strikes to the stone floor stun me still.

"*Who goes there?*" a voice as old as creation calls.

My heart is in my throat, and my eyes dart to the dark spots in this room. Finally, they rest upon a figure up ahead, right where a simple, yet warbled, iron throne sits, perpendicular to a cold, empty fireplace with white ashes scattered about. Sunlight silhouettes the figure, letting me see a crown on a man's head, the light's grip around the serrated points reflecting gold. "Who intrudes upon the castle of the Fisher King? State your name."

Rufus touches my shoulder to pause me. "My lady, let me bear this burden."

I shake my head, though it comes about without any credible courage. I cannot let the blacksmith do this. This is my task, my quest, and I remember the despair written on Marcus's face when he believed his father died in the inferno of Morgan's war. I cannot allow that sadness to have been in vain.

I free myself from Rufus's grasp and walk toward the voice, keeping close watch on the details of each darkened corner, each spider's mosaic webbing, each bit of dust I breathe in and expel into the atmosphere. There might be a trap in this test. I must be on guard.

Finally, the silhouetted figure is much clearer once I've passed the sunbeams. It raises a shaking hand. "Come no further. Why is there a girl in my midst? Who are you?"

I take a long breath. "My name is Vivienne. The sorcerer Merlin sent me to find the Fisher King." And now Rufus will know the truth, that Merlin, our shared mentor, sent me here, not Azur.

The figure responds with a heavy scoff that turns into a laugh. "Merlin. You lie, girl. There's no way in heaven or on earth the demigods would have allowed that thief to exist for as long as this." Words pass through dry lips, shaky and angry and full of hate.

I feel a frown crossing my face at the insult, but I'm not sure the wisest thing would be to respond.

The figure sits taller. "Though indeed I've spent much time imagining him here with me. If the demigods kept tally, they'd know the sense of thievery was stronger in me than the wizard of Camelot. But Merlin...Merlin fell prey to the allure of *deception*." He spits the word in such a way that his bitterness is palpable. "If you claim to be one of his kin, I should expect nothing different from you."

I've already guessed the answer to the question on my mind, but I must know for certain. "Is it you?"

The shadows vanish with my last step, and the face leans closer and peers at me. A man as old as Adam, tangled in gray hair and a long beard that tumbles to his waist, speckled with what looks like seaweed and barnacles. His skin is a cross between mildew and stone that might crumble at but a touch. His garments are of the old-fashioned sort—elaborate robes more flamboyant than practical, with long, royal blue threads and silver harpoons embroidered throughout. A matching trident stands tall in his right hand, and the man stares at me with eyes so small they've nearly fallen into the back of his skull.

"You know who I am. If it was *Merlin* who sent you, then you know I'm the Fisher King." He looks upon me with more scrutiny now. "By Jove. It cannot be. Remarkable." He stares at every part of my face.

"What?" I forget propriety for curiosity.

He narrows his eyes. "You look so much like her."

"Who?"

"The Lady of the Lake, of course. Centuries ago. When she was very young, and I was still a wealthy king." He shakes his head in disbelief. "I knew her as Vivienne."

My breath leaves me. I think of the gypsy in the village of Camelot who only one day past threatened me with violent magic. I remember the shine of the gold coins she gave to the young mother who'd been caught in Morgan le Fay's flames. But even more so, I remember how the old woman's strange, bright eyes widened in surprise or satisfaction when I told her my name. *A good name.*

The Fisher King won't dwell on that revelation, though. "It seems we've much to discuss, my dear. My subjects reformed the castle and all its traps for the rise of the mechanical arts. All in hopes someone able to pass these tests would free me. Magic had been stripped of the entire kingdom except for the curse vehemently set upon me."

Whatever evil the demigods ordered in this castle to guard the Fisher King, the curse's legacy depended on a well-meaning thief of magic finally giving in, not the rise of the new science against which it had no chance. And so I see how the scales were tipped, and I consider how the Holy Grail is meant to balance them.

The Fisher King sits back in his throne and laughs dryly. "Now nearly everything in this godforsaken place is a mere afterthought of magic, and the rest is a twisted, watery version of those blasted mechanical arts you and yours are so fond of. It'll stay this way until someone arrives in my kingdom, someone whom even the demigods might fear. That person will save me from my torment here on earth. Through *his* efforts, I'll finally be released from my curse's hold."

He lifts his arms draped in their fine threads and lets me see the seaweed serving as chains or handcuffs, rock and coral forming around his wrists as though binding him. He gives them a quick tug, showing their strength.

"So imagine my surprise now that I know it just might be the girl painted on my ceiling long ago. The girl painted by mystics and seers. The girl who was supposed to be an homage to the demigods or connected to the legend of the Grail—I can't remember which."

I'm not sure where I should begin, and so all I can manage is, "I share a name with ... " before I've lost any sense of coherency. The Lady of the Lake had known my mother before I was born and decreed I'd be of much importance to Camelot. But to have her *name*. "It was the Lady of the Lake who cursed you. Wasn't it?"

The Fisher King's eyes trace the lines of muck and dirt on his wrists. "Through much resistance on my part. Yes."

"She promised to protect me in Camelot. Why would she curse you if your destiny aligns with the Grail's?"

"While you were *in Camelot*, she promised. But you aren't anymore, are you, Lady Vivienne?" A smile of outright cruelty draws itself upon the Fisher King's face. "She is more concerned with her role in the Grail's discovery than the affairs of mankind. They all are. We're nothing but *beetles* to them." He sneers as he emits the word and struggles more against his bindings.

I cannot dwell here any longer. If Marcus and Owen are still missing, Rufus and I have to hurry. "Tell me how to release you from this."

The Fisher King laughs loudly, and it echoes against the stark bare walls. "Release me? You? Even Merlin would fail a task as monumental as this."

But why would Merlin send me to the Perilous Lands only to fail? "I've passed the tests—" And then my mouth shuts abruptly, right when the Fisher King's eyes widen at my words. We both note my error.

"No, dear," he says. "Not the last one."

I glare at his mocking smile. "Then why did we find you first?"

Rufus shifts uneasily. "Perhaps we missed a corner or a path."

"You didn't," the Fisher King asserts.

I pace in front of the throne. "Tell me what I must do. I killed Morgan le Fay not six months—"

Wind and thunder and icy rain spill around me until I'm sure I'll drown in a storm that shouldn't be. It vanishes as quickly as it came. Rufus and I are left drenched in snow and water and ruffled by gusts of air. But the Fisher King remains untouched.

"Morgan le Fay was a child in the world of magical

thievery," he huffs. "And I could show you what sort of power I can wield myself, foolish girl so sure she can save a thief of magic from his own fate."

I'm cold and tired, and I stare at the rotting face of king in front of me and feel a rise of anger.

"I left the only home I've ever known because I have to believe *all* of this—this Grail, this quest to beat the Spanish rogues, it could save lives. I'm here because the person I admired most in this world gave his soul so the Grail could eventually be found. He told me it was only through you that Camelot might claim it. But the Spanish rogues have attacked Jerusalem, and I cannot go there myself, and it is very possible that it's already too late. And still, Merlin told me my place was *here*."

He sits back, his hands shaped into a temple at his chin as he thinks. Rufus stands next to me and crosses his arms over his chest. The Fisher King knows that leaving is not an option for either of us.

He clears his throat, and now, he speaks with humility. "You'll need the coordinates to Avalon."

I take a breath. It's time to speak the truth out loud. "I have them."

His tiny eyes grow larger. "Then it's true? It's you who will lead the knights to the Holy Grail? It's your mind, the treasured sacristy?" He laughs.

I feel my eyes sting with frustrated, exhausted tears. "Does the thought amuse you so greatly?"

"Oh, certainly not!" he says through louder laughter that borders on cruelty. "It's just that I know what sort of path lies ahead of you, Lady Vivienne!"

The blacksmith huffs and regards the column standing beside him. With one swing of his iron hook, the column collapses into dust and rubble, and the Fisher King is silenced.

"We've come a long way, my lord, with much at stake," Rufus growls.

The Fisher King regards the blacksmith. "Ah. Blacksmith. The demigods are chatty; they've been particularly interested in what'll become of your boy." He snarls a smile, risking some crumbling of skin and bone. Then the old man glances at me. "Tell me first what you want in return. I do not accept charity, even in such a desperate state."

I don't need to think about the question. "You're connected to the fate of the Holy Grail. Give us what we need and set us on the correct path that we might claim it quickly and find the knights. This is what Merlin told me must happen."

He nods slowly. "Very well. Take me to the highest point of my castle, where you'll be presented with the third test, one of right judgment. If you pass, I'll go to meet death, and the path to find Avalon will be unlocked to you. If you fail, my fate will fall upon both of you."

I imagine myself tied to a throne such as his, starfish and barnacles cuffing my wrists. But I will not be afraid. "All right."

"Patience, Lady Vivienne. There's another undertaking that would assure me you are, in fact, suitable for this task." He shuffles his robes until two knobby knees are in perfect view. I blink several times when I glance at what lies below: dust, rubble, as though his legs faded away long ago.

"I'll need a new set of feet, you see."

FIFTEEN

The iron piping torn from the heavy doors works splendidly for any appendages the blacksmith and I could build. I have some of Merlin's *jaseemat* in my possession, and I prep two small, gear-work hinges that would attach to the Fisher King's knees, allowing Rufus's primitive iron legs to fuse to what's left of the cursed man's body.

The Fisher King nods when I inquire. "Every few hundred years or so is the only time parts of me turn to dust."

I keep a watchful eye on him, a man who's sat only in a throne for centuries. He cannot seem to go ten seconds without laughing quietly under his breath. And he won't tell me what amuses him so—won't even give me a hint. Eventually, I'm furious, but forced to let it be so I can help Rufus.

"Your legs, *my grace*," Rufus says. The makeshift feet are flattened beds of wood inserted into a set of old, pointed shoes. I adjust the appliance and add a small bit of *jaseemat* that spills temporary life into the legs as we attach them to the Fisher King's rotting knees.

He's intrigued by the devices. "Impressive. Clearly derivative of Merlin's work. Has he told you much about alchemy, my dear?"

I ignore the taunt in his voice. "It'll work only for a short amount of time."

"It will be long enough. We're but minutes away from the end of all this."

The old man's eyes rest on mine as Rufus's iron hook slashes through the seaweed cuffs. I help the Fisher King to his feet, and the blacksmith and I each take an arm, leading him out the door and into the foyer where there is no way to approach the stories above us, lest we were to forge a quick-winged aerohawk to take us there. I hold my breath at the thought that we might need to return to the watery trenches where a sea monster might wait for a second go at my feet.

The Fisher King points ahead. "Look."

I glance up. The window on the other side of the room right above the descending stairs lets in the sunshine, but as I peer closer, I realize it's not a window but a yellow-painted door leading higher in this castle. My lips part in awe. "But how do we—"

The Fisher King takes my chin between two old fingers and tilts it so that my line of vision changes, and I see his world in a new way. In fact, the set of stairs that descend to the water are now ascending to the sky; shadows and platforms transform to take us to the next floor.

"That's impossible."

"By definition, perception is subjective, Lady Vivienne. There is no need to return to where you came from. Now, your journey lies straight ahead. Shall we?"

He takes that first step, and Rufus and I drop his arms so that the king's trident can lead us to the summit.

At the top, I can already see the brightness of the white sky. The light falling into this part of the castle sparkles like the moon on lake water. I know Marcus is somehow on the other side of this monumental task, whatever right judgment might entail. My brother, as well. And the lives paid in Morgan's war will finally have meaning if Camelot can find the Grail.

The light grows strong enough to nearly blind me. I shield my eyes and look out, finding the Fisher King hobbling toward some widely spaced parapets, where, beside him, Caldor sits, its head cocked in my direction. This balcony reminds me of how the Round Table looked over the whole of Camelot with nothing but stars and navy sky as company. Summer had made the world bright and lovely and full of rich vitality then; here and now, in the dead cold and infertility of winter, the world is so much more brutal.

"Now, dear girl, the third test. I'll have to ask your companion to keep his distance this time."

The Fisher King reaches the edge, and as my eyes adjust, I see a tall, lanky figure join him out of nowhere, as though born of the old king's silhouette. Or perhaps this man has been waiting just as long as the Fisher King. The old king sets a warm, welcoming hand on the younger man's shoulder.

"This test is my favorite. Because no matter who was to pass the first two, once they arrived here, it was guaranteed to be a surprise."

Finally my eyes adjust, and I look ahead at the man in question. Just as his face turns to mine. Dark hair longer now, smile a little more worn for wear. Eyes violet as they've always been. And that smile, that same nonchalant smirk.

Oh my God.

I'm staring at Marcus.

My breath caught in my throat, I race for the edge, but Marcus makes no move to greet me. Instead, the Fisher King steps forward, his trident's three prongs holding me back.

"Marcus!" I shout as the sun somehow brightens. I turn quickly to the blacksmith who looks at me in confusion. "Don't you see? What's the matter with you? It's your son!"

I turn back. Behind the Fisher King, Marcus's face is blank, eyes empty and without the ability to recognize mine. It's not Marcus.

"This is the third test," I whisper.

The Fisher King inclines his head. "With no haunting whispers of magic to lure you this time. At stake, we find the life of this boy, a life you value. Particularly interesting since it's a fate I know well—the demigods have loose tongues when it comes to the mortals they find to be of special interest. And so your test of right judgment is this: shall his life pay the price for the Holy Grail?" In his gray, powder-like hand, he now holds a matte cup whose grip is worn leather and studded with iron. I blink in the sharp light of the sky. The Holy Grail, surely.

As my eyes lock onto the chalice, the vision of Marcus hops upon the parapets, his back to the frozen land. I inhale sharply; it's just as it was all those months ago, when Marcus balanced atop the balcony overlooking Camelot and told me of his life as a squire.

But this isn't real. And so it wouldn't matter how I'd respond. "It's not him."

"Ah," the Fisher King says, steadying his trident so it returns upright. "Do not be fooled, Lady Vivienne. As we saw in the stairwell, perception is in fact subjective. Just because this isn't the version of Sir Marcus you know doesn't mean it isn't the truth in front of you. In fact, Sir Marcus is in a more dangerous place than this, isn't he? The vision you see might fall, but all that'll happen is a puff of smoke as it hits the icy ground beneath us. The real boy is out there somewhere. Is he safe?"

My mind fights to assure myself *it's not Marcus,* and yet I can't look away. "Then what is the test?"

The Fisher King takes another step. He lifts the dull chalice high. "I've already said: the Grail, or Sir Marcus?"

The echo of the Lady of the Lake's prophecy rings in my ear. I shake my head stubbornly. "They're not separate paths; one follows the other. You promised you'd give me a clear path to—"

"To Avalon. Yes. And it'll be up to you to reveal it once you're there. Regarding Sir Marcus, it might be true that the boy's destiny is one of imminent death, but that death might allow the Grail to be Camelot's."

I know this. But I also know what the Lady of the Lake said: Marcus's fate could just as easily be one of betrayal. I don't know which might be worse.

"So I must decide which I'd prefer—Marcus's life or the Holy Grail for Camelot?"

"No. You must decide which would be the right choice."

My lip quivers. This might affect Marcus and the real Grail waiting to be found. What I choose might create the sacrifice. Does the Fisher King possess that sort of power? Would the demigods allow it in the course of releasing this man of stone from his curse? A bout of frustration comes over me. I'm just a handmaid; I was just a handmaid.

Rufus approaches, and even though he looks straight at Marcus, his eyes waver instead at the dead scenery beyond. "My lady, I can't see ... but you have to know what Marcus would want."

I do. I know Marcus would never want his mother's death to have been in vain. But I also know he never wanted to be a knight. Instead of the honor the quest would bring him, he longed for escape, just as I did.

I take a breath. "But could it mean Marcus's life is lost?"

The Fisher King lifts his chin. "You must choose."

The vision of Marcus steps closer to the edge, his foot swaying over the nothingness below.

With timid steps, I walk toward him—toward this vision or ghost or trick of the mind. With every step, he becomes more glorious, more heavenly, like he's long since died on the quest for Avalon and returned as a spirit before ascending to heaven. His blank eyes watch me without the happiness the real Marcus would boast, and I step up onto the parapets with him, my boots finding their grip as the Fisher King watches us in the blinding light. I touch Marcus's hand, arm, neck, his skin is softer than a serf's could ever be. Proof it's not him. His violet eyes blink like a child's would, and he watches me wearing a ghost of a smile I beg to be real.

"I know what you'd want. I know the right answer, Marcus."

I lift to my toes, making myself tall enough to plant a small kiss on his cold, ghostly lips, and I feel warmth cross my skin with an easy sense of peace. When I pull away, I realize he was never really part of the kiss in the first place.

The words I speak do not seem to arise from any part of me, and yet they come forth, loud and declarative to the waiting Fisher King: "Camelot must have the Grail."

Marcus leans back, shutting his eyes. He falls from the parapet, and even though I know this is not real, I cannot look. I listen for the thump from the fall of his body, and that dreadful sound never comes. I breathe and open my eyes. But Marcus is gone.

The Fisher King nods. "You have passed."

I hold the Holy Grail in my hands, and it shines like a mirage and cannot be real. It's heavy and dull and so ordinary—

And suddenly, the world around us turns into an inferno of heat and wind, and it spills around the Fisher King, lifting his body and taking him into the next world, a world of death, a world he'd longed for as his limbs fell to dust while the memories of his loved ones didn't.

"Remember, Lady Vivienne, to reveal Avalon only when the time is ready. You can do so once; to conceal it again would mean the kingdom and the Grail it guards would be lost in seven days." The tension and anger in the wrinkles by his eyes smooth over with relief, and he smiles. "Thank you."

I step closer, the light nearly blinding me. "Wait. Marcus's destiny. Will he soon die? Is he already dead?"

The Fisher King shakes his head. "Sir Marcus has a different fate."

And then he's gone.

My hands are empty. The Grail, lost again. In its place now is a heavy and old signet a king would use to seal documents. I think for a moment that it must belong to the Fisher King, but the material is not wood or silver or even iron—it's dark, heavy marble with ridges on the side that renders it similar to a puzzle piece. On the rounded top is an engraving of a chalice, the same shape painted in that third panel in the castle. From the song children would sing in Camelot, we knew machines guarded Avalon. This small piece of marble might be what Merlin told me I'd need to claim the Grail. Confound it all—another key, of sorts.

Rufus and I look out across the Perilous Lands, and the clouds part in front of us, galloping across the sky and letting a shade of winter blue spill over. A gentle and quiet snowfall accompanies it. A return to the natural cycle of the seasons. A voice against my ear sounding of the sweetest harp opening up a part of my mind that, until now, I hadn't been able to explore myself.

> *Where rogues make their port.*
> *Where sea and sky and sand consort.*
> *Ninety degrees in angle and heat.*
> *No king to fish, no knights to meet.*
> *But one found long before her age.*
> *Alive from portrait to show the stage.*

An array of numbers, a flash of gray stones against breaking waves, an erratic form of sandy shores offsetting a nearby aeroship port. And then Avalon. The kingdom I've seen in dreams and wake for as long as I can remember.

Oh, I know how to get there and claim that glorious chalice. All I need is my aeroship and more *jaseemat* to get it. The Fisher King unlocked the coordinates in my mind, and I have a signet unlike any other in the world that will grant me entrance to Avalon.

Rufus takes a heavy breath. "Lady Vivienne. You did it."

"Yes," I say. Though there's a small bit of uncertainty inside me, and I don't understand it until I realize the Fisher King's last words and how they relate to the Lady of the Lake's prophecy. I realize I'm more afraid for Marcus now than ever.

Because if Marcus won't soon die, it means his betrayal is inevitable.

SIXTEEN

For a while, I stare at the spot where the Fisher King once stood. Gone now. Vanished. In the world after death, with no proof of him ever existing in the first place, except for the makeshift iron feet that clattered to the balcony. I don't know if I should expect the Perilous Lands to become lush with pine trees or firs—they don't. The only difference now is the impression of life in a castle where there'd been nothing but dead silence. Now, the humming of winter insects, the presence of wind sculpting branches of trees. There's a change, but it's a subtle one.

Every time I blink, I see Marcus falling from this balcony. I see his foot drifting to the side of the parapets, and my heart splits. I feel like I might simultaneously laugh and cry at the idea of him teasing me on that warm June day. The day we ran through the castle together with his rough hand gripping mine and his eyes alight with excitement as we sought Excalibur. Compared to the ghost from the Fisher King's test, I don't know how I could ever have mistaken such a shell of life for Marcus.

The tests. And now I cannot think of anything else. My head knew the right answer to the third test, but my heart felt quite differently. I don't know if I could have let Marcus die, even if it meant Camelot would lose the Grail. And so, in a way, I failed.

Rufus stands with me. The clouds are tumbling outward, showing us a clear path that somehow leads to Avalon, but the sky has fallen dark from dusk, and soon, night will follow.

"My lady, you should rest now. Best to leave the Perilous Lands at first light. This place is known for privateers who might find interest in your aeroship." He steps away from the parapets, returning to the stairs. "We'll start our search for Marcus tomorrow."

A sharp bite of anxiety hits my heart at his declaration. That's right: I agreed we'd both search for Marcus. But something nags at the cogs spinning in my mind: if Rufus comes with me, he might bring Marcus and me back to Camelot and take on the task of delivering the knights to Avalon himself. Perhaps he'll hold the instructions on how to create *jaseemat* over my head, not as an adversary, but a father. Rufus is clever.

I close the signet into my fist. "Give me the instructions, blacksmith," I say before he can make his descent.

Out of my periphery, I see Rufus glance over with a semblance of uncertainty falling over him. "You told two lies to me in the short time since you found out who I was. Why should I trust you with these?"

"We're out," I declare. "What I used for the Fisher King's feet was the last of it. We can't hope to reach Camelot now, let alone the wilderness beyond to find Marcus. I need to make more."

It's a reasonable request. Rufus slips a hand into his

pocket, withdrawing that folded piece of yellowing parchment. I note the crisp edges, the small tears in the corners. My fingers are itching to touch it. My eyes crave to read Merlin's own script. My head begs to know what that parchment contains and how it might change my understanding of alchemy forever.

Rufus stares at it, tucked between his fingers. "It's the wrong path, my lady. This science, this exploration of manipulating the elements. It's only grand for so long. And then it'll refuse to sustain your interest." His eyes are solemn with images dancing in his irises I could never hope to understand, a look I'd seen in Guinevere as she silently mourned Lyonesse. Rufus clutches the parchment tighter. "I'll give you these instructions so we can find my boy. But promise me: once this is over, you'll give them back so I can destroy this knowledge. No one else can know of it. It can only end badly."

I scoff inwardly at such dramatics. "Don't patronize me, blacksmith. I can tell the difference between alchemy and magic," I say loudly, though my voice betrays me with a wobble of doubt.

Rufus grabs my hand and squeezes tightly. "Vivienne," he says, and I don't miss how he doesn't use my title. "If you pursue alchemy, it'll take you to a threshold of magic, and by then, you'll already be a thief yourself. Please."

Azur warned of the same thing. But Merlin, when I claimed oh so long ago that only magic could bring my violet-and-dragonfly hairpin to life, assured me alchemy was nothing of the sort. Come to think of it, though, the old man had hesitated.

"Very well," I say. "Afterward, we'll destroy the instructions together."

He smiles sadly and presses the parchment into my palm. "I'll collect the charcoal," he says. "Let's get this over with."

I stare at the splotched ink and the smudges from the blacksmith's nervous palm. Unfolding the parchment stamped with the green phoenix, I read the title: HOW TO CREATE THE ELEMENT *JASEEMAT,* WHICH GIVES LIFE TO THE INANIMATE.

The way to do so involves charcoal and fire, dissolving the makeup of burnt wood so that it could be reassembled through vials and glasses into a rough element, then refined as it's filtered through boiling water. From there, it is smashed and smashed again, until its makeup is indistinguishable from golden powder.

But then, an element I never expected. "Blood?"

A chill falls over me. I study the handwriting. Merlin's instructions call for a human contribution to balance the natural elements. A few drops of blood could do it, but there's more—it must be the blood of someone the alchemist cares for. The stronger the connection, the more powerful the *jaseemat.*

I shake my head. "Can't be." It doesn't sound like alchemy, like instruction to the elements. It sounds...darker.

I read on: *The elements of charcoal have learned to react to the alchemist. Where there is love, there is always life, and through sacrifice, that life comes about in a most divine and intriguing way.*

"Now you know," Rufus says behind me. I turn to his

devastated face as he glances at the parchment in my hand. "There comes a point in the exploration of alchemy where one can no longer go any further without crossing a line."

I don't speak; I nearly wish I hadn't asked for any of this. Merlin's *jaseemat* was always weaker than Azur's—whose blood did each man take for their batches? Who did Azur hold love for? And Merlin?

Rufus steps forward and drops the pile of charcoal he was carrying at my feet. "But it's for my boy." He holds out his palm.

I glance up at him. "What is?"

Rufus stares right through me, and for as long as I live, I don't think I'll ever forget the love I saw in his eyes. "You need blood. Take mine."

_____

The vials from Merlin's satchel separate the elements easily. It's not a simple process, but it's relatively fast. The first batch of *jaseemat* I collect I test on Caldor. The falcon comes to life much faster than it does from Merlin's *jaseemat*. So much that I'm shocked by its strength.

Rufus grunts in surprise. "I didn't..." He narrows his eyes on Caldor as though thinking of the proper words to choose. "I didn't realize how much you cared." Without waiting for me to respond, he takes the stairs to the Fisher King's throne room.

My cheeks warm. I understand what he meant, that my love for Marcus enhances my love for his father. A love once-removed, but a love nonetheless. Caldor's ability to move is strong, but still rather primitive, as though the falcon must get used to my life-giving powder. It might be the same reaction for *CELESTE*.

The air crisps up around me. Tonight, up here, I've never felt more alone. I glance up into the dark nothingness, and I lift Marcus's quicklight high, using my other hand to navigate the approximate direction to Camelot. Home. Caldor waddles toward me, its head cocked in innocent curiosity. I pick it up and set it on my arm, the usually-sharp talons gentle, nothing more than a kitten's needlepoint claws. If I had been able to obtain blood from the mirage of Marcus somehow, I wonder how much stronger the falcon would be.

Hours pass, and I don't sleep, obsessed with tweaking my *jaseemat* as much as possible.

And then below, I hear shouts calling for a handmaid and a blacksmith. Slow and bouncing off the bricks of the towers in a voice I had nearly forgotten. I rush to the parapets and look down. Sir Tristan commands his men in their native tongue with little distinction between their accent and his. He might be around Lancelot's age, but as he's already seen so much of the world that he might as well be a thousand. They're still searching for us, even though they—

Dawn. They'll leave at dawn. By then, they'd have to give up on us, and I wouldn't blame them in the slightest.

I let a horrible thought pass through my mind—*please take the blacksmith with you.*

And then I decide to ensure that future for myself. I pull the hood of my cloak over my hair, even though there's no reason to stay hidden in this abandoned castle, and certainly I'm the only girl in these parts. Taking the multi-perspective steps that now lead straight to the courtyard, in sight of Tristan's aeroship, I find myself in the sailors' presence.

One calls to the others in Arabic, and Sir Tristan runs to meet me, surprised I'm still alive, perhaps, or surprised another soul would be stupid enough to be out in this freezing weather.

"My lady," he says. "We nearly thought you both dead."

I bite my lip. Rufus might never forgive me. "The blacksmith. He must go with you."

Tristan glances behind me as though expecting to see another person there. But I'm alone. "Why are you so concerned about your manservant?"

"Sir Tristan, you must take him with you."

Tristan's eyes narrow on mine, and his head is slow to incline to the side, as though he's incredulous of my request. "My lady—"

"Please," I say, stepping closer, my hands clenching his.

Now Tristan's eyes are harsh. "And you? Where will you go?"

I hold his gaze for as long as I can handle it. "I have a different path. Surely, you can understand how I must find it on my own. Even the blacksmith won't be able to deny that. One day."

Sir Tristan glances at his aeroship, letting me study the intricate wrapping of his turban loose around his head and neck, tucked into the furs necessary in these Perilous Lands. Then he lifts his eyes to the sky, and together we note how the world around us has changed. Surely he must realize that the Fisher King has been saved.

And perhaps he does. "I assume I couldn't begin to understand what sort of burden you might have upon your shoulders." His bright eyes find mine, and their harshness has melted, allowing understanding to bore through. "Likewise, I suppose you haven't asked the blacksmith to refrain from accompanying you."

I shake my head, confirming his suspicions. "He'd never let me go alone."

"Should I?"

I think about his question. "You, my lord, should go and aid Jerusalem. If, by chance, you were to find Lord William there, you should tell him his daughter Vivienne survived the Perilous Lands." I don't say if Lord William's daughter will return home. Because in all likelihood, that girl never will.

Tristan straightens. "We leave at sunrise, Lady Vivienne." He hops aboard the aeroship and helps straighten the newly repaired wings. "Best for you to be on your way a good hour before then."

———

I spend the rest of the night readying *CELESTE*. My fingers are stained black from a quill I found in Merlin's satchel. It bleeds over my fingers as I scrawl an apologetic message to Rufus. I wedge it under his iron hook, letting its crisp edges stick out enough that he wouldn't miss it. One quick, silent goodbye, glancing upon his sleeping figure, the father of my beloved. Perhaps our paths will never cross again. Perhaps he'll hate me for this.

I leave the castle and reach my aeroship, signet in hand like a sword in its own right. The damage on the wings and sails is bearable as long as I can use the navigational mechanism to avoid any heavy storms. I board *CELESTE*, my sleeves rolled up as I submit my own alchemic powder to the engine—it spreads through the veins of the ship, reaching the wings and sail above. Caldor is on my shoulder, and my crossbow is on my arm—I set both aside. I must be fast.

When the stairs crank up, I hear a loud, panicked cry. I jerk toward the castle to see Rufus running for me, a vision of Marcus as he sprints from the lowered drawbridge. I can no longer hide my deception. In truth, Rufus shouldn't have given me the instructions on how to create *jaseemat* just yet. He should have known.

"My lady! Please. Don't do this!"

Rufus is close. But I've already yanked on the lever to free the helm, and *CELESTE* jerks across the ground. Rufus runs beside it, but the ship speeds up.

"Stop! Vivienne!"

"I'm sorry," I whisper, knowing he'll never hear it. But it must be this way. "It's my burden, not yours." I remember the iron wording on the cross in the catacombs; I remember Elly. "If I can save you from her fate, let me."

Rufus grits his teeth as his flesh concedes before his spirit will. "At least tell Marcus I'm alive!" he calls, voice desperate and sad. He slows as I outrun him. My aeroshop's wings grip the swaying currents and glide above them, and I look below at the small speck of a man standing in the middle of a forgotten place. I know Rufus won't try to convince Sir Tristan to come after me. Rufus will let me go.

He'll let me go as long as I tell Marcus that his father survived Morgan le Fay's war. It's the least I can do, and we both know this.

And so I take comfort in knowing I'll find his son.

SEVENTEEN

The winds in the high skies are heavier, sharper, piercing like icicles on my skin. The currents wail like a banshee, too forlorn ever to find peace. I've encountered the storms of winter on the path to Avalon, and as I follow it, I can feel each snowflake slicing against my face until I must draw down my goggles to keep my vision intact. My *jaseemat* does nothing to smooth out the ride or strengthen the wings, but at least it keeps the fire burning and churns the propellers higher in the sky.

When I've surpassed the thunderous clouds and their chaotic bolts of lightning, the sky turns bright blue, curving over me like a sphere. Beyond, the black night might still dwell. Indeed, stars shine just as they always do, but now, it's in a realm of perpetual calm. A bit of quiet heaven. *CELESTE* steadies on a current, and I set the lever between the spokes of the helm to keep my aeroship southbound.

I walk the deck. The shuttering of propellers fades into the background, and my own ragged breath vies for gulps of air to steady my heart and keep me alive. Merlin's handwritten instructions I clutch against my chest.

"I'm sorry, Rufus," I whisper. Every time I blink, the

devastation in his violet eyes haunts me more and more. "I'm so sorry."

But he must understand. And surely, he will go with Sir Tristan and his warriors to Jerusalem. He will offer to repair any damages that might come about to their own flying ship. While working, he'll realize why I couldn't let him come with me, not when Marcus had already lost one parent and might have soon lost another.

Caldor flits to the table where I set the excess *jaseemat* from my satchel while the signet remains safe in the pocket of my cloak. I find Merlin's forgotten scrolls tucked beside a journal and crouch awkwardly, the firelance in my holster hitting the floor until I must shift to my knees to stay comfortable. My fingers drift over the thick, grainy parchment. I'd forgotten about these, and I have yet to see if there are any other hidden pages I might have missed. And so, I unravel one. Like the sorcerer might have forged them out of thin air himself, these are as brand new as a forthcoming day.

But, no, I don't believe the words I'm reading. Because even though they're scrawled beautifully in Merlin's own version of the Latin alphabet, there's no way these words strung together like a necklace of glass beads are anything but magic.

To blind a man. Yeuxeuse fambratcricoh kemphah solohite.
To resurrect. Redia chatusolach azah morterejiakah.

I slam my hand over my mouth as my eyes pore over lines and lines of the stolen words Merlin never destroyed. Words that might have easily fallen into the wrong hands. Words I tossed against my back without any concern for the supposed maps or sketches I thought would help Rufus and me in the

Perilous Lands. Words horridly easy to memorize—and just as difficult to forget—like the spell to bring a man back to life, a horribly tedious task, only doable in an hour's time. The same one Merlin mentioned in his letter to Azur. *Redia.*

The one that would bring about a horrible fate to the thief of magic using it.

Redia chatusolach azah morterejiakah...

But the journals don't end there: they contain the history of the Holy Grail and how it contains sumptuous power craved by the demigods. I'm nearly sick at the thought of Morgan le Fay finding something as precious as this. On the second page, the scrolls have lists and words I don't recognize. More spells. Merlin's own or stolen from a demigod, in all likelihood the Lady of the Lake. I tear them from their bindings as though to separate them from the journals would make them less real.

"Oh, Merlin, why would you have kept these?" I whisper. And why would he have told me to bring them?

A way to move through space, a way to raise a heavy object from beneath the water, or rein it in from the sky. To conceal. Manipulating the laws of nature. Diagrams of a human corpse and how dead blood could serve as a makeshift essence of life. Mechanical people not unlike Mordred, turned into monstrous machines not because of a weakened life, but enhanced on top of their own perfect bodies.

"Fascinating, is it not?"

I jump as the smooth voice of the sorcerer whispers into my ear. Quickly, the spells are stuffed into my dress's pocket, and my firelance is cold and quick in my hand as I aim at the empty space around me. But I'm alone. Merlin's not here, and even if he were, was I supposed to fire *this*? A firelance I got from the madman's very own clock tower? One I managed to find in lieu of his missing pistolník?

I inhale the wind like it might make me powerful, pressing my palms against my eyes until the pressure is relieved. "Calm down, Vivienne." Naturally, all of this is from hunger, or exhaustion, or fear. So much has happened since I left Camelot but a day ago. I'm bound to feel a little out of my mind.

"Don't be foolish, girl. You know what laws of the universe I'm able to transcend."

I whip around, following the voice. A flash of Merlin's cocked brows, gold-rimmed eyes, tattoos on his shorn skull, phoenix feather woven through his small goatee. I see a glimpse of the emerald stone in his wooden cane; I see the long robe he set upon his shoulders. And then he's vanished.

"Merlin? Merlin, if you're really here, show yourself!" I call. The firelance trembles in my hand, and nowhere can I see the man who was my mentor. Certainly, insanity has found me instead.

"Or perhaps I'm more real than ever," comes the whisper again. This time when I turn, Merlin is there. In front of me and in my mind at the same time. Just as he was in the woods with the Lady of the Lake, using a spell that lets him do so.

Sensu ahchla tetay meo loqui havahchi...

He's real, and he's fading in and out of existence. More so now than before. Any stress or pain in his face from the curse Morgan le Fay inflicted upon him—and that he readily took for himself once her sword dug into his heart—has faded for a sense of addiction and delight. He looks as he did when he stole magic to hide Marcus and me all those months ago: strong, valiant, able to withstand any attack and offer brutal retaliation. "Perhaps I'm here to ensure you're on the right path."

I grit my teeth at the venom in his voice. "No, you're nothing but a figment of my imagination. A thief of magic who never gave it up, but hoarded it in his tower for years!" I'm ready to pull free the parchment from my pocket to prove it.

He circles me like I'm his prey. "A figment of your imagination? Huh! Hardly. While you are brilliant, there's no way you could have imagined the likes of me as I am now." He presents himself, and indeed he's different from the sorcerer I knew. He stands tall without his limp, and while his eyes carry such wisdom only a man of countless eras could ever possess, his skin is radiant, shining. His gaze crawls over every corner of my aeroship. "A fine attempt. Could have used Lena's expertise, perhaps."

I frown. "Who?"

Merlin smirks. "Someone you've yet to meet, experienced in the ways of maneuvering vessels and toys affiliated with the mechanical arts. She could have helped you forge a secret passageway or a storage chamber, one that would let you hide the most valuable trinkets and information you have on this ship."

I shut my eyes and rub them. Perhaps Merlin's lost what's left of his mind and thinks he speaks to another. I feel the energy of the past two days finally subside for exhaustion. "You're a hallucination from lack of sleep or food—"

"I'm as real as I'll ever be, girl." His walk toward me is as smooth as the wind. "Azur couldn't contain me for long. How could I remain in a vault when instead I could witness the days soon to come?" When he speaks, it's like he's planning for a funeral instead of a jubilee. "To let you carry out your quest, I've locked the Lady of the Lake in the woods, a trick from an old foe I never imagined would come to mind."

He speaks of Morgan. Oh God, he speaks of Morgan.

"You have one focus now," Merlin continues. "When you first became my apprentice, you longed for the opportunity to learn more about the mechanical arts, how they could enhance the world in ways you could only dream. Once you saw my mechanical falcon take flight from my window, you had to know more."

He's circling me, and I feel like I'm at the gates of heaven on trial for sins I've not yet committed. "You're the one who taught me," I reply. "Or has your memory escaped you with your sense of right and wrong?"

"Do not speak against me, Vivienne, dear. This is not about me; it's about the apprentice I left behind, unaware of the danger I put her in, yet seeking to dive straight into it."

"How so?" I think of Azur's frightened eyes when he told me about alchemy and magic.

"Now you'll want the Grail," Merlin continues, "but not for Camelot or your mother's ensured safety or even for love. No, you'll soon long for the Grail to know what sort of power it might have. Yes, you'll want to study it, learn more about it, see if there's not only a way to use its magic for good, but perhaps your own creations as well. After all, good and evil are two wildly opposite ideas, and yet, subjective. Perhaps your definition of *good* would differ greatly from, say, Sir Marcus's, or mine."

Now I feel the unmistakable call of the Holy Grail, and I'm cloaked with the prospect of absolute knowledge and wisdom. I cannot deny how it fascinates me.

"So what, *pagan*?" I spit back, angry at how well he knows the workings of my mind.

Once I uttered that slur at Merlin, and he flinched as though I'd slapped him; this time, the word passes through his transparent being as though it might not exist any more than he does.

"You saw how magic destroyed the Fisher King, and yet, that doesn't discourage you." Suddenly, he steps closer, and I know he must be real because now he speaks as a mentor, not a challenger. "You must understand the severity of all this, Vivienne."

I firm my jaw. "I will not turn into the Fisher King. I want the Grail for Camelot, Merlin. For Azur's sake. Jerusalem's. Otherwise, I would have left for safer grounds long ago."

"You wouldn't have, as your lover seeks the same thing," he retorts.

"That's not why I do this!"

A frightening calm comes over Merlin. A smile of distrust swerves to the side of his face. He leans closer, forcing me against the helm. "We shall see. You managed to evade the temptation of magic, and you passed the Fisher King's tests, but can you rise up to a far more difficult challenge?"

With one quick reach, he's got the helm in his grasp and twists it until the lever holding the trajectory snaps into two. The deck under my feet turns sharply—I scream. My hands reach for anything that could keep me upright, but before I can seize the helm myself, I've fallen. And when I look up at the traitorous sorcerer, he's vanished.

He's sent my aeroship soaring for the ground.

I stumble to my feet and retake the helm, but it's stuck now, and the furnace is out, even though I'd cast more than enough *jaseemat* inside. I look at the clouds I'm diving into, at the satchel and all its contents spilling out around me, at Caldor slamming against the railings and chirping wildly, steam valve whistling. The clouds vanish. All I can see is the earth coming at me.

Oh God.

Desperately, I set all my weight upon the helm, begging and praying for its shift. *"Merlin!"*

But my aeroship hits thick, snowy trees and snaps across the ground, and all I can do is grab on tightly and pray that death will come swiftly.

EIGHTEEN

It feels like I'm caught at the forefront of a mountain as it crashes into an ocean. A burst of snow sprays like a volcanic eruption of ice instead of lava. My body bangs against a railing, and I grit my teeth and fall, readying to feel the shattering of my bones into bristly shards.

It never comes.

A ringing sound thuds at the inside of my skull, like my aeroship's furnace might still be popping with fire and charcoal, and as I find the courage to open my eyes, the sputter of the furnace dies. The propeller spins like mad against the snow, chopping up the tougher clumps. The nose of my ship has been completely obliterated, but God bless the Norwegian steel Rufus used to reinforce my vessel with the strength of dragon scales.

I release my breath, and with it comes sob after sob and hot tears. I pull my legs close and tighten my arms around them, rocking back and forth and letting myself cry the tears I've wanted to shed ever since Camelot fell, since Arthur's death, since I saw the utter despair on Marcus's face after his childhood home fell to the flames' wrath. All of this blasted work—all of the hours I put into this horrid vessel, only so it'd crash into this barren wilderness. I'll never find Marcus now. I'll never find the Grail. I might never find my way back home.

I want nothing more than my mother's arms around me, my father's stern yet loving presence beside me, assuring me in the kindest way he can manage that everything will be "quite all right, Vivienne, dear." I even wish Owen were here to gently tease me like only a brother could.

My mind drifts to Merlin. It couldn't have been real, having him in the air with me. It was only my imagination. That's all. Just my imagination, and I crashed because I couldn't handle the ship as well as Rufus could. Merlin never would have put me in such danger; he never would have tried to kill me, for goodness sake. This was my fault.

After what feels like forever, I've cried all my tears, and there's nothing left but an insatiable hunger and a terrifying realization: I'm alone in this now. Before, at least I had Rufus as company. But now, I don't even have a horse. All I have are a few scrolls and journals containing the sorcerer's words scribbled at the height of his thievery of magic. A supply of hastily made *jaseemat* that hasn't been tested to its full capacity. And the knowledge that I abandoned Marcus's father so he wouldn't have to go on a dangerous quest.

You did this for the magic, Vivienne, dear. Don't delude yourself.

I banish the quiet whisper from my mind. My eyes are heavy and swollen from crying, and I wipe my cheeks dry. The stairs lower to the ground, past the broken wing that makes me pause. I remember building these wings. It was autumn and still warm enough to be in Merlin's clock tower without requiring an abundance of furs. I'd been proudest of the wings; I'd used the sewing tricks I'd learned from my mother, whose meticulous fingers could weave spun gold into kingly garments in less than a day's time. She'd be proud to see the silk-sheet wings and their lassoing iron hooks, now jagged, threadbare edges dancing like flags in the wind, the loose strands pulling free of the mast and sailing over the trees.

How will I rebuild *CELESTE*? The task is more impossible now than ever, but I cannot worry about that, despite the despair that's come over me. I need to find the nearest village before nightfall. I need food, an inn. Above, the clouds promising awesome storms are warning enough to get out of the countryside.

I land on the snow and steady myself. My feet and legs wobble from being in the skies for so long. A swift current of air bites at me, and the hood I set atop my hair does absolutely nothing for the chill.

"Think about the cold later, Vivienne."

I set Caldor on my arm and pour some *jaseemat* into its steam valve. "You're all I have right now," I whisper. "You and the promise that something great will come from all this." I whisper the proper words to bring the falcon to life, and as the golden powder illuminates the tiny machine, I set its navigational gauge to take me southeast—inland. I'll follow the woods until I reach a body of water—a river, perhaps—and then continue on until I find a village. I send Caldor into flight and hold Merlin's glass-covered navigational piece in my palm. The arrow spins in circles and finds its path.

With my tools in Merlin's leather satchel, I glance at my

aeroship. At the Norwegian steel bound to be pillaged if I'm not quick to return in a few days' time with the tools and textiles necessary to fix it. When I'd built a miniature version of it using Merlin's hookah, it'd simply been to calm crying children at feasts in Camelot. But this aeroship is more important. To bid goodbye brings all sorts of strange and confusing melancholy. But I must find shelter.

At least I had the clever foresight to wear my high leather boots.

———

There'll be miles before I'll see another living soul, and there are miles behind me as night draws closer. Caldor keeps my pace, and my lungs are on fire from running for so long. After a while, everything blends together with hunger and exhaustion, and only the short bursts of delirium keep me from falling flat on my face. I cross a frozen stream, my boots sliding across the slippery surface, and come out on the other side to a bough of evergreens. Tall and majestic and of significant difference from the forest I'd just left. This might be a good sign.

And then, from beyond the trees' edge, comes the telltale crackle and hiss of a fire. No strong, thundering winds like the infernos Morgan le Fay set upon Camelot, but a campfire. I freeze in case my footsteps on the crunchy snow would be loud enough to warrant unwanted attention. But when I glance about, there are no shining eyes staring at me from amongst the trees. I take a leap of faith and another step. The smell of sweet-burning wood finds me, and I follow the plumes of smoke and ash grasping at the evergreens' branches. As I approach, the voices accompanying the fire grow louder.

"...On purpose, you know." The voice belongs to a man, words stretched as though he might have food in his mouth, and accented as well. I don't recognize where in Britannia he might come from, if this is still Britannia. "They've scoured the entire countryside for nothing else other than our gold, leaving us hungry and hopeless. Mark my words: it's *on purpose*. They already know the Grail isn't in the countryside."

"Why would they bother? The Black Knight has enough wealth to sustain a kingdom for eons." The second voice is a woman's. Older, and with the same accent as the man. "The sight of my mother's gold necklace is nothing compared to the Grail, and they know that. That's why they tore apart the Holy Land. Eat your food."

There are gentle scrapings: the scratching of tin and iron. A gear system set automatically with a wind-up tension cord, I'd guess. Then nothing. I peek around a thick fir at two figures sitting side by side on a fallen tree with a small fire blazing between them. They have a boiling pot sitting atop with a wooden spoon that when stirred sends the smells of cooked meat and spices into the air.

My eyes lock onto the steaming pot and nothing else. I'm wild with hunger, and all I want—

"What have we here?"

A lurking figure appears on one side of me, and then a taller one arrives at the other. I jump in surprise. Each grabs an arm tightly enough to hurt. A hand clamps over my mouth before I can scream.

"Looks like we have a visitor," the second says.

I shake my head in protest, but they take me into the range of the firelight, and through it, I look at my captors. Two burly men with scowls on their ice-burnt faces. The first one drops his dirt-caked hand from my mouth.

I swallow hard. "I'm passing through. I didn't mean—" I pause, and their eyebrows lift, waiting for me to continue. But I cannot tell them about the aeroship, the crash. That alone would lead to other questions, approaching too closely the idea of Avalon. "I'm not—"

"Drop the girl," the woman says from the other side of the fire. "I'll see her for myself."

The men do so, and I dare not move as the woman steps around the fiery cinders for me. When she steps past the flames, I see how her dark red hair has been tied at the back of her neck with a threadbare kerchief to keep out the cold. The furs around her shoulders are heavy, a tribe of foxes lying on her arms. Her eyes are light and older than mine, and from what I can tell, they're all villagers, but the woman carries an aura of wisdom that gives her rank.

She comes close enough to study my face. "You're not from these parts. Look at her skin." She grabs my hand and casts back the sleeve of my robe, revealing my bare arm. "She hasn't worked outside a day in her life, has she, Seamus?" A flick of her wrist drops my hand from hers, and the men grab me again, in case I were to run. She circles. "Where are you from?"

I stay as close as I can to the truth. I'm too exhausted to lie. "The north. I lost my way."

"How? What are you doing in these parts?"

I hesitate. I shouldn't tell them about my aeroship. "I'm looking for someone."

Her eyes crinkle with suspicion. "Who?"

Then I realize something that might put me in her favor. Anyone in these English-speaking parts would know of Arthur and Camelot. They'd prove to be an ally. I must trust in that. "A knight of Camelot."

The three men laugh wildly, as though I might have mentioned Hercules or someone just as impossible. The man Seamus bounces in his seat, laughing through a gap-toothed smile. But the old woman doesn't flinch. She stares at me. Finally, she holds up a hand, calling for silence, and the men obey. "You must know how ridiculous of a quest that'd be, my lady. In a land infested with rogues?"

I didn't know there were rogues here, but I pretend. "Of course. But I'm desperate."

The man who took my arm first chuckles. "What of her, Briana? Let's take her back to the village. She might bring in a pretty penny."

Briana cocks her head to the side. "Yes. She's young, likely still pure, and her appearance is rather striking. We could sell her to the inns and taverns before calling her family to pay up." A plotting smile spreads over her face, and the meaning behind that sentiment sends a bout of dread across mine.

I shake my head. "Let me go." I pull my arms from the grips of the two very strong men, but they don't let up. "Let me go now!"

"Quiet, you," the first one says.

I don't know what else to do; I struggle against the two men. I have a firelance hidden at my hip, and they've missed Merlin's sword on my back. But neither are within reach.

Briana taps my chin. "Nothing personal, dear, but ever since rumor spread that Arthur of Camelot fell, there's been nothing but havoc in these parts." She gifts me with an overly patronizing smile. "You understand, this would be the only way we wouldn't have to eat squirrel and the rotting roots too good for them. Have wine for the first time since our king turned into a pillar of dust."

They're descendants of the Fisher King's subjects. How many generations have been without a kingdom since the curse fell upon him?

Briana smiles. "'Course, it would—"

"Hold on," Seamus says. He takes a bite of meat and spits out a long, thin bone, one too small for a chicken. "Seeking a knight of Camelot? Who'd you say you were?"

I keep my mouth shut. I won't give them any more information, not if they already have plans to sell me to the men of their village. I yank my arm, good and hard, but I'm still their captive.

"What difference does it make?" Briana asks.

"Because," Seamus says, standing and wiping a greasy mouth on his sleeve, "just this morning I heard from the cobbler's wife there was word of a girl of some importance, what have you, who escaped from Camelot." He makes his way to Briana's side.

"Is that so?" Briana says, glancing back at me.

I feel my lip quiver in fear, but I must be strong. I look

straight into the older woman's eyes. "I'm not from Camelot; I said I sought a knight from there."

"You wouldn't know of too many knights otherwise, girl. Not with your status. You wear the clothes of a queen, not a harlot. Your words and the way you say them indicate you're castle-born. Your mannerisms, likewise. Who are you?" Both of them inch forward. These two might be demigods themselves, controlling the men whose hands bruise my arms.

"I'm no one," I whisper.

"Not only that," Seamus says, ignoring my answer. "Seems as though someone in Camelot found the coordinates to Avalon. Seems as though someone *knows* them. And wouldn't you guess who that was, Briana?"

"I guess it was probably a foolish girl who made the silly mistake of trying to get that information out of Camelot without anyone noticing."

A smile stretches Briana's face until the lines deepen around her eyes, and the two men lift me so only the toes of my boots touch the snow.

Suddenly, a sharp whistle pierces the air. A whistle of urgency. Of danger. Briana and Seamus dart their eyes toward it. The hands on my arms loosen. And their allure over me breaks.

"Rogues," Briana whispers, her voice dripping with resentment and leaving an aftertaste of horror. "Leave the girl. I'm not losing my neck if they're looking for her, too." The men toss me into the snow, and I cover my head as they kick ice and dirt over me in their attempt to run.

Desperately, I look for signs of danger, and suddenly I

hear breaths of commands shooting into the air like cannons. Up ahead, boldly colored garments contrast with the dull trees and snowy wilderness, the same yellows and oranges and purples Gawain told me rogues traditionally wore. Through the fog in the distance, the steady sound of horses galloping grows louder. A dozen makes their way through the barren trees, breaking through the fog with long, curved swords.

The Spanish rogues are here.

And they're riding straight for me.

NINETEEN

I should run. I should follow Briana and Seamus and the two burly men to whatever village or shelter they might find refuge in; I should seek the closest aeroship port and find my way back to Camelot before it's too late.

Caldor flies straight for me—I can hear the mechanical caw made richer with my *jaseemat*—and a rush of courage invigorates me. Merlin's silly invention might buy me time. The falcon lands, sputtering nearly empty, and the musical notes of the rogues' calls rustle with the shine of their raised, extended blades. I wrench Caldor's steam valve open, take out the small purse of *jaseemat,* and cast a handful inside.

"*Yaty ala alhyah.*"

The *jaseemat* dances over the copper feathers and its iron beak. Black eyes stare at mine, and they've never claimed to hold any sort of life—even with *jaseemat*—but there's a change, and Caldor comes to life. Wings broaden, their span longer than both my arms stretched as far out as I can manage.

"Fly!"

Caldor leaps into the air to catch a breath of wind. I'm on my feet and backing away, snow finding its way into my leather boots and my hair as I run. I glance over my shoulder at Caldor flying straight into the band of rogues. The falcon's wings flap wildly—they slice open the necks of the unlucky two at the front. Shred their brightly colored garments. I tear away from the sight, at the horror of their blood on the ground. I run. Caldor will find me.

I race through trees dark like shadows, branches bare, trunks tall and unlike anything I've ever seen in Camelot. I've lost track of where Briana and Seamus ran to, and I must find a place to hide rather than try to outrun those who evaded Caldor's deadly wings. Every path looks the same, every tree a withered twin of the next. There's nowhere to hide.

"You cannot hide, Vivienne. But there is a way," Merlin's voice whispers in my ear. As I run, I turn to the translucent blue eyes lined in gold staring at mine through the atmosphere. It's delirium; it has to be. *"You know it already, girl. You have everything you need to beat them."*

A nudge at my memory reminds me of the spells in my pocket. Magic, yes. That could fend them off. I face my own mortality now, and magic would ensure I survive. But how could I think of doing such a thing? The spirit of Merlin is tempting me for a reason I still don't understand, but I won't let him win.

Besides, I have another choice. "If you mean your own sword, old man, so be it. Gawain was an excellent teacher."

I stop running and seize Merlin's sword from the holster on my back, holding it high. Merlin vanishes before I can see the outrage on his face for claiming his weapon as mine. Gallops—many gallops. I glance over my shoulder. Horses. Seven. Each carrying a rogue dressed like a prince of the skies: long coats lined in embroidered silver silk. Swords tinted gold bending with their arms. Devious smiles. One drops from his steed and steps forward. His eyes shine as brightly as the gold in his ostentatious blade.

"Why do you outrun us, little girl?" he says in fluid English, his vowels like music. "What is it you hide?"

I hold my sword tightly; I lift it higher.

Merlin's voice is relentless. *"They'll slice you into two, Vivienne. You can't win against them."*

I ignore him. I have to try. I cannot give in to the test of magic he's put upon me. "Nothing you can claim for yourselves," I declare to the rogue.

He has his chin in hand, raspy with black whiskers, and he smiles at his comrades. When he turns back, his face is one of immortal stone, and his blade shines brightly enough to sever the moon from its place in the sky. The sword slams down against mine with such ferocity that fighting the wraith in the Fisher King's castle might as well have been practice. My sword rattles from the blow, and I step back to collect myself.

The rogue's black eyes run over my body. "Come on, little girl. Put away your plaything, and the punishment will be ... lessened."

I know it's hopeless, but I will not surrender.

"There's another way, Vivienne," Merlin tells me.

My shoulders lighten with his truth. "You're right."

Once the rogue is far enough away to turn his back and jeer with his friends, I reach for my firelance. I lift it high, click back the hammer. The rogue hears the sound and turns, just in time for me to send a bearing straight into his forehead.

My lip quivers at the quick death, but there's no time to mourn. I stare at the other rogues, whose mouths drop, who reach for their own firelances. I aim quickly. There are six left. I step backward, and I fire thrice more, hitting another, but not killing him. Now I'm out of bearings.

Now I have to run.

I race into a clear meadow, and suddenly, the ground under my feet shifts, no longer stable. My feet slide, and I look down in horror at the shine of ice. I'm on a lake.

"Vivienne!"

"No, Merlin!" I cry in a state of panic. "No more!" But his voice was strange that time. It was younger, frantic. It was a voice I recognized—

An iron bearing slices the air by my ear, and I jump and scatter further back onto the frozen lake until it cracks loudly. I patter away from the weak spot spidering out in breaks of ice and water, preventing me from returning to shore. I have to go the other way—I have to risk it. Their horses won't cross it. The air is cold enough for me to believe the ice is sturdy—

"Vivienne!"

I ignore the voice for the rogues, who fire and call after me, calling me *bruja*, a witch, a demon girl, the sorcerer's advocate who might know the coordinates of Avalon the rest of the world simply cannot find. *How would they know?*

I keep running. If I can make it to the other side of the lake...

A whip of sharp pain strikes my arm. I cry out. My hand reaches for my torn sleeve, pulling away with thick blood staining my fingers. The shock of a rogue's firelance's bite sends me into a bout of shakes. Soon, they'll finish me off.

But there's one thing I haven't forgotten: one final resort.

And if I don't employ it, all hope is lost. The demigods would have to understand, especially the one who gave me her name.

I remember the words in Merlin's journals as easily as I remember the layout of the clock tower.

"Do it…" Merlin whispers.

"Vivienne!" It's not Merlin. But the voice mingles in my mind with the sorcerer's like I might be possessed. "Get off the ice!"

I dart my gaze at the five rogues in front of me. The ice has made them cautious, but their faces are indicative of their determination. They're not about to let a girl escape them.

My chin lifts, and I utter the spell, God save me. I utter the spell that would blind a man.

"Yeuxeuse fambratcricoh kemphah solohite."

Each word rolls off my tongue like sweet honey I could happily drown in. A pull of my chest and a wave of heat in my veins rush over me like sunlight on my skin. An emptiness in my mind begs to be filled over and over with the same words that seem to expand into the most delectable song, and certainly to take these words as mine could never be wicked.

I aim the spell at each of the rogues. They come to a confused stop, like their surroundings have shifted into an unrecognizable place. Red trickles from the corners of their eyes, mixed with acidic fluids. A gasp escapes my lips, but not out of horror—on the contrary, I'm fascinated, and the longer I watch, the juicier the sweet taste on my tongue. The rogues touch their cheeks, pulling their fingers away to see bright blood. And then their eyes burn.

Burn. Oh God, what have I done? My fingers spread widely in front of me as though I expect to see them wilt into nothingness from my thievery. But nothing happens.

Now the rogues panic. Their hands scratch at their sockets in desperation.

"Vivienne!"

My focus returns, and my eyes dart to the source of the voice. In the distance and through the trees, a man yanks his horse's reins to bring the animal to a stop, and then he leaps from its back.

"Get off the ice!"

His eyes are big and round, and from the time passed since I last saw him, they've grown tired, too. Older. His body is just as lean and athletic as it was on that last day, the furs about his shoulder and the leather across his back worn from weather and battle. He runs toward me, and I'm unable to move in my surprise.

"Marcus," I whisper.

The ice breaks beneath me.

I fall in, frozen water encapsulating me, and through it all, I swear I hear my own name calling back to me. It's from above, surely, or it's the Lady of the Lake's eerie voice born of the water while a signet of sculpted marble loosens from my cloak's pocket and floats away.

My arms flail through the heavenly and terrifying song for the surface, for the signet. Unable to find both. Rogues have followed me. One is slammed to the ice, his face held down by a thick leather boot that must be Merlin's as his pistolník sends a blast straight through the rogue's skull.

My last thought before I fall into a deep sleep is one of certainty.

But it was Marcus I saw, not Merlin.

TWENTY

The air around me is hot and dry, and I'm no longer drowning in an icy lake. Now, I'm walking down a sunlit corridor.

The floor is carpeted with a long, crimson runner, similar to the one in Camelot's main castle. My footsteps render a hollow sound muffled by the fabric. But there's an echo following me. One I cannot place.

The walls are lined with windows where once there might have been gas-lantern candelabras or oil portraits of princesses or monsters. The sills frame a horizon split into two colors: countless sands and endless sky. The caws of seagulls are washed away by the ocean in the distance; I know it's not the fresh water lakes in Britannia from the tang of salt in the air, the dryness against my cheeks, the wind tugging ruthlessly at my hair.

I continue onward, confused and lost and without a very important weight in my cloak's pocket, but somehow certain I'm heading in the right direction. At the end of the corridor, the hall feeds into an enormous room protected from the sky by long sheets held taut by iron bars separating a balcony looking over the desert below. Sands are shadowed by scores of aeroships hanging in the sky, cannonballs sailing through the air from one to the other. There are flashes of explosions, so distant they're nearly beautiful. The colors and scents of a war far away, though war nonetheless.

I glance back down the corridor; there's a room at its end. In the middle is a familiar hookah, one I turned into a toy aeroship long ago. Smoke rings climb the walls and escape out the verandah.

It's hard to see in here with so much light coming through. But clearly this place is much more progressive than Camelot, and war is either a frequent occurrence, or simply not as interesting as the scientific focal point of this room. Every few feet stands a mechanical man the sorcerer once told me about—*automatons*, only found in the Holy Land because of its advancement in the mechanical arts. No longer are machines simple parlor tricks, like Caldor, but actual people, serving cloths about their arms and trays permanently soldered to the hands that boast miniature glass goblets of hot tea.

Someone sits in a fashionable chair inside the room at the hall's end. "Step inside, please."

If the register of his voice had ever evaded me, I certainly would have recognized the tattoos etched onto his skull.

"Merlin," I whisper. My feet pick up, running past the beckoning copper faces boasting the lush turbans Azur wore. Women with silk scarves across their faces stand beside them, a trio putting final touches on a newly made automaton. Final twists of wrenches, soldering of iron, and perhaps one of these women is Lena, whom Merlin told me of. Someone able to create or find secret passageways in aeroships.

At the end of the hallway, the hypnotic octaves of a playing harp fills the open space. And as I enter the room, Merlin looks sideways at me, a breath of green smoke escaping his lips while dancers of flesh and blood move around him.

I stop at the door's entrance. Merlin turns fully, his eyes a sobering mix of white and gold. The blue irises once so kind and mischievous are gone, turning him into an image of pure magic.

"Merlin," I whisper. "What happened? Where are we?" I remember flying through the sky, a rush of wind and snow around me. I remember the sorcerer sending me to my own imminent death by crashing my aeroship, and the dreadful memory of how delightful it was to speak magical words and claim their power.

One of the women sets down a long, copper tool on a small table beside Merlin and beckons a servant carrying a tray of vanilla-scented biscuits and a bowl of shelled pistachios.

Merlin stretches in his seat, ignoring the food. "Welcome to Azur's palace, Vivienne, dear. It's about time you joined me here." His hands gesture to the jewel-toned drapes, the plush cushions, the wall-lining contraptions that crush open pistachios, leaving the nuts inside perfectly intact.

The servant boy no older than ten prepares a dish of pastries. I can smell cinnamon in the hot, dry air with more spices I only ever associated with Merlin's alchemist mentor. "Azur. Where is he?"

Merlin smiles, and it's a smile I've never seen before. A sure-fire guarantee that to ask again would tell me something I'd beg never to know. I can almost see his thoughts scratched onto his golden eyes.

"Merlin, where is he?" My voice wobbles. "What happened to you? You're supposed to be locked up, but in the woods—"

"Magic was always the right path for me, Vivienne. It was only a matter of time before I'd return to it." He leans close to one of the women and touches her chin. The woman's smile is cheeky.

I shake my head. This isn't my mentor. "No. You're wrong. Whoever you are, you're not Merlin. This isn't real. I'm not really here. I'm..."

I'm in the snow or I've frozen in the lake, drowned by ice. But wait, there was something—

Merlin's pistolník.

It sent a bearing into a rogue's temple. I'm watching it happen again and thinking back to the euphoric rush of magic I'd only stolen just minutes prior, but I'm also looking at Merlin, whose cocked eyebrow seems to indicate he knows exactly what I'm thinking. "Lose something, my dear?"

"No," I say, unsure if he indeed means his prized weapon. It was in Marcus's hand—not Merlin's. "But that's impossible. It's yours. You'd never give it away."

The thief Merlin sneers. "Ha! Thinking about gadgets and weaponry when really you should be asking something else. Haven't you wondered why it is I sent you to the Perilous Lands? Crashing to the countryside? Why I put you straight in Sir Marcus's path? Go on, Vivienne—ask."

The violent tremors in his voice shake me. Suddenly, there's a sharp pain in my right arm, spidering down the length of it, and I can no longer bear it. "What, Merlin?" I hold tight to my shoulder, hoping to ease the pain, and when I look at it for myself, I watch blood ooze through my fingers.

Merlin moves faster than sound, and suddenly he is straight in my face. The whites in his golden eyes turn bright red.

"Ask me what I've told Sir Marcus, but not you."

═════════

A loud crackle punctuates the sorcerer's final words and wakes me from my dream, but I do not open my eyes. A quick pop follows a rush of warmth around me, and I steal seconds to rest in this peaceful limbo. It's a heavenly winter morning, and I'll have tea with my mother before kissing my father on the cheek as Owen drags me out the door. He'll go to the knights' quarters to show off his archery skills, and Guinevere and I will go on a hunting day trip with Arthur.

No, that's not the world I live in anymore, and that truth twists my stomach into a knot.

I open my eyes to a threadbare woolen blanket around me. My hair's draped over my shoulders, tangled, but dry. I'm in a small room. Layered stones and bricks serve as walls, and a fireplace crackles away. The room is decorated with oak furniture and noble gray-and-black furs. Not Camelot; not home. Even poor Caldor is nowhere in sight.

I realize I'm on a soft bed, and through my foggy vision, I spot a lean figure move in front of the fire. My heart skips a beat when I remember the vision of Marcus pulling me from the water to safety, the muddled memories of him wrapping furs around me and lifting me atop his horse. Now he crouches in front of the hearth. The fire is well-tended to, and he stares absent-mindedly into it. Lost in thought and a million miles farther than that.

Marcus. Here. *Real.*

Suddenly, all the times I've wondered if he was alive or dead mean nothing—how could they when my illogical heart always knew I would see him again? That no matter what, there was always hope when it was a question of whether we should love.

I watch him for a long time: fine, pointed nose, unsure violet eyes, the rounded shape of his lips over a graceful chin. I can't see the inked dragon climbing his neck, but his piercing has healed cleanly, an arrow's shaft flying through two spots in his ear and disappearing under his tangled hair.

His worn leather breastplate has vanished for a black woolen tunic, light enough to sit in front of the flames as he uses an iron fire poker to usher the red cinders around the fireplace. He doesn't notice me watching from his periphery. His eyes are captivated by the hearth. Breathing steady and mouth serious. Alive, real, and here, like a dream coming to life as I will it.

When I can bear it no longer, I speak. "Marcus."

His eyes, kohled but smudged, snap over to mine, and his face fills with relief.

"Vivienne," he breathes, the hardness in his face vanishing. He comes to the bedside and presses his lips to my forehead, tangling his fingers in my hair. "I was so scared." His arms tighten around me as he draws me into an embrace on the bed. A dullness throbs in my arm where the rogue shot me. But I don't care. I can't care. Not now.

I pull him closer. "I knew I'd find you."

When I close my eyes, I feel the icy bite of the lake fighting me in the water. I feel Marcus's hand wrap around my wrist, a gigantic tug akin to being slammed through a pane of glass. I hear his voice shouting my name, muffled, muted.

"It was impossible," I say, "and there was no reason to believe… especially with the—" The pistolník, I want to add. But I don't yet understand my dream of Merlin in Jerusalem, and I can't bear to decipher it now.

His warm hand cups my face. "When you fell through the ice, it was like seeing the farmlands burning all over again. What happened? How did you *get* here?"

The rogues' gleaming eyes might haunt me forever. "I crashed. Or, at least, my aeroship did." Merlin's chilling presence is gone. I don't know what possessed the sorcerer to send me to the countryside, nearly killing me in the process. Perhaps he's completely turned to magic now. Or perhaps it really was to send me straight into Marcus's path.

Marcus is quiet, thinking, and I'm ready for the next five or ten or ten million questions he'd have, but instead, he leans against the pillows beside me and presses his hand to my forehead. "How do you feel?" His words are quick and clipped, without their usual warmth, and neither of us has mentioned the rogues yet.

My fingers fall timidly to his soft tunic in hopes touch could bring back that warmth. His body feels firmer, stronger. I think about his question, but I'm dizzy, tired, hungry. Eager to keep my fingers wrapped up in his shirt.

"It's been a long few days," I whisper. Then, another thought. "Where have you been? Kay arrived in Camelot and said it'd been over a month since anyone last heard from you!"

He exhales, eyes taking his attention elsewhere as the back of his hand runs blissfully over my cheek and down my neck. He's thinking of how to answer.

But then I remember the fall into the ice more clearly, and oh God, tell me I imagined the signet floating away from me. "Where's my cloak?" I whisper, frantically searching the room for it.

"Wait, you're hurt—"

Marcus's hand touches my shoulder to help me sit up, and I cringe. A shooting bolt of what lightning must feel like courses through me, and all thoughts of ice and water vanish. He pulls his hand away.

"Sorry," he says with all honesty. He tightens his lips for a brief second, as though searching for uncomfortable words. "I, um..." He gestures to my hurt arm, and when I move again, I feel thick fabric bound to my bare shoulder under the blanket. Completely bare. A rosiness warms my cheeks.

"A fine sleeve was sacrificed for the sake of your arm." Marcus emits a quiet laugh. Then his eyes widen. "Oh! I didn't see anything. I swear."

The bandage is too tight, and I twist to relieve the tension. It must be clear on my face, because Marcus frowns. "Can I?"

I nod, and he pulls the blanket to my waist. He's completely torn off the arm of Guinevere's dress, and the fragments left behind he's tucked into the ridge of my corset.

I'm startled by my naked shoulder in full view of Marcus's wide eyes, but he does his best to avert his gaze and focuses on the white cotton tied around my arm.

"Let's see," he whispers, shuffling my legs away so he can get an easier look. His fingers untie the knot, and his cheeks redden as he works. He blinks too often for complete focus, takes a long breath, and glances up until we're staring at one another. "Behind you."

I look over my shoulder at the strips of cotton lying on a small wooden table beside us. My free hand finds a few, and I give them to him. "You didn't say where you were."

His eyes settle on mine, and he tucks strands of tangled hair behind my ear. In his gaze lingers a scene he won't let me see for myself. "I was...on my way back." Now his neck reddens, too, and I'm not sure if it's because of the fire burning too ferociously in this small room, my skin under his sneaking eye, or a blatant lie I don't believe he'd ever tell me.

I cock my head to the side. He must see my incredulity. "On your way back? Sir Kay made it to Camelot before you could."

"Honest." He removes the bandage, and I cringe at the wound's fiery ache, the bold red of my blood spilling from the dent in my skin. "But the quest is strange. Unlike before. We're so close—*they're* so close." He shuts his eyes in frustration. His hand darts to his neck, where his dragon tattoo has long since healed, but is covered in obsessive scratches.

I gasp at the sight of them and pull his hand from the reddening skin. "What happened?"

His furrowed brows deepen his eyes. "The ink marks

us terribly out here. Arthur meant it to, but what I wouldn't give..." He takes a breath, and then the subject changes. "Owen has gone mad."

I sit up. "Where is he?" Worry for my brother pulsates through me.

Marcus gently ties the bandage around my arm and then reaches for my hand. "The land is raw and dead surrounding Athens, and there is no way a place such as Avalon could be anywhere near it. The rogues retreated, but it didn't bring us any closer, and that sent Owen into a craze, forcing Galahad to banish him from Camelot."

Banishment? Sir Kay never mentioned this. Oh God.

"I couldn't stay," Marcus continues. "I—" He freezes, his mouth formed around the words he wants to say, but a strange sort of connection between us shatters, and there's no sense in hoping for him to continue now. I remember the pistolník that killed the rogue, and I wonder if Marcus happened to come across one similar to Merlin's while out here.

Marcus lets his eyes drift out of focus on the fire. "We'd already lost a handful to the Grail's allure. But then there was a brawl." Now he grips my hand. "Owen and Galahad... God, it was nearly to the death."

I find the will to breathe. "Is Owen all right? Galahad?"

Marcus nods tensely, but he stares through the bedspread we're sitting on, lost again.

"Is that what made you leave?" I try. I can't help the rise in my voice, thinking of the black lace Lancelot tossed on the table in front of me, now around my wrist. Marcus's words send surges of sharp energy over my skin.

"No. Not exactly. Being on a futile quest made me leave."
But as he says it, he averts his eyes. "The Grail won't be found
or it doesn't want to be found or it isn't real. This whole thing
has hurt us more than it's helped."

"But the Lady of the Lake," I say, clutching his hand
tighter. I can't believe she'd mislead us.

He squeezes back. "The Lady of the Lake might not have
known if it were real or fabled."

My eyes widen at his doubt. Though I cannot confess to
Marcus about Rufus just yet, there is something else he must
know. "No. I've seen the Perilous Lands and the Fisher King
there. I went and saved him from the curse the demigods set
upon him. He was the key! Of course you couldn't find the
Grail before. You didn't know what to look for. I can reveal
Avalon now!"

But Marcus has grown stubborn. Much more than he
was six months ago. He shakes his head, refusing my words.
I wait for him to ask more about this legend of the Fisher
King, but perhaps he doesn't care. "It doesn't matter." He
takes a breath and cups my cheek in his hand. "We have to
leave. We have to get out of here."

"Do we?" I challenge. He told me he'd go on the quest
for the sake of Camelot's destroyed farmlands, and now when
I blink, all I can see is Rufus calling to me from the Fisher
King's castle, begging me to tell his son he's alive, if nothing
else. But if I were to do so, Marcus would want to return to
Camelot, and I cannot go back. Not without the Grail. Not
when I've come this far and endured so much.

When he finds out the truth, Marcus will hate me, surely,
for keeping news of Rufus from him.

We study each other like we're seeking the truth between us that neither will share, and it's just like it was before, when I was hiding my apprenticeship with Merlin, and Marcus knew about me long before I ever met him. Only now, our secrets are darker.

I stole magic, and oh how lovely it was. But Marcus can never know.

He squints into the fire, violet irises dancing with flames swirling in his pupils. His lips part as a thought comes to him, but when a line deepens between his brow, he shakes it off. The seconds that pass are quiet save for the crackling fire.

"Marcus, we must—" I begin, before my eyes flash white and a whirl of dizziness comes over me. I grip his hand tighter as he clutches me.

"Careful," he says as the wave of it passes. "Are you all right?"

I don't answer because I'm looking at him and my breath catches. Were his eyes always so deep, so warm, so full of an ancient sadness? Has the bed beneath our bodies grown softer, temptingly soft? And the hearth, too warm to warrant the conservative ties of his tunic?

His worry fades with a quick swallow. "You must be hungry," he says to break the silence.

He pulls back to reach for a wooden bowl set far from the lingering fire and sets it in my lap. I have to convince him to come with me to Avalon, but instead I smile meekly, my body overruling my mind. For now.

Red and green apples and a small knife to cut them with, half a loaf of bread, a slab of white cheese. After so long without food, it's a small feast. He hands me the knife, letting me peel an apple, and sneaks his hand over to touch my wrist, my arm, drifting delicately at my shoulder, steering clear of the bandage.

His forehead leans against mine until I can feel the warmth from his body envelope me. "They didn't have your favorite blend of tea," he says in a low voice. "I told them you'd be furious, naturally." A smile.

I'm using the small blade to slice apart apple skin from its flesh, but I cannot ignore the familiar roughness of his fingers. "Where did all of this come from?" I stutter the words and hide it by slipping a cut slice into my mouth.

"I gave a few pieces of silver to the barmaid downstairs for our stay and told her to bring our meals up. An additional gold coin ensured she wouldn't tell anyone a knight brought—"

Our eyes lock and, like a tether, they draw us closer as he nearly mentions the thought so obviously drifting between us. For Marcus to have brought me to an inn alone in the middle of the countryside...

"What did she think—" I can't even finish the question. My skin is lit, like the hearth's flames have crawled onto our bodies without either of us noticing.

Marcus shifts against me, settling closer. "I'm a knight. I took a vow. And I'm not to be alone with a girl. They know that."

They know it, but we might not. Because as he speaks, I can't stop from tracing his arm to his open palm, resting in my lap.

Still. "Surely it wouldn't have been any problem. It's not like we're—"

But then Marcus's fingers drift across my collar bone, finding its hollow, and I've lost the sentence on my lips. He stares at my parted lips for too long, and then he locks onto my eyes. "It was best to pay the barmaid."

I sweep the bowl aside in time for his fingers to slip into my hair. He crashes his lips to mine, and finally we disappear into a corner of the world where no one will find us: no rogues, no Merlin, no promises of death or betrayal. The fruit is sweet on my lips and even sweeter on Marcus's.

As I move closer, the thin woolen blanket at my waist rides up with my skirt, and I vanish into a fantasy where his bare legs entangle with mine underneath it. I think back to the night in the barn and realize that, here and now and with no one to find us, it could be very easy to lose ourselves in each other. There's a storm inside him that refuses to be still; it springs to life in his quick breathing, his steeled eyes locking onto mine before squeezing shut, his long, firm body pressing against mine. His hands are fast to clutch me as though to let go might mean either he or I would disappear. The feather pillows on this bed are useless, scandalously tempting us with a less-than-formal sitting arrangement.

I peek at him as he kisses me. I watch how his fluttering eyelids show how he thinks—or doesn't think at all. His arms go around my waist and pull me closer, and to run my fingers through his hair and against the back of his neck is like I've brought summer to chase away a thousand winters. Between kisses he whispers, *"I can't believe you're here."* And when my palms press against his chest, he runs his hands down my waist and over my hips, until he's found my leg, which has revealed itself from under my dress.

With a quiet gasp, he stops. Our eyes flash open to each other. I can't tell what he's thinking—usually I can. Usually, Marcus is a wealth of anything I'd ever want to know. But I'm not sure if he's worried we've crossed a line, or wondering if this could lead to something more.

Without breaking our gaze, his fingers trace my calf and under my knee, sending a shiver through me. Slowly, he savors the touch. Memorizes every bit of it. Suddenly, I couldn't care less that my shoulder is bare to him. I press my lips to his, quick and full, but then he pulls away, denying us the chance to feel the kiss properly.

I feel my lips swell as he jerks his hand from my leg. His eyes are desperate, but sad, and they linger on my mouth for a moment too long before he takes a deep breath.

"That barmaid might get an extra gold coin tonight," he whispers through a short laugh.

Somehow, Sir Kay's words return. *With all the attention the girls of Corbenic gave him...*

Marcus sits up. "You should rest. I'll—" He rests his elbows on his pulled-up knees and searches the room as I sit up myself. "I'll check on my horse and settle with the innkeeper so we can leave at dawn, when no one's likely to be awake. They saw the ink on my neck."

Propriety. Yes. In the middle of the snowy wilderness, his knights' vow of celibacy still holds until we find the Holy Grail and bring it home. But he's distant, and an entire month passed when no one knew where he was.

I try to hide the disappointment in my voice. "You'll stay in the barn? With the horses? On a snowy night like this?" I tilt my head so he can see how pitiful the excuse is.

The smile that follows is a nostalgic one. He pulls to his feet. "Well, the last time I spent an entire night in a barn, it wasn't so bad."

I follow him to the door, the blanket covering my shoulders. When his hand finds the doorknob, I touch his fingers, pausing him. "Marcus, it's been six months," I whisper, feeling my heart flutter as I lift my gaze to his. *Six months without your lips pressing against mine.*

His eyes, so heavy and so deep, pierce my eyes with a hint of melancholy and want, as though I might be a vision from a dream. "And we have the rest of our lives." But his voice betrays his belief in that.

To return to Camelot, all we'd be granted is the slow journey there. A knight who abandoned his infantry and returned Grail-less? And a handmaid destined to be safely imprisoned in a foreign nunnery? There'd be no hope. My eyes well as I stare at him, seeing this future in his. We both know it would be the most likely result. And yet, he stands here perhaps willing to see it through.

Marcus presses a fast kiss to my forehead. "Sleep," he says, and pulls away as though it might be impossible to stay any longer. He drops my hand and shuts the door behind him.

"Good night," I whisper.

Through the window, the last of night pours inside. Dawn will arrive in a few hours. I have to convince Marcus to come with me to Avalon. He must understand it'd be the only way to part from Camelot honorably and return whenever we wished.

I peer through a small gap between the door and its frame. Marcus is still there, staring at the floor. He shakes his head long and slow.

"Merlin, you monster. Please be wrong."

I don't know what he means by that; I wait and listen in case he'll say something else. But no such luck. He presses his hand to the door, and from the other side, my own hand matches it. There's no warmth penetrating the wood, but regardless, I send him a silent message: *What is it you won't tell me?*

But Marcus pulls away and leaves down the stairs.

TWENTY-ONE

The window pane is frosted over come dawn, and bits of sunlight spill through the cracks in the glass, like snow-flakes caught in a clear web. I press my fingers to the surface, and the coolness melts around my skin. Five foggy prints let me see the outside of the inn and its surroundings—Marcus and I are in the countryside, where there is nothing but trees and snow-covered paths. No ocean or sea or lake in sight. No landmarks I recognize. In Camelot, whenever the sky was overcast like this, I felt strangled, unable to see past the clouds to the day ahead. But in this beautiful wilderness, it feels like a piping-hot cottage.

"Not too often we see knights in these parts so close to Christmas," an old voice says over the whinnies and neighs of the horses in the stables. I peer down at a balding man with a long nose and an inventors' apron. He tightens the gears on the right side of Marcus's saddle as the knight watches. I've only ever seen a mechanism like the one he's affixed once or twice before, and it was always after a knight returned from the quest. It's comprised of two pathways of sprockets and a lever attached to the rider's preferred side. An easy and convenient place to safely lock in a firelance or a fusionah. "Right then," the old man continues. "If you say you wish to keep your *sword* tucked away instead of your…mechanical trinket, we can certainly oblige, my lord."

Marcus studies the land as though expecting a visitor. He runs his gloved fingers through the back of his hair. "I've lost my taste for the blade," he says, a forlorn look in his face before he remembers his status in this innkeeper's eyes. "And you might see more knights sooner than you think."

"Oh? And why's that?" The man gives his wrench a final tug and stands, letting Marcus study the handiwork and test the contraption. Marcus rotates his sword into the pathway and clicks down the lever in an attempt to withdraw it. The blade is securely fastened against the saddle.

"Rogues will head for these parts." Marcus ducks to tighten the saddle and then stands, giving the horse a pat on the nose. "By now, the rest of Galahad's infantry will have retreated from the quest to seek the Black Knight's head."

Marcus's firelance glints at his waist, and the innkeeper does a double take. "Goodness, my lord, that's a fine looking pistolník. Didn't know knights used anything that didn't boast at least one blade." He laughs a high-pitched chuckle. From my window, I can't make out the details of the weapon.

Marcus's hand flocks to his holster. "It was entrusted to me." Then he pulls his furs closer to conceal it, the same pistolník that killed the rogue on the frozen lake. I know it. There was no hesitation in Marcus when he fired a weapon so close to the likes of—

"Knight of Camelot!" breaks the silence of this tiny village.

I look out at the dirt path beyond the inn. Marcus, likewise, whips his head toward a rider headed straight for him, cloaked in the vestments of Camelot.

"Blast!" he growls before throwing his effects into the snow and running for the inn's door. The innkeeper calls to some attendants to prepare a room and bath.

I hear Marcus gallop up the stairs as I wipe the window pane to see better. When the knight arrives, I gasp. Because it's not a knight at all.

"It's a squire!" the innkeeper calls to his stable boy, readying to take the horse.

The rider comes to a fast stop. He yanks on his horse's reins and casts a stoic gaze over the entire land. When I last saw him, he was equally full of ambition and humility. But that boy has changed these past six months. That boy is nearly unrecognizable with a light beard on his face and coldness in his eyes.

"Owen," I whisper.

I tear away from the window and seize my thick furs to tie around my shoulders. I adjust my torn dress so it's at least remotely wearable as Marcus throws the door open. "Did you see?"

I nod. "How did he know to come here?" I grab my satchel and lead Marcus down the stairs, my hand inching toward my cloak's pocket, but I don't understand why it would.

"It's a popular rest stop. The innkeeper knows Lancelot well."

"We have to speak with Owen," I say. My father was worried about him. I have to know my brother is all right.

But not only that. My brother's highest ambition is to become a knight of Camelot. To find the Grail would cinch that—having Owen on my side once I tell him I know Avalon's coordinates would convince Marcus to continue on the quest. The three of us could seek the Holy Grail together, and then, I could stop whatever forthcoming horror that might come after me for stealing magic. Because I can no longer ignore that.

At the bottom of these stairs is a tavern, and together we get stares and bitter looks from a row of drunkards at the counter despite the early hour. A barmaid with gold in her eyes and silver jingling in her apron's pockets steps between the tavern patrons and me.

"Hope you're feeling better, my lady. Your *brother* was worried." She flicks a knowing eyebrow at Marcus.

"Vivienne," Marcus says, pulling me close before we can open the door to the outside. Eyes are still on us, but the barmaid's loud declaration has lessened the chatter. "Owen has changed. He's angry, and he's resentful. If I didn't know any better, I'd think he'd been switched entirely with someone else."

Owen and his sleeping demons. Those demons might have been resurrected out here on the quest. With one look at Marcus, I make sure he knows I understand. And then I open the door and walk out.

Owen's hair is also longer, as though none of the knights had the foresight to bring proper grooming shears. A sharp gaze shines with anger, eyes blinking wildly when they settle on mine, full of surprise. But then he sees Marcus walk out after me, and his gaze changes entirely.

"Owen," I say, heading straight for him. "What in God's name happened to you? Kay told us you fought Galahad."

Owen drops from his horse and storms through the snow toward us. He tries to brush past me for Marcus, but I seize his arm. His furs carry the scent of smoke and ocean, and his eyes on mine are crazed, just as Marcus warned me. "What the hell is she doing here?" he says, looking at me, but not speaking to me. Then he turns to Marcus. "And with *you?*"

"Calm down, Owen," Marcus says, his voice too low for safety.

Owen's face twists into a bitter frown. "It'll be a cold day in Hell when I take orders from a *serf.*" He shoves Marcus, eyes widening with anticipation as though he might hope Marcus will return the cold greeting and perhaps give him a reason for retaliation.

Marcus's eyes fall elsewhere, ignoring Owen, his lips pursed in anger.

But Owen isn't done yet, and he flicks a tempting eyebrow as he offers one last jab. "Couldn't wait any longer to make my sister your harlot?"

My breath escapes me at the insult, but before I can slap my brother's cheek, Marcus gets to him first and throws Owen to the ground. The leather plates of Owen's armor dig into his neck, and Marcus holds them there. Owen kicks as he tries to free himself.

"Stop!" I scream, flocking to Marcus's side to pull them apart. Owen sees me, and one strong kick sends me onto my back and into the snow.

Looking out the tavern's windows are the curious eyes of its patrons, and they take in every bit of this brawl between a knight of Camelot and a squire—every strike, every hit.

"Enough!" I shout, to my feet and pulling Marcus off. He brushes the snow from his cloak and furs in a clumsy way and presses a quick palm to his jaw. My brother got a few choice hits in.

Owen saunters toward me until he's right in my face. "You won't have a place in Camelot, Viv," he declares in a voice that strives to growl, but settles on a sob. I have to hold Marcus back from striking him again.

But I won't be made into a distraction. "Tell me what happened."

Owen relents. The whites of his eyes are colored blood red with dark circles underneath, as though his exhaustion has permanently bruised the skin there. "Galahad—" He bites his tongue on the knight's name. "Forget it. There's something more urgent at hand. I passed through a village last night and caught wind of peasants' gossip. They claimed they'd found Merlin's apprentice, that *she'd* left Camelot, but rogues attacked before they could bring her into the village. The entire countryside thinks she might know the coordinates to Avalon, and now they say Spanish rogues seek her."

My lips part. Only two days past, a handful of subjects from the Fisher King's castle plotted to sell me in exchange for food. A wave of fear runs through me, and it locks me still.

"Vivienne." Marcus touches my elbow. His eyes full of worry look so much like his father's. "We have get out of here. Go to Camelot, even. Lancelot might know what—"

"So it's true. The Spanish rogues are looking for *my sister*. The Black Knight seeks *Vivienne*?" Owen growls. "You're damn right she's going back to Camelot, Marcus." He steps closer with a fist ready to strike.

"Owen, stop!" I shout, coming between them. My breath hitches at the idea of returning home when this is the closest I've come to Avalon. I turn to Marcus. "I know how to find the Grail. You *know* that. It won't take more than a few days. A few days, Marcus. All I need is my aeroship, tools to fix it, and the *jaseemat*—"

Marcus reaches for my hand and layers our fingers together in a tight clasp. "What the Black Knight can inflict upon his prisoners..." He pauses to think and looks over my shoulder at my brother. "Owen, go back to Camelot with Vivienne while I go after the rogues. Despite what you say about the Round Table, it's all you've ever wanted, and you know I could easily get you back in Galahad's good graces."

"Marcus!" I pull away from his touch. "You don't get to decide this."

Owen scoffs. "The Holy Grail is still missing, *Sir* Marcus, and to hell with the knights. I'll seek Avalon myself. Where is it, Viv?"

I blink and see the floating castle high in the sky above the Great Sea of the Mediterranean. I've known for as long as I can remember that Avalon floats south from England. I know the knights searched Greece top to bottom. But it's *there*.

"You won't be able to find it without me," I say.

"Can't matter." Marcus shuts his eyes through his impatience. His eyes open slowly to mine, and he squeezes my hand. "I need you to do this. I'll backtrack to find the rogues and lead them away. I'll be only a week behind you both."

I feel my eyes widen with amazement. How can he

think this way? "And do what?" I counter, to which he has no response or viable plan. "I can take us to Avalon! Let's return to my aeroship so I can fix it. Then all we'll need is—"

"No, Viv," Owen says, pacing restlessly behind me. "Rogues are soon to swarm this land. To head straight into the thick of them would be suicide. The serf might be a *deserter*, but he's right about that." He keeps a steady glare on Marcus.

Marcus sighs loudly, like this is an accusation he's heard before. "I didn't desert—"

"Then tell us why you left the entire infantry in the middle of the night. What captivated your interest so much, you'd abandon those you called brothers?" Owen steps forward. "Or tell us *who*."

I let Owen's words churn in my mind and feel Marcus tense up behind me. I duck my vision over my shoulder at him, thinking of the Lady of the Lake's prophecy, of how death or betrayal was foreseen in Marcus's future. But he wouldn't betray Camelot.

Marcus chooses his words carefully, but I don't miss how he refuses to address my brother's accusation. "Travel by day; they won't expect it. Rogues will recognize me, and if they know this much about Vivienne already, they might think I can lead them to her. It'll give you time to make your way north."

Owen doesn't answer. He turns on his heel and storms back to his horse. "Viv! We're leaving." As he passes the stables, he slams an angry fist into the wood, sending a young boy watching to jump straight into the cold air.

"Vivienne," Marcus says with a gentle tug of my hand.

I'd forgotten he was still holding it, and I snatch it back. He steps closer. "Please."

I look into his violet eyes, the ones that would always show me the truth whenever I asked for it. I want to ask Owen's question again—*Who were you with, Marcus?*—but I'm too furious at Marcus's orders and how he pulled rank, and I'm scared of the two bleak futures facing him.

Marcus takes my cheek in his hand, and our lips are so close it nearly kills me to want to kiss him. "A few weeks at most. I swear. And then we can go wherever we desire. Don't think I want this."

He presses his lips to mine, despite the curious eyes watching, the ones he paid much gold to avoid. Even though a traitorous part of me wants to melt in his arms, I pull away. "I'll ride with my brother, *Sir* Marcus." And with that, I turn on my heel and head the other way, my lips chilled from early morning frost and deception, but my determination strong like fire.

Marcus follows me to the stables, footsteps heavy and angry. As I mount Owen's horse, Marcus leaps onto his and rides off without another word.

————

Owen and I will travel with Marcus until we reach a fork in the path in two days that'll take him east and us north. My brother is less than thrilled with this arrangement, but I'm already pondering how to convince him to seek Avalon with me instead.

"Damn serf. Doesn't deserve to be called a *knight*."

I'm sitting in an awkward sidesaddle position while Owen holds the reins. Marcus is at least twenty yards ahead, well out of earshot.

"Stop this, Owen. He was your friend once." I stare at the flat, snowy scenery, wishing for the familiar mountains and cliffs outside of Camelot. It's hard to imagine ever missing home, but I do.

"Father will never agree to it," Owen hisses. "You know this as well as I do. It cannot happen. Not with a serf. Even still, Marcus is a knight now. He's bound by the law Arthur set for those who would be a part of his Round Table."

I grow quiet. I won't remind Owen of the condition Marcus agreed to in order to become a knight. That if he were to bring the Grail to Camelot himself, he could relinquish his vow without banishment. And if that were to happen, perhaps Lord William would welcome Marcus. I'm not sure what sort of ire that would ignite in my brother. Anger clearly clouds his memory—it was Owen, after all, who told me all this before he and Marcus rode out with Galahad's infantry in the spring.

Marcus gallops further ahead as Owen's horse steadies into a slow walk. It gives me time with my brother, time I didn't think I'd get. "What happened, Owen?" I whisper. We both know I mean Galahad. Perhaps sympathy is the best way to Owen's sense of reason.

I know he's heard me because he takes a long, winded sigh. One of exasperation he would emit whenever we fought as children. He'd play up the dramatics so our mother would side with him. It usually worked.

"The world is different from what I expected."

It's a weak excuse, and it makes me angry to hear such an excuse to explain how he viciously attacked a knight. "And so that difference forced your aim at Galahad's neck?"

He yanks on the horse's reins in response. "Viv, you don't know what it's like, to search for something that knows the evilest part of you and wants to use it against you. Do you think I *wanted* to pull a firelance on Galahad? Don't you understand how *ashamed* I felt that I let anger get the best of me over something as simple as—" His words choke, and from how he clears his throat, I know my brother is trying to keep from losing a most vicious temper.

"As simple as what?" The black lace Kay brought back to Camelot is warm around my wrist. There's no way I can show it to Owen.

My brother scoffs quietly. "Simple jealousy, it seems. None of us were oblivious to the fact that the Grail was turning us into the worst versions of ourselves. All but Galahad, frankly, and God knows how he could have been strong enough to resist. But what about Marcus? Did you ever stop to wonder, Viv, what his vice was?"

I glance at the tall, lean outline of Marcus riding in his dark furs. I remember running my fingers through his hair only last night, how heavy his eyes were with the fireplace's heat dancing on our faces, the feel of our lips locked. How close we were to going just a little bit further, and how he stopped us before we'd gone too far.

Marcus's gloved hand points east at a village named Asto-lat, whose chimney shafts send spiraling clouds of gray smoke into the air. The shine from the little sunlight in this country-side reveals the sea beyond it. The three of us will convene in the village for the night. Close to the sea. Possibly near aero-ship ports.

I don't have a plan; but I do have a brother as determined to find the Grail as I am. But Owen's question—I don't know the answer. Marcus's vice? I think back to the times we were together and alone in Camelot, to the jokes he told that bordered on scandalous. I consider his quick winks, his horrified embarrassment when the oafs Stephen and Bors told of his attraction to me at Arthur and Guinevere's wedding. Percy is on a quest for honor. Owen is on a quest for power. Lancelot was on a quest for glory. And Marcus?

Sir Marcus of Camelot didn't want to be a knight at all. He wanted to escape with me to wherever I would go.

"You know, don't you, Viv? You know the only reason I would ever strike a brother in arms as I did just now," Owen whispers.

Marcus's horse rears and then gallops faster, kicking out dirt and snow from under its wild hooves toward the village. Behind it, three aeroships lift into the sky, each heading in its own direction.

"I'm angry not just because he's a serf honored in the kingdom before I was. I'm angry because he claimed to be honorable, and when some of the more idiotic knights found warm beds to share with harlots of the villages, he stayed behind. Until one night, he didn't, and then in the morning, he was gone."

Despite the cold air, my blood heats up with hurt and anger. "What is that supposed to imply?"

Owen snorts. "It's a rite of passage, Viv, for new knights to have at least one night of debauchery in these parts. How noble do you think Marcus is?"

I don't answer. My heart is still heavy with anger at the insult Owen cast in my direction back at the inn. Marcus was right: Owen has changed, and I'm not going to let my brother's demons force me into a state of madness. "Owen, you have to come with me to find Avalon. You have to help me convince Marcus of the same."

Owen twists his face into something vile and stares at the horizon, a low scoff escaping him. "Not going to let Marcus get my sister killed just because she doesn't want to spend her life in a parlor."

I press closer to him. "You want to go after the Grail anyway!"

When I face him, the brown eyes he inherited from our mother are full of a rage I've never seen in him. "No, Viv. I'd kill Marcus if something were to happen to you."

The truth in his words haunts me, and with that, I cannot engage in this discussion anymore. Ahead, Marcus disappears into the village as we follow. Owen kicks our horse into a gallop, and soon we're riding through a town with thatched roofs built around stout chimneys. Gas lanterns line the snowy streets. In these parts, street entertainers have molded wooden and gear-work dolls into moveable puppets that lift their knees high and their smiles even higher. Children laugh, and mothers draped in wool shawls point at the tiny primitive machines.

All of it is lost on me. In another world, I might have

been delighted by all of this, a vision of happiness and inge-nuity. Here is a place untouched by rogues, but all I can think of is how the Fisher King told me the fate of Marcus did not include death. Then, if what the Lady of the Lake told me is true, the only other option is one of betrayal.

And what Owen suggested might be as simple as Sir Marcus of Camelot betraying the girl who worked away in Merlin's clock tower for six months, waiting for the chance to find him and take him into the skies.

We reach the inn with a swinging sign out front, wooden doors, and windows with clouded glass. Marcus steps off his horse and hands the reins to a small boy.

His eyes are on me as Owen brings his horse to a stop. I stare right back, reinforced with my brother's anger, but not saying a word. Marcus holds out his hand to help me down, and God help me, I take it, squeezing my fingers around his. My sleeve lifts, and the strip of black lace around my wrist reveals itself.

"What's this?" he asks. Clearly, he missed it when he was tending to my arm.

Steady on the ground, I pull my cloak tightly around my shoulders. "A forgotten memento, it seems."

I stride past him toward the inn door. Inside is a bevy of people and a roaring fire, a dozen tables filled with candlelight and pints. Tiny glass bulbs of lantern oil have been set aflame and strung across the ceiling in a way that looks like stars are shining down on the tavern's patrons.

"Hello!" A girl about my age steps in front of me. She has a beautiful face with sharp gray eyes and heavily arched brows that give her appearance an aura of drama. Her raven hair is tucked in front of one shoulder, long and straight, and weaves into the lace of her low peasant's blouse, blue and silver, luxurious colors mixed in a familiar tartan. "Get you a warm drink, my lady? Or are you looking for a room for the night?"

Behind me, I hear Marcus's distinct footstep, and the girl glances over my shoulder. When she sees Marcus, her smile vanishes and a look of surprise replaces it. "Marcus," she says.

I turn in time to see the identical look of surprise come across Marcus's face. His lips part, and he doesn't blink for nearly a minute.

"Lena," he replies.

TWENTY-TWO

The blood rushes from my face when Marcus says that name. *Lena*, the same name Merlin said in my dream, on my aeroship. And then, there's the remark Kay made to Lancelot back in Camelot—*"With all the attention the girls of Corbenic gave him, I half-expected him to follow in your swaggering footsteps!"*

An older woman dressed in peasants' attire leans close to Lena, a scrutinizing eye on every part of Marcus without subtlety. Her passing whisper cinches the horror in my chest. "Handsome, Lena. This the one you told us about?"

Lena nudges the woman with an air of playfulness. "Away, you!" But she denies nothing.

Of course. I was so foolish. The possibility of betrayal was the likeliest of futures for Marcus, and I arrive at it with Marcus beside me, not knowing my humiliation because my last bit of dignity is wrapped up in the calm façade I'm desperate to cast into the crowd. But my heart—my heart is as cold as the approaching night, and just as dark.

A smile crosses Marcus's lips, though I'm not sure he heard what the other barmaid said. "What are you doing here? Last time I saw you was—"

"Hold on," Owen says behind me. He narrows his eyes at Marcus. "How do you know her?"

Lena smiles. "Corbenic," she says. My heart plummets as I relive Sir Kay's accidental taunt over and over; it shatters when I remember how Marcus was gone for a month. That's more than enough time to reach Corbenic in the north of Britannia and return on the quest, possibly finding me in the countryside on the way. This is why Marcus has been so distant.

What Owen feared was the truth. Camelot wasn't betrayed—I was.

I feel like a fool, standing here with all these drunken eyes upon us, staring at Marcus as he subconsciously rubs the ink lining his neck.

Lena's face breaks into a bigger smile, and she steps past me to embrace Marcus, wrapping her arms around his neck. "Don't just stand there as though I were a stranger! My God, it's spectacular to see you here!"

Marcus smiles until his eyes crinkle, and I haven't seen him smile like this since the spring. He returns the hug, watching me the entire time. My throat chokes me with my sobs, and my dying heart begs for the release.

"I never thought I'd see you again," she tells him, the true and honest words shutting his eyes with melancholic happiness.

Owen scoffs. "I knew it," he whispers under his breath.

The voice of Merlin is a horrible truth in my ear. *"Oh, there's Lena."*

How could the old fool know about her? *How?* I step backward, unable to breathe, unable to find air in this smoky tavern. Those drinking their ale at the tables whisper, and certainly it's about this liaison between a barmaid and a knight everyone knew of but me. There's no other possibility.

I'm about to ask them both, but to hear Marcus admit it with so many watching...that would be unbearable. I'm holding my breath, and the room is spinning around me, and my eyes are burning with hot tears. And so I turn on my heel and run out of the inn.

"Vivienne?" Marcus says, as his arms drop from Lena's waist. "Vivienne, what—"

But I've already slammed the tavern's door behind me.

━━━━

Vivienne, you damned fool.

Happy laughter surrounds me from passersby on these streets as twinkling gas lanterns rock in the wind above in long crisscrosses. Though the cold is biting, and my boots aren't thick enough to protect me from the knee-high snow, I will not stay in that tavern only to be humiliated. I want to forget Marcus, forget all of this ever happened. I want to return to a state of normalcy and staunch logic.

The inn door cracks open behind me. "Vivienne!" Marcus calls, and I hear him running after me until he catches my wrist.

I yank myself free and turn on him. "Stay away," I warn, my voice quiet and low. A voice he's never heard me use; a voice I don't think I've ever used myself.

His eyes are wide and scared and confused. "What...where are you going?"

I turn my back to him and storm away. "To find the Grail and bring it to Azur," I answer, not caring who can hear. "It's the only honest thing I can do, and I'm leaving before you and Owen try to force a different future upon me." I push through the villagers captivated by a puppet show with Marcus close on my heels. I head in the direction of two landing aeroships. The ports must be close by, and I have my fair share of gold.

"Vivienne, stop—" Marcus calls, his pace quickened as he tries to keep up.

He must think I'm an absolute fool. I spin to face him. "Everyone in that tavern knew as soon as you stepped inside who you were in Corbenic. Everyone but me. Were you ever going to tell me, or are you satisfied to have me find out on my own? Why did you bother coming here with me, and why, *why*, Marcus, are you so determined to keep me from Avalon?" At the very least, he should be able to answer that truthfully.

But Marcus is too surprised by my frantic questions to respond. I give him ten seconds of silence, more than enough time to come up with a diabolical *lie*, but he can't even do that. He can't deny anything now. Those passing us come to notice our lovers' quarrel, and I no longer care. Several villagers stop, whispering and pointing, carrying on with blatant eavesdropping as though we might be actors in a street performance.

"You don't know what..." he finally manages. "You don't know what it's been like out here—"

"Then tell me, you bastard!" I scream. "Tell me the truth

instead of ordering me around and carrying on like you ever felt *anything* for me!" And now we're gathering a bigger audience.

As some onlookers chuckle, Marcus eyes them with viciousness and steps closer to me. His eyes well with angry tears, and he's too furious to blink them away before they fall. "What is it I'm supposed to explain? You have yet to tell me."

I ready myself for the truth that'll slice me piece by piece in these streets. "Where were you for that month?"

He freezes. Wherever he was falls over his eyes, like he'd pushed away that memory for days or weeks. The seconds drift between us—more and more—until I realize he's not going to tell me.

I step away, but then he draws closer. His voice is low. "I was worried about you *long* before I saw you fall through that ice. Seeing you out here means whatever is destined to happen is already on its way."

He already knows of the Lady of the Lake's prophecy. That must be what he means.

"No, Marcus. It's already happened." I feel tears stinging my eyes, and the crowd offers their low calls of witness and heckles. I have to leave now. I have to leave this village and do something with an ounce of integrity. "Leave me alone."

He's quick to grab my arm, but I turn and slap his face. My eyes widen at what I did, but I stay strong. He sets his hand to his reddening cheek, just as surprised by its sting.

I turn and run through the crowd, deeper into the village.

Marcus calls after me. "Vivienne—"

"Leave me alone!" I feel him following, and a band of

older villagers have noticed my tears and the knight two steps behind me.

One heavily moustached man nursing a tin pint and dressed in the ornate costumes of the town steps forward. "Oi! The lady said to leave her alone, didn't she, mate?"

Another likewise steps forward, eyes lingering on Marcus's dragon tattoo, but not intimidated by it. "Causing problems for the lass, boy?"

I back away as the brutes stall Marcus. Defeated, his shoulders slump, but his eyes not only plead for me to come back, they ask me with blatant confusion why I'm leaving.

I turn, and I know I'll never see Marcus again, and that thought makes the prospect of crying stupidly attractive. My pride won't let me ask once and for all how he came to be acquainted with Lena; instead, I run through the crowd that's long forgotten us, past a puppet show performing on the other side of the street, complete with whistles and metal-work dolls that send the entire crowd into fits of delighted laughter.

When I've turned the corner, I look back at the crowd swallowing Marcus up. My back against the stone wall, I fall to the snowy ground, pull my knees to my chest, and cry.

———

When it doesn't seem rational anymore to sit in the snow and cry as villagers stroll past, I dry my eyes with the backs of my hands and stand, certain of one thing: I have to return to my aeroship, fix it, and go after Avalon myself. Find the

Grail and learn more about its powers. Learn why the Lady of the Lake and I share the same name. Flee to Jerusalem to help Azur defeat the Spanish rogues. Maybe I could even find Galahad's infantry. But no longer can I dwell on the humiliation of Marcus and Lena. Instead, my heart jumps into my throat when I remember the Fisher King's signet. It's no longer safely tucked in my cloak's pocket, but at the bottom of the frozen lake. I'll have to backtrack first. *Blast.*

It's grown late enough in the day that aeroships flying through the air are no longer visible—not only that, but clouds drift over the village, shielding any ascending or descending vessels from me. I spot a young man and woman walking arm-in-arm, and I touch the lady's fine mauve sleeve to halt her. "You wouldn't happen to know how to get to the ports, would you?"

The man's eyes widen as he recognizes me. "We adored your performance earlier. These parts are frightfully dull with the same old minstrels and their pathetic, wilting damsels. It was refreshing to see a vision of broken love instead." The woman nods vigorously in agreement and clutches his arm tightly. Their shared smiles and tilted looks of fawning are enough to make my stomach turn.

I turn my lips up, though it nearly kills me, and utter, "Thank you," as quietly as I can manage without breaking that delicate lump in my throat. "The ports?"

The man points to a tavern on the other side of the village. "You're looking for ol' Bill, if you seek an aeroship. If he's not in the skies, he's romancing a pint."

That tavern is alive with gas lanterns and music, jovial laughter, and hearty cries for hot mulled ale on a cold evening. As I make my way through the crowds, I find a numbing peace inside, like a dam has been put up between my sense of logic and the emotions rattling me with shaken nerves. I hold my head high, though I know the slightest nudge of that dam will cause it to collapse.

I must stay rational, but by God, I wish Caldor were with me instead of lost in the countryside or drowned in icy waters. My falcon's existence between life and the mechanical arts would at least keep me grounded and remind me that once I had a mentor who was an insufferable fool, yes, but even more so, a friend who would never let me face the goliaths of life alone.

In the tavern, I stand out painfully in my Camelot garments. These men wear serfs' clothing, many dressed like Rufus. And, oh God, Rufus. I never told Marcus his father was alive. For a second, I think he might not deserve to know, but then I take it back. No one deserves that sort of cruelty.

An old man with wire-rimmed spectacles resting atop the end of a long nose welcomes me with a polite nod as I find the counter. "Drink, my lady?"

I shake my head. "I need an aeroship. I was told to ask for Bill."

The barman leans back to follow the line of men sitting at his counter. He sends a whistle through his teeth, and two men glance over. "Get Bill."

The two men step aside, revealing a patron leaning against the counter, halfway through an engrossing tidbit of gossip. "…Hasn't been seen in ages, then. Sir Tristan of Camelot, on his way back to the Holy Land. Something must have stirred up if it meant he was forced to abandon the quest."

Sir Tristan. With Rufus, surely, as the blacksmith wouldn't simply return to Camelot to tinker with ironwork if the rogues' attack on Jerusalem were something he could fight. I know this.

"Oi! Bill!" the barman calls.

The man glances over as the barman juts his chin at me. Bill eyes me up and down with a face too red and sweaty not to have already enjoyed his fair share of mead. His dirty hair isn't dirty enough to cover the white from age. A belly indicative of constant attendance to a tavern hangs over a leather belt. "What have we here?"

I feel the drunk and yellowing eyes on me, but I cannot appear afraid. "You have an aeroship," I say more than ask.

The old man flicks an eyebrow. "What of it?"

I reveal my small purse of gold and withdraw several coins. "I require passageway to the eastern countryside. I'll pay handsomely if you take me there."

Bill's lips pull back over shining teeth in a sneer, contagious enough that the rest of the scoundrels around him laugh quietly. Then he leans forward. "What kind of a castle lady wanders into a village at this hour, demanding to be flown away? Go home, girl. Whoever your father chose as a husband for you isn't worth getting killed over." The laughter coming from Bill's company is obnoxious, and he turns back on his stool to his band of friends.

"Please," I try, my voice louder now. "This is a matter of urgency. If you won't take me, at least point me in the direction of someone who will."

Bill's eyes sneak over his shoulder at me. "Careful, dear. You're in the thick of a village where rumors of Merlin's apprentice carrying some very valuable information run rampant. Don't want to stand out now, lest some desperate souls were to think you're her."

I meet his eyes and lie perfectly. "I know nothing about that."

Bill turns on his stool, the gratuitous sight of his twisting stomach off-putting as he faces me. "That so? They just let girls wander into these parts of the countryside, then? Well, much obliged for educating me, miss. If it's true, you got nothing to worry about." His voice softens, and he shuffles closer to me. I jerk away, my fingertips grazing my firelance, ready to seize its cool metal hilt and fire if necessary.

But then a long, curved sword splits the space between us and slams into the counter. Bill's drunken eyes cross as he looks at the sharp silver beneath his nose. The patrons freeze. The barman steps back.

"The lady asked a simple question, and you have yet to provide her with an answer." The voice sounds like tobacco and old spirits, a lifetime of leadership shouting orders to a crew. Magical and fluid, as though it knows well the Latin languages of Rome or France.

Bill backs away in complete recognition of this new character as the length of the sword follows.

I gather the courage to face the blade and then the blade's

owner. I look at the white lace at the wrists, cuffed to luscious black cloth. I look at the detailing in the seams, the golden thread not unlike the kind my mother preferred. The long, fitted gentleman's jacket, midnight black above a pair of dark trousers with buckled shoes.

Then I glance up, up, up, into an olive face with a square jaw, a dark, curled moustache and groomed beard fashionably set around full lips. A green eye looks back at me from under dark brows. His right one is covered with a golden patch.

I don't miss the cap. A rounded hat, set to the side, the brim embossed with decorative goggles. These goggles are brass and impractical, the sides boasting a kind of face: gaunt cheeks and a tilted cross underneath.

He cocks an eyebrow. "Hello, darling." Romantic, like music. "It seems you're in the need of an aeroship, yes?"

That isn't a face—it's a skull and crossbones. Like the emblem air pirates—

Oh God. The Spanish rogues.

The Black Knight offers a smile that tilts unnaturally, like a crescent moon's constant watch. "It seems we were both fortunate to cross each other's paths tonight."

TWENTY-THREE

My fingers fly for the sword at my waist. But faster than the alarm of danger ringing in my mind is the Black Knight as he grips my arm. He slams the blunt edge of my blade against my shoulder. Holds it there. Squeezes my wrist until I drop my weapon and cannot move. He grips my wounded shoulder until my vision is a cascade of stars and then touches his head to mine as he hushes my cries, his lips grazing my ear.

"Now, now, Lady Vivienne. You don't know how difficult you made it for me to find you. With your permission, we'll talk."

His breath is sweet with absinthe, and his voice is a lullaby filled with promises too sanguine to trust. He doesn't wait for my *yes*; he releases me, certain I will not run. And I won't— my hand clamps onto my throbbing arm, and I futilely pray it could stop the pain.

The tavern's patrons have stalled in their drinking and philandering. Their pints float in front of their faces as they watch this legendary ally of the Spanish rogues confront a girl from the north. Then, as his gaze steadies on the Black Knight, the barman reaches under his counter and pulls out a tarnished firelance.

But perhaps the Black Knight is a devil or perhaps he

saw the reflection in my own frightened eyes. He sighs in annoyance and withdraws his own firelance—a polished silver barrel twisted against a steel blade with Spanish insignias carved into the handle—and throws the weapon across his chest, lazily aiming behind him. A blast of smoke shatters my eardrums, and the barman falls over dead.

The Black Knight sets his weapon on the counter with careful fingers. Specks of ashes linger on the smoking barrel. His well-polished fingers brush them away, steering clear of his immaculate garments.

"Anyone else wish to stay to *chat*?" he declares, too preoccupied with the lapels of his coat to look around. Instantly, the patrons and barmaids leave, and cries of "*The Black Knight!*" echo into the village as he adjusts the lapels on his gentleman's jacket, rustled from seizing me and the inconvenience of a rebel barman.

I'm trembling underneath my strong façade of narrowed eyes and heavy furs. He knows who I am. Word spread about me leaving Camelot as fast as Merlin's absinthe would disappear during feasts—I wonder if it'd been my father who sent word to neighboring kingdoms—but even more frightening is how the Black Knight knows my *name*.

I must think. Calmly. Now's not the time to be rash. He'll try to force Avalon's coordinates out of me. He might use torture similar to Gawain's hacked-off arm. Or blackmail. I imagine what sort of sinister plans he has concocted for those who would cross him. But the seconds are passing, and I have no plan other than to keep the Black Knight stalled for just a little longer.

And so I whisper, "How did you find me?"

He touches his chin absentmindedly and looks off, like a fond memory has found him. His words tumble from his lips like the smooth smoke of a hookah. "The squire in my hold is blond, curly-haired, looks a bit like you. Before we caught him, he'd been tracking my rogues for some time, but I'm not sure he realized I was with them. To disappear into the background is not hard for demigods."

Owen. He has Owen. But that's impossible—it's only been an hour since I left Marcus and my brother. Were the Spanish rogues following us even then? My hands shake uncontrollably under my cloak, but I can't let the Black Knight see that.

I swallow. "They say you're a devil amongst men." I force a smirk so that perhaps the wolf in front of me might think me just as sadistic; I likewise make sure he sees how I study his luxurious garments. "But certainly, it's a vast exaggeration." Do I speak to gain the truth or to anger him?

"Oh, Lady Vivienne. I don't need to prove anything to you. The wonderment of who I am is much more enjoyable, don't you think?" He speaks as though considering tomorrow's weather. "I could see days ago how this would all end, though with you it was a bit more difficult. You're quite hard to read from a distance." He taps his fingers to his temple, slow and purposeful, like this about me annoys him. "Your mind is too much like the sorcerer's, I wager."

I suddenly feel like the Black Knight can see the magic I stole written all over my face. I press a palm to my cheek to soothe the warmth, but keep my hounding smile. "A compliment from a devil. Lovely."

He stares. His one eye pierces mine like he's hoping my secrets would be carved straight onto them. There's a look of inquisitiveness, and there's a glance of caution. Then he scoffs. "And still…" He strolls the empty tavern, his walk indicative of what power runs in his veins.

I'm looking for a way to escape and trying to understand the meaning behind his words, but—

"What I wouldn't give to see Master Owen's rage now." The Black Knight laughs jovially. "Indeed, people are fascinating when they lose their tempers! And then, there's the knight."

I freeze. I realize I hold love in my stupid heart for Marcus.

The Black Knight takes another clacking step, its echo like a thunderstorm of danger. "Specifically, the knight's face when he realizes I'm closer to you now than he is…"

I don't know who'd be angrier by the Spanish rogues' ability to outsmart us. Marcus would be furious that my wayward brother led the rogues straight to me; Owen would blame Marcus for his sin, stating it was because of him that I left, only to find myself in the Black Knight's clutches. But they must realize it was my own fault. *It was my doing.*

Something inside tells me to protect Marcus and Owen as much as I can. That intuition, strong like a rumble of thunder in a spring storm, forces me to stand straighter and fold my hands together. My governess would be so proud of the lady speaking.

"I don't know whom you mean, my lord." I speak in hopes the Black Knight wouldn't bother dealing with those I claim not to know. But my lie is horrid, and my voice breaks as I speak. Perhaps they've already killed Marcus and Owen; perhaps they'll hold Camelot over my head now as the price for Avalon.

The Black Knight doesn't blink. People never go this long without at least a twitch of an eyelid. "They're your brother and your lover, certainly, darling, and I don't tolerate lies."

I hold my tongue, though inside, I'm a mess of rebellious tears and anguish.

"Lady Vivienne, just as many people are searching for you as they are the Holy Grail these days. The girl who knows where Avalon hides." He saunters toward the bar to help himself to a pint of hot ale and swings around to lean an elbow on the counter, lifting the glass to toast me. "What good fortune I had tonight."

Still, I am resilient. "I'm not her."

He slouches against the counter now, his gaze averting mine. Then he takes the forgotten glass of the drunk Bill and smashes it against the wall. I jump, my cold blood poisoning my strength.

"I said I don't tolerate lies." A jagged-edged dagger with an emerald handle finds itself in his tight grip, and the Black Knight slams the point into the counter. "You might be able to fool *them*, but you cannot fool me. I'm very good at carving dishonesty free from mankind."

It's the first time in my life I can claim to be Merlin's apprentice, an inventor, an alchemist, as I've always wanted, but it's the truth that's put me in danger. But I will not be afraid. I look into the Black Knight's face, inches from mine and full of brutal threat.

"I'm not lying. I am Merlin's apprentice, yes. But this business about knowing the coordinates to Avalon is absurd. If I knew where it lies, why would I be here looking for an aeroship home? A smart girl would have gone straight to Avalon from Camelot."

I cannot read the Black Knight's face, and I desperately hope the Lady of the Lake has kept him ignorant of the Fisher King and the marble signet. The Black Knight is quiet, fingers tracing the rim of the pint glass he's barely sipped from. He watches me as though trying to decide whether to believe me and tilts his head with curiosity.

"Quite convincing. But you must realize I simply can't take your word for it."

A surge of hope runs through me as I realize he hasn't killed me yet. He hasn't killed me because he needs me.

But Gawain warned: *He can keep a man alive for as long as is needed.*

"So," the Black Knight whispers, "conveniently enough, I do have an aeroship in my possession..." He turns for his pint.

Under my furs and at my waist sits my firelance, and the Black Knight has looked away. I seize my weapon and pull it free, my thumb clicking back the hammer, my index finger finding the trigger. The Black Knight turns back quickly.

I aim it. "Fly it to hell, for all I care." The firelance blasts, but the Black Knight ducks out of the way. The bearing misses, hitting a bottle of mead on a shelf, which explodes like a tempest of snow. I run for the door, ignoring the melodious clang of Merlin's blade catching on a chair and promptly falling from my waist to the floor—I can't help that now.

Outside, the village has been abandoned. I duck around the tavern's corner and run straight into the snow-covered woods—

"Lady Vivienne, really!"

The Black Knight's voice is like warbling steel, confusing me and my ability to tell up from down. It forces me to stop running so I can search amongst the trees, black as a hellish abyss. All from him.

His laugh is demonic; no, his laugh is playful. *"You really think you can run?"* He *tsks* three times like a mother scolding her child for stealing sweets in a market.

A rush of determination sends me onward. Branches scratch me from the trees I dart through, and my breath hitches from exhaustion and distress. I spill out into a meadow and come to a fast stop. Then I gasp.

The sky is empty of stars, and even the moon wouldn't dare show its face. Taking up the space above me is a fleet of rogue aeroships, anchors keeping them to the ground.

Laughter pulls my gaze across the terrain. Only a hundred yards away are scores of rogues themselves, sunburnt skin shining under the light of their gas lanterns, cloaks and vestments ornate and lush, like the Black Knight's. Their rugged faces and crooked smiles suggest I might be a table of sweetmeats, and they've been sailing on a wind's current for months without a taste. Sabers hang at their sides, firelances affixed beside them.

Some have bloodied lips and bruised jaws. Those worse-off hold iron restraints tied to heavy shackles.

And in those shackles are Marcus and Owen.

TWENTY-FOUR

I can't breathe. Not when the knight I still love and the brother I'm afraid I've lost are made into captives, bloody and restrained. Marcus glances up, and his face falls with relief to see me. But Owen is unreadable.

Footsteps crunch on the dry snow behind me. Slow, heavy. "Darling, for someone whose fate might change that of the world, you certainly act carelessly."

The Black Knight appears in my periphery. He dusts fallen snow or leftover glass from the forearm of a sleeve as I turn. The green in his iris brightens in the moonlight, and I cannot look away. I'm bound to him, and perhaps I'll never be free again.

He stops within steps of me and glares. "The coordinates."

I shake my head. "I'll never tell you."

His full lips turn up in a smirk, and he takes a careful step closer. The snow under his feet softens, like he's docile, safe. His green eye seems all the more childlike the longer he stares at me, as though trying to trick me by appearing as innocent as a dagger-wielding lamb.

"Stay away from her!" Marcus growls, struggling against the three brutes holding him. Blood spills from his nose.

The Black Knight raises an eyebrow. "Perhaps there's an easier way to get Lady Vivienne to talk."

He nods once at a rogue, and suddenly that rogue elbows Marcus in the face. I want to cry out as Marcus keels over, wincing in pain, and it takes every bit of strength to stop myself. *If I react, the Black Knight will know he has me in the palm of his hand.*

But neither does the Black Knight react himself, and that is worrisome. Instead, one pristine hand lifts his golden eye-patch, revealing not a blind eye or even a socket, but a round contraption with a glass lens. A scar runs diagonally across the skin; the extraction of his eye must have been particularly painful. His thumb and forefinger adjust the lens carefully to extend the glass—cloudy and mechanical—and he peers at me as though to study me.

It's futile even to blink, but if I were to try, it'd be of no use. The glass has enchanted me with a glowing, emerald light, and I can't tear myself away.

"Do you know what it means to see a rogue with a golden eye-patch, darling?" The other eye he covers with the patch to focus better, letting me see up close how the sinew of his facial muscles overlaps to compensate for the gash.

I shake my head, lost on words.

"It means he once battled a worthy opponent, a well-respected enemy. I lost my eye to a great man, someone it would have been an honor to kill." The backs of his fingers brush against his lapel. "Horribly disfiguring, clearly, but sometimes things happen for a greater reason. Even to demi-gods. This artificial eye forged for me by glass-smith Druids is stronger than my real one ever was. Able to see greater distances than a normal person, able to see in the pitch-black of night. Even able to surpass the limits of time or memory."

The allure has nearly claimed me, but I fight for rule of my mind. "And yet, here you stand without the Grail in your grasp, nor any idea of where Avalon lies."

Now his glass eye casts my own reflection back at me. I look desperate, and my skin is wind-burnt. The Black Knight smiles. "My, you're a brash one, aren't you?" A laugh, but there's a strange sense of nervousness to it. "It's true Avalon has been a little more of a challenge." As though he were explaining the rules of etiquette at tea. "Location is all that stands between the Grail and me. The temptations these two faced"—he seizes my wounded arm, forcing me to cry out in pain, and faces me to Marcus and Owen—"slowed their quest to an embarrassing pace. For me, it'll be faster. I am immune to the Grail's temptation."

I can feel hot blood spilling from my arm through my sleeve. The Black Knight's tight grip reopened the gash.

"The Grail can only be found by someone pure of heart," I rasp, the wobble in my voice telling of my anguish. With the stain of stolen magic on my soul, it cannot be me who claims the Grail, but there are others who can.

"Correction," he says, adjusting his mechanical eye so it retracts back into its socket. The golden eye-patch covers it, and he focuses his true sight on his prisoners. "It can only be found by someone whose soul has no blemish. And since I have no soul to begin with..." He lifts an eyebrow. "A delightful loophole, yes?"

I stare in fury. I've never felt more hatred for another.

"And so," he says, "I need the coordinates. You have them. I've asked several times now, and all I've gotten from you is *lip*." The way he says the word comes out like an exploding cannon, adding wrath to his already vengeful presence. "But you'll tell me, you know," he whispers low enough that only I can hear. His fingers find my neck and trace its line—his touch is cold and patient. "Because right now, I have thirty-score rogues in the aeroships above me, and they have fire-lances pointed straight at your loved ones' hearts."

I glance up at the gleam of iron barrels lining the aeroships.

"I'll let them go. I'll let *you* go free to live your life without me to bother you. All you have to do is tell me which godforsaken isle or valley I must search. Where is Avalon?"

I'm silent for too long for the Black Knight to believe I'll tell him.

A dirty-faced rogue behind Marcus slams the heel of his boot into his back, and Marcus falls to his elbows, pain twisting his face. It'll be him the Black Knight tortures first if I don't speak. And it won't be another kick in the back. *He knows how to keep a man alive for as long as possible.*

Like my mind is nothing but an open scroll for the Black Knight to read, the devil nods once at his rogues. "Do it!" His fingertips rest on the back of my neck now, pressing into the base of my skull so I cannot move.

They yank Marcus forward, and through the awkward chains about his wrists, he falls to the snow with a grunt. I twist against the Black Knight's hold, terrified of what might come next, but his grip is like an iron vice. The rogue pulls on the thick iron links between Marcus's wrists until he's dragged him toward a snow-covered stump, setting his bound hands on top.

"What are you—?" I shout. "What are you going to do?" My breath is short, and my words and thoughts are frantic, jumbled.

Marcus glances left then right as two more rogues close in on him. His face hardens with ferocity, like he might try to fight, but deep in those violet irises, I see how frightened he is.

One rogue with sunburnt cheeks and a black leather eye-patch pulls a firelance free from his waist—no, it's not a firelance. I look closer: it's all silver gears and spiral drills built into the hilt. He lifts it against the black sky to reveal a shining, twisted point. With a pull of the trigger, the drill spins, and the sound is loud and choppy and a clashing of metal against metal in a way that digs into my bones without ever touching me.

"Stop," I whisper. The Black Knight's fingers press deeper into my neck.

Marcus's eyes widen, and he yanks his bound hands from the tree stump, but the rogues holding him in place are strong. Marcus grits his teeth as the rogue with the drill presses the point into his palm, held flat by the other two. Owen's hands slam over his mouth, and I'm screaming for them to stop, not even feeling my own wounded arm with the Black Knight's fingers tightening around the gash. The rogue pulls the trigger again and the drill presses slowly—horribly—into Marcus's palm as he screams through gritted teeth.

I watch blood and flesh spill over the sides of his fingers. *"Stop!"* I shout, as loudly as I can. "I'll tell you!"

The Black Knight raises one halfhearted, indifferent hand, and the rogue pulls out the drill from Marcus's palm. Marcus yanks his impaled hand to his chest and falls onto his back, his face soaked in sweat and agony.

The Black Knight lets go of me and waits, the brow over his eye-patch cocked. I breathe long and slow, and the fury in my heart sends my blood coursing like a river through my veins. "But you won't be able to claim the Grail, even if you are a *demigod*." I say the word with acid.

"Please do not suggest I'll need something as ridiculous as *alchemy*," he mutters with rolling eyes. "Demigods have no need for your childish world of science."

I look straight into his eye and smile, thought it might very well cost me my fingers. "I'll never say."

But then a rogue next to him with eyes shining like a black cat's leans close. "One moment, Captain," he says in the same eloquent English as the rogue I killed on the lake. "Rumors of this girl came from those who claimed to be of the Fisher King's people. If what they believed is correct, I'd wager you'd need a sort of puzzle-like contraption."

I feel the blood pool from my face; I think of Briana and Seamus and the two burly men who held me still while I was studied like a plate of meat, fit for selling. What sort of fate met them in exchange for this information?

The rogue's eyebrow, curved like a hill of desert sands, jets up at the surprise on my face. "Their legend states that to claim the Grail requires the seal of Avalon. If this one freed the Fisher King, she'd have the signet needed to open the castle's gates."

The Black Knight shifts his gaze toward me. In his green eye, curiosity and wonderment, but most of all, a sense of victory.

I shake my head at the rogue's words, thought it might not do me a lick of good. "Foolishness. I know of no such thing."

The Black Knight thinks. And then he leans closer until his lips brush again my ears. "The apprentice from Camelot is a shrew, aren't you, darling? Does the knight know the secret I can see written all over your face, the secret that would wreak destruction and vengeance upon you and yours if the demigods were to realize it? Does he know how you *adore* the taste of magic? Come, now. I can see right through you."

His eye welcomes me into a world of debauchery and thieving, and for a glorious second I feel like the Black Knight might understand me better than Marcus would. I let my eyes fall shut, and the only warmth I can grasp on to is from the tears gleaming at my lashes.

But then they freeze, and my blood follows. "I'm telling the truth." It comes out thick and heavy, and there's no reason for the Black Knight to believe me.

There's a tinge of fear surrounding him when he looks at me, though, and it ruffles him enough that he steps away. "Very well, then." One quick glance at Marcus. "Take his hand."

Rogues make for my beloved, and his eyes widen as he desperately backs away. My heart is stuck in my throat, but still I scream in protest. "No!"

The Black Knight waits. I'll speak the truth now, and I don't know what he might do when he hears it. "The signet. I crashed my aeroship and lost it when I fell through the ice."

Marcus rises to his knees, his injured hand still vulnerable against his stomach. "I know where it is!" he shouts, clambering to his feet. The bruise on his face has already deepened in color, and his palm is spilling over with blood. "It's yours. I'll get it myself, but not until you let Vivienne go."

No, Marcus.

The Black Knight shoves me off to a pair of rogues whose grips on my arms are painfully tight and saunters toward Marcus. "Your eyes are quite captivating. Quite . . . how shall I put it? *Regal.* And yet you're nothing but a farmer's son given the wasted chance to prove himself as a knight." He strolls toward Marcus as rogues hold tight to his arms. "Why should someone of my caliber trust you?" The Black Knight leans in to study Marcus. "Besides, why negotiate? I think you'd rather kill me, would you not?"

Marcus's voice trembles with rage. "In a second."

The Black Knight laughs loudly, a horridly jovial sound that suggests he has been nothing but entertained tonight. "I don't blame you, Sir Marcus." He sets his golden eye-patch to the side and focuses his mechanical eye on Marcus.

Marcus pulls away, but rogues push him forward, and a spark of white light brightens his pupils as the Black Knight explores his thoughts.

"Hmm," the Black Knight mutters. "I didn't recognize you, all this time." He turns back to me, one cloudy eye watching for my reaction as I ponder what the Black Knight could have seen in Marcus.

The Black Knight's chin tips upward as though speaking at court. "Well, Sir Marcus, clearly there's some honesty in what you say."

Marcus struggles, but the rogues hold him back.

"But in addition to a missing trinket, Lady Vivienne has coordinates I need, and there's no way I'll let her go. Nevertheless, I'm willing to negotiate. Bring me the signet she spoke of. I'm a patient man, but I'm not going to waste any more time." He spins on his heel to pace. "You know of the rogues' port in the Mediterranean, yes?"

Marcus nods. "Yes."

Owen glares at him.

"Wonderful!" the Black Knight says. "We'll convene there in two days' time, and as long as I have what I need to get to Avalon, you can have Lady Vivienne back. Two days is long enough, isn't it?"

The Black Knight isn't killing them. He drilled straight into Marcus's hand. He tore off Gawain's arm. He has the power to kill all of us right now, but he's … letting them go. I don't understand.

Then, perhaps a miracle. A propelling sound in the distance churns the air around us, and I look up. The Black Knight hears it, too, and regards the scores of aeroships soaring across the skies. Marcus and Owen and the rest of the rogues likewise cast their gazes high—we stare at a new fleet arriving, only visible because the shy moon has come out to illuminate the hope making its way toward us.

Marcus's mouth drops in utter disbelief. "Galahad!" he shouts.

I watch as the aeroships draw closer, riding the waves of the night winds with Galahad at the forefront, blond hair unmistakable and stoic face determined.

Galahad's infantry has found the Black Knight and the Spanish rogues. And now they've found us as well.

The Black Knight growls like a wolf. "Take her aboard *MUERTE*!" he calls as the most ominous-looking ship in his fleet drops a set of extending stairs. I jerk away from the rogues around me, but too late—they pull me toward the ascent, lightning-fast.

"Let go of me, you bastards!" I scream.

"Don't take her! I'll go with you!" Marcus shouts. The knights of Camelot are too far away for him not to negotiate with every last second. Marcus gestures to my brother. "Owen can find the aeroship. He'll bring the signet to you. Let Vivienne go!"

"No, Marcus!" I shout, my eyes holding his for as long as I can bear it. I won't have him die for me.

The Black Knight smiles gleefully as he pulls back toward the stairs. "Master Owen doesn't think you should be sacrificing all this for one person, even if it is his sister."

Marcus tears his gaze to Owen. My brother's face reddens with bitter guilt. *Oh Owen, what happened to you?*

"Two days to bring me what I need to get to Avalon or else Lady Vivienne will be kept alive for longer than you'd ever wish." The Black Knight climbs his aeroship's steps and signals to those above. Anchors rise, and sails extend. A storm of wind spirals around us from the steam valves that'll send us flying like hawks across the sky.

"Release them," calls the Black Knight, and from his tone, I can tell he doesn't care in the slightest what sort of peril that'll put his rogues in once Marcus and Owen are free.

The unlucky rogues holding them unlock their chains and cuffs, and when they do, both knight and squire tackle them and seize the firelances from their crooked hands, Marcus's reclaimed pistolník a gleam of ancient bronze stained red from blood. They leap to their feet. Owen fires straight into one's temple, and the rogue falls over dead.

The Black Knight drags me up the steps. He hasn't forgotten how my right arm has been weakened, and his grip tightens, forcing my submission. My face twists in pain, but my defeated heart hurts even more.

"I think you'll like *MUERTE*, darling," he says.

Despite the aeroships quickly leaving and those hurrying to arrive, the rogues' aims at their enemies are careful and calculated. The stairs slowly lift and retract as we reach the deck. On the ground, Marcus halts, his body shaking with cold and shock. He catches my eye and mouths my name, *Vivienne*.

"And," the Black Knight says, tipping my chin with one finger that utterly repulses me, "I think you'll *adore* the Great Sea of the Mediterranean."

TWENTY-FIVE

When we reach the aeroship's deck, the Black Knight drops my arm so he can shout orders to his scurrying rogues. He faces Galahad's approaching aeroship and withdraws his pristine firelance from his inner jacket pocket. Sets the scope against his real eye. Smiles. I dart my gaze across the storm between aeroships at the tired, thin faces of knights I know. Particularly the one at the forefront.

Percy. The Black Knight is aiming at Percy.

I run at the brute and seize the barrel of his firelance just as he fires. "No!" It sends the bearing scattering into the sky.

"Damn you!" the Black Knight shouts, grabbing my hair at the base of my neck and lifting most horribly until I'm on my toes. He studies me like a vagrant wolf might study a dying cat, but though the delicious thought of tearing me limb from limb has certainly crossed his mind, he does nothing of the sort.

My fingers reach for the firelance at my waist—to kill him, to strike him, to do what I can to make him drop me— but he finds it first and snatches it from my grasp.

"You just signed his death warrant, girl. And it'll be *slow.*" A bearing from the other aeroship nearly catches on his ear, whizzing past both of us. I squeeze my eyes shut and wait for the second attempt, for Death to call me. But the only thing the Black Knight does is plan for retaliation. "Lift anchors! Set the fleet to full speed ahead! We return to the Mediterranean, with or without these bastards on our tail!"

Cannons from Galahad's aeroship fire. The Black Knight throws me to the deck and sheaths my firelance for himself. The planks of floor holding up this vile flying vessel shudder from the impact of iron. With the ship's instability, I tumble into the mast and grip the rough wood tightly, wishing for Merlin's sword, dropped at the tavern.

The Black Knight gnashes his teeth through a vengeful growl. "Greet them in the same way they've greeted us!" he shouts. He heads for the helm and the rogues manning it.

It'll be another full minute until Galahad can fire the cannons again. More than enough time to take in the spectacular bat-like wings of the Black Knight's aeroship—boldly colored and massive in span. The rich golds, burgundies, and emeralds are prominent, like this is not just an aerocraft, but a world of luxury where only the finest tapestries and linens could ever enhance the aesthetics of such violent contraptions aboard. The helm is solid gold facing the pointed bow where a naked mermaid encased in bronze looks out. She wears goggles that curve into teardrops, the points of which line her eyes like a cat's. She has a fish tail, and sprockets for scales.

Above the wings, a massive gray body is the real monster behind *MUERTE*. Long and pointed and smooth, the rogues call it a zeppelin, and it seems to be where they store the power that sends us flying across the sky at unimaginable speeds.

Another cannon blasts into us. I grab the mast tighter. Galahad wouldn't know I'm aboard; he might not even know I've left Camelot.

A third cannon, and this one slams into the sail whose mast I'm gripping, sending me straight to my knees with my arms covering my head. I'm desperate to breathe, but there's no way I could. I panic for the air I want, and I pray for the home I left.

I look up in time to see the Black Knight smiling at my brush with death. "To the Mediterranean!" he cries to his rogues.

And they cheer. The zeppelin above us churns, and we soar across the sky.

I press against the splintered mast as though it might absorb me into its wood. The Black Knight glares at me with diabolical thoughts, perhaps entertaining the possibility of slicing me piece by piece, as he tried to with Gawain. Only the start of his planned torture for me. He might have his rogues pierce my palms, the same way they did to Marcus, before finding enough reason to dirty his own hands. And this could very well be his plan, for suddenly he is at my side, and the sharpness of his small, jagged blade bites into my neck.

"I'd be honored if you joined me in a more private place, Lady Vivienne," he whispers. "We have much to discuss. I won't hurt this pretty neck of yours, not after seeing how Sir Marcus looks at you. What he'd love to do to you exceeds the neck, I'm sure." His free hand grabs my arm to lead me below deck. Before we can take the first mahogany step toward a well-lit cabin with an exquisite red door, he turns to his rogues manning the cannons. "Get word to the other ships. Half the fleet will fight alongside *MUERTE*; the rest will return to the village. Burn it and the people there!"

"No!" I scream, pulling from the Black Knight's grip to no avail. The memory of burnt land, burnt people, the woman whose hand I held in the middle of Camelot's courtyard. Marcus's mother and the apron of ash tied to her waist. I can't bear it. "How could you be so cruel? They've done *nothing* to you!"

The Black Knight might feel nothing at my words. "They knew I was there, darling, and they might send word to other villages. And they knew *you* were there. Had you not run, perhaps none of this would have happened."

I feel the weight of Atlas atop my shoulders. So this is what it feels like to steal life without ever firing a weapon.

As the Black Knight's commands are relayed across the whispers of the skies, I watch a half-dozen aeroships steer away from this battle for the village we've left behind. I remind myself that the villagers ran as fast as they could once they saw the Black Knight in the tavern. They've certainly escaped. Their homes might be forever gone, but at least they're alive. Marcus and Owen, too. Surely.

The Black Knight takes me to his private quarters.

I hate how it reminds me of Merlin's clock tower in its size, its world of craftsmanship and planning, its intricate details each with a history of their own.

A creak sounds from a nearby closet matching the tilts and blows from the battle above. I struggle to stay upright, but the floor is unstable from the winds, and the world even more so. I glance out a foggy window at Galahad's English-styled aeroship coursing along the skies, fighting to keep pace with *MUERTE*. It vanishes from sight, sailing overtop to attack from the starboard side. Once it's disappeared completely, I take in the entirety of the cabin. A counter sits beside me, set up with spirits and ales. In the opposite corner is a long day bed, complete with pillows and blankets of silk and wool. But nothing of comfort that could ward off the chill of fear from my skin.

The Black Knight is cool and stoic as he saunters in next, shutting the door with an air of elegance and chivalry. But there's also frustration as he goes to his spirits' counter and slams down his firelance. Such annoyance undoubtedly comes from the cannons' blasts ringing in the air.

"Galahad's talent of being a thorn in my side has outdone itself tonight. Even the realm of the demigods wasn't this irritating."

The winter skies follow him inside this cabin, but such a monster might be unaffected by the cold. When he sees me shiver, he points at the unlit hearth next to the day bed.

"Where are my manners? You must be chilled to the bone." A wave of his hand sends flames to rise from the wood. It reminds me of the fire Marcus built for me in the barn, and perhaps the Black Knight knows that somehow.

"I'm not," I reply, hiding my shivering arms.

"Always with the lies." He shakes his head as he pours himself a drink from a crystal decanter.

Perhaps Gawain was wrong, and the Black Knight is

nothing more than a trickster, an illusionist. I've heard of them before: traveling merchants who will take your money once they get you to look the other way.

My arms will not stop shaking, and I nearly hate myself for letting my furs and cloak drop in the village snow. I take a woolen blanket from under the decorative pillows and wrap it around my shoulders while the fire grows strong. There's another call from the knights' ship for cannons and steel sabers from deck, and I send a prayer to whoever would listen that Galahad might at least start with crossbows, which would never shatter these walls.

In the meantime, I need to find something that could free me from the Black Knight's clutches. Perhaps a looking glass. If I can find one, and if he leaves, I could get in touch with Azur, since my soul isn't tainted—

I draw in a sharp breath. But my soul is tainted now. I stole magic, and it was remarkable and horrifying, and the power in my hands was unlike anything I'd ever built, greater than forging the mechanical dragon, Victor. Even forging my aeroship. And although Merlin was able to use looking glasses to help me finish up the monster we'd hoped would defeat Morgan—after stealing magic in the woods, at that—I can no longer believe that Merlin was always truthful with me.

I shake the thought free. Something else, then. The cabin is full of globes and maps strewn across luxuriously lined tables that would cost an entire kingdom. All major ports on those maps have been marked and targeted, pinned and circled. Trade routes have been traced, and islands conquered have been marked.

Oh God, there seems to be nothing. I take a breath and will myself to be practical about this predicament, to search for an advantage against the Black Knight. But I can't move. I've never been in such danger before, and I can't see a logical way of ever getting out of it. Instead of a step forward, I take a step backward, and to take another is tempting indeed. It sets me straight against the aubergine walls within reach of silver trays boasting preserved fruits and meats—all fit for a king or demigod. Despite my terrible hunger, to eat now would nearly be traitorous.

Instead, I force my eyes at a map of the world with pins and pins and pins on it. There's no pattern, but I force myself to count them, the ease of which lets me trap fear inside me and turn it into my own captive, not to be freed until I can kiss the ground in Camelot's gardens.

But then I pause in my counting. I step closer to the map and lift my right hand, despite the sharp pain ringing through my arm. Ladies in Camelot do not take up the study of cartography unless they are queens, but Merlin was of the opinion that a girl of intelligence should know how to navigate. My finger drifts over Britannia. *Home.* The range of mountains I could see from the height of my bedchambers, the forestry that takes over a good part of the English countryside and carries the subtle aroma of wildflowers once the month of May has bloomed. There it is, even the cliff where Excalibur waits in an anvil for Camelot's future king. I let my fingers drift over it. My home. The home I might never return to.

A pin marks it, and I frown.

When were the Spanish rogues there? I think back to all

the times aeroships docked, how I watched them from the balcony that circled the knights' verandah with Marcus. Those were aeroships of trade, of commerce. They were nothing out of the ordinary in a country at peace, though on watch for a witch.

But, no, there was another aeroship that came to Camelot. When the subjects evacuated, when Morgan's armies were about to attack. I watched from Merlin's tower as it pulled to the cliff.

"No, that can't be right," I whisper.

"Darling?" the Black Knight asks with an air of indifference, turning to me from the task of fixing himself a drink.

I shut my eyes, forcing myself to think further back. My stomach twists in a way I don't understand. I see my mother's face in my mind's eye. I see her board with the rest of the nobility and serfs.

Now I'm worried that the flags, the sails, the burgundy—Oh.

The Spanish insignias, the unassuming call and response for help when Camelot needed it. In the midst of a crisis in the kingdom. Arthur wouldn't have paid attention; aeroships were called for, and aeroships answered. We're allied with the kingdoms of España, and perhaps one was set to come to our aid. The perfect cover for air pirates whose treacherous flags bear similar markings. My hands are shaking, and it seems like there will never again be peace in my heart.

I trace the rest of the landscape surrounding Britannia, unexplored and wild, and run my finger between the two bodies of land leading me from Camelot to a flattened bit labeled *the Kingdom of Jerusalem.* Worlds away from where I am now, home to a new war to lure Arthur's knights from the Grail quest. It was supposed to have been a way to slow us down, but here is the Black Knight, like he might have known I'd go after Avalon myself, right into his waiting clutches. My finger pauses on the Holy Land, where there's another red pin, and perhaps a fleet of aeroships carrying Camelot's subjects.

"Rogues took them."

I sent my mother to those ships.

TWENTY-SIX

How stupid were we in the face of danger to ignore something so perilous? How stupid not to realize deadly enemies were right on our doorstep, as well as in our farmlands? In all likelihood, Arthur didn't even bat an eye, not when he was going mad—and his wife and champion were caught in each other's arms. Perhaps they were told it was, in fact, an allied kingdom sending help. Oh God, what if the ship my father sent for me had been a rogue ship, too?

Another of Galahad's cannons hits the deck above us. Shouts are indecipherable and layered and panicked from such danger, and I can only hope that the damage is enough to give Galahad a chance to end it all.

The Black Knight turns to the door at hearing his rogues' cries. He squeezes his fingers around his goblet, tighter and tighter and tighter, until there's a loud snap and a chime, and every piece of glass flies outward against the dark walls. I cover my eyes from the flying shards and peek through my fingers. A lone line of blood trickles down the devil's skin, but he is unfazed.

"A drink, darling?" he says nonchalantly. He picks up an unopened green glass bottle and readies a comb of shredded silver with a square of sugar atop. Absinthe. A ring on his hand has a strange compartment set on top. As the drink settles, he opens the tiny chamber, filled with white powder, and presses a fingertip of it to a nostril, sniffing loudly as he inhales.

I can smell the fragrance of the anise from where I sit, but I look away, making sure he sees my grimace.

"Suit yourself." He drinks the entire shot. "I need inspiration, Lady Vivienne. I need to come up with the most exquisite way to kill Galahad. And then I need to find a way to convince you to give me the coordinates to Avalon." He holds up his empty green glass and looks through it at the gas lantern's light. "How will I ensure you tell me? Maybe we should discuss the situation regarding … Camelot."

My eyes find their way back to the maps. "It was you, wasn't it? You came to Camelot for its exodus?" I can't help but give in to the turmoil he'll set upon me now.

And suddenly, the Black Knight is next to me at the maps, glancing at the array of red pins. It appalls me to have him so dangerously close; it sickens me even more to think of his aeroships not a mile from my bedchambers. He has another shot of green fairy in his grasp, one I didn't see him make. "It was my men, yes. But this map is out of date. Your kin aren't in Jerusalem anymore. Still in the Holy Land, though, if memory serves."

"Where are they, you monster?" I try to sound threatening, but I come off as weak and trembling. I think of my mother's look of horror once the façade of who their saviors were was revealed. How she would have had to be strong for the rest.

The Black Knight inclines his head at my pitiful insult. "Don't be absurd to think you're entitled to any answers yet, Lady Vivienne."

"Answers?" I say. "I demanded one and no more. What else is there for me to know?"

His breath is spicy licorice, and his green eye is all the greener. "A lady of your standing shouldn't raise her voice to such heights." But he cannot hold my gaze for long. A shudder as I stare back and a breath that speaks loudly of his discomfort are all too obvious, and he turns away as though to hide what I now recognize as fear.

Perhaps he holds no power over me after all. He could have tortured me by now. He could have cut my fingers clear off my hand with the jagged dagger tucked inside his jacket. But instead, his fists are clenched tightly, ready to strike, though to him perhaps it's impossible. There might as well be a wall of impenetrable glass between us.

My God, there's so much danger here, but none of it has touched me. "What has you so afraid of me?" I ask.

And then I see the slightest dip in his confident green eye, as though I've touched on something I wasn't to know just yet.

"That," I continue, pointing. "What is that? Why do I scare you? You could have easily killed or hurt me, but you haven't. You could have slain the knight and squire, all in one go. The signet would have required a bit of a hunt, but the world is finite enough. You could have found the Grail yourself eventually. Why go through the trouble of keeping me alive?"

He swallows the rest of his green spirit as he returns to the decanter. His hands shake more noticeably now against the table as he pours a third, and the decks above us rumble from the pains of war. He glances at me. "As it is practice for men to share drink when they discuss matters of the world, shall I now pour one for the lady?"

"I think I've found my thirst."

He reaches for a second glass goblet, miniature and carved with a cloudy dragon on the front. He paints the animal green with the drink and hands it to me with an ironic smile. "Fitting, no?"

I hold the glass, waiting for his explanation. Now, I'm not afraid.

"Your mind, Lady Vivienne," he finally says, "is untouchable."

I narrow my eyes at his likely ruse in the making. "How so?"

He lifts his eyebrows and his glass, but I refuse to clink mine with his. It'd be wrong to toast with such a monster. "You don't know what the demigods say about you?"

I kiss the glass, and the cool absinthe washes down my throat. It's harsh, but refined. "I certainly wouldn't be surprised to hear they've declared to the entire world that I'm the new inventor of Camelot with the coordinates to Avalon," I manage through the burn.

The Black Knight drinks his absinthe, but no bout of green comes over his face, as though the liquor has not rendered him drunk. After three!

He takes my glass and sets it on the table. It lands with

a heavy clank, nearly breaking into pieces. "Fascinating. I wonder what it'd be like to see the contents of your mind."

My head starts to swim, and I'm wondering now if he's passed on his drunkenness to me in the same manner he was able to light the kindle in the hearth from afar.

"What?" I say, frowning as he drifts into two people, mirror reflections of the other. The room shifts, as though the aeroship were a spinning top dancing in the sky. Cackles come from the ship's bow, where I know the Black Knight's men fight, where they wield the wind as their weapon. The rush of fear is a hurricane coming back to me, and I'm losing my control of it. "What are you talking about?"

"Dizzy, love?" He tilts his head in a pitying manner.

I force myself to face him; I push aside the hold nausea has on me. "What's happening? What was in that?"

I focus my gaze on my empty glass, the one with the dragon bursting free from its cage, flickering flames made out of spun sand. The rim of the glass is coated in something; perhaps a fine salt, or sugar. I'm dizzy, but I wipe my finger across the surface and taste it.

"Opium?"

He has a pipe in his hand, and as he smokes, bellows of green plumes surround me until the room disappears into a fog. "Despite all the time spent with Merlin, you have no idea how opium works."

I cough and cough, and it's of no use because the smoke gets thicker until the entire room disappears, and I'm left in a world I cannot understand.

"Be still, and let it work. I won't harm you, as you've

already come to realize. But your mind must be loose." Another breath.

I'm fighting for air and failing. My lungs burn with fire and ash, and I can't find my way through the smoke. Oh God, if he is a devil, he might be immune to whatever he's putting me through. And after how I taunted him, how I realized he wouldn't kill me—no, not when there's clearly something he fears about me. What is it? What is that voice, that honey-coated voice screaming behind the soundless smoke?

"Wake up, Vivienne, daughter of Carolyn!" thunders in my ear, and I breathe a gasp.

The Black Knight is closer now, and he's uncovered his mechanical eye. He stares into my gaze. I feel the same pull I felt only once before—when Morgan le Fay tried to steal the coordinates to Avalon from my mind. And perhaps the Black Knight is trying to do the same.

"Vivienne! Wake up!" the woman bellows again.

It's the Lady of the Lake, who promised she'd protect me. Who might have freed herself from whatever hold Merlin set upon her in the woods. And with that, I realize what the Black Knight fears.

I snap free, and in my hand is his firelance, its barrel aimed at his temple. He's shocked by the gentle flirting of skull and iron, and oh God I'd love nothing more than to steal magic to torture him before sending a bearing straight into his head.

"You have her eyes," he says with a tone of amusement covering his humility.

I shake my head. "I have my father's eyes. And I may

not be able to kill or hurt you with this firelance, but I am creative, too."

He cocks an eyebrow. "I am immune to stolen magic as much as I am immune to the copper that killed le Fay."

I incline my head. "The magic wouldn't be stolen if it were a gift, though." I feel the Lady of the Lake's protection. Even in the sky, so far from her element of water, she'll still protect me. "As for bearings, well. I'll certainly call your bluff."

The Black Knight drifts closer, as though to captivate me by way of his elegance or his chivalry. "Oh, darling. You think you could ever hurt me. We're high enough in the clouds that you'd be properly tortured before the Lady of the Lake could have her revenge."

I smile sweetly. "I think not. *Do not lie to me.*" I press the barrel against his temple. "*Darling.*"

Through his defeat, he raises his chin. "Where is Avalon?"

I look deep inside my earliest memory. At the clear picture of a castle in the clouds. It's plain as day and only made more real by what the Fisher King unlocked. "You'll never know." I click back the hammer.

The Black Knight smiles as though his death is not seconds away. "You'll show it to me."

I shake my head. "It'll never be yours." The barrel digs deeper into his temple.

His smile remains tight on his face, but he holds up a halting finger in pathetic protest. "It appears, darling, your mother is quite as determined as you are to survive."

I freeze. The firelance loosens from his skin, and I feel the weight of it fall to my side.

He glances at the map next to me. "So, the Holy Land. Is that where I sent Camelot's subjects? To a world you longed to escape to anyway, even if hundreds—no, *thousands*—of rogue aeroships have invaded its skies? If so, do you really want to spend all this time in Greece instead? Be reasonable, Lady Vivienne. I could send you in your own aeroship to meet the ridiculous alchemist fighting to reclaim his home, or the mother who fights more viciously than you do with a blade. You could be away from all this Avalon nonsense."

I cannot let my face give away my thoughts. I blink away the tears that want to rise out of fear for Azur and my mother. I lift my weapon high again. Press the barrel deep into his temple so that the Black Knight grits his jaw. I harden my face, ready to kill.

His eyebrows slowly rise. "Wait. Let me gain your trust. I'm a demigod of my word. To prove as such, I have something important for you to see about your beloved knight and the barmaid."

My heart skips. He's bluffing.

He's bluffing, he's lying, whatever it takes to get the coordinates to Avalon. I must have heard him wrong—I *know* I heard him wrong. It's the absinthe talking, and perhaps this is all just a nightmare, and I'll wake up tomorrow in my warm bed. I'll wake up, and it'll turn out all this never happened. My brother didn't find us. Marcus didn't save me from the icy waters. The Black Knight is a man I made up myself, using the lens from Caldor's eye when Merlin and I conquered the woods Morgan bewitched, and the crisp green eyes of Arthur, whose death I still mourn.

But no, the Black Knight looks plainly at me, hiding nothing, letting me see everything his soul encompasses. He is a walking paradox: his soul gone and his body here. Not a ghost in the machine, but Merlin's antithesis.

He smiles as his hand tilts the firelance away from his temple. And, God help me, I let him. "You want to know, don't you? Isn't there part of you just *dying* for the details?" His voice drawls into a raspy whisper, graceful in its waver.

Anger crawls over my skin, and I cast it away by shoving the barrel under his throat. "You don't get to mention him; you haven't the right."

He suppresses a choked cough. "Just one more taste of green fairy. For someone protected by the Lady of the Lake, for someone whose mind is eternally locked from my mechanical eye, it'll be nothing more than the sweetest-tasting honey you've ever had."

My mother's kind eyes, brilliant mind, warm touch ... I imagine her in turmoil. How could I ever trust the monster standing in front of me?

The Black Knight's green eye shines. "Let me tell you about Sir Marcus and Lena. To ease your mind, to show you can trust me."

He's lying. He's bringing this up to control me. *I cannot trust him.*

"Do not mention him again," I warn. But I cannot kill him now. He speaks of Marcus, and God, Marcus—

"Darling."

I pull away in defiance and drop the firelance; I'm as far from the monster as I can get and as far as my dizziness will allow for. He flips his golden eye-patch to the other side, letting me see my rounded reflection in his mechanical eye. Another miniature goblet of absinthe has found its way into his grasp. "I know the truth."

"How?"

Even without a real eye looking back at me, I know what he says is true. "I looked into Sir Marcus's eyes and saw it for myself. Whatever fate you believe to be his was an intentional lie told by someone you trusted once."

"Why?"

"To mislead."

It doesn't make any sense. The booming cannons above threaten to throw me off-balance, and the Black Knight seizes my wrist to keep me from falling.

"To mislead whom?" I ask.

And then, the light changes, and there's movement in his glass eye piece, similar to how Merlin's looking glass would turn at the beckoning call of Azur's *jaseemat*. The Black Knight offers me the miniature goblet.

I seize it. Lift it to my lips and tilt it so that the cool green liquid can touch my lips.

"To mislead you, darling," he answers.

As the drink flows down my throat, I look straight into the Black Knight's mechanical eye to see for myself.

TWENTY-SEVEN

A fire-breather blows a mouthful of oil across the lit torch in his hand. Flames flare above the small children who reach into the sky to grab hold of one, cheering in hopes the festival entertainer will do it again. But like a mischievous minx, the fire-breather runs off with those children running after him. The Black Knight saw these memories when his mechanical eye bore into Marcus's, and now, so do I.

I'm a stranger in this land, a phantom never to be seen. I transcend the laws of the world to follow my beloved and witness King Pelles and the people of Corbenic, long before the threat of Morgan le Fay was a whisper in Britannia, celebrate the summer solstice, the Festival of Lights and Stars.

Those honored stars cast their glimmer on the drunken Pelles, and to that, he calls for more ale from atop his wooden throne, under tapestries of cornflower blue and silver strung overhead, mingling with tiny gas lanterns in the courtyard. Subjects dance while Pelles's nobility watches, their visions as glazed as their minds. Girls' hair weaves around the red and yellow hydrangea crowns atop their heads. Glorious yellow dresses sway as the crowd claps in rhythm to the minstrels' song.

I pause from searching the crowd as the song ends and

another entertainer steps forward: a girl with long, raven locks whose mask shields her eyes. Her hair is too wild to hide, but a tall hat does its best to try. With dramatic flair, she creeps through the people, a cape about her shoulders, and under it, a small mechanical animal—a bronze rabbit—she sets in the middle of the grass. I take a seat next to Pelles, stinking of too much ale and chicken grease from the plate in front of him.

"Watch, now. She's been working on this one for weeks," the king slurs to the man on his other side. I glance over, seeing only the hand of the gentleman in question.

The girl calls for attention. "Gather 'round, if you dare, to see the mechanical arts distort and amaze!"

She withdraws a long steel wand from the inside of her cloak and casts aside the garment entirely, revealing a low-cut silver gown she wears boldly and happily.

As lords and dandies offer their whistles, she shakes a finger at them. "That's another show, my lords. One I'm afraid none of you could afford." The crowd laughs.

She flicks her wand into the air for effect, and the children who've lost interest in the fire-breather sit at her feet and giggle. There's one tap of the bronze rabbit's head while her other hand sneakily finds the key built into its back, turning clockwise.

"Come to life!" Her voice bubbles with so much confidence that all attention is hers, and when she throws her sleeve off the rabbit, it clatters and waddles around on the grass. The entire company claps politely, and the children gasp in awe at the "magic" they've witnessed.

"Wonderful!" Pelles says, standing and clapping, nearly

knocking over a goblet of wine in the process. Instinctively, I reach over to steady him, but the man on Pelles's other side gets there first.

I'm surprised to see Sir Lancelot, young and at ease before Arthur's death will come to pass. He sits at Pelles's table an honored guest of Corbenic, a castle he knows well. His smile crinkles his eyes, and his untamed black and curly hair sits about his shoulders as he sips from his own goblet.

Pelles takes his seat and beckons the illusionist over. "Elaine! Come, dear girl!"

The girl makes no motion to remove her mask, running over with a smile as wide as the crescent moon. "It was delightful, wasn't it?" With one look at Lancelot, that smile softens, and the knight inclines his head politely before looking elsewhere for something to sustain his tired interest.

"Sir Lancelot, I present my daughter, Elaine of Corbenic," Pelles says mid-gulp of wine.

Elaine ignores her father's lack of propriety and offers her hand. "I've heard great things about you, Sir Lancelot. Many stories I imagine have been wildly exaggerated." Her smile shines brighter, and she refuses the opportunity to relinquish any boldness on her part.

Lancelot kisses her hand. He holds it in his glove for quite some time as he looks at her. "Terribly so, I'm afraid, if your father was the one to tell them." He glances to the side where Marcus sits, chin rested in his palm as he struggles to keep his eyes open. Lancelot elbows him. "My squire, Marcus. He's not usually this dull, but we did just arrive."

Marcus's violet eyes shoot open at the sound of his name,

and he looks at Elaine, offering a polite nod, which Elaine returns. The girl has handmaids much younger than herself, three of whom huddle in a small circle, pointing at Marcus and giggling, and a fourth bold enough to tap him on the opposite shoulder and run off when Marcus turns to see no one standing there.

I watch their encounter closely in case there'd been a chance I missed a romantic spark, but Marcus is distracted enough that he does not speak with Pelles's daughter. By merely looking at him, I see his thoughts written on his mind: those of Camelot, of his life back in the farmlands, of his mother, his father.

"Where did your travels take you this time, my lord?" Elaine asks Lancelot as she takes the free seat across from him.

Lancelot stares at the blue of the sky on the cusp of turning black. His face falls into a subtle state of melancholy. "To the south. Four or five countries. After long enough, you lose track of which is which, isn't that right, Marcus?"

Marcus, leaning on his elbow now, lifts his head and offers a tired smile for an answer.

Elaine touches the sleeve of Lancelot's gentleman's jacket. "Come on, then. Tell me one place. One place I should visit."

Lancelot stares at the gas lanterns hanging above. "Lyonesse is quite beautiful."

"But Lancelot," Pelles calls. "It's the only kingdom left in Britannia that still embraces magic! Puh!"

"No," Lancelot replies. "Not all do."

Pelles and his stewards argue on the matter for some time longer, debating kingdoms and demigods with enough ale and spirits to sustain the discussion long past dawn. Elaine listens with exaggerated interest, rolling her eyes at Marcus once her father has emptied his goblet. Pelles speaks out of turn regarding Arthur keeping a sorcerer in his kingdom, not only a subtle mockery to demigods, but a *"blasted drunk"* as well. Through his ramblings, Marcus and Elaine hold their laughs, and Pelles's advisors rush to quiet their king on the matter.

But Lancelot says nothing after that.

———

"He doesn't remember me, does he?"

Marcus opens one eye, but otherwise doesn't move from his stretched-out position, lying on his back in the grassy courtyard as I find my place in this memory from the following week. In Camelot, it'd be against propriety for a squire to appear so inactive. But Corbenic is different. Marcus glances up at cloudy shapes he might have seen as animals if he'd been a child. Lady Elaine sits next to him by a stream, but I cannot clearly see her face, as it is shadowed by a hickory tree.

Marcus shuts his eyes again. "What do you mean?"

But I can tell by the way he avoids eye contact that he knows exactly what Lady Elaine is thinking. And then the Black Knight shows me another memory from the grand hall only the other day—Marcus had witnessed Lancelot and Elaine when they'd thought they were alone. The memories fly past me as though I'm watching a performance. The knight had strode through the corridor with much on his mind—Lyonesse, for example—and a girlish voice had followed him.

"I see you," she had sing-songed.

Marcus had watched a frenzy of raven hair disappear behind long, blue tapestries. He'd witnessed a smile of amusement appear on Lancelot's face, along with a sense of long-lost fun he hadn't seen since well before their journey to Lyonesse. Lancelot had run after the girl, calling at her to come out.

"Forget the Grail, Sir Knight! This is your quest now!" she'd responded.

Once the hallway had ended, Lancelot had tiptoed to her stilled body, his hand trapping her inside the tapestries. When he'd swept them from her face and touched her cheek, her smile had disappeared. She'd leaned in and kissed Sir Lancelot.

Now, Elaine seizes a handful of grass and weeds and throws it at Marcus. "Hey! You got your fill of sleep days ago. Wake up!"

Marcus grumbles as dirt falls into his eyes. Pelles's daughter certainly commanded an audience wherever she went; if not, she'd force one. She and I are so different from one another.

"Does he remember you? Lancelot?" Marcus looks toward the courtyard, where the knight in question strolls with Pelles, a much happier man now that they were days away from their time in Lyonesse. The next stop, Camelot. "Of course he does. You were in a dream of his weeks ago and haunted him while we crossed the eastern plains."

Elaine scoffs, and part of her cheek falls into the sunlight. Marcus peeks at her as she blushes at the thought, eyeing the knight who hasn't yet spotted her. "Do not mock me, Marcus. Otherwise, I'll be forced to square off with you in the courtyard and put your swordsmanship to shame."

Marcus laughs under his breath. "Wouldn't want that. You're good enough with a blade to beat me one day."

"Two years past you both were in Corbenic. You weren't his squire yet; it was a blond boy, the most serious-looking fellow I'd ever seen. I'm not sure even my father was successful in getting him to crack a smile."

"Galahad," Marcus says as the memory clearly returns. He shuffles to a sitting position. "Arthur knighted him a short while after. Were you there? I don't remember."

Elaine's gaze flicks skyward in exasperation, still in the hickory's shadows. "You wouldn't, scoundrel. I was with my father to greet Lancelot. Just a girl of fifteen. Terribly forgettable."

Marcus watches Lancelot laugh with Elaine's father. Perhaps the knight had a vague memory of a black-haired girl the last time they'd been to Corbenic. "Come now. How could anyone forget you?"

"An excellent answer," Elaine responds with a winning smile. She picks at the grass. "But Arthur's court will demand it of Lancelot, won't they?"

Marcus takes his time to find a suitable response. "My lady, what do you expect from him? He is and will continue to be your friend—"

"Friend?" she says, stumbling on the word and withdrawing herself in a way that seems unusual for Elaine of Corbenic. "I suppose he would think that. Perhaps I'm as forgettable now as ever."

Marcus stands and offers her a helping hand up. But she refuses and gets to her feet herself. Marcus scuffs his boots across the grass. "Lancelot is a knight of Camelot, bound to the Round Table."

Elaine shrugs, and it's an oddly vulnerable gesture. "Perhaps if I were to join you on your adventures, then. Or perhaps if he were to leave the Round Table."

Marcus's eyes shoot up to hers in surprise, and instantly, the pitiful girl must know what she is suggesting has bordered on the impossible.

"My lady, don't lose your heart to someone who could never offer you his," Marcus says. He takes a step back as strolling subjects make their casual and indifferent hellos to Elaine. "Perhaps Lancelot and I are overstaying our welcome."

"Perhaps you are." Elaine's voice trembles with humiliation, and Marcus hesitates before leaving her to greet the subjects with a princess's smile, the biggest lie of all.

———

Marcus had slept for nearly a day and a half after arriving in Corbenic. Lancelot was involved in assemblies with King Pelles regarding the Holy Grail, so it wasn't an issue. But after so much rest and inactivity, the wind in Marcus's sails certainly begged for movement and practice, and now I see his desperation to wield a sword.

The next morning, he finds the artillery room and explores Pelles's selection of fine, steel-based weaponry. Corbenic is slower than Camelot in terms of implementing firelances and pistolníks in battle, much preferring to employ the mechanical arts to enhance the imagination and provide entertainment at festivals. For years, Pelles asserted a sort of divine perfection in the sword—what could a few cogs and gears add that wouldn't render the weapon clunky and over-stated?

Marcus draws his fingers across the blades glinting on the walls. One by one, he meets and admires them before moving on to the crossbows. I'd never known him to be an archer, but the finely polished bows of Corbenic made of applewood and sculpted like hourglasses are works of art themselves and beg praise.

"Marcus!" a girl's voice hisses, breaking his concentration.

Marcus nearly drops the crossbow in his hand as we both spin around to the door. A girl stands there, a heavy hood covering her face, but dark locks spilling through.

"Please don't make a sound!" She removes her hood from the top of her head and sets a shushing finger to her lips.

Marcus recognizes her immediately, and so do I. "Lady Elaine, I—"

"Please, Marcus. You're my friend. You can call me Lena." She checks the corridor to make sure the halls are empty and shuts the door. "But you cannot tell anyone you saw me." She strides past him and the ghost I am to the swords he'd been admiring and chooses one. With a quick move, she flicks it around her wrist and into a hidden holster at her waist, buried underneath her cloak.

Marcus watches. "What are you doing?"

"Leaving Corbenic."

His brows shoot up at that. "Leaving? Why?"

Her eyes shine at his, full of adventure. I don't know why the day before he expected her to harbor feelings of resentment or despair over Lancelot; in these few memories, I've seen how Lena is strong in her ability to retain her independence.

"Because I've always wanted to. Because there are countries whose tongues I don't speak. Because I've never seen the sea to the south. Shall I go on?"

She finds a selection of monocles that have been formatted to gauge far distances and chooses one for her pocket. "Marcus, I cannot stay. Not when there's an entire world out there just waiting to be explored. I never realized how badly I longed for the life you and Lancelot live."

Marcus looks up, catching the sadness in her voice when she utters his knight's name. But he says nothing.

"Really, I'm fine," Lena says, snatching up a rope and winding it around her palm and elbow until it's a bunched loop. "Besides, the mechanical arts here are nothing more than illusions, and beyond these shores, there are kingdoms where they've built entire cities all with labyrinths and passageways. I must see them. There's even word of an innkeeper in the countryside who's begun building escape routes in his tavern. I've already sent word that I'd work as a barmaid if only he'd teach me—"

"Don't leave your home because Lancelot—"

"This isn't about Lancelot," Lena says firmly. "This is about me. For three years, I was foolishly in love with him. I wasted time. I already knew, Marcus." But even though it might be true that Lena is free of loving Lancelot, the tears that collect in her eyes are enough to show Marcus she still has to grieve.

She takes a large satchel and fills it with all sorts of gadgets and tools: thick, heavy rope, a monocle like the viewers I'd construct in Camelot, a crossbow. She straps a grappling hook to her back that Marcus's own blacksmith father could have forged. Then she meets Marcus in the middle of the room.

"My letter to my father will inform him that I've eloped with a foreign prince who wants to take me around the world in his golden aeroship. It's just the sort of dramatics he'd expect, and he'll be thrilled to let this story turn into legend in Corbenic. I had to bribe my ladies-in-waiting to keep silent, and I have nothing else to offer for your own—"

"I won't tell," Marcus promises.

She throws her arms around his neck and kisses his cheek, and where I should feel jealousy, I feel happiness for Lena instead. "Thank you. Goodbye, Marcus."

He holds her tightly, the friend he met too late. "Godspeed, Lena."

She makes for the door. When she opens it, and it creaks loudly against the quiet air, she turns back. "Marcus?"

He glances up.

"I'm not sure Arthur knows what he's asking of his knights when he offers them a place at his Round Table. Never put duty above love. All right?"

Marcus says nothing, and Lena slips into the night, never to be seen again in Corbenic.

The squire shuffles in the quiet that follows, perhaps contemplating Lena's advice, but then he shrugs. His knighthood will save his mother. His sacrifice will have to be enough. Certainly, there isn't any other way. Is there?

"Next stop, Camelot," he says. Perhaps starting with a quick detour to the same village where he first met Lancelot, Marcus leaves the artillery room with a broken crossbow in hand, whose string is not nearly taut enough to fire properly.

Perhaps with an idea of how to fix it.

TWENTY-EIGHT

The Black Knight's mechanical eye cuts me free of Marcus's memory, and I return to my place in the cabin of his aeroship, where I scramble to understand everything I just witnessed.

Lena is Elaine of Corbenic, the girl Sir Kay mentioned and mocked as a thick robe of melancholy draped over Lancelot's tired shoulders my last night in Camelot.

What the Black Knight showed me might have been the last time Marcus saw Lena until we arrived in the village, or perhaps not. Marcus was missing for a month. But from the memories I saw, they were friends and nothing more. It wasn't betrayal.

And so death must be Marcus's destiny, despite the Fisher King's assurance to the contrary—was he wrong? Did I really send Marcus to die as soon as I stepped outside of Camelot?

I'm reaching for stable breath, and the much-louder and more-frequent booms of the cannons above deck are no help. The Black Knight moves his golden eye-patch over his mechanical lens to watch me.

"Lena was the girl Lancelot—"

"Lady Elaine was no harlot, and she was nothing more than a friend to your lover. Pride is your biggest flaw, Lady Vivienne, and look where that got you. You couldn't even ask the knight to confirm the truth for himself." The Black Knight finds a well-used pipe on a small table beside his day bed and fills it tightly with feathered bits of herb. He lights it, and the smoke of the *hashish* sways into the air. "The misdirection of suggesting betrayal was someone else's doing. A demigoddess who didn't realize just how determined you'd become to find the Grail."

The last words Lena gave Marcus before she left Corbenic come back to me: *Never put duty above love.* Only last spring, I'd told Marcus the exact opposite when he asked me to leave Camelot with him. That we had a duty to be there.

"Duty, right."

He'd listened, and because of that, his mother stayed in Camelot to burn with its farmlands.

"This is my fault," I whisper. The Black Knight is right: it was pride. Pride I'd never boasted before, not until I could be away from Camelot, finally see the world on my own, and embrace that which I'd promised I never would. I couldn't even have simply asked Marcus for the truth—I assumed, and the prospect of humiliation was enough to turn my assumption into fact. I hurt us both with my words and actions. If our hearts could be one, I've shattered it. "This is my doing."

I lean over my knees, letting my hair drape around my face. As I do so, the part of me determined to make up for my sins madly searches the Black Knight's cabin. Hearing the vision of Lena speaking of passageways reminded me of what Merlin said aboard *CELESTE* before he sent it crashing to the ground. This aeroship is much more luxurious than my own, but there might be tricks to the design.

Tricks like passageways that could somehow let me escape this cabin and take this ship as my own. Passageways a demigod might never realize exist.

But a desperate inventor would, and a desperate inventor is someone the Black Knight should fear. Enough so that the words of magic I read in Merlin's journals and heard while in the realm of the Fisher King come rushing back to me, and I have to silence them before I steal again.

The Black Knight's footsteps on his cabin floor are quiet. I feel a soft pat on my shoulder.

"Be enlightened, Lady Vivienne. Learn from your mistake. You might never again see Sir Marcus—"

Another loud boom and shuddering of wood and sails.

"Regardless, you have the chance to do some good. You could seek Camelot's subjects, fight the fools I sent there to lure Arthur's knights and the rest of the world from Avalon." Another long inhale. "I'll sweeten my offer. Show me how to find the Grail, and I'll show you how magic could be employed for a greater purpose."

I'm running what he said over in my mind, and I feel Merlin's spells burn in my pocket. I know the spell that would blind a man. Perhaps there were more in Merlin's clock tower than just those I snatched to bring with me, spells the sorcerer would use to offset the weight that is *Redia*, the spell to resurrect. Oh how lovely it'd be to kill the Black Knight right now and commandeer this aeroship myself, even if it would be at the cost of my own soul...

I snap free from the temptation and think of Camelot's subjects. My mother. I can only pray Marcus chose the nobler path, deciding against seeking the Fisher King's signet from my aeroship wreckage, instead joining Galahad and Percy in attacking *MUERTE*. They could rise up against the Black Knight. Defeat him. Then we could return to my aeroship and retrieve the signet ourselves. And perhaps this want I feel for magic could be stopped once the Grail is in our hands.

The Black Knight kneels next to me, and I feel a wisp of smoke cut against my cheek.

"I know you worry about the consequences of magic. I know you think of le Fay or the sorcerer. Perhaps you look back fondly upon memories of Arthur's queen and the stories she told you of Lyonesse. Perhaps they were enough to send nightmares to every child in all corners of the world. But it's not like that. To embrace magic, Lady Vivienne, is to realize there are some of us who can rise above humanity and become *great*. Nature does value the strong. You've known this your entire life. Think about the ingenuity you employed when you built a toy aeroship that amazed even Merlin."

"How could you know that?" I whisper. I wonder if he might try again to use his mechanical eye on me. If I've finally weakened. Surely, the Lady of the Lake hasn't abandoned me now, but she might have discovered I've stolen magic. I could be lost forever.

"I might know you better than you think, Lady Vivienne."

I won't believe that. "No, it's that you're more afraid of my connection to the Lady of the Lake than you dare admit. That's why I'm still alive. You cannot use torture to extract the coordinates of Avalon from me, because her vengeance would be worse than anything you could conjure up." I'm nearly enjoying taunting him. We draw closer to Avalon the higher we fly, and the limit of my patience is being tested, and suddenly Vivienne, the former lady-in-waiting, has become Vivienne the Conniving.

A sneer crawls across the Black Knight's jaw. "Do not tempt me," he growls through gritted teeth. "There are many ways she could destroy me, but I'd most definitely make her retaliation worth it."

He returns to his spirits' counter to set his empty miniature goblet. The shine of the glass shows me a faint rendering of my own twisted reflection: my eyes are wild. In them, a fast flicker of gold, like Merlin's, before they flash back to my own. Or like Morgan's, as she sought coordinates from me. Guinevere's, once, strangely enough.

"The handmaid has two days to consider my offer." He glances one last time at me. "We'll reach the Great Sea of the Mediterranean then." He leaves, closing the door behind him, and instantly I hear him shout orders to those fighting a war of the skies.

Then there is nothing. Only the memory of Marcus's time in Corbenic, which I must push away and consider later. I wish for escape, but the gears and cogs spinning in my mind assure me I'd need another set of hands if I were to pull it off, let alone a bloody aerohawk if I were to go anywhere. *Blast.*

I don't know what will happen once we arrive in Greece. I don't know how the Black Knight is so sure I'll tell him where Avalon lies. Beneath these questions is another, one that was quiet once, but now grows into something I can no longer ignore—why do I so desperately want to find the Holy Grail?

I already know what my vice would be. The way magic tasted when I stole it, and the way it felt as it sprang from my lips...oh God. I might have been wrong to think I understand the power magic has on the world.

I must find the Grail fast. But would that save me, or destroy me?

A creak breaks the silence, and I dart my eyes toward it. A chirp, a bit of a whir. Sounds of the mechanical arts that are as familiar to me as my mother's voice. I search the room, furrowing my brow and glancing about, but perhaps it was a drunken rogue outside my door fiddling with a broken firelance. Perhaps it was the wood adjusting to the cold air at this height.

Another creak. An iron coat hanger and a selection of fine jackets hides the Black Knight's closet from view. The same closet creaking from before. I inch closer, as quietly as I can manage. It must be ajar, that's all.

A small finger sets itself between the door and the frame. I yelp in surprise and cover my mouth with my hands. A burst of copper wings and beady black eyes find its way into the Black Knight's cabin.

"Caldor!" I exclaim as my mechanical falcon takes flight around the Black Knight's spirits' counter and lands on the floor beside me. But this is impossible!

"You have no idea what sort of a challenge it is to keep a determined mechanical falcon silent, my lady," a girl's voice says. I glance at the closet as a face I've just seen—in the tavern and in several of Marcus's memories—peers out at me. "Thankfully the devil left when he did."

Her eyes are wild with adventure, and her lips are smiling with pride.

Somehow, Lena found a way aboard the aeroship *MUERTE.*

TWENTY-NINE

"Lady Vivienne. We were parted too quickly the last time we met," Lena whispers as she ducks her head around the closet door and checks the cabin. There is no sign of the Black Knight or any of his rogues, and that doesn't seem likely to change. Another cannonball strikes the aeroship, another shuddering of wood and iron, but it's of no concern to Lena, who draws back her hood and smiles. "Hope you don't mind company."

From what I saw of Lena in the Black Knight's mechanical eye, I realize that to see her as a stowaway is not surprising in the least.

But still, "What are you doing here?" I say too loudly, before I remember to lower my voice. Oh God, what she might have heard the Black Knight say . . .

Lena's eyes shine as she pulls her arsenal from her back. "Oh, I'm always game for a little adventure. And since Marcus gave up everything to ensure your safe return, I figured what little I could do to help must be done."

My eyes widen, and a gasp escapes from my lips as she reveals Merlin's sword and presents it to me.

"You dropped that. Thought you might want it back."

Then she pulls out a firelance and a crossbow and hands

them over, too, reserving a long-barreled fusionah with a wraparound blade for herself. "I figured you might be low on bearings. Probably not used to firelances like ours in Corbenic, but it should do the job."

"How did you get aboard?" I ask, unable to sheathe the marvel in my voice, though I do miss my own crossbow, rescued and reinforced by Rufus only to be lost in *CELESTE*'s crash.

Lena straightens in the same low-cut peasant blouse from the tavern draping across her arms and décolletage, but she's covered her shoulders in a deep Corbenic-blue cloak lined with silver embroidery. "When a ruckus broke out in my tavern, I took an underground route to the next inn, which let me witness you aiming a firelance straight into the Black Knight's ugly face. After he followed you, I found myself face to face with this little chap—"

She sets her arm next to Caldor's sharp talons, and it hops aboard. We pet the copper feathers at its chin.

"Caldor was covered in snow and ice, and nearly running out of steam." She shakes her head in amazement. "Never before have I seen such a magnificent illusion, my lady. You'll have to show me how it works."

I can't help but steal a second to be proud of Caldor; I open the compartment in its chest and pull out the reserve of Merlin's *jaseemat* for the bird. Lena watches me cast it into the steam valve, and when I utter the instructions to bring it to life, Caldor inflates with vitality and flits around the room, wingspan broadening past our arms.

"Magnificent!" Lena exclaims.

Her voice is loud, and with that, I run to the door and peek through the slice of light from the war outside this cabin. The Black Knight is occupied with Galahad's battle; the cannons have slowed as each aeroship repairs their sails and masts, but soon they'll start up again. I shut the door and rest my back against it, clicking over the lock and sliding a chair under the knob to keep it locked from both this side and the other. Caldor flits to the counter and tucks its feathers close to its body.

Lena's amazement fades for a somber look. "Where are we headed?"

"Greece. If we don't crash first." I strap the crossbow to my back, ensuring Merlin's sword is much more secure at my waist. The firelance is comfortable in my grasp.

"Let them worry about crashing," Lena says. She glances around the room. Her smile comes about her face easily and with a sort of zeal I can't help but envy, like this is not a terrifying predicament but a glorious adventure. "There's a trick to these sorts of aeroships. Weak spots, you see, that we could employ for the sake of commandeering this vessel. I learned all about them in Corbenic from old illusionists who showed me how to make rabbits disappear."

"Yes, I know," I reply. "I mean, I know of what you speak. But I have nothing I could use to expose their vulnerabilities." It feels strange talking to the real version of the girl I just saw in a memory, and I ignore the discomfort by studying the firelance she gave me. It's got a longer barrel than those from Camelot, and the chamber holds eight iron bearings rather than the six of Merlin's pistolník.

Lena stares at me, her lips pursed in thought before she speaks. "You all right, my lady? I thought you'd be relieved by the idea of hijacking a rogue aeroship."

"It's simply that…" I stare at the weapon in my hand and think about the dead shock on Morgan le Fay's face when I fired a bearing straight into her forehead. "Nothing. And you needn't call me that. I was just a handmaid." In fact, I should be the one addressing Lena as such, if she's a princess of Corbenic.

But Lena's silvery eyes shine at mine. "A lady is never *just* anything, Vivienne."

———

Hearing how Lena boarded the aeroship *MUERTE* through passageways in the village was remarkable. The Black Knight had been much too self-absorbed to realize the window to this cabin was poorly locked, and thus easy to pick. Marcus and Owen were more interesting playthings anyway, shackled on the ground while Lena cast her rope and grappling hook to scale the side of aeroship and shimmy up to the sill. Helping me escape once *MUERTE* had taken flight seemed safer than engaging the rogues in full out battle in the middle of a snowy meadow.

"Oh, the blond one saw me. I don't know if Marcus did, though," Lena tells me. "I never knew him to pay that much attention to things occurring in the background."

Her smile is subtle, but happy, and I know if I don't ask now, I'll never know for sure.

"You were friends in Corbenic."

Lena glances at me. "Yes." A moment passes, and Lena shows no sign of discomfort, but perhaps she doesn't know what Marcus means to me. "Didn't think I'd ever see him again, actually. But when the three of you arrived, I could tell with one look he'd taken some advice I'd given him long ago, and that brought me much delight." She turns her smile to me and reaches for my hand. "I'm happy for you. Or I will be, I suppose, once all this Grail nonsense is sorted out."

The next breath of air I take cleanses the idea of betrayal from my heart. Marcus wasn't with Lena during that month he was missing. But then... where was he?

I can't think about it now. "Why did you do this?" I ask, gesturing to the cabin. I pace in front of the door in case rogues would pass by and try to enter, or the Black Knight himself, and I'm more than ready to slam the door onto his fingers. "Did it ever cross your mind that perhaps you'd die on this ship?"

Lena leans against the wall and shrugs. "Not really. The world was already a dangerous place for me once I left Corbenic. I didn't know if I'd make it a week before I'd starve or be murdered or abducted for ransom."

With a giddy look in her eyes, she sneaks to the Black Knight's bar to help herself to a quick shot of absinthe, her eyebrows raised at mine. I shake my head. One trip into the mechanical eye of the Black Knight was enough for me, and one trip was all it took to lose my liking of green fairy.

"Besides," she adds, "this is the finish line now. Civilizations are closing in on Avalon, and according to the Black

Knight, you're the one who's going to find it. How could I *not* want to be a part of that? Aren't you thrilled?"

Thrilled. More like wobbling on a line between magic and fear. "I'm not sure it's as easy as that."

"It won't be," Lena says. "But even so, this is the dawn of something new. The Holy Grail is meant to balance the scales between the mechanical arts and magic. The world is going to change."

The world has already changed a hundredfold for me—I'm a prisoner flying through the clouds in the middle of a violent, bloody scrimmage.

And still, "How?" I ask. "Truly, I have no idea how something so mythical could even exist, and beyond that, I don't know how such a balance between two starkly different elements would work."

Lena's shoulders fall, but it's out of uncertainty and not defeat. "I don't know. But I'll stick around to find out. Can you imagine what sort of wonders must exist in Avalon?"

I want to indulge in a bit of fantasy and consider what the elusive castle in the clouds must be like. Staring out the window, I watch the stars drift by and listen to how silent the aeroship has become.

But then Galahad's aeroship drifts into my view.

Then closer.

And when it's close enough that I can make out the fine grain of the wood on its side, I feel my heart stop.

"Look out!" I shout, in time for both Lena and me to take cover.

The aeroship slams into *MUERTE* to cries echoing

above. The wooden beams lined in thin iron on the ceiling crack and crumble, and much of it falls over us. The floor shakes. I stand and look around as Lena does, brushing off the shards of wood from her sleeves and coughing in the fog of dust. I run to the window and peer out at Galahad's aeroship and the iron-tipped wing spiked with hooked prongs, able to grab an aeroship's body and yank parts of it free—oh God.

The wing is too far to reach from the window, but a plan shapes in my head. "Where are the passageways, Lena?" I turn to her. "If there were any in an aeroship, where would they be?" Merlin said Lena was an expert on these sorts of details. Certainly that's what he kept from me but told Marcus. Certainly.

Lena's face freezes in surprise, and I know she's wondering how I could ever realize this about her. But instead of questioning me, she says, "In the captain's cabin. Facing the stern."

She points, and I follow her finger toward the spirits' counter. On the other side is a mantle holding glasses and the Black Knight's absinthe decanter.

I run to it, gauging the perimeters of the wall and spotting a faint outline that's long since caked over with dust and age. The cannons are rising again, and I must be cautious. I press my ear to the wood and knock once: the sound echoes. Hollow. I push gently, and it's tightly sealed, but when I realize it swings on an axis, just like the stone wall to Merlin's catacombs, another nudge breaks it free of the wall.

Lena and I stare down a passageway dark and damp and full of cobwebs, beams of wood, metal gears. An impossible path while an aeroship is in motion, lest we would be crushed by the slamming steel pistons churning the ship's propeller.

Nevertheless, there's no other way, and I have little time before the Black Knight will try to free his aeroship from Galahad's grasp. And so Lena and I won't seek to commandeer this aeroship.

We'll escape from it.

"Lena," I say. "I'll need your rope."

———

We switch out my crossbow for her firelance, setting it across my back so it won't get caught in the folds of my dress or clatter against the pistons as I make my way through a hellish obstacle course. I pull back my hair and secure it atop my head in a spare steel netting of Lena's, my fingers trembling as I set the pins.

Lena watches me. "Let me do it."

I shake my head, glancing through the door. I've already begun memorizing the pattern of the pistons' rotations on the path to a solid wood door, taking me straight to what Lena and I believe is a chamber adjacent to the wing. I take off my shawl and furs and hand them to her, feeling the chill of winter bite at my exposed, wounded arm. The blood has started to dry, and the wound no longer throbs. I unsheathe Merlin's sword from my waist and give her the blade.

"Guard it."

She cocks an airy eyebrow. "I will. Better than you did."

Lena will stand watch until I've made it through to the wing; she'll follow me once, God willing, I can disengage the mechanisms from the other side, letting the aeroship glide across the currents. From then on, we might have minutes to cross to Galahad's aeroship—I'll have a thousand things to do all at once before the Black Knight notices the stalled ship, realizes Lena stowed away, and discovers we're both on the path toward escape. But I cannot think about the repercussions now.

Click, click, click go Caldor's wings as I add more *jaseemat* to its steam valve, bringing life to the falcon in a way only alchemy could. I usher the bird to my left shoulder and pray it doesn't drag its sharp talons across my neck to my unclothed right one.

I nod once at Lena, who returns it. She angles her body to face the door in case she'll need to fire her crossbow—hopefully not. I stand at the threshold of the pathway, my fingers hitting my leg in rhythm with the churning pistons. My eyes shut, and I listen. I could almost pretend I'm back inside the mechanical dragon, Victor, and my mission is to pour Azur's *jaseemat* inside the clockwork heart and iron lungs. I open my eyes and let them adjust to the dim light; on the other side, the outline of the wooden door tells me it'll take but a few seconds to get there.

The cannons boom loudly, and a crack of the ceiling straight above my head shocks me still.

"Don't think about it," Lena calls. "You cannot hesitate!"

She's right. I set my eyes on the door, blocking out the unstable feel of air under my feet, the deafening cries of rogues, the sharp metal scent of blood spilling from knights who might have made it to this aeroship's deck, or perhaps the other way around. The pistons slam against the propeller every two and a half seconds, but it's every tenth that there's a six-second gap. Long enough for a girl to get past five. If she's quick about it.

Slam! goes the first piston.

"One," I count. "Two. Thr—"

Slam! it goes again.

I step as close to the first piston as I dare, only inches away come the next two and a half second mark. I feel the wind as the heavy steel pillars pass me. Another cannon strikes the deck, and I shake enough that my hand accidentally catches on a piston, scratching most awfully against it. I wince, pulling further back, but only so that on the tenth second—

Slam!

I run.

I'm holding my breath, and I've got my skirt in my fists, and I'm running like my life depends on it, and surely it does, and Caldor chirps by my ear, and the damned thing might be sentient enough to be afraid. There are still three pistons to rush past, and the shuddering of the aeroship from another cannon sets me off-balance. I might be crushed, but my boot catches friction on the wooden path, and I can hear the winding up of the mechanism that would send the pistons straight into me, and it forces me faster, and just as the blocks of steel crash into each other, I reach the end and slam into the door.

My hands press against the blessed wood, and my ears fill with the split-second crashes. Below, the propeller spins like mad, and above, the Black Knight and his rogues cry orders to kill the knights, slice them, decapitate them, keep them alive long enough—

"Viv!" calls Lena from the other end.

I nod and look about for a way to open this door, praying I won't come face to face with any rogues in the meantime. It nudges open and leads to the navigation room—empty, thank God. A small box of a chamber, only big enough for perhaps two, and a world of pulleys and gears hanging from every part of the ceiling and walls. There's a table in the dead center covered in parchment and levers, the gauges likely measuring the aeroship's ascent, using the same knowledge as Merlin's navigational device. Caldor flies to a windowsill as I step up to the table. I have to turn off the propellers so Lena can pass through. And then we must use the wing hooked to escape to Galahad's aeroship. I glance past Caldor out the window—we're right above it.

I turn back to the controls. "All right, Vivienne, you can figure this out."

I'm the inventor who built Merlin's mechanical dragon. I'm the lady-in-waiting whose firelance shot and killed Morgan le Fay. I'm the girl who freed the Fisher King from his earthly curse. Surely, I can manage to override a few measly mechanisms.

"Can you, now? Or is that more pride talking?" Merlin's spirit whispers.

I shut my eyes at the memory of his voice and find myself wishing the old fool were really here.

"I am here, girl. Look around you."

I open my eyes, and the ghostly wisp of Merlin with his shocking gold-white irises materializes into the man I once knew. He rushes back to his form, and it's no longer the masked man who was about to transform into a dragon's spirit or even the smooth, easy-walking figure in the woods. Now he's the Merlin I know, with his inked skull and emerald-stone cane and the limp that requires it. His eyes are old, but his, and there's no longer any sharpness to his appearance.

"Vivienne."

I want to burst with happiness. And with only a smile, Merlin has lost years off his face. I rush forward and embrace him. His shaking hand clasps over the back of my head and holds me close as though he's just as shocked as I am that he made it here.

"How is this possible, Merlin? Did Azur—"

"No, girl. I still have much work to do."

The impossibility of it forces me to pull away. "Then how are you here? How can I touch you? Why did you take control of my aeroship and send me crashing to the countryside? Why aren't you helping Azur with the chaos in Jerusalem? Merlin, what happened?"

The sorcerer wields a long, slow breath. "So many questions whose terrible answers you already know." A glint of copper catches his eye, and he ducks his gaze to the sill, where Caldor sits. Merlin chuckles and reaches to scratch the mechanical falcon's chin. "Hello, old friend. Didn't think I'd get to see you again."

"Merlin," I breathe. I think of his hateful words, his taunts. "You were so cruel."

He sighs, and immediately, I've lost him to the void inside his mind. "I can't ask for your forgiveness for the monster I've become. Truthfully, I'll never deserve any pardon." A pause, and then, "Vivienne, do you know why you are so special?"

His words are strange, but more importantly, they're irrelevant now, too.

"I hold the coordinates to Avalon. How long have you known?"

"I always suspected, but I was never certain. There was much the Lady of the Lake and I never saw eye to eye on, and there was no way for me to confirm it, certainly. It was only when Morgan suspected, caught wind of it that day she tried to take you captive, that I guessed. But there's more to you than simply that."

Outside, rogues grow wild with the realization that Galahad has locked his ship to theirs. I think of Lena waiting in the Black Knight's cabin and wonder if they've caught her yet. I feel the weight of her firelance on my back, and I'll only have eight shots. "Merlin, what must I do now?"

He strains, as though to hold his form here is too much. "Azur will call me back soon, and his world needs help just as much as Camelot. You're on the right path, Vivienne. Whatever it takes, lead the knights to Avalon. Only you can pull back the concealment that keeps it safe. Only you. Otherwise, the future of Camelot will be lost, and there will be no other way to get it back." Sweat beads across his forehead from sheer exhaustion.

And suddenly, there's a banging sound at the Black Knight's door. I turn and look through the doorways at Lena's pale face and parted lips. "Vivienne!"

With utter desperation, I turn back to my mentor. "Merlin, help me take control of this aeroship!"

He smiles sadly as he fades into a ghost again. "I'm sorry." And then Merlin is gone.

Lena calls for me, but I do not move; I forget the thunderous slams at the door. Splinters of wood fly all around me from the cannons on Galahad's ship, catching in my hair, scratching my cheeks, forcing my eyes shut as they prick at my lids. But all of this feels like a dream.

"Vivienne!" Lena screams again, like her own blood is too hot and burning her alive.

It stuns me from the haze Merlin left me in, and I turn fast to see her watching me from the edge of the door, just as the Black Knight and his rogues burst inside from above deck. Instantly, her crossbow's only bolt flies into the chest of the closest rogue, and Lena casts the empty weapon aside.

In front of me is a lever, and it shines like copper in twilight, and I don't know what it'll do, but I grab it with both hands and yank it forward. The aeroship sputters, and the pistons slow and pull back, leaving a clear path for Lena to run through just as the Black Knight's mechanical eye, black and twisted and clicked forward, falls upon us.

"Run, Lena!" I scream.

And she does. She has more weapons in her hands, and as the Black Knight points at us, Lena spins on her heels to fire her fusionah at the rogues sent after her. The bearings are disastrously potent—they strike the chests of a few unlucky rogues with shards of metal that burrow deep, bloody holes into their bones instead of the clean deaths the bearings of Camelot offer.

The Black Knight follows. Lena fires at him, but she

must be missing her target because still he walks slowly for us. Calm, deadly calm. Too angry even to crack an expression.

Once Lena makes it to my side, she slams the door shut, the Black Knight still in his private quarters. I push all my weight onto the lever to restart the pistons, crying out as I move it back into place. The aeroship springs to life again. The pistons churn against one another, and the propeller restarts. As it happens, the rogues unfortunate enough to be caught in the crossfire cry out as they're crushed. My eyes shut, but that only makes it worse, because then I can hear the crunching of their bones. "Oh God."

Lena presses the door slightly ajar, and together we peer into the passageway leading to the Black Knight's cabin. He stands there, watching, unmoving. He hasn't attempted to cross the churning pistons; he stayed behind, and he's unaffected by the deaths of his men. I don't know what he might do, but before I can wonder out loud to Lena, he leaves his cabin.

Lena and I edge the door shut. I consider the means of torture to come if we're caught.

"We need to lock ourselves in here." I run to the control room's door and lean against it. "Give me the sword!"

Lena tosses it to me, and I catch the hilt. The door has a heavy iron ring built into it, and the latch is strong, and I slam the blade between both to keep it from budging open. But as I do so I have to laugh through my exhaustion—this won't stop a demigod. It'll only buy me a minute, at best.

Lena and I face the glass window. She lifts her skirt to

her knees, revealing thigh-high black boots with a heavy heel. With one kick, that heel slams through the glass, and the window shatters into the sky. She uses the butt of her fusionah to slice away any sharp remnants, and together we stare at the stretched silk wing of *MUERTE* and the diabolically hooked wing of Galahad's aeroship. The wings' masts connecting both are slim, but they're flattened and rough, and someone could certainly cross them in the most ideal of circumstances. Winds blow around us, and it'll be nearly impossible to switch aeroships as we fly so close to the heavens.

Nonetheless, Lena grabs my hand. "Come on!"

"Wait." I release Lena's rope—heavy on my shoulder as it is thick—as Lena stands guard with her fusionah aimed at the door. We have little time, but I have to steal a minute.

I drop into a crouch and usher Caldor down my arm, copper talons that much colder with the glacial airs surrounding us.

"What are you doing?" Lena cries, her melodious voice mixed with the wind's song.

"I have to send word." And this might be the only chance I get—I cannot use mirrors anymore, and Azur must know I've left Camelot. He must know about Rufus and Marcus and the Black Knight and the aeroships that arrived. He must know how I found myself here. Seizing a piece of parchment from the table, I recall the events until now in as little script as I can manage and set the folded message inside the belly of the bird. I spill the rest of the *jaseemat* into its valve. God help me—there is no more after this. "To Jerusalem, Caldor."

The mechanical falcon chirps, its valve shuts, and I cast it out the window. Caldor swoops and swerves on the mighty winds, steering away from the rainfall of iron seeking Galahad's aeroship and *MUERTE* just the same. I watch it fly, just like a real falcon, its source of life the last of the sorcerer's alchemic dust.

I can't help but think that it's as it should be, and that if Caldor runs out of steam before it reaches Azur Barad, at least the falcon went down with the same alchemic life it was born with.

THIRTY

Galahad's aeroship has its talons tight into *MUERTE*'s wing. I stare into the blowing wind at my destination and plan for its impossible fruition. Aboard, knights aim heavy cannons at the Spanish rogues. My heart leaps with joy at the sight of Percy alive, though a little worse for wear, his ragged, brown hair in his eyes and a thick beard across his jaw. He relays Galahad's orders to the others with his usual zeal, and I know for sure that none of them will rest until the Black Knight is defeated. I'm certainly not in this alone.

My plan is to aim the grappling hook at the railing of the aeroship so it can guide Lena and me as we walk from our wing to theirs. With one unexpected gust of wind, we could fall to our deaths. Rope is more than a simple luxury.

I tighten the excess around my wrist three times for safety's sake. And then I step onto the window's ledge and set my back flush against the ship's body. I shouldn't look down—I know this. But as I grip the wood behind me, I feel the wind cast its power, and though the sail's mast has a rough surface, my boots lose their grip. Before I know it, I'm looking down at the swirls of clouds spinning below me the way an autumn breeze might conjure leaves to dance. I exhale loudly at the sight—oh God, there's no land beneath me, and even more terrifying are the churning propellers that might chop me into bits on my fall through the clouds. My hand slams over my eyes, against the tears gathering on my lashes.

Then, "Vivienne!" comes from the other aeroship.

I open my eyes to Percy leaning over the railing. His usually stoic face is wrought with panic at seeing me. "Cease fire! Galahad! Cease fire! Prisoners aboard!" He drops to his knees at his post. "God's sake, Viv! Get back inside!"

Stubbornly, I shake my head and lift the grappling hook. I'll need to step out onto the wing's mast, and this will be the biggest risk of all. The aeroships spin wildly in the sky, and the Black Knight's rogues are trying to free themselves from Galahad's grasp. But I stand directly under them, and they haven't spotted me. Yet.

I lower myself into a crouch, ignoring the hair across my eyes, the cold so sharp against my skin, the cannons and the endless taunts of death. The line is tight around the hook, and I swing it several times to gain momentum, careful to keep the points from catching onto *MUERTE*'s sails, and then with a strong step and a loud cry, I cast it, and it lands straight on the wooden railing of Galahad's aeroship, only feet from Percy's reach. He runs to it and ensures the hold is tight just as I've thrown the excess line back to Lena. She catches it and ties it around the iron ring of the door, looping it into the lock.

I fling myself back against the aeroship, my forehead against the rough wood. The wind rises beneath me, tasting like salt in water or blood spilling over the sides of both these great and terrible vessels.

"Ready!" Lena calls.

I open my eyes as she rushes to my side. We look across the winds at Percy, and I can't believe I have the strength to speak. "We're two, and we're coming across!" I call to him.

Galahad arrives, the gallant knight much older now than the twenty-five years he should be. Dark circles line his eyes like shadows, and blood tinges his lip. He spots me, and his voice is commanding when he shouts, "Vivienne, stay there!"

Again, I shake my head. Cries from above deck shout for the sorceress of Camelot, for the girl with the coordinates. For me. I scan Galahad's aeroship at the infantry so much sparser than it was in the spring. Marcus isn't with them. So he did go to retrieve the signet for the Black Knight. He put me above defeating the demigod. He put me above the Holy Grail.

I cannot think about that now. With both hands around the line, I guide myself upright and step away from the body of *MUERTE*. My feet are trembling, and I'm holding my breath, and Lena calls to me to be careful, but I have to ignore everything—debris from the shards of splintered wood, the burning stench of the cannons. I have to cross. I focus on the width of the sail's mast and follow it step by step, reaching the halfway point to the iron talons of Galahad's ship. I haven't taken a full breath in nearly a minute, and I'm shaking like mad and holding tightly enough to the line that I'm sure it's burned into my palms. I don't realize I'm crying until I look up at Percy's terrified eyes, one of his hands tight around the embedded grappling hook, the other extended toward me.

"A little further, just a little further! Come on, Viv!"

Behind him, Galahad shouts at his knights, "Ready to

release them! On my command!" He holds his hand upright, and the other knights wait, but then Galahad's eyes flicker behind me, steadying on Lena, I'm sure. Lena, who hasn't stepped onto the mast yet. No, not when it might jostle the line and send one or both of us plummeting into the sky beneath.

My feet are at the edge of the sail, where the wood starts to bend from my weight. I press my toe to it for an idea of its strength, and a gust of wind forces me back another step.

I can't breathe, I can't breathe, and now I know I've gone too far. I should have gone north instead of searching for Marcus and Owen. I should have stayed in the clock tower instead of finding myself in these damned skies, forcing my own people to save me instead of defeating a man of magic.

"Oh God!" I cry, my fists tight around the line, my teeth chattering from cold and fright.

Percy and Galahad won't give up. Percy leans further toward me, his hand so close to mine. "You can do this, Viv! A little further! Don't look down!"

But I cannot move.

"Ready to release!" Galahad shouts, a somber look back at Lena.

"No!" I shout. I cannot leave Lena to die.

A whipping sound slices past my ear, and I jump. A bearing hits one of the iron talons. I scream. Someone shot at me. I know who.

From my periphery, I see Galahad and Percy fire relentlessly at the aeroship I'm escaping from. But I'm a wounded sheep in the middle of a field, and they're about to send in the dogs to finish me off. I want to scream at Percy to give up, to defeat the Black Knight, to let me go.

But then an arm goes around my waist, holding me upright.

"Hold on, Vivienne!" Lena says. She's followed me onto the mast. Merlin's sword is against her back. The line is tight in her grasp, and she lifts her own fusionah at the rogues above deck trying to knock us off.

Her aim is ruthless. Two fall over the railing, streams of blood trailing in the air from their chests.

I could nearly forget we're between two aeroships in the middle of a war in the skies. I glance over my shoulder at Galahad organizing a defense while Percy waits to catch my eye. "Come on!" he shouts.

Rogues are making their way toward us on the wing, and the footing I've found is more stable than Lena's. I draw Merlin's sword from her back and step in front of her protectively, though it might not do anything in the slightest.

"Go, Lena." I'll guard her as she crosses, as she's more liable to fall than me. Only a few steps…

Lena finds herself in Percy's range. He grabs her wrist and pulls her to the aeroship's side. As the devil-eyed rogues make their way closer, I take a careful step backward.

Suddenly, the Black Knight appears on deck with his long, elegant firelance. I feel time slowing as he lifts his weapon to his green eye and squints, aiming. I feel the air whipping around me. *Fires.* I drop to the mast in time to miss the shot that strikes Galahad's aeroship instead. My scream overwhelms the blast.

But then I look at the splintered mast, married to the other aeroship by way of iron claws, and realize what the Black Knight meant to do.

Galahad's aeroship pulls away from *MUERTE* with Lena aboard. The Black Knight's aim knocked free the talons. I whip back to face the devil himself. He smiles a smile of triumph and aims again. The line tethering the aeroships snaps, and I must clutch *MUERTE*'s splintered mast to hold on for dear life.

"Viv!" Percy shouts, the taste of blood in his words.

I wait for the fall, but it never comes. There's no wind racing me toward the ground, no burst of ice from the winter skies, no propellers slicing my limbs from my body. No—when I open my eyes, I see the Black Knight's arm outstretched for me. I see myself hovering above the breaking wing. I feel that familiar taste of honey in the air and hear the whispered words of forbidden magic in my mind.

I'm torn from the space and thrown onto the main deck of the enemy ship. I land with a crunch, a wince sprawling across my face and Merlin's sword at my side. Around me, some of the Black Knight's rogues circle as the rest fight the knights of Camelot for reign of the skies.

Galahad's aeroship has lost the edge to one of its wings because of the Black Knight's perfect shot. It sets the knights' aeroship into a tailspin, and they're too preoccupied with staying alive to fire back, and Lena is screaming so ferociously at losing me to *MUERTE* that she's just barely pulled over the railing. I hold my breath, my hand over my mouth as I watch the spectacle in horror. A long minute later, when the aero-ship is too far off to make out fully, I swear the sails regain balance and stability. I have to believe they saved themselves.

The Black Knight doesn't watch his enemies struggle to stay alive, because now we're too far ahead for them ever to catch up.

"Wind in the sails!" he shouts to his rogues, who scurry around adjusting masts and lines to gain speed.

The Black Knight briefly eyes me like I'm a mirage after weeks of wandering a barren desert. He lifts an eyebrow.

"Lady Vivienne, you've caused me a lot of trouble." Then he gestures to a nearby rogue. "Kindly take her weapon before I use it on her myself—"

He bites on the words like he's holding his temper together with nothing but a lone thread.

"Or we can do this in a way that allows me the *sincere* pleasure of tearing off the limbs of Lady Vivienne's cham-pion."

Before they can so much as touch me, I yank my fire-lance free and point it at the Black Knight. I let the bear-ings fly free, damn it all. Slam straight into his forehead. His green eye turns strange and shifts in color so that it is more golden now. I pull back and watch, wondering if I was able to kill the Black Knight, and pray the bastard will fall quickly so that I might claim control of *MUERTE*.

But the Black Knight cocks his head at a strange angle, and his lips form a straight line. "You forget, Lady Vivienne. Death is no match for me. Not by a mere mortal, anyway."

The bearing pushes itself from his skull and drops to the

aeroship's wooden floor, clanking by his boots. He rolls his head on his neck, and as the blood on his forehead disappears, the skin around it closes up.

I clench my teeth in anguish, swearing under my breath as I fire again and again, until I've run out of ammunition, and there's nothing left for me to do but throw the gun at him as he laughs.

I've failed.

THIRTY-ONE

The Black Knight steps toward me, the girl he cannot hurt.

Firelances may be useless, but maybe the sharpness of a blade is a stronger threat. I retrieve Merlin's sword from the deck as the Black Knight comes closer. Perhaps I'll be able to slice the bastard into pieces, but what if it's not enough? What if his bones are like steel? What if he's more machine than I originally thought, like Mordred?

Nevertheless, "Stay where you are," I say, hoping my voice won't give way to fear.

The Black Knight's gaze falls upon Merlin's sword, and he shifts away from me. "Where did you get that blade?"

I hold it higher, and Merlin's sword shines. "You know whose it is."

The Black Knight recoils, fingers curling into claws and inching towards his mechanical eye in a way that indicates fright.

Do you know what it means to see a rogue whose eye-patch is gold, darling? It means he once battled a worthy opponent; not someone in passing, but a well-respected enemy.

I grind my gaze into his. "It was Merlin who took your eye."

The Black Knight's mouth quivers involuntarily. A desire

for vengeance crosses his face in a dangerous way. "Give it to me so I can destroy it."

A current of air gliding us through the clouds throws the entire aeroship into a spin of wind and sunlight, and my footing stumbles from its ferocious stance. Suddenly, the Black Knight has seized Merlin's sword from my grasp and holds it to my throat.

He won't kill me, I tell myself, though I gasp at the sudden move I was too slow to see. *He won't kill me. He can't.*

"Although," he continues with a smile of satisfaction, "this *is* a rather fine weapon." Then, "Take her below deck," he barely whispers.

And then rogues swarm me by the dozen. As they do, my patience reaches its limit, crossing the border into desperation.

"You'll never get to Avalon! I swear it! For as long as I live, I'll never tell you where it is!" I shout as loudly as I can, and through it all, the Black Knight responds with not a word.

His vile men take me down the stairs, past the monster's cabin, straight to a cell. Two guard me, looking as though they'd love to slice me into pieces.

The winds lift *MUERTE* into the clouds, denying me the chance to hear the echoes of my protests. I stand at the door, and my hands clutch the iron bars. "You'll *hang* first, you bastard! Merlin's sword will take your second eye, but it'll be in my grasp when it does!"

"Shut it, you." A guard's fusionah slams against my fingers until I pull back, the sharp pain throbbing my hands. "Bad luck having a woman on a ship, but this one is a league of her own." The voice grows quieter as the rogues leave back up the steps.

The room is small and dark, and a strong current pushes me straight into the wall. I fall to the cold floor and curl my legs up to my chest. Tears come quickly, tiring but cleansing. With no one around to comfort me, the sobs in my throat are heavy and deep. I sit for a long time, willing away the anguish. And then I do something I've been dying to do ever since I left Camelot, since I took *CELESTE* into the skies, leaving Marcus's father behind, since I ran from Marcus and Owen at the inn.

I fall asleep.

——————

There's a small window in my cell that lets me see the blue sky and an occasional puffed cloud. Birds are no strangers to aeroships, even the large ones—hawks and falcons and other birds of prey who take to the high skies. They soar past me, free, while I press my cheek against the windowsill and watch. The Black Knight has kept me locked in here for the past day and a half, and it's been maddening not knowing where the knights are, or Lena, or whether any of them are even still alive.

I glance at my feet, next to which sits a china plate with delicacies such as pistachio-flavored pastries, cinnamon-dusted crumpets, and bland, sugarless tea. Even the most loathed prisoner, it seems, should have afternoon refreshments, regardless of her crimes.

Loud footsteps startle me, and I sit upright. More rogues—two, from the sound of it. They reach my door and peer through the iron beams. One sets his long face prickled with black whiskers against the bars. "We're taking you to the main deck."

They pry the door open and seize my arms, pulling me up the stairs before I can gather the strength to argue.

Above deck is like being transported to another world.

I breathe in the saltiness of the air and look around. But the ear-splitting thumps from the aeroship's mechanisms below are enough to stimulate my imagination into coming up with all sorts of torturous ideas they might soon inflict upon me.

The Black Knight is a vision in a crimson robe lined in black leather, though not weighted with it. He smiles when he sees me.

"Ah, right on time. Lady Vivienne."

He leads me to the bow. Merlin's blade finds its place at my neck, cold and sharp, and I can already feel its ruthless bite against my skin. "I present the Great Sea of the Mediterranean and the Grecian shores," the Black Knight declares.

Tall, skinny trees with branches bright green breach the aeroship's railings. There's no sense of death or desolation—it's as though lifting the Fisher King's curse has rendered this land fruitful, too. The sea is a sheet of sparkling diamond water both loud and boisterous with power, and tranquil and soothing as night. In the distance is an aeroship port with the telltale rogues' dead-bones-and-cogs emblems marking each ship while bands of them run about, readying sails for the quest to seek Avalon.

Avalon.

I sneak a hopeful glance at the sun-soaked sky, remembering what both the Fisher King and Merlin said—the kingdom whose coordinates I know will only appear once I reveal it. The rogues and the Black Knight himself look about obsessively for the lost kingdom in this plethora of rich sea life, but they haven't looked high enough. Nor have they seen the strange shape of clouds that have cloaked themselves, where the sunlight is a little more golden, and the depth of the sky, a little more fitted. I stare harder, and I can see it: Avalon, a floating city in the clouds made of gold and shining even more brightly so. The path of the Fisher King has led us here.

"Lower the sails! And keep your eyes on the skies for the knights hot on our trail!" the Black Knight calls to the response of much laughter. He tilts his head toward mine and whispers, "They're not here yet, but have faith, darling. I don't think Sir Marcus is about to let you pay the price for the Holy Grail."

With the curve of Merlin's blade in the corner of my eye, I glance down the long spread of the Grecian shores at sands so infinite and so white, like the sun spilled its whole self to live by the waters forever. It doesn't seem like any place could be more beautiful. I search for riders or horses or even aeroships Marcus and Owen might have employed, but there is no one, and I'm terrified of what'll come to pass once they arrive.

"And then there's the question of the Lady of the Lake's prophecy," the Black Knight continues. My pulse quickens against the blade at my throat.

I force myself to remain stoic, but I truly don't know what he means, or if he really is just referring to the coordinates locked away in my mind. But it must be about Marcus.

"You won't kill him," I whisper, deciding we speak of the same thing. "You won't kill him because then you would never get the Grail." I'm not afraid to look him straight in the eye as clouds weave through us.

The Black Knight smiles in reassurance. "Who, Sir Marcus? Oh, Lady Vivienne, I wouldn't dare of it. He has a much more interesting fate awaiting him."

"What does that mean?" I say through viciously gritted teeth.

The Black Knight jets an eyebrow high, setting his gaze on a spot in the distance. "Your knight approaches."

I whip toward the shore, and the brightness of the sun reflecting upon the sands nearly blinds me, but as my eyes adjust, I make out a lone rider. Above, the sensation of the Grail's allure is so strong, like nothing else could possibly exist unless I were first to deny myself air. The soft gallops in the sand grow louder, only drowned out by the jeers and shouts coming from the rogues behind me.

The rider comes into focus—Marcus, with no sign of my brother anywhere. Marcus, whose hair is wild and scattered across his face. Marcus, whose eyes are bruised and blackened, and even without a dusting of kohl, they're as dark as night. Marcus, whose lip is bloodied. Whose face is exhausted, deluded, and mixed with the kind of wrath I've only ever known Owen to have.

"Marcus, no," I whisper too low for even the Black Knight to hear.

"Welcome back to Greece, Sir Marcus!" the Black Knight calls, Merlin's blade now holstered and a firelance steady in his grasp, aimed at its target as the aeroship floats above the sands.

When Marcus's heavy eyes fall upon mine, his expression softens. But when he sees the Black Knight, his brows draw together in fury. He clutches the reins of his horse tightly lest he would lose his temper.

He reaches inside his thick cloak and furs—he never took the time to remove them in this heat—and withdraws a heavy, marble signet. Two fingers stained red from the make-shift cotton bandage soaked around his wounded hand hold it high. "Shall I cast it into the sea? Let Lady Vivienne go."

The Black Knight lowers his lips to my ear. "Remember your mother, darling," he whispers. He leads me toward the stairs, pushing me down the first two. Rogues behind him cackle. "Does he have what I need?"

I have to focus. I squint into the bright sunlight at the signet in Marcus's hand. "Yes," I whisper. God knows how he managed to retrieve it from the icy lake.

Suddenly, I'm pushed in full view of Marcus, and the deadly click of the Black Knight's firelance sounds loudly beside my ear. "The signet, Sir Marcus, and you can have your *wench*."

Rogues laugh and taunt at a near-deafening volume. I almost expect Marcus to leap off his horse, run at the aero-ship himself, and slam the Black Knight straight into the splintered mast behind him. To act in haste, as he did when he discovered Owen had told all of Camelot about Lancelot and Guinevere's affair.

But Marcus is deadly calm, as though the months away from Camelot forced unnatural patience upon him. Or maybe not.

"You heard me. Vivienne walks free right now, or I'll rip your fucking eye out."

The Black Knight's eyebrows lift. He glances at his rogues, who offer mocking chuckles. "The boy speaks like a man!" he shouts. Then softer, to me, "He asks for his own death with words like that."

I cannot think of how this might be the moment when the Lady of the Lake's prophecy becomes truth. For Marcus to die—

No. Good is supposed to *triumph*—it has to. It always did in the fairy stories Owen told me through gaslit shadows and silent nights.

The Black Knight throws me into three more rogues who seize my arms, and I'm too weak to fight back.

They take me off the ship and toss me into the sand just as Marcus leaps off his horse, dashing for me and wrapping his arms around me. I sink into his embrace, more at home now than ever, and he brushes the hair from my eyes, but all I can think of is my mother and how Marcus's father is still alive, and maybe it's too late for any of this.

Suddenly, about ten rogues swarm Marcus and yank us apart. "Marcus!" I shout.

Their firelances click back and ready, all pointed at his heart.

Marcus watches each with hesitation, but his face is wiped of surprise. He glances at me. "You won't tell him the coordinates. Please say so. You wouldn't."

But this might be what the Lady of the Lake saw—this, right here, right now. God help me, I cannot let that happen if I have the ability to change it. "I'm not going to let you die," I whisper. "I have to tell him."

He stares right at me, those beautiful, stormy eyes so happy and hopeful once. "No, you don't—"

One of the Black Knight's rogues seizes the marble signet from Marcus's grasp, and he makes no move to stop that. They back away onto the aeroship, their aims steady on Marcus.

"Lady Vivienne, the coordinates."

My name is spoken through impatient, clenched teeth. It's spoken with power held over another, power I hate and wish I could overcome, and yet, I hesitate. I duck my head to the side to peer at the monstrous demigod behind me.

The Black Knight waits. He waits and waits, and my silence is long enough to assert my refusal to speak. He nods suddenly, as though he knows this, even if he might cast death upon those from Camelot through whatever anarchy the Holy Land holds.

"Very well," he says. "Kill the knight."

Rogues lift their weapons and aim, and I realize now Marcus's role has been played out, in the Black Knight's opinion. Completely dispensable. Now able to die.

"No!" I scream.

The Black Knight leans on the side of the aeroship beside rogues boasting firelances too large to be conventional: iron-barreled and resting on each man's shoulder, all aimed at Marcus. "Ah. Because there *is* something our heroine wants. Let's try again, then, shall we? The *coordinates*, love."

I breathe in sharply.

"Vivienne—" Marcus says behind me, his voice heavy with exhaustion and defeat, and his gaze on the firelances aimed to kill him if I choose not to oblige.

The Black Knight flicks an eyebrow. "I'll call your bluff, darling. Is this really the fate you'll choose for him?" But instead of ordering his rogues to fire, he raises his own firelance and clicks the hammer back, aiming with purpose, and I can already see how close the shot is to being freed into the air.

My heart falters. "Stop!" I shout. The Black Knight pulls back his aim and waits, bold enough to tempt my wrath and that of the Lady of the Lake when we're so close to water.

But she is nowhere to be found, and so I glance skyward and dig into the place in my mind where there are more instructions now, but for me alone. Instructions as to how to peel back sky and time and space and magic and illusion to show the world what sort of power the Grail boasts.

It'll be because of my own selfishness that I reveal Avalon to the world. And I will it so. My eyes fall shut. I feel the warmth of this land and the sinking feeling of the sand beneath my boots, and suddenly, everything becomes more golden, and I hear the awestruck cries of the Spanish rogues on the Black Knight's aeroship. I open my eyes to see it for myself.

The entire sky fills with a floating island, whose ground has been pried from the earth and soars toward the Holy Land. The castle shines, gleams, sparkles more brightly than gemstones. There are towers and parapets striking the sky.

And despite the grandeur of this elegant kingdom, despite its size and marvel, it's as far away as perhaps the moon and stars. It's a journey itself, just to gaze upon it.

Beside me, Marcus's eyes fill with amazement, and on the Black Knight's aeroship, the demon himself has to stagger back a few feet in order to see it properly.

"All this time, you've been hiding in the sky, you beautiful world," he says through a mischievous smile. "Start a course for Avalon!" he calls to his bewildered men, who frantically move about to get the aeroship airborne.

"Start a course!" one cries.

"Secure the lateen!" calls another.

I panic. The Black Knight is going to leave before I get what he promised. I run toward *MUERTE*, wind spilling around my hair and dress and behind me Marcus calling my name.

"Where are they?" I cry frantically, running as close as I can get to the aeroship's bird-like wings. "You promised. You made a deal. Where did you send them?" Marcus grabs my arm and holds me, his touch letting me know he's there, he's here, he's not going anywhere.

But the Black Knight looks down upon me with pity. "Darling, really. I never *actually* promised to tell you their fate. If you don't believe me, you can look into my eye at the memory for yourself." He pauses and removes his golden eye-patch so he can stare at the glory of Avalon through his mechanical eye. "Besides, Lady Vivienne, with your alchemist mentor in a city I've taken for myself, you have much bigger problems ahead of you."

He might have already sent word to have the subjects of Camelot be executed or tortured. An entire kingdom of people. My mother.

The Black Knight's teeth shine between his smile as he lures my wrath. His firelance lifts high, and I see how the next blast will be reserved for Marcus, but when I step forward, he pauses. A mutual understanding regarding Marcus and the element of water next to me, and perhaps he momentarily regrets the death he so carelessly threatened upon my beloved.

And so he sheathes his firelance. "Enjoy your last days, knight." He tears away from us to order his aeroship higher.

There's a spell in my head, a thief of magic that wants to break free. For Marcus. For Merlin. For the chance to be rid of this. For the chance at another life.

Don't... comes from a place inside my mind, from that of someone who shares my cursed name. *Don't give into magic. Be strong. This is not your destiny. You can choose. Remember how you're being tested.*

Tested. Tested by her and the Black Knight and Merlin and the Fisher King—all treating me like a plaything, a doll with strings like the ones I saw back in Lena's port-side village. Keeping the truth of the Perilous Lands from me. Merlin crashing my aeroship to the ground, straight in Marcus's path. Being told Marcus's future was betrayal or death. The strange words Marcus said as he left the inn room.

Merlin, you monster.

What sort of hell are the demigods sending us through? Why would Merlin put so much magic in place just so that I would have to avoid it? He really is a monster.

MUERTE ascends. The Black Knight will claim the Grail, and perhaps he'll keep it for himself instead of selling it to the highest bidder, as Gawain speculated, making the demigod unstoppable if he ever desired to take the rest of the world for himself. I watch *MUERTE* soar into the clouds toward a world I promised he would never see.

The Black Knight, now bearer of Merlin's prized sword, at that, will see Avalon before I will. And this might be the worst part of all.

THIRTY-TWO

Marcus seizes his pistolník and fires like a madman. The aeroship breaks over the currents of the wind and sails higher. Bearings ricochet off the masts rendering *MUERTE* unharmed.

"God damn it!" he curses.

We watch the Spanish rogues escape to a faraway cloud of shining towers and jagged parapets and bridges with ivory molding and oh the Holy Grail inside. Just as I saw it in my mind all those years. "Avalon," I say through a quivering, breakable voice.

But Marcus doesn't care. He lets his pistolník fall to the sand and grasps my face with both hands.

"God," he says. "Are you all right? What deal did he mean? Vivienne, I didn't know if I'd ever see you again." All calmness dropped, he's frantic and terrified.

I wrap my arms around his neck as he embraces me. "I'm so sorry, Marcus. I thought..." My fingers ache to soothe the bruises forming on his cheekbones from God knows what brawl. I want to admit my hastiness, my pride, is what got us here, but a wild exhaustion twisted up in disappointment pauses me from that thought and turns my focus elsewhere. "Why did you go back to my aeroship? I had to reveal Avalon, and you just gave him the signet! Why didn't you go with Galahad and Percy to—"

"Because I love you." He rests his forehead against mine. "Avalon be damned. The Grail be damned."

I remember our fight on that dead winter evening with silent snowflakes floating around us. I thought Marcus had been with Lena. In this Mediterranean paradise, it seems like a lifetime ago, but it was only two days. I'm about to speak, to apologize for all that happened as a result of my stupid jealousy, to return the words he just told me, but all I can do is collapse onto the sand as he falls with me.

This wouldn't have happened had I never run off; it never would have happened had I simply told Marcus about the Lady of the Lake's prophecy or heard him out about Lena before the Black Knight could tell me first.

"I'm sorry, Marcus. All I could think of is the Lady of the Lake, and then what Owen said, and Lena was there, and, oh God, this is all my fault." I repeat my words over and over through my pathetic sobs until they get muffled into the air.

Marcus brushes my hair from my face. "What? What do you mean? What are you talking about?"

I take a deep breath, feeling the sobs subside, but just barely. "I left Camelot when Sir Kay told us you'd gone missing, and it changed things. The Lady of the Lake wasn't sure if your future would entail death or betrayal. Or if Camelot would even get the Grail, and..."

I gesture to the gold-filled sky and the Black Knight's aeroship on its way toward it.

"We've lost. All because I thought—"

"Hold on." He wipes the sleeve of his tunic across his tired eyes. "I don't understand. You thought I betrayed...you? You thought I betrayed you with Lena?"

Shamefully, I nod.

He breathes out long and slow. "Don't tell me you thought—" He bites his lip at the sheer idea, and his shining eyes glance around at the empty seas and sands before finding me again. "Vivienne. It's only ever been you."

His words cast a warmth over me. "But you were so distant." My voice is pathetic as I say it, but I have to know.

"Because I thought the Grail was impossible, and to return empty-handed would mean no chance to relinquish my knighthood. Or it would mean exile. There was no hope, unless we were to..."

He pauses, his lips slightly parted, as though he's about to ask the same thing he'd asked so many months ago, when the people of Camelot took all they owned to escape a kingdom haunted and damned. When his hands captured my tear-stained face in the privacy of the royal stables. *Leave with me.*

And we could. We could run away to another world and leave all this behind.

But it's not about that anymore. Merlin said Azur would need the Grail to defeat the rogues. Jerusalem will fall and people will die if we don't stop the Black Knight.

I touch Marcus's face with my fingertips. "Someone once told me there was always hope when it was a question of whether we should love."

Marcus breathes out long and slow, eyes heavy with tears and exhaustion. Then he smiles, just as he did six months ago.

A boyish smile. A smile that tells me my words have loosened a weight on his shoulders.

But I haven't said everything just yet. I glance at my sandy hands and silently beg Marcus to forgive me for what else I must tell him. "When I saw the Fisher King—"

I pause, uncertain of how to say it. Marcus is here, and he's listening, and he'll hate me for this, and I cannot put it off any longer.

"Marcus, your father is alive," I say quietly.

For a long time, he doesn't move. He stares like he might not have heard me. His lip quivers, and he frowns, forming his mouth as though to ask *What?* but losing the will as he pulls away.

"I'm sorry," I whisper, breathing my apology. "Marcus, I'm so sorry. He helped me free the Fisher King in the Perilous Lands. It would have been impossible without him. He stayed in the infirmary after Morgan's war and only left to forge the sword Guinevere knighted you with. He watched the ceremony, Marcus." I think of the tall, dark figure leaving the grand hall after Marcus was made a knight of Camelot and wonder again how I could have missed it.

Marcus's eyes widen, and he stumbles to his feet, momentarily losing his balance in the sand. He runs to his horse's saddle, where his sword has been holstered, and pulls it out of the mechanism. He studies the blade, the hilt, finding a small artisan signature engraved into the steel.

"I thought it was a spare they'd had, or ... "

I stand, but I do not move to his side. I watch his hand clamp over his mouth as the fullness of the truth comes over him. I watch his shoulders slouch and shake from the same sadness I saw in him when the farmlands in Camelot burned.

"Marcus, I—"

He faces me. "How could you not tell me this?" he shouts, throwing the blade across the sand and letting it stick out of the ground. "You've known this whole time and you didn't say a *thing*? How could you *keep* something like that from me?"

My face is wet with tears, and my fingers steeple over my mouth as I watch him pull back to curse into the air, his anger echoing wildly against the sky.

I find my breath. "I thought you'd want to return—"

"*Of course* I want to return, Vivienne! Do you think I actually *wanted* to be a knight? I only did this for their sake! So their deaths would mean something! Were you so set on keeping my status raised to that of a knight's that you felt such a horrible lie necessary?"

I should be devastated that all of this is coming out of him now, but then a surge of anger comes over me. "That's not why I didn't tell you! Do you think me that shallow, Marcus, just because I grew up inside the castle instead of in the farmlands? There are people in the world who need the Grail more than ever—"

"No." His anger subsides only a bit, and he shakes his head. "It's not my problem."

"And had we returned to Camelot empty-handed, there would have been no way to help them! Are you too selfish to see how the Grail—"

"*Selfish?*" he shouts, matching my voice's volume. "After

all the years you worked with Merlin, can you honestly say this has *nothing* to do with wanting to know more about the Grail? It's the only *logical* reason you're here."

I feel my eyes widen in vehement anger. "I left Camelot because the people I care about in Jerusalem are in danger! And because Kay told us you were missing for a month! A *month*, Marcus! And you won't tell me where you were? I had every right to assume you'd betrayed Camelot *or* me."

His eyes fall shut. "You know the truth. I didn't betray anyone. Especially you."

"Then you'll die, Marcus!" I shout, and now I know his death is inevitable. I cannot stop the welling tears from spilling over my cheeks. "Marcus, I can't just wait for you to die."

And maybe we could go back to Camelot, to the safety of the Lady of the Lake's protection. But what if my failure has undone her promise and Camelot is just as deadly a place for Marcus to be as these shores with their scents of war and rogues? Jerusalem was attacked, why wouldn't our home be next? At least here in Greece, I'm with Marcus—if I were locked up in Camelot's towers or sent north, I could do nothing to save him.

Marcus's anger softens. I cover my eyes and wipe away my tears. I feel him step closer and pull me into a tight embrace. His fingers run through my tangled hair.

"Viv," he says over and over, and it's the first time he's used my nickname. "I won't die. Not for many years. The Black Knight abandoned us, and there are no rogues for miles." He takes a breath, and it shudders with a sob, leftover from the bout of tears we both spilled. "We could leave.

We could find my father, go to Jerusalem, bring Merlin back somehow. I'll go with you. I'll follow you anywhere. But we can't stay here."

I'm staring into his eyes, wondering why he'd ever give up on the Grail when we're so close, and to leave could mean him relinquishing his vow, and oh I'm so tired, and the Grail is right there...

"Vivienne, please. Let's go." His eyes lock with mine, and I look deeply into them, and maybe the Lady of the Lake was wrong and Marcus won't die. He presses his lips to my fore-head, and I want him to hold them there forever. "I cannot bear this ruthless part of the world anymore."

But if all this proves to be too much, and you can no longer bear such magic in a ruthless world, turn back. Won't you?

I blink. Those were Merlin's words Marcus just spoke.

But that's impossible—a coincidence. So I consider Marcus's suggestion. What would happen if we simply left? We could go to the Holy Land to help Azur and leave the task of stopping the Black Knight to someone else. We could search for Camelot's subjects. Perhaps this could be our destiny. Perhaps destinies aren't always written in stone.

But, no. "Marcus," I whisper, pulling my hand from his stubbled cheek, "I have to stop him. Lena followed me onto his aeroship, and escaped to Galahad's. Their aeroship caught in a tailspin. I watched them fall from the sky. If they didn't make it, I can't let that be for nothing. You under-stand that, don't you?" I search his eyes until I know we're both thinking of his mother and how it was the only reason he told me not to give the coordinates to the Black Knight.

Our fingers fall in line with each other. There's a seawater wind around us and a sweet and familiar home between us, as though home is something you make with the ones who hold your heart. I press my lips to Marcus's cheek and hold them there.

He wipes the back of his hand against his lashes, freeing exhausted, frustrated tears. "All right."

There's no need for a plan. In his violet eyes, I see how he thinks. Only a half-day's trek up the shore is another aeroship port free of rogue ships, occupied with commercial ones—I can see the port from where we stand, the fluttering of wings, the rotation of propellers. We'll return to the countryside, to *CELESTE*. Fix it together. It might take a day, but with its speed and with the *jaseemat* I'll create, we could catch up to the Black Knight and stop him somehow. There will be no time to trek back to see if Galahad and Percy and Lena survived, but our hands clasp tightly together, and I know Marcus will follow me to the stars, if I were to ask him.

Then I remember what he confessed to me only moments ago, and though I'm choked up and exhausted and devastated beyond belief, what I feel for Marcus transcends even that.

"I love you, too," I whisper against his sun-kissed skin. No matter what sort of motives I might have for finding the Grail, he must know.

He pulls back to look at me, eyes welling like an ocean. And then he presses his lips against mine, his skin raspy and scratching my cheeks, but I don't care.

Even when I shut my eyes and see the chalice the Black Knight seeks, with Marcus's arms tight around my waist, I couldn't possibly care about a damned thing.

The sky is pink with the falling day, and the sun's light flickers on the small waves, but the sea cannot hold onto those rays forever. We'll make camp tonight and set out for the aeroship port at dawn.

Our fire burns strong. We built it together, and as we piled the wood, I gave Marcus his quicklight, even though I'd long since missed his early December birthday. *"A debt repaid,"* I'd said of the peace offering, reminding us both of the one I used to blow up a harvester in the farmlands. He'd taken it and rolled it in his palm to see the engraving, running his thumb over the letters of his name. And smiled.

Then Marcus set off in search of more dried leaves and shipwrecked wood, and as I wait, I watch the glow dance across the sand, climb the kindle, his heavy cloak across my shoulders as the night sea air brings a chill. Every so often I glance up at the budding stars and let myself feel the absolute peacefulness of these parts. The wind is silent, and thus, so is the sea.

When he returns, he doesn't speak right away, and when he sets down a bushel of dried branches, I feel the thump once they've fallen into the sand. He's still angry. Whenever I think of what Rufus asked of me, a wave of guilt threatens to drown me, and I wish it'd be quick about it.

"Where is he now?" Marcus says with an irrefutable sharpness to his voice. He's crouched in front of his supplies, sifting through his satchel in a way that demands attention. "You said he went with you to the Perilous Lands, but from there you came after me, and I found you alone in the countryside. Where is my father?"

I remember the look of utter disappointment in Rufus's face when he realized I'd leave without him. "Sir Tristan's aeroship crashed in the Perilous Lands," I say. Marcus glances sideways at me, but I cannot read his expression yet. "They managed to survive; they were fixing their aeroship by the time we arrived. The knight allowed your father passageway to Jerusalem. I wouldn't have just left him alone in a desolate place."

Marcus doesn't move for a long minute, and then he returns to stripping wet leaves from the branches he's collected in fast, vicious strokes. As he works, I glance up at *MUERTE* ascending. It's nowhere near close to reaching Avalon. I shut my eyes and see the map in my mind for myself—the Black Knight still has three days of journeying.

Marcus brings the freshly cleaned branches to the fire and drops them. He sinks onto the sand next to me and stretches his legs out, crossing his boots at the ankles. In the barn, back in the farmlands of Camelot, he looked the same way, but his appearance has roughened even in the two days since I last saw him. His eyes are heavier with melancholy, and his frame has grown stronger, like he's become a man in these six months.

When he leans back, a wince crosses his face, and he sits up, his wounded palm bleeding through the bandage. I take his hand and unravel the cloth covered in sand and sea water.

"I'm not sure what I'll say when I see him," he says as I change the bandage to a clean one. "The last time we spoke wasn't a good memory."

"Why not?" I ask quietly, not sure if I've won the chance to inch closer.

He shrugs. "It was before the trial." He doesn't say he means Lancelot and Guinevere's, because the memory of that day has been branded onto our minds. "My mother had lost the right to stay in the infirmary, and my father had arranged for a neighbor to take her back to our farm. I argued with him that I could bring her to another kingdom..."

I tie the bandage in place and drop his hand. He looks at me, and I remember how after the trial, he tried to convince me to join him in leaving.

"But he was convinced my knighthood wasn't far off, and that would be enough. We had to stand by each other, like a family." He looks into the fire. "Did he ask of me?"

I watch the last six months melt off him like he's turned back into that mischievous boy. When he glances at me again, his eyes are so big and round, and the young beard on his jaw is misplaced against his features.

"Yes. Of course he did," I whisper.

Marcus swallows. "What did he say?" His voice breaks at the end of his question.

I think back to my memories of flying against the sky with Rufus. Of constantly quarreling with him. I think of how much he resembled the son I fell in love with. "He said he was proud of the man you'd become. He said he put too much on your shoulders, and that he'd give anything to have you back."

Marcus looks straight into the fire, and I watch his lip quiver and a tear smear across his cheek. He wipes it away, leaving there streaks of sand and dirt from the branches he collected, and shuts his eyes. I draw away to give him space, but his hand seizes mine.

"No. Don't. Don't pull away. And never let me draw away from you again." His watery eyes find mine in the moonlight. "Promise me."

I nod and press my lips to his temple.

He takes my cheek in his palm and pulls my lips to his. A fire rushes through my body at this kiss, so different from the others he's given me since he found me in the countryside. It's a kiss of honesty, of knowing the truth we were keeping from each other has been set free, despite the consequences.

He breaks our kiss, stares at me. And he's never looked at me that way before. It's a way to ask what hasn't been asked, or a way to let souls whisper to one another, making sure one wants what the other is desperate for. He bites his bottom lip and creases his brow, and then he moves closer until our bodies are inseparable, but still it's not enough. Another kiss.

But then it's a kiss that wants no boundaries, that wants to return to the barn in the farmlands with rain pouring down on us and wet linens between us and a vengeful witch seeking us and vow and reputation ruling over us. That wants to touch skin, taste skin, breathe skin. That wants my nails running across the dragon inked on his neck.

It becomes a kiss that wants to find the inn where people saw Marcus's tattoo and knew he was a knight of Camelot and ignore them for the warm bed beneath us. It's a kiss that knows we're completely alone on these beaches. Of his fingers digging into my hips and clenching the folds of my skirt, of my nails in his hair and running down his chest, untying his tunic and losing all control of my fingers in the process.

It's a kiss peppered with the quiet whispers coming from lips pressed against ears, and furs and blankets binding us together, and it's a kiss that wants the cover of night to stay forever.

THIRTY-THREE

The sea spills over my feet as I scrub sand from the brackets of my viewer. Once shining, they reflect dawn's sun and the dark shapes of gulls flying over these shores. I can't believe in other parts of the world dwells winter when the air around me is this warm.

Behind me, Marcus packs our weapons and tools onto his horse. I hear his nearly silent footsteps in the sand and turn. He stuffs his hands in his pockets, his tunic left untied and open to the heat. He smiles a crooked smile at me as his eyes lock onto mine.

"Should get a head start before the sun breaks past the horizon." His hands run over my hips and around my waist, and he presses a kiss to my forehead. His voice sounds different now, breathier. Husky and wild, like his whispers in my ear while night cloaked us from the world.

I look up to the sky at *MUERTE*'s voyage. Its propellers are magnificent, and its sails are breaths of mighty wind captured. Just as magnificent was the Black Knight's mechanical eye, and I find myself wondering if he's able to see me right now.

Marcus takes my hand, and together we walk to his horse, but before we can ride off for the aeroship ports, I realize Marcus might not know everything I've learned.

"Marcus," I say, dropping his hand. "The aeroships that left from the cliffs before Morgan's war."

"What about them?" he calls, reaching the horse and strapping my satchel to its saddle.

"They were rogue ships."

He shakes his head and sets his pistolník into the locking mechanism in the saddle. I still haven't studied it for myself, but there'll be another time for that. "That's impossible. Arthur wouldn't have allowed something so dire as an evacuation of his own people go unchecked." His words are terse; he might be thinking of the devastating memory of Arthur's fall. But as he fiddles with the saddle, I realize he's no longer paying attention. I take his hand so he looks at me.

"I saw it on the Black Knight's aeroship. Their map, they'd had it pinned. The monster himself told me so. Marcus, my mother. That was the deal he and I spoke of. We have to send word to Lancelot when we reach the aeroship ports."

He thinks for a long time, so focused, before he blinks himself free of whatever thought has nearly consumed him. A quick nod. "We'll send word."

Curiosity has claimed me. "What is it?"

His face hardens. "I was thinking that it could have been the Black Knight's way to encourage you to hand over the coordinates instead of using torture or ... magic. And how thankful I am that didn't happen, but it is strange ... "

And then his cheeks and ears and neck warm from surely what is the growing heat of day, but I can't help but wonder if the worry in Marcus's eyes is about something else. He takes a quick breath, like he's bracing himself to ask.

"Vivienne, what happened before you fell through the ice?"

Before I fell through the ice, I stole magic to save myself from rogues. I look at Marcus, and I do not blink. I feel my pulse pound against my neck and wrists as seconds pass between us. Finally, I gather strength, but my voice is weak. "What do you mean?"

He searches me. "The rogues' eyes were gouged out, and there was no way anyone could have done that with a fire-lance." A step closer. "What happened?"

"Nothing," I say, in a clipped voice.

He traces my neck and shoulder, watching the path his fingers makes. A lazy shrug sets his mouth into a line. "Strange. It seemed like...like there had been magic nearby. And that wasn't the only time. I mean, the Black Knight had every reason in the world to torture you, and he didn't." He looks at me with a face I cannot read. "He didn't hurt a hair on your head, like you were..."

I wait for him to finish, but he doesn't. I think of how frightened the Black Knight was of me. How I called him out on it. "The Lady of the Lake is protecting me, Marcus." And I pray she never finds out about the magic I stole.

"Certainly. And she did a hell of a job when the Black Knight took you aboard his ship."

"That was my folly."

There's uncertainty in his gaze. "It's almost like...there was a reason she turned a blind eye."

Finally, I recognize the look he wears. It's the same look of denial or disbelief as when he paused on the other side of our room's door at the inn, not realizing I was watching. He was lost in thought with only the sorcerer on his mind and a familiar pistolník at his waist.

"Where were you for that month, Marcus?" I ask, turning around the interrogation. "It wasn't Corbenic; that much I gather now."

He draws in a nervous breath.

"And who were you with?"

He rubs his stubbled cheeks with his palms, weary exhaustion from our lack of sleep falling over his eyes. "I can't tell you. Not yet." He presses forward, those roughened palms on my cheeks now. "As soon as all of this madness is over, I'll tell you everything. I swear it."

It's strange, but I have to believe him now. Not because of the love we've admitted to each other, or—

Oh God. Merlin.

For an entire month, Merlin was also unaccounted for, according to Azur.

But I don't mention that. I smile warmly and nod, pressing my lips to Marcus's cheek and wrapping my arms around his neck. I want Marcus to confirm that Merlin is involved, but part of me wonders if somehow that would mean Marcus knows of the magic I stole. If Merlin had been able to tell him.

Or warn him. And pass along a prized pistolník in the meantime.

And once again, there are untruths between Marcus and me.

The sands go on forever, and each cliff we pass is even more gargantuan than the last. Marcus holds me as I lean against him, riding sidesaddle, the reins in my hands. The aeroship ports are only hours away now. *"Almost there,"* he tells me over and over.

Then, down the way, a rider makes for us, and as soon as he breaks into a gallop, Marcus grabs the reins, drawing our steed to a halt. I feel a rise of fear in my throat at the thought if it being a rogue who might try to kill Marcus, but then I bring out my viewer, elongating it to see better. It's not a rogue. No, it has the armor and shape of a knight of Camelot, but as I focus a little more, I make out the face.

"It's Owen," I say, relieved.

"Damn," Marcus growls.

Owen, who wanted the Grail even if it meant his sister would remain in the shackles of the Black Knight.

"He would have been off his feet for a day, I wager," Marcus says in a low, dangerous voice, "after what I put him through."

I look through my viewer again. "He's furious," I say, but it's more of a question.

"He should be happy to see you alive and well."

Owen's steed kicks the sand out from under its hooves. My brother sees us, but doesn't wave, doesn't offer a greeting. On the contrary, I've never seen him so angry. His body is beaten up from Marcus's heavy punches, and he winces through his injuries as the horse's hooves thump in the sand. There might as well be whites in his pupils, golds in his irises.

"I'll talk to him," I tell Marcus.

"I should."

"He's my brother."

"He's my adversary."

Marcus and I drop from the saddle. He storms toward Owen, arms lifted in spiteful surrender.

Owen's steed reels to a stop. A spray of sand hits Marcus in the eyes, forcing him to turn and grunt.

My brother looks at me. "Stolen from the Spanish rogues and then returned unharmed. I suppose marble signets are to thank for this?" His voice is different: harsher, resentful. Full of hatred. "And now the Black Knight will claim what should be mine."

Marcus faces my brother, hands still raised in case Owen would turn quickly on him. "Vivienne is safe. That's what's important. If you want something to do, return to Camelot and tell Lancelot—"

"That's *not* what's important," Owen growls, his face drawn up in a sneer. "The Spanish rogues have all they need to use against us. You fools."

Marcus steps forward. "Owen, step down. Talk to me on my level."

But Owen's bruised and bloody chin jets up in defiance. "Why would I lower myself to a *serf's* level?"

Marcus flinches at the insult. He lowers his hands. "Your mother," Marcus tries, slowly, patiently, with much anger dancing on his own voice. "The rogues have Camelot's subjects. They might have even captured the rest of the infantry."

Owen shakes his head. "You're taking the attention from

the Grail, trying to force me to do the same. Now that Avalon is revealed, you want me distracted so you can seek the Grail for yourself." He spits at Marcus's feet.

Marcus ignores the gesture and steps forward. "Hear yourself, Owen! We have to send word to Lancelot—"

Owen shakes his head. "Let them save themselves. The strong amongst them will rise up. The strong always do."

I brush past Marcus for my brother who now notices me with much indifference. "You don't see how the quest has changed you! You don't see how heartless you've become!"

Owen's cold eyes shoot ice at mine. "I see how much time I wasted in Camelot. Now that I've left its restraints, I've only become stronger. Being banished from the Round Table is the best thing to have happened to me."

Marcus shakes his head. "Forget that, Owen! Vivienne said your mother was amongst them!" His voice wavers, and I know he must be thinking of his own mother. "Please, know the torment I felt. Find them while we go after the Black Knight."

Owen seethes. He glares at us, at our entangled hands, our bodies pressed together in urgency and love. He doesn't know about the Lady of the Lake's prophecy, about Rufus, or what the Fisher King told me about Marcus. He doesn't know how we must follow the Black Knight.

I swallow. I have to find the Owen I once knew. "Owen, please. We're wasting time fighting."

But my plea is lost on my brother. The Owen I grew up with no longer exists. He might as well be on his way to becoming a rogue.

"You stand before me declaring all this, but all I see is a whore who gave herself to a lowly serf, no more worthy of her than she is of him."

My heart shatters, and before I can stop him, Marcus drops my hand and runs at my brother. He tackles Owen off his horse and slams him into the sands.

THIRTY-FOUR

Marcus's fist clashes with Owen's jaw, hitting him three times or more.

"Marcus! Stop!" I shout.

Owen shoves Marcus so he can sit up and grab a long dagger from his boot, aiming the point at Marcus's neck. Owen readies to strike, but Marcus's heavy grunts give him the force he needs to wrench the dagger from Owen's hand and throw it aside. The blade lands point down in the sand.

"Stop! Both of you!" My voice is frantic, but amongst the heavy waves and the terrifying grunts and shouts of pain, I can't get a word in. My enraged heart pattering against my chest, I run to the horse and seize Marcus's pistolník and fire it twice into the air, shattering the sky with loud bursts.

Marcus sees me armed and stands, slumping a bit with his hands on his knees, breathing heavily. Owen's face reddens with fury, and his nose swells from a break.

And then his hand slips to his side.

"Marcus!" I scream.

Owen is on his feet before I can blink, and he frees a fusionah from his holster, but Marcus is just as fast and wields his own blade, lifting it high and saving himself from losing an arm. Each points their weapon directly at the other: Marcus in defense, Owen to kill.

"Owen!" I scream, running for them, but before I reach his side, my brother's quick punch sends Marcus to his knees, and then he twists the barrel out from the blade's hilt, pointing it directly at me.

I stop quickly in the sand and stare down the black tunnel belonging to the last person I thought would ever cast a weapon in my direction. Before I realize what I'm doing, Marcus's pistolník in my hand aims right back at my brother. I hear the click of my fingers pulling back the hammer.

"Stay back, Vivienne," Owen says purposefully.

I don't move; I don't breathe. My feet sink into the sand, and my heart pounds against my ribs. "How did this happen, Owen?"

Marcus finds his feet, eyes manic and wild. He runs at my brother with his blade and slams it down just as Owen turns, the long, steel barrel of his fusionah horizontal at eye-level.

"Threaten her again, and it'll be me who kills you," Marcus growls dangerously as Owen backs away to gain balance.

My brother swings his own blade viciously. Back and forth they go, back and forth until their blades are at a standstill.

Then the sword forged by Marcus's father shatters Owen's steel into three pieces that fly across the sand.

Marcus pulls away, and I sigh in relief, lowering the pistolník.

Owen steps back, back, back toward his horse. Not in a way that indicates surrender—as though he might have a cannon to trump Marcus's blade.

And that thought sends my heart into a panic. "Owen, what are you doing?"

"Owen!" Marcus shouts, lowering his sword. "It's over!" His voice is gruff and on guard.

Owen reaches his horse and disappears into the carriers and furs it boasts. Marcus storms toward him as though his ferocious step might startle Owen into yielding. Owen retrieves his dagger from the sand and attacks Marcus with it.

I dash across the beach, over sand and water, as I follow them at the sea's edge.

When Owen's dagger catches the hilt of Marcus's sword, Marcus's weapon tumbles from his grasp. He loses balance and falls to his knees, glancing over his shoulder for his blade lost in the sand. His eyes full of urgency, he scrambles for it and then stands again. But when he faces Owen, a crossbow my brother had retrieved from the horse and hidden on his back, aims at Marcus's heart.

With a cruel smile of power and victory, Owen releases the arrow.

It strikes Marcus in the chest, extending to the other side.

The iron plates click outward in a horrible, deadly rhythm into a complete circle, locking the arrow inside him.

No. I didn't see this. I hear myself scream from a far-off place, but I know my eyes were tricked by the shine of the sun, the reflection against the water. It didn't happen. My feet wobble in the sand, and I'm not sure I can move, but somehow I'm running quickly to Marcus. I watch as he glances at the arrow that couldn't possibly be stuck in his chest. I watch as Owen regards the empty crossbow in hand, blinking as though he'd been under a spell. He stares at Marcus, who looks back as though thinking, *How could you?*

Marcus falls to his palms. A trickle of blood spills from the corner of his mouth, trailing down his chin and onto the white sand. He falls onto his chest, landing with a soft thump so much quieter than the waves.

My head is not with me, and my feet are no longer of my own control, and I slide in the sand to reach Marcus, pulling his body and turning him over, a waterfall of hot blood spilling over his clothes and skin. He writhes in pain, his eyes a horrid gray, blood staining his teeth and mouth.

"Marcus…" I'm too shocked to cry. I look at Owen.

My brother's mouth is agape. "He shouldn't have fought me," he whispers, sounding like the boy I once knew and loved when we were children.

I shake with anger. I can't control myself anymore. *"What have you done?"*

Owen steps away as though by doing so, he might somehow undo such an awful mistake.

My hands flock to Marcus's heart, where the gentle thumping I love so much has slowed to a horrifically sluggish beat. He fights for breath, and his eyes gloss over, glancing everywhere in a fast panic.

I lean in to kiss his face and lips, feeling the thick warm blood coat mine as well.

"I'm here. I can—I can save you." I nod to reassure both of us. "I'll find charcoal. I can turn it into gold, and from there, I can make *jaseemat* to keep life within you. Alchemy…" I trail off when I see how his face twists in agony, how he cries without realizing it, how his body shakes like his life is trying to escape this horror. "There's always a choice. Hold on, Marcus."

Owen watches.

I glance sideways at his still figure. I cannot look anymore at him. "You're no longer my brother."

Owen says nothing. Perhaps he regrets his actions. Or, perhaps, he's looking at the girl he called a whore and is hating her with every inch of his being. Perhaps he's nothing more than a boy desperate for the Grail for his own selfish reasons.

Owen sputters for speech, but no words follow. He backs away to his horse, and I hear the gentle gallops of his steed take him far away, off these shores, out of Greece, and from my life forever.

===

My tears drench Marcus, cleaning off the blood still warm, still spilling from his mouth. He's in great pain, drifting between delirium and awareness. The arrow hit his heart, but not cleanly enough that death would be immediate.

"I can fix this, Marcus. It's what I do. I fix things," I tell him, my hands already moving and itching to construct, even though I know he can't hear me. I look around, but there's nothing. Only sand and rocks. No *jaseemat*. Oh God.

But I have to do *something*. Perhaps if I ride back to where we slept last night, I'll find the remnants of our fire. Merlin's instructions are lost in my aeroship's wreckage, but I'll remember how to make *jaseemat* as I go. My hands are much wiser than my head sometimes. I could use the blood trickling down his chest to make the most powerful *jaseemat* of all. But I can't bear to leave him, not when he could have minutes left, and I might miss the last—

No. I cannot think like this. I must remain logical.

"Vivienne," a voice whispers. I ignore it, holding Marcus's shaking body against me. I don't want that strange, confusing presence near me now. *"For God's sake, girl, wipe away those tears and save him. You know how, and the clock is ticking."*

I shake my head, though in my mind's eye, I see the scrolls the sorcerer told me to bring. The scrolls he told me I'd need. The spell to resurrect soon after death. They're safe in my pocket. They're with me. And the power they carry dies in an hour's time. *Redia.*

"There's always a choice. You've been tested, and perhaps now it could be for good. Did you ever consider that?"

"Leave me alone," I whisper low enough that Marcus cannot hear.

I rock Marcus's head so he looks at me. His eyes roll and settle upon mine. His hand clenches my fingers with little strength; he cannot speak. I lift my eyes to the pistolník I dropped, and a small part of me—the logical, rational, always questioning Vivienne—wonders how on God's green earth Marcus got ahold of that weapon.

Because it is Merlin's.

"Yes, it is."

Marcus's violet eyes are fading, until finally, they're nothing more than a memory of my favorite flower.

"Marcus?" I shake him gently. "Marcus, don't—"

His eyes roll in pain. In desperation, I grip the bolt, because perhaps there's a mechanism on its feathers that would let the clasp release, letting me at least remove this horrid thing of destruction. But it's stuck; it won't move. Damn it all, I cannot free him!

"Marcus!" I say louder. My hands shake, and I might be sick. No, no, no...

He breathes in and then releases it.

My fingers stroke the side of his cheek and the stubble there, and then I touch his bloodied lips.

Death really does make people cold when it steals a life.

"Marcus," I whisper. My hands shake. "Marcus!" I scream until it echoes against the sea.

I lean my forehead against his and cry. Marcus's hand drops from mine. His eyes won't open. And I don't want them to. I don't want to see the grayness. Not when they should be violet.

But... what if they could be again?

The spell *Redia* would have no consequences for the one saved. It would only affect those who'd stolen the magic.

And I'm protected by the Lady of the Lake.

Maybe it won't affect me either. Maybe this is what Merlin means.

"He wouldn't want that," I whisper. "He'd rather be dead."

"He'd be alive, and you'd be together. He never wanted to be a knight, Vivienne, and there are ways to steal magic for good."

I stand, feeling the damp hem of my skirt hit my feet. The wind blows my hair around my face. The salt water sings a song that brings with it a honey-like sensation of wonderment.

Perhaps Merlin is right. All I'd have to do is take those precious words from the demigods too stupid ever to hide their glorious powers from humanity. Then, Marcus and

I could find the Grail to save me—while my soul is tainted with magic, his isn't. He could claim it. And then we could find Camelot's subjects. Help Azur and the whole of Jerusalem. A small, temporary sacrifice on my part could save many.

Yes, magic could be used for good, surely.

I feel in my eyes a strange sensation, and somehow I know there are thousands of shades of white and gold coming over them, making them glimmer in this quiet morning. I hear the gentle singing of the Lady of the Lake's quiet *"no"* whisper through the water and in my blood as Merlin's *"yes"* hisses louder in the marrow of my bones.

Marcus died too soon. He was stolen from a thankless world, and his destiny lies in my hands.

Call me a thief, but the magic to restore his life will be mine.

The End.

Acknowledgments

Special thanks to my husband, Justin, especially on the days it seemed impossible to write a sequel. To my mother, who told me, "I can't wait to find out what happens to Vivienne next," and never realized how badly I needed to hear that. To my rock star sisters, Sarah and Monica, for your constant, unconditional support. To my family and friends in Canada and in the States for your enthusiasm, excitement, and love.

To the amazing group of writers I call friends. Special shout outs go to Elizabeth Briggs, for saving Lena. To Sara Raasch, for the Merlin love. To Lisa Maxwell, for helping me see beyond Camelot's horizon. To Rachel Searles, Jessica Love, Dana Elmendorf, PK Hrezo, Helene Dunbar, AdriAnne Strickland, and Kate Bassett, for your precious friendship. To the OneFours, so many hugs forever.

To my brilliant editor, Brian Farrey-Latz, for being in my corner. To Mallory Hayes and Ed Day, and to everyone at Flux. To Brittany Howard and Marisa Corvisiero, eternal thanks.

To my readers—You Wonderful People You. Thank you for the retweets, the emails, the love letters. You are made of stars.

And a special reiteration of this book's dedication. One day, I brought my Kindle to my grandfather's house and showed him the first page of *Camelot Burning* long before it became an advanced copy. Hearing him read the first line I'd come to know so well continues to be one of my proudest moments.

Papa—I wish so badly you'd been able to see that book hit shelves. You are well and properly missed. This one's for you.

© Jenn Verma

About the Author

Kathryn Rose was born in Toronto, Canada, and grew up in the Kitchener-Waterloo region of Southern Ontario. After graduating from York University, where she studied literature and philosophy, she relocated to Los Angeles, California.

When she isn't breaking up fights between her cat and dog, Kathryn can be found writing and reading mostly speculative fiction, cooking with her husband, or listening to rock music.